HT
SHOT

Charlotte Hughes

ISBN 1-55166-941-2

HOT SHOT

Copyright © 2002 by Charlotte Hughes.

Visit us at www.mirabooks.com

Printed in U.S.A.

CHARLOTTE HUGHES

66863   A NEW ATTITUDE   ___ $5.99 U.S. ___ $6.99 CAN.

(limited quantities available)

TOTAL AMOUNT $_____
POSTAGE & HANDLING $_____
($1.00 for one book; 50¢ for each additional)
APPLICABLE TAXES* $_____
TOTAL PAYABLE $_____
(check or money order—please do not send cash)

To order, complete this form and send it, along with a check
or money order for the total above, payable to MIRA Books®,
to: **In the U.S.:** 3010 Walden Avenue, P.O. Box 9077, Buffalo,
NY 14269-9077; **In Canada:** P.O. Box 636, Fort Erie, Ontario
L2A 5X3.

Name:_____
Address:_____ City:_____
State/Prov.:_____ Zip/Postal Code:_____
Account Number (if applicable):_____
075 CSAS

  *New York residents remit applicable sales taxes.
   Canadian residents remit applicable GST and provincial taxes.

MIRA®

MCHU0902BL

If you enjoyed what you just read,
then we've got an offer you can't resist!

Take 2
bestselling novels FREE!
Plus get a FREE surprise gift!

Clip this page and mail it to The Best of the Best™

IN U.S.A.
3010 Walden Ave.
P.O. Box 1867
Buffalo, N.Y. 14240-1867

IN CANADA
P.O. Box 609
Fort Erie, Ontario
L2A 5X3

YES! Please send me 2 free Best of the Best™ novels and my free surprise gift. After receiving them, if I don't wish to receive anymore, I can return the shipping statement marked cancel. If I don't cancel, I will receive 4 brand-new novels every month, before they're available in stores! In the U.S.A., bill me at the bargain price of $4.74 plus 25¢ shipping and handling per book and applicable sales tax, if any*. In Canada, bill me at the bargain price of $5.24 plus 25¢ shipping and handling per book and applicable taxes**. That's the complete price and a savings of over 20% off the cover prices—what a great deal! I understand that accepting the 2 free books and gift places me under no obligation ever to buy any books. I can always return a shipment and cancel at any time. Even if I never buy another The Best of the Best™ book, the 2 free books and gift are mine to keep forever.

185 MDN DNWF
385 MDN DNWG

Name	(PLEASE PRINT)	
Address	Apt.#	
City	State/Prov.	Zip/Postal Code

On a warm September night, in a San Francisco law office,
a client and his attorney are gunned down.
It is just the start of what will be
the biggest squeeze play the city has ever seen....

Squeeze Play

Nick Sasso: A disgraced ex-cop whose brother has
been "borrowing" money from the family restaurant.

Billie Fox: A tough-talking defense attorney
whose ex-husband is murdered.

Dickson Hong: A homicide detective looking
for the case to finally make—or break—his career.

Henry Chin: A district attorney with his eye on the mayor's
office—unless the corruption scam he's at the center of is exposed.

Igor Sakharov: A retired hit man with a heart of
gold who's been offered one last job that he can't refuse.

Jolie Hays: A novice hooker who lands the wrong john and
comes away with a piece of information that will make her a target and
provide her with the opportunity to change her life...if she survives.

**A novel filled with suspense, adventure, craziness—
and a cast of characters you'll never forget. Sit back,
take a deep breath and experience the unpredictable
trip that is SQUEEZE PLAY.**

R.J. KAISER

MIRA®

*Available the first week of September 2002
wherever hardcovers are sold!*

Visit us at www.mirabooks.com

SUSAN WIGGS

On sale
September 2002
wherever
paperbacks
are sold!

ENCHANTED AFTERNOON

Beautiful, charming and respected as the wife of an
ambitious senator, Helena Cabot Barnes is the leading
lady of Saratoga Springs. But beneath the facade lies a
terrible deception. Helena married for all the wrong
reasons—and discovered too late that her husband is
a dangerous man. Fearing for her safety, she ends her
marriage and flees to legendary Moon Lake Lodge.

But Helena can't outrun her past, and in desperation,
she turns to Michael Rowan, a man she once loved, a
man who broke her heart. For Helena, the road to
trusting Michael again is long and hard. But Michael
has just discovered a shattering truth…and a reason
to stay and fight for the woman he once lost.

MIRA®

New York Times Bestselling Author

DEBBIE MACOMBER

204 Rosewood Lane

Grace Sherman
204 Rosewood Lane
Cedar Cove, Washington

Dear Reader,

If you've been to Cedar Cove before we've probably met. I've lived in this town all my life and raised two daughters here. But my husband and I—well, about six months ago, he disappeared. Just…disappeared.

My hometown, my family and friends, bring me comfort during this difficult time. And I'm continually reminded that life can and does go on. For instance, my best friend's daughter impulsively got married a little while ago. My own daughter Kelly recently had a baby. And my older daughter, Maryellen, is seeing a new man, but for some reason she won't tell me who it is.

But that's only the beginning…. Just come on over and we'll talk!

Grace

MIRA®

"Stress?" Frankie asked. "I invented the word. But you needn't make excuses for my behavior. I'm a grown woman, and a professional police detective. This is child's play compared to what I've seen."

Orvell started to say something, but Matt interrupted. "A real police detective, huh? Well, I'm impressed. How about you, Orvell?"

He gave Matt a funny look. "Yeah."

"And a damn good one at that," Frankie replied, unaware of the looks the men were giving each other.

"So, what brings you to Purdyville?" Orvell asked.

"Job transfer. I'm going to be working for the Purdyville Police Department. And believe me, it won't be easy working with a bunch of good ol' boys after the pros I've dealt with. What can you tell me about the police chief?"

Matt and Orvell exchanged amused looks. "Oh, well, he's a nice enough guy," Matt said. "Good-looking, too."

The other man chuckled. "And don't think he don't know it. Why, half the women in town are hot for him."

"A ladies' man, huh?" Frankie snorted. "Just what I need. Another man whose brain is located behind his zipper."

Matt frowned. Orvell roared with laughter.

"Did I say something funny?" Frankie asked.

Orvell stepped forward. "I'd like to introduce you to Purdyville's esteemed police chief, Matt Webber."

Also available from MIRA Books and
CHARLOTTE HUGHES

A NEW ATTITUDE

WITHDRAWN

To Susie O'Neal, my advisor on life,
love and happiness, and the only person
who will tell me the truth when I ask,
"Do these pants make me look fat?"
Also, to Jane Dowdney, who taught me
that not every little thing is a crisis,
even if we all love being drama queens.

ACKNOWLEDGMENTS

Many thanks to my agent, Al Zuckerman,
and to my editor, Miranda Stecyk,
for their enthusiasm and support.
My heartfelt appreciation to Dr. David John Berndt,
for his friendship and promotional skills.
And, as always, a big hug to Janet Evanovich,
my friend and inspiration, and the only person
who truly understands my sick sense of humor.
That's scary, Janet.

One

Detective Frankie Daniels was mad enough to spit a barbed-wire fence, and the oppressive July heat only made it worse. She gritted her teeth in annoyance at traffic sounds that were so much a part of her life she had made a habit of not noticing them. Strangers bustled by on their way to work, cutting in front of her, bumping against her with purse or briefcase, and she longed to turn her rage on them.

As she stepped inside the first floor of the Atlanta Police Department, the cool air hit her face like a soothing balm. She paused, took a deep breath and swiped one hand against the back of her neck, where it was already damp despite the early hour. The elevator was packed with uniforms, people she had worked with for years, but today she refused to make eye contact. She got off on the third floor and marched toward Captain Dell Wayford's office—backbone ramrod stiff, lips pressed into a grim line—determined to ignore the stares of her co-workers. She was wired, having drunk a pot of coffee and smoked an entire pack of cigarettes since climbing out of bed at five that morning.

She could just imagine what they were calling her.

Home-wrecker.

Slut.

Whore.

Frankie squared her shoulders. At least she didn't look the part. She had replaced, at least temporarily, her jeans and T-shirt with khaki slacks and a starched white oxford-cloth blouse. She'd pulled back her dark hair, twisting it into a tight, demure knot like her grandmother had worn for as long as Frankie could remember, forgoing her usual wash and curl-as-it-fell look.

She had *respectability* written all over her. And the no-nonsense attitude she'd earned after more than a decade with the department, three of those years as a plainclothes detective. She'd pulled her weight in a male-dominated field and had earned the begrudging respect of her fellow officers.

Then she'd gone and blown it all to hell by sleeping with a married cop—her own partner, for God's sake.

It didn't get any worse than that.

Well, okay, the fact that her ex-lover, Jim Connors, was the police commissioner's son-in-law, wouldn't win her any commendations.

How could she have been so stupid?

Frankie paused at the captain's door and rapped on the frosted glass with her knuckles, then entered when she heard a grunt from the other side. This was going to be about as pretty as a drive-by shooting.

Captain Wayford's shirt had already wilted from the heat and looked as if he'd slept in it. A nonfiltered Camel cigarette dangled from his lips. The only reason it wasn't lit was because smoking had been banned from the building two years before. Wayford had never forgiven the powers behind that decision. Most of the cops Frankie knew smoked and drank too much, and they swilled coffee as though it were the elixir of life. As she tried to gauge the man's mood, she noted the fleshy face, flushed crimson against his light gray hair, and a bulbous nose where red, spiderlike veins on either side gave evidence of years of boozing. She knew why he drank. Still, as much as she loved and respected the man, Frankie wouldn't have given ten cents for his liver.

Wayford wore a look that said "Don't piss me off." Retirement was only a few months away; the last thing he wanted was a problem.

Frankie stepped up to his scarred metal desk and pulled her service revolver and badge from her purse.

Wayford leaned back in his chair and regarded her quizzically. "You gonna shoot me, Detective? Or do you plan to turn that gun on yourself and save me the trouble of killing you with my bare hands?"

She laid the gun on his desk and pulled off her badge. "I'm resigning, sir. I'm an embarrassment to you and the department."

He pulled the cigarette from his mouth. "An embarrassment?" He gave a snort of disgust. "No, Daniels, you're more like a boil on my ass that won't go away. A seed wart that keeps coming back each time it's burned off. An abscessed tooth—"

"I get the message loud and clear, Captain."

"But you're a damn good detective, and I expected better from you. If someone had told me you were doin' the police commissioner's son-in-law, a *married* man with three children, I would have pistol-whipped the SOB and thrown him out of my office."

"Captain—"

"Sit, Detective."

She sat.

"I'm just glad your old man ain't alive to see this."

Frankie flinched. Wayford had just struck a nerve, and he knew it. "If you have a problem with my job performance or the way I've conducted myself, fine. But I'd appreciate it if you'd keep my father out of this.''

Wayford ignored her. ''Frank Daniels was my best friend, and the finest cop this force ever had.''

Frankie knew all that. She had spent ten years trying to fill her father's shoes. Not an easy job. Her father was a hero and an icon as far as the force was concerned. He and Wayford had been partners way back when, and her father had taken a bullet for the man. His only request as he lay dying in a cold alley was that Wayford look after his kid. Dell Wayford had honored that request, but he was hard on her. He expected a lot, and she'd worked her ass off to give it to him. Somehow, it was never enough. Wayford had made her jump through hoops to make detective, even though she had earned it more than others.

Frankie clenched her hands in her lap. She felt the sting of unshed tears. ''Sir, for the record, Jim Connors told me he was separated from his wife and in the process of a divorce.''

''That's the oldest line in the book, Daniels. Why do you think he was transferred over here? I'll tell you why. He was humping the dispatcher at the last precinct.''

Frankie's shoulders slumped.

''I've already had a visit from the commissioner,'' he said, reaching into a desk drawer and pulling out a bulky manila envelope. ''Bet you didn't know Connors's wife was having him followed. Jesus Christ, Daniels, they've got footage of the two of you in bed doing everything except the hokey-pokey. You want me to stick this in the VCR so we can take a look?''

Frankie suddenly felt dizzy and a little nauseous. The absolute last thing she wanted to do was watch a video of her and Connors in the sack, and she was humiliated beyond belief that Captain Wayford had seen them.

"Don't worry, I haven't looked at it," he said as though reading her mind. "Believe it or not, I got better things to do. And frankly, I don't care who's doing who, as long as I don't have to hear about it and it ain't on company time."

Frankie gulped in air. How could such a thing have happened? Had someone installed a hidden camera in her bedroom, for heaven's sake? "Whoever took those videos did so illegally, sir," she managed to say. "This person had to have broken into my house."

"You planning on pressing charges?" Wayford chuckled. "Yeah, I'd definitely want to drag this into court. Every lech on the street, including the ones in this department, will have copies. We'll play 'em at the next Christmas party."

Frankie stared at the toes of her shoes. She *was* thankful her father wasn't alive to witness her humiliation. "I'm sorry I disappointed you, Captain."

"Oh, you're going to pay for this little indiscretion," he said. "Connors's wife wants you out of here, and her daddy's gonna see that his little girl gets exactly what she asks for."

"So I'm fired," Frankie said. Ten years down the toilet, she thought. She felt all used up.

"Hell, no. Firing is too good for you." Wayford placed the envelope on his desk and, without warning, reached for Frankie's gun and smashed the video inside with the handle. He slid the gun across his desk and tossed the envelope in the trash can as Frankie stared, openmouthed. "I worked a deal with the commissioner. The only reason he agreed to it is because he doesn't want this to get out."

Frankie looked up, feeling hopeful for the first time since the affair had become the topic of lewd jokes. "What kind of deal?"

"A new job. You disappear quietly, and none of this will go on your record."

"A new job?"

"Yeah. I've already found a place—hopefully you won't screw this up. 'Course, you'll have to take a pay cut."

"I don't make that much to begin with."

Wayford leaned forward and clasped his hands together. "Do yourself a favor and take the deal, Daniels. I found you a job working for my nephew. You don't take this, you're going to be working in a doughnut shop. Besides," he added, "you won't need much money where you're going."

She looked at him. Already, it didn't sound good.

"I'll call you when I finish the paperwork. In the meantime, start packing." He was already shuffling through forms. "You're dismissed."

They exchanged looks. Dozens of pictures flashed through Frankie's head. Baseball games the two had attended, complete with cold hot dogs and greasy chili. John Wayne movies on Saturday at the old Plaza Theater with buttered popcorn and chocolate-covered peanuts. Wayford cheering her on at her soccer games, even though, afterward, he always insisted she could have done better. He was the first one she'd told she wanted to be called Frankie, after her father, instead of Francis, her real name. "The name fits you," he'd said.

But that was a long time ago. A lifetime.

"Thank you, Captain Wayford," she said stiffly, rising from her chair.

Wayford swiveled around in his chair and stared out the window wordlessly.

Frankie exited his office, fighting back tears. She wove her way through a maze of cluttered desks, thankful that most of the detectives had already left on assignments. She smiled stiffly as she neared the desk of Hank Adams, a veteran cop who some joked had been with the department since before inside plumbing. Frankie had learned a lot from him.

"You okay?" he asked, somber brown eyes fixed on her. His hair had receded to the center of his scalp. The top of his head was red and freckled, a result of the sun bearing down on him in summer. In winter it grew dry and flaky.

"I'm history."

"Jim Connors is trash. Not worth the bullet it would take to put him out of his misery."

Frankie wondered if there was anyone in the department who didn't know about the affair, but then, Hank knew everything. He was different from the rest, though. He listened, but he kept his mouth shut. "Yeah, well, that's the breaks. I've received my shipping orders. Just waiting for the name of the port." She opened the middle drawer in her desk and fumbled about. Her throat ached.

Hank put his hand on her shoulder. "I wish there was something I could do."

Frankie stiffened at the show of kindness. She was too close to tears. "Wayford should have fought harder for me, Hank."

"He did fight, Frankie. I came in early to catch up on paperwork, heard the whole thing." Hank wiped his hand across his scalp. "But he lost. That's what really has his goat. He's so angry right now he doesn't know what to do except bark at everyone who comes within a foot of him." He paused. "So what're you going to do?"

She shrugged. "I have no choice but to take the job offer."

"Connors won't last. You've got my word on that."

Frankie noted the determined look on his face as she grabbed a black marker from the drawer. ''Thanks for being on my side, Hank.''

''Everybody's on your side, but they need their jobs as much as we do.''

''Would you excuse me? I have to take care of something.''

''Sure, Frankie. You have my home and cell phone number. Call anytime.''

''Thanks.'' She made her way to the ladies' room. Inside, she found another detective. She had worked with Anne Roberts on several cases and had found her more than competent.

''You don't look so good,'' the woman said.

Frankie uncapped the marker. ''I'm being shipped out.''

''I sort of figured that. Jim Connors's daddy-in-law is going to take care of his boy. But don't worry. This department will freeze him out in no time. Once he realizes nobody is going to cooperate with him, not even the crime lab, he'll beg for a new assignment.''

It was the second time Frankie had been told as much in the last few minutes. There was some small victory in knowing Connors wouldn't get off the hook so easily. She had seen firsthand what happened to detectives who weren't accepted into the department, the cocksure who played by their own rules and refused to accept constructive criticism by supervisors or share information with their partners. There were a few, but they didn't last long.

Frankie turned to the wall and began writing in big letters. Anne remained quiet. When she finished, Frankie replaced the cap and faced the detective. ''What do you think?''

Anne stepped closer and read the words aloud. ''Jim

Connors has genital herpes.'' She looked at Frankie. "Is it true?"

Frankie didn't care whether or not it was true, she was seeking revenge. "It's my story, and I'm sticking to it."

"Hey, it works for me. I'll see that word gets out."

The next morning, Frankie was in the process of packing her dishes when her mother called. "I'm getting a new job, Mom," she said. "In a place called Purdyville, North Carolina. Isn't it exciting?" Frankie held her breath.

"What did you do this time?" Eve Hutton asked matter-of-factly.

"Thanks for the vote of confidence, Mom." Frankie had no intention of telling her mother the truth. As ludicrous as it sounded, the woman thought her daughter was pure as distilled drinking water. Saving herself for marriage, she bragged to the blue-haired ladies in the beauty parlor, where she went once a week for her shampoo and set. Frankie didn't have the heart to tell her she knew every trick in the book when it came to sex. She had always felt a sense of protectiveness toward her mother, and she knew it was because Eve Hutton had never gotten over losing Frankie's father. Nor had Frankie. She had been eleven years old at the time, and a daddy's girl.

The silence on the other end of the line told Frankie her mother was pondering the news. Frankie envisioned her sitting in her compact kitchen, wearing a bright floral caftan, painting her fingernails and checking her roots in a hand mirror to see if she needed to have them touched up.

"They need a good detective in Purdyville," Frankie said at last. "You wouldn't believe how many people put in for the job, but Captain Wayford chose me." Wayford had called an hour ago with Frankie's destination. They were just waiting for the paperwork to go through.

"I can tell when you're lying to me, Francis," Eve said. "Don't think for one minute you've got me fooled. And you know I'll find out eventually."

Frankie's irritation flared. She wished she and her mother didn't have to go to battle over every little thing. "You're right, Mom. If you must know the truth, I got bagged for sleeping with my partner, who just happens to be a married man and the police commissioner's son-in-law. Satisfied?"

"Fine, don't tell me."

Frankie lit a cigarette and inhaled deeply. There was no way to win where her mother was concerned. It was times like these that Frankie wondered if her father had thrown himself in front of a bullet just to escape his wife's constant nagging. God, she missed him. "Mom, could we not fight over this?"

"How much are you smoking these days?"

"I've cut back."

"You say that every time I ask."

"Stop asking."

"You're in a mood," Eve said. "I've never even heard of this place, Purdyville. You say it's in North Carolina? What big city is it near?"

Frankie heard the rustling of paper and knew her mother was pulling out a map. "About fifty miles from Raleigh. It's a small town. You know how you're always worrying about how dangerous it is here in Atlanta. I understand the crime rate is very low in Purdyville."

Eve sighed from her end. "Well, that's a relief. At least I'll be able to sleep nights, for a change. I still don't see it on the map. Are you sure they said North Carolina? Maybe you misunderstood."

"I wrote it in the palm of my hand as soon as Captain Wayford told me. Of course I'm sure."

"Stop being fresh, Francis. I'm just trying to find out where my only child is moving. Is that a crime? You must be having your period. I can always tell, you get so testy. I'm surprised they let you carry a gun when you're like this."

Frankie hated being called Francis, and her mother knew it. She was tempted to tell the woman she hadn't been a virgin since she'd done the nasty in the back seat of Ronnie Lee Patterson's car on prom night. "Mom, that is the most sexist remark ever to come out of your mouth, and I'm going to pretend I didn't hear it."

"Do you need money?"

"No."

"I wish you'd let me help you. You know I can afford it. Your stepfather, God rest his soul, left me very comfortable."

Frankie was grateful for that. Eve had remarried shortly after Frankie entered high school, an older man with health problems. It had been a perfect union. Lamar Hutton needed a caretaker; Eve craved security. Somewhere along the line they'd learned to love each other. Not the kind of love that Frankie had seen on her mother's face when her father used to come through the door at the end of the day, but a mature love born out of two individuals meeting each other's needs.

"There comes a time in your life when companionship is more important than passion," Eve had told Frankie after Lamar's marriage proposal.

Lamar Hutton died shortly after Frankie joined the Atlanta Police Department, leaving Eve financially secure. She had moved into an upscale retirement community in Miami, Florida, where she played bridge once a week, attended plays and concerts with friends, and had her nails silk-wrapped.

"I'll let you know if I need something, okay?" Frankie said. "Right now I have to pack."

"This is all so sudden. Would you like for me to come up and help you move?"

That was the last thing Frankie needed. Her mother had a tendency of getting on her nerves and in the way. "No, I've got everything under control. I'm supposed to report for duty early next week, so I'm kind of rushed."

"Do you have a forwarding address?"

"Not yet. I called a Realtor in Purdyville this morning and she's checking on it." The woman had not sounded optimistic. Good housing was apparently scarce in that area.

"Well, don't go without letting me know how to reach you."

"I'll call as soon as I know more," she promised. "I'm sure we'll be in touch before then." She could count on it.

By midnight Frankie had packed her entire place, except for a few items she would need in the meantime, which wasn't much. She lived on coffee, cigarettes and fast food. She could stick the rest of her belongings in her car at the last minute. Sad as it was, everything she owned would fit inside her small compact. She had nothing to show for her life except a color TV, a nice stereo, a decent car and a modest savings account. Her dishes didn't even match. Furnished apartments did not come cheap in Atlanta. She could only hope housing was not as costly in Purdyville, since she was taking a pay cut.

Frankie stepped into a hot shower a few minutes later, giving in to the tired, washed-out feeling that had plagued her all day. Hot tears streamed down her face as she lowered herself, sitting, in a corner of the shower, the only place she found refuge after a bad day. She could cry and nobody would be the wiser.

She had seen the aftermath of so much violence these past ten years. She had visited crime scenes that had shocked even the most seasoned detectives. Some of the pictures never faded from memory. They found their way into the subconscious, spilled over into dreams, made the nights darker and longer and dimmed the light on a sunny day. As hard as Frankie tried, it was impossible to remain professionally detached from everything she saw.

Sometimes, one or two details stuck in her mind: a woman's bloody hairbrush, a child's bicycle that lay on the street, bent and broken after the accident that had snuffed life from the youngster. Details of human life, flesh and bone, that would soon become case numbers. Sometimes it was not the crime so much as those details that seemed to take on a life of their own, attaching themselves like cancerous cells to a vital organ, eating at it slowly, like parasites that eventually destroy their hosts.

Some cops drank.

Frankie cried in the shower.

She had witnessed such a crime the day she ended up in bed with Jim Connors, although, in all honesty, she had already been feeling vulnerable. She'd celebrated her thirty-second birthday the week before and she'd realized that, with the exception of her mother, she was alone in the world. There was no significant other and no prospects were on the horizon. She'd watched her friends marry and have babies, and she'd pretended, even to herself, that it was not what she wanted out of life. And it wasn't likely to happen, what with her track record. The few men she'd dated were turned off by a street-smart woman who chain-smoked, packed a gun and discussed autopsy findings over dinner. She had screwed up so many blind dates that her friends had stopped setting her up.

She had been an easy target for a man like Jim Connors, who went through women like her mother did panty hose.

Frankie wondered if she was losing her femininity. Not that she'd ever been a real ''girlie'' girl to begin with. Her father had taught her to shoot when she was eight years old, and she'd been a better fighter and tree-climber than the boys on her block. She'd had the scruffy knees and elbows to prove it. When she'd developed a crush on Davie Brown in third grade, she'd punched him in the face to get his attention. Davie ended up with a nosebleed and she a good paddling by the school principal. Davie had started hanging out with Pammy Wilson on the playground. Pammy wore pinafores, socks with lace around the edges, and Mary Jane's. Frankie wouldn't have been caught dead in such an outfit. Against her mother's will, she dressed in jeans, T-shirts and old sneakers. Her dark hair, as unruly then as it was now, forever needed combing. Eve tried braiding it or pulling it into a tight ponytail, but by the end of the day it looked as though it hadn't been brushed in a week.

Face it, Frankie told herself as she continued to sit beneath the spray of water that had grown cold, she was a failure at being a woman. In fact, she didn't much care for women's silliness. She didn't go ballistic over the latest lip color, and the only reason she wore the slightest bit of makeup at all was because her mother had shamed her into it.

''You're a beautiful woman, Francis,'' Eve Hutton had once said, ''and I'm not just saying that because I'm incapable of giving birth to an ugly child. But you need to do something with yourself. Have you ever heard of eye makeup?'' Eve had eye shadow in every conceivable color.

Jim Connors had claimed he liked strong women who knew their own minds and didn't come with a bunch of frills. He'd said Frankie was a refreshing change, that he admired her intelligence and the fact she didn't use feminine wiles to attract a man's attention.

Jim Connors was full of shit.

And she had believed every word of it.

Never again.

Two days later, Frankie walked into Captain Wayford's office. Her car was packed. She had changed her oil, replaced her spark plugs, checked the transmission, brake and power-steering fluid, and added air to one tire. She had washed and waxed her car by hand, then cleaned her apartment from top to bottom, so that it looked better than when she'd rented it. She had fought back tears all morning, but she was determined to see it through like a professional.

The Purdyville Realtor had called. A small house had just become vacant on Elm Street. It sounded perfect, and even came with a fenced-in yard. Frankie had always wanted a dog; perhaps this was her chance.

A fresh start, that's what it was.

So why wasn't she excited?

Wayford had a cigarette tucked behind his ear. "You see the morning paper?"

Frankie shook her head. "I don't read the paper. Too much violence."

"There was a drug raid night before last. Connors was in charge."

"Good for him," she said dully.

"Only problem, they raided the wrong house."

Frankie couldn't hide her astonishment. "You're kidding."

"You're never going to believe this, but Connors and his team got the address mixed up somehow, and they raided Judge Henry's house."

"Oh, my God!"

"The judge is mad as hell. He was giving a dinner party for a bunch of hotshots, including his priest, the mayor and Connors's own father-in-law. The mayor's wife fainted. They thought she was having a heart attack and dialed 911."

Frankie couldn't believe her ears. Sure, there were screwups in the department from time to time, but this was a major one that would embarrass the department. "How could something like that have happened?"

Wayford shrugged. "Connors claims he was set up, says his snitch gave him the wrong house number. Like I told Connors, we've been working with this snitch a long time, never had a problem." He paused. "I figure Connors was in such a hurry to look like a hero that he wrote down the wrong number."

"What's going to happen to him now?"

Wayford shrugged. "I had no choice but to suspend him until we look into the matter, but I have a feeling he's going down on this one and there's no way I can prevent it from going on his record. Gonna make him look real bad, trying to bust a judge and sending the mayor's wife to the hospital and all. Way I figure, he'll probably end up behind a desk doing grunt work."

A look passed between them. Suddenly, Frankie understood. "Sorry to hear it."

"Yeah, I knew you'd be brokenhearted over it." Wayford handed her an envelope. "Everything you need is in here, including your severance pay and whatever else I could get you.''

''Thank you.''

Wayford leaned back in his chair and grinned. ''Hey, I hope the two of you were practicing safe sex.''

Frankie arched one brow. ''I beg your pardon?''

''Word has it, Connors has a serious case of herpes.''

Frankie tried to maintain a sober look. ''Gee, the guy sure is having a streak of bad luck. But don't worry about me, Captain, I know how to take care of myself.''

He gazed at her a long moment, as though pondering something in his mind. ''Behave yourself, kid,'' he said, sounding like the man who'd driven her home after ball games and soccer practice. ''I'm going to be checking in on you from time to time.''

Two

Police Chief Matt Webber rubbed the grit from his tired eyes and tried to concentrate on what the fire marshall, Orvell Dean, was saying. After hours of sifting through rubble in what was left of the small frame house, Orvell had finally come to the conclusion that the fire was an act of arson. The fact that there were two gas cans present was all the answer Matt needed, but Orvell insisted on knowing the point of origin. As he'd crawled about, he'd regaled Matt with his latest fishing stories, of which there were many. Matt personally didn't give a damn *where* the fire had started or that Orvell had won the Purdyville Fishing Tournament two years in a row; he wanted a shower and some shut-eye.

"What d'you say we wrap it up?" Matt suggested, hoping Orvell had run out of fish tales and they could be on their way.

"I only got one thing to say," Orvell began, tucking his ink pen in the pocket of his stained uniform.

"What's that?" Matt asked, trying to walk through the muck created by the hundreds of gallons of water it had taken to put out the fire. His shoes made sucking noises each time he took a step.

"I feel sorry for Irma and Homer Gibbs."

Matt had to agree. The elderly couple who owned the rental property had enough problems, what with Homer having suffered two strokes in the past year. Word had it he was bedridden. Matt knew the couple, who were both approaching ninety, depended on the extra income to make ends meet. "I don't know how they'll manage," Matt said, thinking of Irma fondly. There was a time, before the woman's osteoporosis had set in, before her hands had become gnarled with arthritis, that she'd been the town's most productive citizen. She'd taught Sunday school at the Baptist church for more than thirty years, visited the sick and organized fund-raisers for every imaginable cause. Homer had contributed, too. As school principal, he'd set high standards for faculty as well as the student body. He'd been tough, and although the kids had grumbled—Matt included—they'd all received a better education because of him. Now Homer was helpless and Irma was doing her best to look after him, because they had no family to speak of.

"This town's a better place because of them," Orvell said, as though reading Matt's mind.

"I think it's time we returned the favor. Do something nice for them." He watched as a late-model Nissan pulled in front of the property and parked. A woman climbed out and peered over the top of the car. At first she just stared.

"Oh, my God!" she cried out. "Please tell me this isn't 414 Elm Street."

Matt walked toward her. She wasn't from Purdyville— he would have noticed her. "May I help you?"

"Is this 414 Elm?"

"Yes, it is."

Frankie slapped her open palm against her forehead. "Aw, shit!"

Matt shoved his hands in his pockets and exchanged

glances with Orvell. "Is there something I can do for you, miss?"

Frankie turned to Orvell and noted his uniform, which indicated he was with the fire department. "What happened here?"

"House burned down."

Frankie sighed and rolled her eyes. "I've already figured that out for myself. How did it happen?"

"We suspect arson."

"Aw, shit. Shit, shit, shit!"

Matt chuckled. As much as he liked pretty women— and this one was easy on the eyes—her language made him think of truck stops and bus stations.

Frankie eyed the tall, dark-haired man and wondered what he looked like beneath the grime and soot. Not that she had any business looking at men, after what she'd been through. "You think this is funny?"

Matt closed the distance between them. She looked mad enough to chew a fence post. He crossed his arms and leaned against the woman's car. "No, I don't think it's a dang bit funny, lady, but there's not much sense in cryin' over spilled milk, as they say. You mind telling me why you're in such a tizzy?"

Frankie would have told him to mind his own business if she weren't so upset. "I was supposed to rent this place. I've driven for hours, I'm exhausted—"

"And irritable," Matt supplied, and received a dark look.

"And now I have no place to live. Well, that's just dandy. Would you mind not leaning on my car? You're getting it filthy, and I just washed and waxed it."

Matt stepped away, noting where the soot from his jeans had smudged her automobile. "Sorry about that.

Guess I'm a little on the tired side myself.'' He wiped the car with his palm, and the smudge grew worse.

"Now look what you've done," Frankie said in exasperation. She felt the beginnings of a headache. "Just leave it alone, okay?''

"No way," Matt said. "I'm not about to dirty up your car. Fine lady like you shouldn't have to ride around with soot all over the side of her vehicle. Orvell, you got a clean handkerchief?''

The man pulled one out of his pants pocket and handed it to Matt, who managed to get most of the grime off. "There now, that's better. I can always borrow the neighbor's hose and wash it if you like.''

"That won't be necessary.'' Frankie didn't like his attitude. As if she didn't have enough problems, she had to run into some smart-mouthed hillbilly who seemed hellbent on making the situation worse.

"I meant no disrespect," Matt said. "Just trying to be friendly. You look like you could take my head off my shoulders with one bite.''

"I reckon she's under a lot of stress," Orvell said, "just arriving in town to find her rental house burned down and all.''

"Stress?'' Frankie asked. "I invented the word. But you needn't make excuses for my behavior. I'm a grown woman, and a professional police detective.'' She motioned toward the house. "This is child's play compared to what I've seen.''

Orvell started to say something, but Matt interrupted. "A real police detective, huh? Well, I'm impressed. How about you, Orvell?''

He gave Matt a funny look. "Yeah.''

"And a damn good one at that," Frankie replied, unaware of the looks the men were giving each other.

"So, what brings you to Purdyville?" Orvell asked.

"Job transfer. I'm going to be working for the Purdyville Police Department. And believe me, it won't be easy working with a bunch of good ol' boys after the pros I've dealt with. What can you tell me about the police chief?"

Matt and Orvell exchanged amused looks. "Oh, well, he's a nice-enough guy," Matt said. "Good-looking, too."

The other man chuckled. "And don't think he don't know it. Why, half the women in town are hot for him."

"A ladies' man, huh?" Frankie snorted. "Just what I need. Another man whose brain is located behind his zipper."

Matt frowned. Orvell roared with laughter.

"Did I say something funny?" Frankie asked.

"Lady, I don't know you personally," Orvell managed, "but I hate to just stand here and watch you dig yourself into a deep hole."

"It's okay," Matt said. "I'm enjoying myself."

Frankie sensed they were making fun of her. "Would the two of you mind sharing your little joke with me? I'm in no mood to play guessing games."

Orvell stepped forward. "I'd like to introduce you to Purdyville's esteemed police chief, Matt Webber."

The color drained from Frankie's face as she met Webber's amused gaze. His eyes were a startling blue. She simply stared, mortified by her own behavior.

"I think she's speechless," Orvell said.

Matt shook his head. "I find that hard to believe."

Frankie coughed to hide her embarrassment. "I… uh…don't know what to say, Chief Webber. I'm Frankie Daniels, from the APD, and I was out of line. I'm sorry. I hope you will overlook my behavior, what with circumstances being what they are." Mustering what little dignity she had left, she turned abruptly, thinking it would be better to get into her car and drive as far away from Purdyville as she could get. There was probably an excellent doughnut shop in the next town. She had always liked doughnuts.

She was not prepared for the patch of mud. Sliding about three feet, Frankie tried to keep from falling, arms flailing, hips gyrating as though she were trying to learn the latest steps to a new dance.

The men watched, brows arched high on their foreheads. Orvell cocked his head to the side as if trying to figure out what she was doing. "You reckon she's trying to do that moonwalk dance like Michael Jackson?" he asked softly.

"I think she's trying not to fall on her butt," Matt replied, at the same time noticing what a nice behind she had. "A dollar says she won't make it." He pulled a crumpled bill from his front pocket.

Orvell produced four quarters. "I don't know. She looks pretty limber to me."

Frankie lost her footing and landed on her backside, all the while cursing. "I hate my life!" she bellowed. "And I hate this town. I have never been so...so damned angry and humiliated in my life." She continued to rant and rave.

Orvell gave Matt his change. "You think she's okay?"

Matt shrugged. "I don't know. I haven't heard screeching like that since I ran into a rabid coon. You think I should shoot her?"

"Naw, she's too pretty to shoot." He looked at Matt. "You think she's pretty?"

"She's not bad. Got a mouth on her, though."

"I'd better head on out of here," Orvell said, checking his wristwatch. "I promised the wife I'd take her to bingo tonight, and I've got a lot to do in the meantime. You planning on going? That redhead will probably be there. You know, the one who wears those tight shorts and halter tops?'' Orvell nudged him and grinned. ''Don't think I haven't seen the way you look at her.''

''I know the one,'' he said, but his eyes were presently glued to the woman in the mud. He stretched and yawned. ''I'll see how the day goes. I may still be out here waiting for this woman to come out of that mud hole by the time they start.''

Orvell chuckled as he began picking up his gear. ''I'll have my report on your desk in a couple of days. You going to notify Homer and Irma?''

''Yeah.''

Frankie was only vaguely aware the men were conversing as she finally pushed herself up. She was covered with mud from head to toe. Why couldn't she have just landed in quicksand and been done with it? She tried to move, but her sneakers were stuck in the goop. She glared at Matt.

''Please don't bother to help me, I'm doing just fine.''

''We didn't want to insult you, what with you being such a hotshot detective and all,'' Matt said. ''Figured you were used to this sort of thing.''

Orvell reached for his coffee thermos. ''I kinda figured you for one of them women's libbers.''

''They're called feminists now, Orvell,'' Matt whispered, ''and we don't even want to go there. Is there something I can do for you, Detective Daniels?''

Frankie stood there a full minute without speaking. Hot tears stung the backs of her eyes, but she would rip her heart right out of her chest before she'd give in to them. Hadn't she made a big-enough fool of herself for one day? She had literally been thrown out of the last town, only to end up in Hicksville, U.S.A., with a burned-down house, and a cocky, womanizing police chief who seemed to find her situation amusing.

She planted her hands on her hips and waited. She would not ask him for help. She would stand there and become fly bait first. Orvell drove off, waving as he went, and still she refused to speak to the tall man standing only a few yards from her.

Matt sensed the woman was at the end of her rope. She might come off sounding tough as nails, but he could see the emotions playing across her face, and he suspected she was close to tears. He stepped closer. "Okay, give me your hands," he ordered. "I don't have all day." He reached for her.

Finally, she relented. This was not the time to let pride stand in the way, or she might very well find herself flat on her behind in the muck once more. She grabbed on to him.

Matt grasped her wrists, surprised by how slender they were, how dainty her stained hands. She came off sounding big, but she was no more than a runt of a woman, compared to the size of her mouth. "Go slow," he warned, looking into smoky blue eyes. He couldn't help notice how smooth her complexion was. Finally, he managed to pull her free. "You might want to hose off next door before you get in your car," he said, releasing her.

They found a garden hose easily enough. Matt turned on the spigot, and Frankie shivered as soon as the cold water hit. Goose pimples stood out on her arms. "It's cool here for July."

"You're in mountain country, but we've had an unusually cool summer."

Frankie had been only vaguely aware of the changing scenery during her drive up. Her mind had been on other things, like what she was going to do with the rest of her life. She had paid little mind to the rolling hills or distant mountaintops, other than to wish she could jump off one and be done with it.

Matt tried not to stare as Frankie washed beneath the hose, the water plastering her clothes to her body. Her nipples hardened and pressed against her T-shirt as though trying to break free of the clammy material. Something in his gut tightened at the sight. Frankie Daniels was going to turn a lot of heads in the town of Purdyville. She reached for the spigot, bending slightly. Nice butt, he thought.

Frankie caught him staring. "Like what you see, Chief?"

Matt didn't so much as bat an eye. "I admire a healthy body, if that's what you're asking." He paused. "What's your story, Daniels?"

"My story?"

"A detective with your credentials has no business working in a small town where the biggest crime is what Alma Grimes charges for a slice of pecan pie at the Half Moon Café."

"Have you looked at my personnel file? Your uncle faxed it to you."

"He was a little vague as to why you requested a change. Something about you wanting to get away from big-city life and live in a small town. Well, this is about as small as it gets."

Frankie tried to hide her surprise. Captain Wayford had obviously doctored her papers. Not that it mattered. Webber would probably fire her, anyway. Not that she had any intention of staying in Hooterville Hell to begin with. The sooner she got out, the better. All she needed was a hot shower, food in her stomach and a good night's sleep, and she was gone.

"I guess it's not important why you're here, but if you're planning on hanging around, you need to know the rules up front. I don't care how many commendations you have or how smart you think you are, I don't give preferential treatment. And I won't have you referring to my men as good ol' boys. I run the show. You have a problem with that?"

Frankie was stunned. "You mean I still have the job?"

"As long as we agree on those conditions. I don't want trouble within the department. Do I make myself clear?"

"Crystal clear. And you managed to maintain that charming disposition at the same time."

He chuckled despite his resolve to remain serious and detached. "Anybody ever accused you of being mouthy?"

"A few people have mentioned it in passing conversation."

He nodded. "I have to go by the Gibbses' place and give them the bad news. If you like, you can follow me and I'll point out Purdyville's motel. Nothing fancy, mind you."

"I'm not looking for fancy."

"Good thing, too. It's the only one we've got." He took in the length of her. She reminded him of a wet puppy. "Hold on." He hurried to his pickup truck and pulled out a piece of plastic. "You may want to put this on your front seat so you don't get mud all over it."

"Thanks." She put it in place. He continued to stare at her. "Anything wrong?"

He just shook his head and started for his truck. Frankie took one last look at the charred remains of the little house as she climbed into her car and sighed heavily. Things were not looking good. She could only hope it wouldn't get worse.

The Pines Motel offered free cable TV, clean sheets and a small coffeemaker in the room for thirty-seven dollars a night or two hundred dollars a week. Frankie decided to pay for a full week, as she suspected she'd need at least that long to find another place.

After lugging her suitcase into a room that had been decorated when foil wallpaper had been the rage, Frankie soaked in a hot bath, washed her hair and dried it on a thin towel that had seen too many wash days. But the mattress was firm and the TV in good working order, so she lay there and smoked one cigarette after another, wondering where she was going to live. She was too tired to call the Realtor. She stubbed out her cigarette and continued to lie there.

At least she had a job, whether she wanted it or not. She was surprised Webber hadn't sent her packing. Damn her mouth. She had never learned to curb her tongue. She lit another cigarette. Well, she had to give him a little credit. He might be laid-back and easygoing but he seemed competent, as far as she could tell. He had set the record straight right away as to what he expected from her and what he would and would not tolerate.

But he was a ladies' man, and that made him her number one enemy. He was no different from Connors as far as she was concerned.

Not that any of it mattered. She had no intention of hanging around any longer than she had to. She would start putting together a résumé immediately. Frankie Daniels was not a small-town cop. She needed to check into big cities, where she could better utilize her skills. She would do a brief stint in this "Andy of Mayberry" town until something better came along, but she was bound for greater things.

Her father had told her so.

Frankie finished her cigarette and put it out. Her stomach growled, reminding her she hadn't bothered with breakfast or lunch, only meeting her coffee quota for the morning. But she was too tired to think about food at the moment. Closing her eyes, she fell asleep instantly.

The room was dark when Frankie awoke, and she was amazed that she'd slept most of the day. Obviously, her body was trying to catch up after the sleepless nights she'd suffered once her affair with Jim Connors had blown up in her face. She pushed the thought from her head and made for the vanity and the coffeepot, trying to avoid looking at herself in the mirror as she put on a cup to brew. Her hair was a tangled mop, but the dark circles beneath her eyes weren't as noticeable.

She drank her coffee and smoked three cigarettes, one after another, as she paced the room and wondered—dreaded, actually—what lay ahead. The telephone rang. Frankie wondered if it was Webber, making sure she was settled in. She answered the phone, and her mother started in on her immediately.

"Francis, the things you put me through," Eve said from the other end. "I should just have a heart attack and get it over with. Is that what you want?"

Frankie blinked. "It's good to hear from you, too, Mom, and we both know you have the heart of a twenty-year-old. What's wrong?"

"What's wrong? How about the fact you didn't call me when you arrived in Purdyville like you promised? How about the fire that burned down the house you rented, and you didn't even bother to call me? I had to hear it from a perfect stranger. I don't mind telling you I had to swallow two nerve pills in case I got a call to come up there and identify your charred body. And I wouldn't have the first clue how to get there because I still haven't found Purdyville, North Carolina, on my map. I'm telling you, Francis, they're going to lock me away one of these days, and it'll be all your fault.''

Frankie wished her mother were locked up right now—without phone privileges. "I was nowhere near the fire when it occurred.''

"How was I supposed to know that? If it hadn't been for that nice policeman—''

"What policeman?''

"Your new boss, I assume. I was ready to call every burn unit within a five-hundred-mile radius when that Realtor told me what had happened. Until that nice police chief assured me you were okay.''

"You spoke with Matt Webber?''

"I most certainly did. How do you think I found you?''

Frankie gave a mental sigh. Webber would think her mother a lunatic. "I was going to call, Mom, after I took a nap. I was exhausted when I arrived.''

"Such a nice man, Chief Webber. He sounds young. Is he married?''

"Happily," Frankie lied. "Four kids and one on the way.''

"You would never have put your father through this sort of thing," her mother went on, changing the topic. "You would have pulled over and used a pay phone the minute you hit town.''

Frankie reached for another cigarette. Here it was. Now she would be forced to hear how she had always loved her father more.

"You always loved your father more, Francis.''

"That's not true, Mom." Frankie yawned. "Look, do

we have to go through this right now? I haven't eaten today, and I have to find another place to live."

"If you had come here like I asked, you could have stayed with me. I could set you up in business, and I would never again have to go to sleep worrying about you getting your throat cut during the night in a drug bust. There's a building for rent not two miles from me."

"I don't want to open a dress shop, Mother," Frankie said, using the tone she used when her mother pushed too far. "I don't even *wear* dresses." Frankie winced the minute she said it. Now her mother would accuse her of being gay.

"It's a wonder you're not a lesbian. You act just like a man. That's why you have trouble finding one. A woman your age should be married with children."

Frankie closed her eyes and counted to ten. "I have to run now, okay?"

"It must be a small town if it's not even on the map. Do you know what your odds are of meeting a man?"

"Later, Mom." Frankie hung up. It was times like this she was tempted to put her own gun in her mouth. No, on second thought, it would be easier to just shoot her mother.

Frankie pulled on a fresh pair of jeans and a sweatshirt from her suitcase, her hunger pains reminding her she couldn't stay in bed with the covers pulled over her head as she would have preferred. Luckily, she'd noted a restaurant next door. She could walk over, order something to go, and then spend the evening watching TV. Anything to take her mind off her troubles.

Virgil's Restaurant and Tavern smelled of mouthwatering barbecue. Rough-hewn walls, an oversize fireplace and plank floors gave the place a rustic look. Pictures of NASCAR drivers adorned one wall; the other was devoted to shelves of bowling and fishing trophies and various plaques, praising Virgil Kellett for his generosity to the Boy Scouts, the Jaycees and various other organizations.

A circular bar dominated the room, surrounded by tables draped in vinyl cloths. Somebody had thought to roll the silverware in paper napkins and put a plastic flower in a vase on each table. Frankie approached a big man standing behind the cash register counting bills. He looked up and smiled heartily.

"Hello, young lady. Would you like a table?"

Frankie liked his voice. "Are you Virgil?"

"Sure am. Virgil Kellett."

"What's the specialty of the house?" she asked, although the smells coming from the kitchen made it obvious.

"Barbecue. The best in town. Ribs, chicken, sandwiches. We also put out a good hamburger or steak platter. You just tell me what you're in the mood for and I'll fix it."

"How big are your sandwiches?"

"How big you want it?"

She made a huge circle with her index fingers and thumbs. He laughed. Judging from the lines around his mouth and eyes, Frankie suspected he did it often.

"I got what I call a monster sandwich, served with spicy fries and a side of coleslaw. Don't know where you're going to put it, skinny little thing like you."

"Trust me, I can handle it."

Virgil wrote out an order ticket. "You just passing through?"

"I live here, as of today."

"Well, what d'you know, we got a new face in town. What's your name?"

She told him.

"I reckon I'll have to buy you a cold beer while you're waiting on your order." He yelled over at the bartender. "Abby, give this young lady a cold one on the house. She just moved to town, so give her the VIP treatment."

"Thank you," Frankie said, warmed by his friendly nature. "Would you make my order to go?"

"Sure will." He headed for the back and pushed through a set of swinging doors.

Frankie made for the bar, choosing a stool at the back where she could watch the door. Habit. Cops always watched the doorways. An attractive middle-aged woman approached her. "Welcome to Purdyville, honey. What'll you have?"

"Whatever you have on draft is fine."

"Coming right up."

Frankie looked about the restaurant as she sipped her beer. The clientele was mixed. A group of businessmen in suits pored over papers at one table, several men in jeans and work shirts sat directly across from her at the bar, no doubt sharing a cold one at the end of the day, and two or three couples sat in booths, obviously the beginnings of the dinner crowd.

She'd only taken a few sips of her beer when the front door opened and four men walked through. The group was led by a stocky, broad-shouldered man who might have been handsome at one time, but was now soft in the middle, his face and neck puffy with added flesh. He had dark blond hair and was dressed in jeans that were too tight to be flattering. He and his buddies took a seat nearby. Glancing up, he caught her staring and grinned. Frankie turned back to her beer.

"Well, now, would you take a look at that, boys? It must be spring, because there's a pretty little flower sitting at the bar tonight."

Frankie knew without looking the voice belonged to the blond. She winced inwardly at the sound of approaching footsteps.

"Hey, there," he said, pulling out the stool next to hers. "Is this seat taken?"

Frankie glanced up and shook her head. He took the stool.

"You're not from around here, are you? I would have remembered a sweet-looking thing like you." He held out his hand. "Name's Willie-Jack. Willie-Jack Pitts."

Frankie nodded but didn't take his hand.

He motioned for the bartender. "Abby, give me the usual, and bring this young lady another beer."

"No thanks," Frankie said. "I'm waiting on a to-go order."

"Hey, it's Friday night. Time to celebrate."

Frankie suspected he celebrated each day of the week. It would explain the paunch. "Thanks, but I'm not interested."

He was frowning as Abby brought his beer. The woman shot Frankie a sympathetic look. "Your order will be ready in just a jiff." Frankie nodded her thanks.

Willie-Jack gave Frankie a come-hither smile. "So, where you from?" he asked. "No, let me guess—"

"Would you excuse me?" Frankie said, sliding away from the bar. She made for the ladies' room. She hoped he would rejoin his friends in the meantime. When she came out a few minutes later, he was still sitting there, talking to his friends from across the bar. Frankie decided to wait for her order at the cash register. Picking up a menu, she studied it. She felt the hair on the back of her neck prickle and knew the man had followed her over.

"Hey, I was beginning to think you'd left on me. That drink offer still stands."

She turned around and found Willie-Jack standing too close. "Look, I don't know how to put this in a nice way," she began, "so I'll forgo the pleasantries. I'm not interested. Get it?"

His smile turned to a sneer. "What crawled up your ass, lady?"

"I don't like men with gun racks in the back of their pickup trucks and Confederate flag license tags."

He looked stunned. "What are you, some kind of psychic? Oh, I get it. You saw me pull in."

"I didn't have to. You've got it written all over you."

Willie-Jack glanced at his buddies, who were watching the entire exchange. He shot a dark look at Frankie. "You've got a smart mouth, lady. I don't like being insulted."

"Do the words *get lost* mean anything to you?" Frankie was glad to see Virgil push through the swinging doors. A frown creased his brow when he caught sight of Willie-Jack. The big man stepped behind the cash register.

"Sorry it took so long," he said. "I had to drop a bag of fries in. I think you'll like them." He took the twenty Frankie offered. "Evenin', Willie-Jack," he said, although he didn't look pleased to see him.

Frankie remained silent as Virgil counted out her change. "Thank you," she said.

Virgil handed her a large, square to-go box and a plastic container with her drink. "Come back and see us, hon."

Frankie smiled and made her way out the door. She hadn't taken more than a few steps when she heard the door open behind her. She kept walking.

"Hey, you!"

Willie-Jack had followed her to the parking lot. She ignored him and kept walking. All at once, he grabbed her arm. Startled, she turned quickly, and the container of food and her beverage slipped from her hand. They fell to the ground, dumping her drink, barbecue sandwich and fries on the asphalt.

"You son of a bitch," she said, jerking her arm free. "Don't you ever put your hands on me."

His face darkened. "I don't take kindly to being called an SOB. You want me to replace your dinner? Come inside and I'll buy you a steak."

Frankie couldn't believe the man was still pursuing her. She wondered if he was drunk. "What's with you?" she demanded. "Are you deaf, dumb *and* stupid? I don't want to come inside with you. What does it take to get through that thick skull of yours?"

His look turned menacing. "You know what I think? I think you're one of the coldest bitches I've ever met."

"And I think there must have been a little inbreeding in your family, mountain man. Get away from me."

Frankie was vaguely aware that Willie-Jack's friends were standing at the front door of the restaurant. Suddenly, he grabbed both of her arms. "Somebody needs to put you in your place, you know that?"

"Let her go, Willie-Jack," Virgil shouted, shoving his way past the group at the door. "I've already called the chief. You don't come to my place and assault my customers."

Willie-Jack's fingers dug into Frankie's arms, his nails biting through the soft flesh. She saw red. All at once, she brought her knee up as hard as she could and made contact with his groin. She saw the pain register on his face. He muttered a foul word and fell forward slightly but didn't release her. His nails broke skin. She threw her head forward and slammed her skull against his nose. He howled and dragged his nails down the insides of her arms. Frankie refused to cry out. She twisted around, foot raised thigh high, and kicked him in the stomach, hard as she could, with the heel of her sneaker. Willie-Jack slumped to the ground, banging his head on the asphalt.

"Holy shit," one of his friends said, but didn't make a move toward him.

Virgil hurried toward her. "Are you okay?"

Her arms were bleeding, but Frankie nodded as she gazed at the prostrate man on the ground. Blood streamed from his nose. All at once, she heard the sound of tires squealing. She glanced up as a squad car raced in her direction and screeched to a halt. Matt Webber climbed from the car and raced toward her.

"What's going on?"

Virgil spoke up. "This young lady just beat the crap out of Willie-Jack Pitts, that's what." Virgil looked at Frankie. "Pardon my crassness, miss."

Matt looked at Frankie, noting the red streaks on her arms. "I assume he had it coming."

"Damn right he did," she said. "I don't particularly like being mauled by some redneck who thinks he's God's gift. I just hope he's had his rabies shots."

"She's right," Virgil said. "He accosted her in the parking lot. I saw the whole thing through the window. Told Abby to call you. This lady was merely trying to defend herself." He wiped sweat from his brow. "Glad you came quickly."

"I was close by."

The man on the ground moaned slightly. Matt knelt beside him. He chuckled. "You want me to call an ambulance, Willie-Jack?"

Willie-Jack opened his eyes. He blinked, tried to focus. His gaze found Frankie. "You're going to pay for this."

Matt whipped a small notebook from his shirt. "I'd

keep my mouth shut if I were you, stud," he said. "You just assaulted Purdyville's new police officer."

Willie-Jack looked surprised as he pushed himself up and touched his nose. "Police officer? You're shittin' me."

"Meet Deputy Frankie Daniels."

"I think she broke my nose," he countered. "That's police brutality sure as shit."

Matt yanked him to his feet. "Sounds like you had it coming. Put your hands behind your back, Willie-Jack. You know the routine."

Willie-Jack opened his mouth to argue, but Matt slapped the cuffs on him.

A second squad car pulled up and a deputy climbed out. Matt shoved Willie-Jack toward the deputy's car. "Run him over to the emergency room so they can check him out, then take him in and book him on assault charges. I'll take care of the paperwork."

"I ain't going to jail," Willie-Jack said.

"You're not resisting arrest, are you?" Matt said. "Go ahead and make my day."

The deputy grabbed Willie-Jack's arm, opened the back door of the car and pushed him inside, none too gently. He slammed the door and took off. Matt looked at Frankie. "You okay?"

"Fine."

"Those scratches look nasty. You want me to take you to the ER?"

She shook her head. "No."

Virgil insisted on going inside for a bottle of peroxide. Frankie stood there patiently as he poured it on both arms and handed her a napkin to mop the excess.

"Is that your dinner?" Matt asked, noting the spilled food.

"It was."

"Come with me. I'll get you something to eat and take your report. Virgil, I'll call you later."

"Sure thing, Chief." Virgil began cleaning up the mess. He looked up. "That man needs to be horsewhipped and run out of town."

Matt chuckled. "From the looks of it, I think he just got whipped."

Virgil straightened and looked at Frankie. "You come back tomorrow night and I'll give you dinner on the house."

Frankie thanked him and followed Matt to his squad car, climbing in on the passenger's side. Matt joined her in the front seat. "You sure you're okay?"

"I've suffered worse injuries." She strapped herself in. "I'm just pissed right now. I'll get over it."

"I hope you're planning to press charges."

She shook her head. "I'd rather face him on the street than in a courtroom."

Matt smiled. "You're tough, Daniels."

"I try to walk away from trouble, but I refuse to take abuse. The judge will give him a slap on the wrist, but I'll pistol-whip him if he comes within a hundred yards of me."

Matt suspected she would. "I hope I don't end up arresting both of you."

"I'll be discreet and wipe my fingerprints off the gun."

He chuckled. "Willie-Jack is a troublemaker, and the town bully. He and his old man have rap sheets a mile long. They've both served time. I locked up Willie-Jack for a month when I discovered he was holding cockfights in his grandfather's barn. I'll see that he spends a couple of days behind bars, at least till he cools off."

"You certainly arrived on the scene quick enough. I'm impressed."

"I was knocking on your door at the motel when I got the call. Wanted to see if you'd gotten settled in okay." He pulled into the parking lot of a restaurant, where a sign read Half Moon Café. Window boxes stuffed with plastic flowers adorned the large plate-glass windows, and a sign on the glass door announced a meat loaf special. The parking lot was full. Frankie figured folks in Purdyville must be fond of meat loaf.

She noted the stares the minute she and Matt stepped inside, especially from two women sitting at a table near the door. A slightly overweight woman hurried over carrying menus. She tossed Frankie a curious look but didn't say anything. "Evenin', Chief. Table for two?" When he nodded, they were led to a booth covered in red plastic vinyl.

"Alma, meet my new deputy, Frankie Daniels."

The woman looked surprised. "Nice to meet you. I'm Alma Grimes. My husband and I own the place."

Frankie smiled. "You obviously do a good business."

"We do pretty good." Alma handed them each a menu. "I didn't know you were hiring a new deputy, Chief."

"Abe is retiring in a couple of months."

"That's right, I forgot. We'll have to give him a little party." She looked at Frankie. "Welcome to Purdyville, Miss Daniels." She paused and blushed. "I suppose I should refer to you as Deputy Daniels."

"Just call me Frankie."

"And I'm Alma. Anybody interested in the special?"

Matt looked at Frankie, who nodded. "Two meat loaf specials," he said, "and an iced tea for me."

"I'll have coffee," Frankie said. She wished she'd brought her cigarettes from the motel room.

"I'll tell Betty." Alma hurried away.

Matt crossed his arms and leaned back in his seat, studying her. "So, not counting your run-in with the town redneck, what do you think of Purdyville?"

"I haven't seen much of it. I took a long nap once I checked in at the motel." She smelled smoke from the booth behind her and turned around. Two men were deep in conversation. "Excuse me," she said to the one who was smoking. "May I have a cigarette? I forgot mine."

He smiled. "Sure." He tapped his pack against his hand and several popped out. "Will three hold you till you get home?"

"Yes, thank you very much," Frankie told him, accepting a pack of matches as well.

"Anytime." He glanced over his shoulder and nodded at Matt before turning around in his booth and resuming his conversation.

"You mind if I smoke?" Frankie asked.

Matt shrugged and pushed the ashtray closer to her. A young waitress appeared in a too-tight uniform and served their beverages. "How are you this evening, Chief?" she asked, setting the glasses on the table. She ignored Frankie.

"Doing fine, Betty, and you?"

She fluttered her eyelashes and sighed. "Better than I was. It gets a bit lonely now that I'm divorced."

He patted her hand. "A pretty thing like you won't have trouble meeting a good man, Betty. Someone deserving of you. Just hang in there, sweetheart, y'hear?"

She gave him a lingering look before she walked away.

"Oh, b-rother," Frankie said, rolling her eyes at the man.

"What?" His look was completely innocent.

"Do women fall all over you wherever you go?"

He chuckled. "Oh, Betty's harmless. She's just a kid." He shot her a speculative glance. "You jealous?"

Frankie groaned. The man definitely had an oversize ego. "Oh, please. I simply have problems with women who simper and men who encourage it."

He looked amused. If anyone had his attention it was the woman on the other side of the booth. Her dark hair tumbled carelessly down her back, slightly disheveled, no doubt from tussling with Willie-Jack, but she didn't seem to care. Most women would have made a wild dash to the ladies' room, but not this one. If she wore makeup, it wasn't noticeable. She obviously didn't spend a lot of time in front of the mirror, but then, she didn't have to. Her smooth skin glowed with a clean, healthy look. The set of her jaw suggested strength and perhaps a bit of stubbornness, but it did nothing to alleviate her femininity.

His gaze fell to her shoulders and, finally, her arms and the scratches and bruises there. "How are your arms?"

"More irritating than anything. I'll be okay."

"Are you all settled in at the motel?"

Frankie lit her cigarette and inhaled deeply. "The room is clean and cheap, so I'm not complaining. Besides, I've slept in a few rough places while on stakeouts. You learn to adapt."

"This is going to be a lot different from Atlanta."

"We'll see."

"You're not planning on hanging around long, are you?"

"What makes you say that?"

"You don't look too happy to be here."

She took another drag of her cigarette and studied his face. Under any other circumstances she would have been flattered to sit across the table from a man with Matt Webber's looks. He was about as good-looking as they came, now that he'd cleaned the soot from his face. She had never seen eyes that blue, and his dark complexion only emphasized their unusual color.

"I've had a bad day, believe it or not."

He nodded. "That's true."

"As for the job, I'm sure it'll take some time getting used to," she said, being deliberately vague. No matter what her ideas for the future, Matt was her boss and she had no intention of letting him know her plans.

"I don't want to invest a lot of time training you if you're going to up and leave the first opportunity you get."

"Train me?" She gave a short laugh.

"We do things differently here. Folks move at a slower pace. We don't run into many drive-by shootings and we don't have a lot of drug lords in the vicinity."

"I'll tell you this much," she said, trying to worm her way out of a straight answer as to whether or not she planned on staying. "I'm not a quitter. I'll try to acclimatize myself to the town and its people." She wasn't sure he was convinced. The fact that she had no intention of staying was her business.

"By the way, how did the Gibbses take the news about their house?" she asked, hoping to change the conversation.

"Mrs. Gibbs wasn't home. Her husband said she ran out for groceries."

"I thought he was bedridden."

"I have a key in case of an emergency. He's on so much medication he's barely coherent, but I think I managed to get through to him because he promised to relay the message to his wife when she returned. I plan to call her later."

"Mrs. Gibbs still drives? How old are the Gibbses?"

"They're almost ninety, but she still gets around pretty good. She's not the best driver in town, but I don't have the heart to take her license. I'm sure she gets tired of sitting in that house all day with an invalid."

"I hope she doesn't kill anybody while she's on one of her outings."

"Folks look out for her." He chuckled. "Some of them pull off the road when they see her coming."

"Why would Mrs. Gibbs leave her husband when he's bedridden? Don't they have a neighbor or friend who could run errands?"

"Irma Gibbs is a proud woman. She refuses to ask for help and people don't want to insult her independent nature."

"Let me get this straight. You have a town bully who causes trouble every time he walks into a place, but for some reason he's allowed to patronize any establishment he chooses. You have a ninety-year-old woman whom you've described as not being the best driver in town, but she's allowed to keep her car keys because nobody wants to hurt her feelings."

"That's the way we do things here, Daniels."

Betty reappeared with two plates and a pitcher of tea. She made a point of leaning over Matt as she filled his glass. "Anything else, Chief?"

"I believe that does it."

"I'd like more coffee," Frankie said. "If it's no trouble."

The other woman nodded and sauntered away, hips swaying provocatively. Frankie rolled her eyes. "Would you feel more comfortable if I moved to the next booth?" she asked.

"Why should I feel uncomfortable sitting with the prettiest girl in town?"

"Save your breath, Chief. That sort of thing doesn't work with me."

He shrugged and picked up his silverware. "Back to Willie-Jack. He's been kicked out of a few places from time to time. He straightens up, and they let him come back until he starts another ruckus."

"And Mrs. Gibbs?"

"She's harmless. Now, stop fussing and eat your dinner. You can't live on caffeine and cigarettes alone, although from the looks of it, I'd say you've been doing it for some time."

"Your point being?"

"You're skin and bones." He took a bite of his meat loaf.

Frankie chose to ignore what she considered an unprofessional comment, even though it wasn't his first. She suspected Matt Webber liked all women. She tasted the meat loaf and knew why the Half Moon Café was so popular. "Do you have any suspects with regard to the fire?"

"I've got someone in mind."

"Feel like sharing?"

"I know this is going to surprise you, but Willie-Jack Pitts was doing some work on the Gibbses' place. He does a few odd jobs to keep himself in beer. Anyway, from what Homer said, Irma wasn't pleased with some of Willie-Jack's work and refused to pay him the entire amount. Naturally, Willie-Jack threatened to get even."

"Imagine that."

"Pretty convenient since I'm locking him up over what happened earlier. I won't have to drive all over town looking for him."

"I'm glad I could be of service."

"How's your dinner?"

"Just like Mom's cooking."

Matt chuckled. "I had the pleasure of speaking with your mother."

"Sorry about that. She tends to get excited over the slightest thing."

"She sounded worried."

They were interrupted when a teenage boy with a bad case of acne stepped up to the table. He looked from Frankie to Matt and back to Frankie again. "Are you the one who kicked Willie-Jack's butt in Virgil Kellett's parking lot tonight?" he asked.

Frankie regarded him. "Why do you ask?"

"My mom works in the emergency room. Said he came in less than an hour ago."

"She's the one," Matt said. "This here is one mean woman."

Frankie shot him a dirty look before smiling up at the kid. "I was trying to defend myself," she said. "Fighting is for ignorant people who don't have enough sense to settle their differences like civilized people."

"Willie-Jack's nose is broken."

"That's too bad," Frankie replied. "Perhaps he'll think twice before manhandling a woman."

"You're the new deputy in town, right?"

Frankie wondered how he knew. "That's correct."

"Sorry I interrupted your dinner. I just wanted to meet the woman who laid out Willie-Jack in Virgil's parking lot. My friends and I sort of have a bet going, and I just won five bucks." He grinned and walked away.

Frankie looked at Matt. "Word travels fast."

"The mayor will probably give you the key to the city for what you did."

Frankie dove into her mashed potatoes. "Does everybody back down from Willie-Jack?"

"I don't," Matt replied. "I have three things going for me. I wear a badge, carry a loaded weapon, and I'm not afraid of him. That doesn't mean he isn't mean as a rattlesnake. I think it's only fair to warn you."

"Warn me?"

"You embarrassed him tonight, and that isn't going to sit well with a man like Willie-Jack Pitts."

Frankie forked a mouthful of deliciously seasoned green beans into her mouth. "I just love moving to new places," she said. "Gives me a chance to start out fresh and make new enemies."

"Don't get too confident, Daniels. You'll have to watch your back from now on."

Three

Frankie arrived at the Purdyville Police Department the next morning at eight o'clock sharp, dressed in her nicest T-shirt and jeans. She'd pulled her hair into a ponytail, and wore an Atlanta Braves baseball cap, the bill facing backward. She pulled off her sunglasses as she stepped inside the lobby and walked to a counter where an overweight, dour-faced receptionist sat. Her nameplate read "Velma Flatts."

"May I help you?" the woman said, taking in Frankie's appearance with obvious disapproval.

Frankie noted the look, and she was tempted to tell the woman she didn't much care for her outfit, either. Did she not know that horizontal stripes were not flattering on someone of her girth? "I'm Frankie Daniels. Would you inform Chief Webber I'm here?"

"*You're* the new deputy?" Velma didn't look impressed.

"That's me." She decided she and Velma already had something in common. Neither particularly liked the other.

"The chief is busy right now."

Frankie leaned over the counter, coming nose-to-nose with Velma. "Fifty cents says he'll see me. Why don't you buzz him?"

"I'm a Christian woman, Miz Daniels. I don't place bets."

"I can tell the two of us are going to get along just fine, Mrs. Flatts."

Lips pursed, Velma picked up the telephone and punched a button. "Daniels is here." She paused a moment before hanging up. "You can go back."

Frankie smiled. "Let's do lunch, Velma."

Matt was standing in the doorway of his office as Frankie made her way down the hall. "Good morning," he said, taking in her attire. "I've already filled out most of the paperwork to order you a uniform. They can send it overnight mail and it'll be here tomorrow. What size are you?"

"Uniform?" she said dully. "Like a French maid or something?"

Matt pointed to his own clothing. "No, like a cop. A deputy, to be precise."

She pointed. "You expect me to wear *that?*"

"No, it'll be too large for you. You'll receive one of your own." He took in her slightly wrinkled jeans. "You'll have to iron it. You *do* know how to iron, right?"

"Yeah, I'm a regular Donna Reed. But nobody told me I'd have to wear a uniform. This is how I normally dress for work."

Matt sighed. "Daniels, I don't care if you're accustomed to wearing thong underwear and a bustier. Like it or not, we wear uniforms here."

"But I'm an undercover detective."

"Not anymore." He noted the disappointment in her eyes, and he knew his words had not set well with her. "Maybe you'd like to reconsider the job."

She wanted to reconsider her life. "Okay, order me two uniforms," she snapped, "so I can have one dry cleaned when I'm wearing the other. Does the department pay for dry cleaning?''

"Nope." He crossed his arms. "And while you're still good and pissed, I may as well inform you I've made an appointment for your physical today at one o'clock."

"I had a physical six months ago."

"And you're going to have another one today. Any more questions?"

Frankie opened her mouth to protest but was interrupted by a knock at the door. Matt opened it. A squat deputy stood on the other side. "We just picked up Bobby Weaver for shoplifting at Moore's Five and Dime."

Matt nodded. "Take him back so I can question him." He turned to Frankie. "Meet Deputy Calvin Rines," he said. "We call him Cooter. This is Frankie Daniels from Atlanta," he told the man.

Cooter nodded and took off his cap. "Heard you was joining us, Miss Daniels. Welcome aboard."

"Thank you," Frankie replied, wondering if the man was being earnest. "In the future, you don't need to tip your hat or refer to me as Miss Daniels. Call me Frankie."

Cooter's face reddened as he put on his cap. "I look forward to working with you."

Matt turned to her. "I'll introduce you to the others later. I keep six deputies on the day shift, including you, and five at night."

"That's all?"

"We don't see a lot of action. You've already met Velma, I assume."

"That pleasant lady out front?" she said. "Oh, yes."

Matt couldn't hide his amusement. "See her about ordering your uniforms, then meet me in room eight at the end of the hall. I want you to sit in on this. Weaver is a habitual offender."

Velma was in the process of giving someone a recipe over the telephone when Frankie went up front. Frankie stood at the counter drumming her fingers impatiently while Velma ignored her. She noticed a woman sitting in one of the plastic chairs in the lobby, wringing her hands, and wondered if she was Bobby Weaver's wife.

"Virdie, honey, I specifically *told* you to buy chopped broccoli because it's easier to work with," Velma said. "You'll have to exchange it."

"Excuse me," Frankie said.

Velma held up her hand. "My peach recipe? Why, of course, sugar. I know it by heart. You need peaches, butter, brown sugar and walnuts. Did you get that? Buy the large cans like they use in restaurants. Oh, and vanilla ice cream. The Piggly Wiggly sells it in big tubs."

"Excuse me," Frankie said, a bit louder this time.

Velma shot her a dark look. "And, Virdie, this is very important—do *not* buy black walnuts because they leave an aftertaste. Ask Alice to go with you to the store. She'll know what quantities to buy."

Frankie sighed.

"Excuse me, Virdie, dear, but I have a visitor up front who looks as though she's about to have a hissy fit. I'll have to call you back." Velma hung up the telephone. She wore that sour look on her face again. "Is there something you need, Miz Daniels?"

"Yes, Velma, as a matter of fact, I do. I would like for you to order me two uniforms."

"The department is only responsible for paying for one. If you require another, you'll have to pay for it yourself."

"That's fine."

Velma pursed her lips. "The uniforms are not cheap, you know."

"I'll open a lemonade stand to raise the money."

Velma looked annoyed. "What size do you wear, about a fourteen?"

Frankie ignored the jab. "That's close, but order me a size ten instead."

"Won't be in for a week or more. Reckon you'll have to wear that snazzy outfit you've got on in the meantime."

"Chief Webber wants it sent overnight mail."

"I'll need a memo with his signature."

"I'll see that you get one. By the way, in the future, you may refer to me as *Deputy* Daniels."

Velma just looked at her.

Matt was leading a young boy toward one of the rooms when Frankie met him in the hall. Cooter was leaning against the wall wearing a grin. "*This* is Bobby Weaver?" she asked, unable to hide her surprise. She had expected a man with tattoos and nose rings.

"This is Bobby, all right," Matt replied. "Don't let his age fool you. He'll steal you blind before you know what's happening to you." Matt motioned to a table with four chairs. "Sit down, Bobby. You know the routine."

The boy was quiet as he took a seat. Matt surprised Frankie further by handing his revolver to Cooter. "Hang on to this. I don't need the temptation."

"Sure, Chief." Cooter took the weapon as Frankie stared in astonishment.

Matt looked at her. "I want you in on this so you can see how we interrogate those who choose to break the law. I just want you to observe and try to keep quiet, if it's possible."

Frankie was still reeling over the fact Matt had handed over his gun. He was obviously out to intimidate the boy, but what he'd done was unconscionable. She had probably interrogated more criminals in the past three years than Webber had in his entire career, and she knew what was permitted and what was not. And she hadn't been dealing with children; she was accustomed to hard-core offenders. "I promise not to steal your thunder," she said, suspecting she needed to see firsthand what went on behind closed doors.

Matt approached Bobby, who sat very still in his chair. The boy didn't look like a thief. He was a clean-cut, red-headed boy with freckles, who looked small for his age.

All at once, Matt yanked the boy up by his collar, knocking over the chair in the process. He shoved the kid against the wall, drawing a dark frown from Frankie. She remained quiet—at least for the moment.

"You've gone too far this time, Weaver," Matt said. "First it's penny candy at the Quick Trip, then comic books at the Piggly Wiggly. Now I hear you're lifting goods at the five-and-dime."

Bobby remained quiet but his eyes were wide, as though he feared he was about to get the worst beating of his life.

"I've had enough of this crap," Matt went on. "You want to be a thief, then you'll be treated like one. This time I'm sending you up the river."

Frankie blinked several times.

Bobby looked frightened. "You mean prison?"

"You got it, kid. And I'm going to see that you're tried as an adult. You're going to be an old man by the time you get out."

Frankie's jaw dropped. She closed it. "Chief, may I speak with you outside?"

He ignored her. "You're a handsome young man, Bobby. You shouldn't have any trouble finding a boy-friend. In the meantime, I'm going to hold you and see how you like living off bread and water for the next few days."

Frankie had had enough. She opened the door and stepped out of the room, slamming the door behind her. Cooter hadn't moved from his spot. He looked amused. "Do you find this amusing, Deputy?" she asked.

Cooter chuckled. "I reckon the boy needs to be taught a lesson. If anybody can do it, the chief can."

Frankie was waiting for Matt—stewing, actually—when he returned to his office, holding his belt in one hand. She jumped from her chair. "I do not believe what I just witnessed."

He nodded. "Yeah, but you missed the best part. I took off my belt and whupped him something good."

Frankie gaped at him. "You're not serious!"

"Tried not to leave welts, of course."

She gritted her teeth. "You just made the biggest mistake of your life, Webber."

"I know. I shoulda used a two-by-four on him." He began threading the belt into the loops on his pants.

She was furious. "I'm reporting you, do you understand that?"

He shrugged and sat at his desk. "Okay."

"Do the words *Internal Affairs* mean anything to you? And that's just the beginning. I'll see that you never wear a badge again."

Matt put his hands behind his neck and leaned back in his chair. "Guess that means I'll have more time for fishing."

"You can joke about it all you want, but—" She was interrupted when someone knocked on the door.

"Get that for me, would you?"

Frankie glared at him as she opened the door.

"Come on in, Eileen," he said to the woman on the other side. "Eileen Weaver, meet Deputy Daniels."

Frankie recognized the woman from the lobby. "Are you Bobby's mother?"

"That's right."

"Then you're just the person I need to see. I want you to know—"

Matt grinned at Mrs. Weaver. "Eileen, I did exactly as you asked. I think I scared the pants off the boy."

"Oh, thank you, Matt. I was hoping you'd put the fear of God into him. I just can't...well...you know. I've already lost one son. I can't lose Bobby." Her eyes glistened with tears.

Frankie looked from one to the other, wondering what was going on.

Matt stood, rounded the desk and put his arms around her. "You're not going to lose him, hon. You're just going to have to practice being tough. I jotted down the number for that support group I told you about." He slipped a card from his shirt pocket and handed it to her. "I'll keep Bobby overnight as we agreed. Give him time to think about a few things. But I'll have to let him go in the morning. Then it's up to you. Don't go getting soft on him the minute you take him home."

"I won't, Matt."

"And be consistent, Eileen. Bobby needs to know there's a consequence for everything he does. You need to ground him for one month. No TV, no computer games, no telephone."

"I promise." Her eyes flooded. "It would be so much easier if his father were in the picture, but God knows where he is. You're the only father figure the child has ever had."

Matt handed her a box of tissues. "And I'll continue to be there for him. I'm his godfather, remember? It's just as important for me that the boy turns his life around. You just keep doing your part, and I'll do mine."

Eileen wiped her eyes and nose. "Did you spank him? His grandmother has told me over and over the child needs a good spanking, but I can't do it."

"Naw, I didn't spank him. I pulled off my belt and threatened to, but you know I don't go for that sort of thing. Consequences and consistency, Eileen. The two Cs."

She nodded. "Will he be okay in there?"

"You have my word. I made sure he wouldn't be near the others. We'll look after him."

"And he'll get a good dinner?"

"I told him bread and water, but there'll be cheese and fruit on the plate, and I'll see that he gets a big breakfast tomorrow. Stop worrying."

Frankie slumped into a chair, not knowing what to make of the whole thing.

Eileen turned to her. "It's so nice to meet you, Deputy Daniels."

Frankie nodded. "Same here."

"I just want you to know what a fine police chief we have in Purdyville."

Frankie smiled. She felt like pulling out Webber's hair by the roots. "I wish you the best of luck with your son, Mrs. Weaver."

Once the woman had left, Frankie looked at Matt. "You could have told me what was going on," she said. "You made a fool of me."

He regarded her. "I don't know what you're talking about, Daniels. You seem to do an okay job of it on your own."

She noted the twinkle in his eyes. "You're having a

good time over this. At my expense, I might add. I still think you were too rough on the boy.''

Matt stepped closer. "Let me give you a brief history on the Weaver family," he said, matter-of-factly. "Eileen and I grew up together. She's like a sister to me. I didn't much care for the man she married, and he proved me right by deserting the family years ago. I've tried to help her as much as I can.''

"You're the boy's godfather?''

"I was godfather to both boys.''

"What happened to the other son?''

Matt looked away. "We lost him to a drug overdose. Buried him several years ago. So, whether you like it or not, I'll do anything short of wringing Bobby's neck to see that we don't lose him, too. Any more questions?''

Frankie shook her head, feeling stupid.

The phone rang. Matt snatched it up and listened. "Okay, tell her I'm on my way." He hung up. "Come on, Daniels, we have to take care of a small problem before you go in for your physical.''

Frankie followed him out of his office and into the lobby. Matt stopped at the counter. "Call Jeeter Skinner at animal control and have him meet me over there. He'll know why.''

"You're up to something," Velma said. "I can always tell.''

"Who, me?" He started for the door with Frankie on his heels. He paused. "By the way, did you give Virdie your peach recipe?''

"Sure did.''

"You told her not to use black walnuts, right?''

"Yes, Chief. But I know she'll get everything fouled up. She always does, bless her heart.''

"If you need to take the day off to help her, let me know."

"I will."

Frankie looked from one to the other. They were on a call, and the chief of police was worried over a peach recipe. She may as well face it. She had landed in Oz.

Frankie climbed into the squad car beside Matt a few minutes later. "What's the big deal about the peach recipe?" she asked.

"Oh, we're holding a barbecue in the town square Friday night. Trying to raise money for Mr. and Mrs. Gibbs. I figured we needed to do something fast, what with them losing the house and all. You just watch. The whole town will be there. That's just the way folks are around here.

"The local radio station is announcing where people can drop off donations in the meantime, and the Piggly Wiggly and the A & P stores are supplying the meat. Twenty dollars a plate for adults. That's a lot of money for some people, but Virgil will be cooking his famous barbecued chicken and ribs, so it'll be well worth it. Every woman in town will be bringing a covered dish. We'll even have a band."

"How did you manage to put this together so quickly?" she asked.

"Velma and her friends from church move quickly. They were on the phone most half the night and all morning, so if she seems grumpy this morning it's because she hasn't had much sleep. You need to put the barbecue on your social calendar. It will be quite an event. Be a good way for you to meet people."

Frankie tried not to stare at the handsome face with the one-hundred-watt smile, but she couldn't tear her eyes away. "Sure," she said. Finally, she turned to look out her side window. "You were right," she said, more to herself than him. "This is going to be a big adjustment for me."

"Sometimes change is good. Depends on how you look at it."

"Have you ever considered leaving Purdyville?"

He shook his head. "No. I know there are fancier jobs out there that would offer me more of a challenge, but I'm right where I belong."

As they drove, Matt gave Frankie a brief history of the town and told her about some of the more colorful residents. The land was rolling and lush, and far off in the distance she spied a mountain range. So different from the Atlanta skyline.

"By the way, Willie-Jack is still in the hospital," he added with a chuckle. "They had to reset his nose and X-ray his skull. He's got a lump on it the size of an egg."

"Now he'll be even more irresistible."

A few minutes later, Matt pulled into a subdivision called Mountain View. "We're here to see a Mrs. Blubaker," he said. "She calls once a week to complain about her neighbor's dog, who tends to bark during the day and keep Mrs. Blubaker awake. It would be easier if Mrs. B. slept at night, like the rest of us, but she's a night owl and likes to read till all hours."

Frankie realized she'd come a long way in her career—from chasing drug dealers to answering calls about barking dogs. "Sounds dangerous," she said. "Wish I'd worn a vest."

Matt laughed as he parked in front of a small brick house. "You may want to run back to the station and get one when you meet Mrs. Blubaker."

The woman in question was standing in front of her house in her bathrobe and was wearing a scowl that would have frightened small children. As Matt and Frankie climbed from the squad car, an animal control vehicle pulled up behind them. A man wearing a uniform and a serious look climbed out, holding a rifle. Frankie looked at Matt.

"That's Jeeter Skinner from animal control. He and I go way back. Let me do all the talking."

"It's about time you got here," the woman said. "That damn dog has barked nonstop since I called."

Matt cocked his ear. "I don't hear him."

"He must be taking a breather. Who is that woman, and why is Jeeter Skinner carrying a gun?"

"He's going to kill that damn dog," Matt said.

Mrs. Blubaker drew back in horror. "Kill him?"

"The dog is a nuisance, ma'am," Jeeter said, "and probably dangerous."

"He's just a little dachshund," the woman replied. "Can't weigh more than fifteen pounds."

"Those are the worse kind," Matt said.

Frankie looked the other way. She knew what was going on, and it was difficult to keep a straight face.

The woman no longer looked angry. "He's in a fenced yard."

"Don't make no difference," Jeeter replied. "If the owners can't keep him from disturbing the peace, we can. They sound like they should be shot, as well."

"Oh, no, the Smiths are lovely people. Both of them are teachers."

Matt whipped out his notebook. "I don't care if they're missionaries in South Africa, they sound pretty selfish letting their dog bark all day, waking up the neighborhood. What's the offender's name?"

The woman looked at him. "You mean the dog? Oh, his name is Smiley."

Jeeter gave a snort. "He won't be smiling when I get through with him." He started for the neighbor's house.

"Wait!" Mrs. Blubaker cried. "You can't just kill somebody's animal."

"I have an order from the chief," Jeeter said. "I'll get rid of that little varmint and he won't know what hit him. One shot between the eyes and he's a goner." He cocked the rifle.

"No!" Mrs. Blubaker shouted as Jeeter walked away. "I'll not have it, do you hear me? You can't shoot a harmless little dog just because he barks. The Smiths would be devastated."

Jeeter stopped in his tracks and looked at Matt. "You want me to just haul the damn dog over to the animal shelter and be done with him?"

Mrs. Blubaker covered her heart. "No! Please, please don't hurt the little fellow. I'll figure something out." She grabbed Matt's arm. "I can buy earplugs. That's what I'll do. Or move to the bedroom on the other side of the house. I have three bedrooms, you know. Why, I've been thinking of redecorating that other bedroom, anyway. Martha Stewart has that new lavender color in Kmart and—" She paused, eyes filling with tears. "Please don't shoot little Smiley."

Matt shook his head. "Mrs. Blubaker, I have dangerous criminals to chase after and I can't keep running over here—"

"I'll go to Kmart today. I'll buy that nice lavender comforter set and a pair of earplugs. Just don't shoot Smiley."

Matt seemed to ponder it. Finally, he looked at Jeeter. "I guess our work is done here."

Matt and Frankie were on their way a few minutes later.

Frankie suddenly burst into laughter. "I'll have to hand it to you, Chief," she said. "You're good."

He grinned. "You liked that little display, did you? And that's not even where I do my best work," he added with a wink.

She felt her stomach flutter. "That was totally unprofessional."

"So it was." He tossed her a glance. "But I've seen the way you look at me. You're curious."

"Oh, b-rother!" Frankie rolled her eyes. "Listen, Webber, I wouldn't think of coming between you and your significant other."

"What significant other? Just so happens I'm not seeing anyone at the moment."

"I was speaking of your ego."

This time he laughed out loud.

"Besides, I don't mix business with pleasure."

"Only problem is, it gets mighty cold up here in the winter. Skinny little thing like you probably doesn't give off much body heat. I'm as hot as a potbellied stove, in case you're wondering."

"I wasn't."

"Whatever you say."

He glanced over at her and Frankie met his gaze. It felt as if he were looking right through her. "Tell you what," she said. "I'll buy an electric blanket so you won't stay awake nights worrying about me."

"Whatever you say, Daniels. But I have a feeling we're both going to have a few sleepless nights thinking about each other."

She grunted as he continued down the road, still wearing a smile.

Four

Frankie's uniforms arrived the next day, both a size fourteen. She glowered at Velma. "This isn't a bit funny," she said, holding one up for inspection. The cap was too big as well. The rim rested on the bridge of her nose.

"You have a problem?" the woman behind the counter asked innocently.

"I specifically requested a size ten."

Velma shrugged. "I suppose I'll have to reorder."

"You do that." Frankie went in back, passing Matt in the hall. "Your dispatcher is a royal pain in the ass."

He looked surprised. "Who, Velma? Why, she's sweet as molasses. Maybe you should try being nice to her."

Frankie started to reply, just as Cooter and another deputy named Buster led Willie-Jack Pitts through the back door. The man wore a white bandage over his nose.

"Hello, Willie-Jack," Matt said. "Welcome home."

"Should I just put him in his regular cell?" Cooter asked.

Willie-Jack spotted Frankie and shot her a menacing look. "What the hell are you looking at?"

Frankie stepped closer to him. "I want to watch them lock you up like the animal you are, Pitts. And when you get out, I'm going to keep my eye on you. If you so much as fart, I'm going to know it."

"Tough broad."

"I kicked your ass once and I'll do it again."

Matt was enjoying the exchange. "Book him," he said. "Then give him his phone call. He'll need a lawyer."

"That's right," Willie-Jack said, never taking his eyes off Frankie. "I'll be out of here lickety-split. I'll be looking for you."

"Don't threaten me, Pitts, or I'll jerk the toilet out of your cell and make you pee in your coffee cup." She turned toward the little hole in the wall that was now her office.

Matt followed and leaned against the doorjamb. He looked curious. "You ever thought of going to charm school, Daniels?"

"Charming doesn't work when it comes to people like Willie-Jack. In my opinion, the man's a sociopath. He's dangerous and it's just a matter of time before he goes off."

"You think I don't know that? I watch him. But you just became enemy number one as far as he's concerned, and I don't want to have to watch both of you."

He looked concerned; worry lines creased his forehead where a lock of dark hair had fallen. Frankie studied his features, the way his thick hair gleamed beneath the fluorescent light, his compelling blue eyes probing hers. He had an air of authority and determination, and a strength that suggested he was not afraid of anything or anyone, including Willie-Jack Pitts. But there was something else, a certain degree of sensuality that drew her to him. She found herself thinking about his wide shoulders and broad chest more than she should, despite her resolve not to get involved. No wonder women found him so appealing; they would be hard-pressed not to.

Frankie made a dismissing gesture. "Willie-Jack is a

small-town thug. I've dealt with worse. I can take care of myself.''

A suggestion of annoyance crossed his face as he turned for the door. "I never doubted it for a minute."

Frankie arrived at Dr. Chalmers's office early, only to discover he was out to lunch. Once she signed in, she picked up a *Cosmo* magazine and read an article on "Ten Ways to a Better Orgasm." She thought of Matt Webber as she read it, and then chided herself. Hadn't she learned her lesson about getting involved with those with whom she worked? Had she not suffered enough humiliation?

Dr. Rand Chalmers was middle-aged and prematurely gray, with a warm smile. Once his nurse gave her a series of tests, he met with Frankie. "So far everything looks good," he said, "but it'll take a few days to get the other test results in." He seemed to study her closely as he spoke. "I see you're a deputy for the police department. How's your stress level?"

If only he knew, Frankie thought. "I don't think I'll be under a lot of stress in my new job."

"Your blood pressure is a little high, but nothing to be alarmed about at the moment. I note on your file that you smoke. Any plans on giving it up?"

"Not today."

"Hard habit to break," he said. "I can prescribe something when you're ready, but I don't want to put you on medication at this time. I'd rather send you to a relaxation therapist."

She groaned inwardly at the thought. "Is that really necessary?"

"Might help with the hypertension, and this therapist is one of the best. She's also my wife."

"Oh, so you're trying to drum up business for her."
Frankie knew she was being impolite.

"Trust me, my wife does a good business, even in a
town the size of Purdyville." He picked up the telephone
and dialed a number. "Let me speak to Alice, please."

"Hi, hon," he said after a minute. "I'd like to schedule
an appointment for the new deputy in town. She looks
like she's ready to burst a vein." He smiled and winked
at Frankie. "How soon can you see her?" He put his hand
over the mouthpiece. "She's checking her book. Says she
thinks she's had a cancellation." He listened. "Hold on,
Alice." He looked at Frankie. "Can you go right over?
Alice's office is on the second floor of this building."

Frankie shrugged. Better to get it over with. "Okay."

"I'll send her down now, hon," he said, and hung up.

Alice Chalmers was a pretty woman who looked
younger than her husband. She welcomed Frankie and
ushered her inside an office decorated in soft mint green.
"My husband seems to think you're wound up tight," she
said, once Frankie took a seat. "Anything I can do to
help?"

Frankie shrugged. "I feel great."

"Good. Let's not waste time fixing something that isn't
broken. How about joining me for lunch? My treat."

"That's *it?*"

"You look disappointed."

"Well, I was expecting you to hypnotize me or to bring
out aromatherapy candles."

Alice laughed. "How about I lend you one of my books
on relaxation?" she offered, picking up a slender volume
from her desk. "If you have problems, my card is attached. In the meantime, I know this adorable little restaurant that serves the best chicken salad in town."

Frankie followed her out, wondering if she'd ever get used to how folks did things in Purdyville. Of course, she didn't plan on staying to find out.

Frankie found herself opening up to Alice in ways she'd never done before as they lunched in an old Victorian home that had been turned into a quaint restaurant.

"And then I got caught doing the nasty with my partner, a married man with children who was also the police commissioner's son-in-law. Someone managed to capture it on video, which meant that person broke into my house at some point."

Alice Chalmers shook her head. "You must've been mortified!"

"That's not even the worst of it. I was wearing thong bikini underwear that night, and I'm sure my butt looked as big as Texas."

"Don't be silly, you have a wonderful figure. As for myself, I prefer something that hides the cellulite, but then I'm older than you and have a little more padding." She paused. "Were you fired?"

"No, but I may as well have been. I was 'offered' a job here, where I will never be able to utilize my skills, and I took a substantial pay cut. I haven't really been able to talk to anyone, especially my mother. We argue all the time, and besides, she thinks I'm still a virgin at thirty-two."

Alice smiled. "Perhaps *she* needs therapy."

"She needs Bellvue." Frankie told Alice about her father's death in the line of duty, and her mother's fear of her dying the same way. "She calls me Francis, even though she knows I hate that name."

"That must've been painful, losing your father when

you were eleven years old.'' Alice patted her hand. ''You don't have to talk about it if it upsets you.''

Frankie suddenly realized she had just told her entire life's story to a perfect stranger in less than an hour. ''I don't know why I'm telling you this. It's just...I feel so guilty. Connors told me he was separated from his wife and in the process of a divorce. The piece of shit even told me he'd caught her running around on him, and he pretended to be so wounded by it all.''

''No wonder your blood pressure is up,'' Alice said, ''what with all the changes taking place in your life.'' She pushed her half-eaten chicken salad away and clasped her hands on the table. ''What I don't understand is why you're taking all the blame for the affair. The man lied to you, Frankie. You were lonely and vulnerable. An easy target. It happens to the best of us, honey.''

Frankie wondered if Alice had ever been through something like that, but the woman looked too smart. She and her husband were obviously crazy about each other. ''I'm so angry,'' Frankie admitted. ''I get up every morning and run three miles, hoping to bring my stress level down. Sometimes I push myself even harder, until I think I can't go any farther, but I still feel like I'm on the verge of blowing up.'' She looked at Alice sadly. ''And when I can't handle it anymore, I sit in a shower and cry.''

Alice patted her hand. ''When was the last time you did something nice for yourself, Frankie?''

She thought about it. ''I bought a new pair of jeans before I left Atlanta.''

''That's not enough. You need pampering.''

''I've never been into that sort of thing.''

''Maybe it's time.''

''That I got in touch with my femininity?'' Frankie replied with a chuckle. "I think I've spent too much time working around men."

"That doesn't mean you have to act like one."

"I do when I'm on the job."

"But you go home at the end of the day."

"You're trying awfully hard to turn me into a girl."

This time Alice laughed. "You *are* a girl. When was the last time you looked into a mirror?"

"I don't spend a lot of time primping, as you can probably tell."

"Because you don't want to be like your mother?"

Alice's voice had become soothing and it tore at Frankie's heart. Somebody finally understood. She struggled to regain her composure. "Damn, you're good."

Alice shot her a rueful look as she reached for the check. "It's always easier to help someone work through their own problems," she said. "If only I were this good with my own."

Frankie snatched the check from her. "This one is on me," she insisted.

"Only if you allow me to buy you a little gift," the other woman consented, as Frankie put money and a tip into a small plastic tray. They left the restaurant a few minutes later and walked several doors down, until Alice stopped them at a sweet-smelling shop.

Frankie paused inside the door. Lotions and bath oils with fancy names lined one wall, and another held an assortment of candles and potpourri. There were beautiful nightgowns that Frankie would have been uneasy sleeping in because she wouldn't want to wrinkle them, and dresses that were both smart and feminine. Dainty throw pillows were piled on a white wrought-iron daybed that was covered in a sky-blue-and-yellow quilt. It was unlike anything she'd seen before. "Wow."

"This is my favorite place," Alice said, holding a tester of body spray to Frankie's nose. "Isn't that wonderful? And smell this talcum powder. It's French milled. I sprinkle it on my pillow at night before I go to bed."

It was the most delicious fragrance Frankie'd ever smelled, and the container that held it was gorgeous. "It's a little sissified, but I like it."

Alice smiled as she carried the powder to the counter and paid. "You just wait. You'll be painting your toenails before long."

"Don't count on it, Alice."

Frankie arrived back at the station at three o'clock, where she was given the assignment of accompanying Cooter to a house that had been robbed and vandalized while the owners vacationed.

"Probably kids," Cooter told the frantic couple. "We'll dust for fingerprints and see what we can come up with. You folks'll have to come up to the station so we can get your prints, as well. That way, we won't confuse yours with the perpetrators'."

Frankie took their reports while Cooter dusted. "Do you have any idea who would have done this?" she asked. The couple shook their heads.

"We don't have any enemies that we know of."

After Frankie took the information, she and Cooter were on their way. Cooter pulled in front of the local pool hall. "Kids have a tendency to brag," he said. "Maybe we'll learn something."

They went in. Frankie was surprised to see so many young faces, especially since there was a bar at the back. "This must be the after-school hangout," she told Cooter, "and not a good one at that. Isn't there another place they can go?"

"The YMCA doesn't have much to offer, I'm afraid."

She followed Cooter to the bar. The owner smiled pleasantly but looked nervous. "This is Hep Whitfield," the deputy told Frankie. "Hep, meet Frankie Daniels, our new deputy." The two shook hands.

"What are these kids doing in here, Hep?" Cooter asked. "Sign at the door says no one under eighteen."

"I've been stretching the rules," Hep said. "The drinking crowd doesn't usually show up till after five, anyway. I make good money off these kids, and they don't cause me no trouble. Hell, I've got kids of my own. I know where you're coming from."

Frankie spoke. "If you're making so much money, looks like you could put a couple of tables for the kids in another room so they don't have to mix with the older crowd."

"And I know you got space," Cooter added, pointing to a closed door, "if you clean up that crap you're storing in the next room."

"You could add pinball machines and games and put in a soda machine," Frankie suggested. "Like an arcade."

"Or you could pay fines for allowing these kids in here in the first place," Cooter said.

"You planning on fining me?" the man asked, obviously alarmed.

Cooter shook his head. "Not right now. I'm going to give you time to think about it. But me and the chief will be back in a few days. Maybe you'll have come up with a decision by then. In the meantime, I want these kids out of here."

Hep scratched his head. "I'll check on renting the equipment," he said reluctantly. "Hell, Cooter, I care about these kids."

"One more thing," Frankie said. "Have you heard any of them bragging about breaking into a residence?" She told him about the vandalism.

"No, but I'll keep my ears open. You know, it's going to take a lot of work to get that room cleared out. It'll have to be painted, and the floors patched. That's a lot of work, and I'm tied up here most of the time."

"Maybe you can get some volunteers," Cooter said. "After all, you'll be providing a service to the community."

"Maybe some of the kids will help," Frankie said, "if they know you're going to put in an arcade."

Hep sighed. "Okay, I'll get 'em out of here."

Back at the station, Frankie and Cooter discussed the problem with Matt. He agreed the town needed something to keep the after-school crowd occupied. "I've been pondering the situation myself," he said. "I just hope Hep follows through."

It was after six by the time Frankie arrived back at the motel, only to discover that someone had thrown eggs on her door. The yolks had dried, and it looked like a hen had miscarried all over the place.

"I'll never be able to get that off," a voice said.

Frankie turned and found the motel manager standing there with a bucket of sudsy water in his hands. "Did you see who did it?" she asked.

He shook his head. "I was in the front office."

Frankie thought of Willie-Jack. But he was in jail...

"I heard you beat up Willie-Jack in Virgil's parking lot last night," the man said, as if reading her mind. "Could have been some of his friends."

"They've got balls, doing it in the light of day," she replied. Noting the surprised look the man shot her, she regretted using bad language in front of him.

"I'll give it a good scrubbing, but it's going to need painting."

Frankie nodded and unlocked the door to her room. The phone rang before she had a chance to lock her door. "I've been calling all day," her mother said the minute she picked up.

"I was working."

"So soon? I would have thought you'd take a few days off before you started your new job."

"I figured the sooner I got started, the better."

"How do you like the place?"

"It's dull compared to what I'm used to, but I'll adjust. You sound down in the dumps."

"Oh, it's Clarice."

"Your hairdresser?"

"Yes. The woman is stuck in the sixties, refuses to try anything new. I told her I wanted to get the orange out of my hair, so she used a new color. My hair is now burgundy."

"Good grief."

"It's awful, Francis. I'm embarrassed to be seen in public."

"Why don't you go someplace else?"

"Clarice needs the business. Her daughter ran off with some man, leaving Clarice to raise her grandchildren. I don't know how the poor woman manages."

"So, you're going to put up with bad hair just because Clarice has to raise her grandchildren?"

"You wouldn't understand, Francis, because you've never had children. You have no idea the sacrifices parents and grandparents have to make. The only person you've ever had to worry about is yourself."

She should have seen it coming. It didn't matter that Frankie had gotten her first job at eleven, baby-sitting three little girls an entire summer while their parents worked, or that she'd worked after school and weekends at a fast-food restaurant for several years in order to help her mother. Eve Hutton had a selective memory.

Frankie decided it wasn't worth arguing over. Perhaps it was time to stop arguing with her mother altogether. It was a battle she would never win, and she didn't always have to be right. Alice Chalmers would be proud of her.

"Other than your hair, how are you?" Frankie asked.

"I'm well. I'm not like some of these women who complain about every little ache and pain. I take it in stride. Have you found a place to live yet?"

"I'm putting feelers out. I've been pretty busy with my new job." Frankie heard a knock at the door. "I have to run, Mom. Someone's at the door."

"Don't open it until you know who it is."

"I'm a cop, remember? I always take precautions." Frankie hung up, checked the peephole in the door and opened it. Matt Webber stood on the other side.

"I heard someone threw eggs at your door," he said, stepping into the room uninvited.

"Won't you come in?" Frankie asked.

He seemed to be studying the room closely. "I've found you a place to live."

Frankie was glad she was a neat person. Although she suspected the room smelled of cigarette smoke, it was otherwise clean. "You have?"

"My cousin needs a housemate."

"I prefer living alone."

"It won't be easy finding a decent place in this town. Besides, Sissy's house is nice and big. You won't even know she's around. You can stay there until you find something else."

Matt had changed from his uniform. He wore jeans and a cotton pullover.

Considering his words, Frankie decided she might have to share a place, after all. Her Realtor was still looking, but she hadn't sounded optimistic. The only rentals she'd found so far were old mobile homes and a few houses she described as unkempt. There was a two-bedroom house for sale, of course, but Frankie assured her she wasn't interested in buying.

"Have you eaten yet?" Matt asked.

The question surprised her. "No, I just got in."

"Why don't you change clothes and come with me? My mother cooked a pot of collards, and she wants me to join her for dinner."

"I'm not really a collards person, but thanks."

"There will be other food. She always goes all out."

Frankie studied him. "Matt, I don't think it's a good idea for us to—"

"Fraternize?" He chuckled. "I'm not planning to announce our engagement. I usually take one of the guys from work, but everybody is busy tonight, so I'm inviting you. When was the last time you had a home-cooked meal?"

She couldn't remember, although her meat loaf dinner at the Half Moon Café had come close. "I just don't want people getting the wrong impression."

"Since when do you care what people think?"

He had a point. But that was before she had been publicly humiliated by her affair with Connors.

"Just change your clothes and come with me," he said. "What have you got to lose?"

Frankie had to agree. She'd pretty much lost it all.

Five

"My parents are simple country folk," Matt explained as he pulled his truck up in front of an old two-story white frame house with brick columns and a wide front porch that held an assortment of rockers and an old swing. "They're laid-back."

Frankie noted the red geraniums blooming in clay pots. Ferns shuddered in the light breeze. A wreath of dried flowers, with a miniature welcome sign attached, adorned the front door. "Place looks comfortable," she said.

Matt pointed to the swing as he and Frankie made their way up the front steps. "I used to do a lot of necking in that swing."

"I would have figured you for a back-seat sort of guy."

He shrugged. "Well, that, too."

The boards on the porch had recently been painted a dove-gray color. From the looks of it, the place was well kept. Frankie wondered if Matt helped out. He reached for the screen door, called out as they stepped inside, and a plump woman with a friendly smile hurried across the room. "Well, now," she said as she regarded Frankie. "What a nice surprise."

Matt dropped a kiss on her forehead. "Mom, this is Frankie Daniels, our new deputy. I figured you could put some meat on her bones. She's kind of puny." Frankie shot him a look.

"Hello, Frankie. I'm Hattie Webber. Matt told me he had a new deputy, but he didn't mention how pretty you are. And I don't think you're puny at all. Come on in."

Frankie stepped into a cozy living room with over-stuffed floral furniture, and a number of antiques that she assumed had been passed down through the family. She could smell collards cooking in the kitchen. "Your house looks very cozy, Mrs. Webber," she said, thinking of her mother's living room with its white sofa and chair and glass tables that showed every smudge. Hattie wore a simple shift and sneakers; her hair, which she was allowing to gray naturally, told Frankie the woman was not much for pomp and fuss. Frankie wondered what her mother, the beauty parlor queen, would make of Mrs. Webber.

"Call me Hattie." She looked about the room as if seeing it for the first time. "We like it fine," she said. "My husband and I have lived here all our married lives."

"Where is Dad?" Matt asked.

"Taking care of the animals." She looked at Frankie. "We have a few cows and chickens, and a couple of hogs. I take care of them in the morning, and Denny takes the evening shift."

As though acting on cue, a big man stepped through the doorway wearing work pants and a cotton shirt, sleeves rolled to his elbows. He had a full head of hair that had turned a battleship gray. "Hi, son. Your mother said you might be joining us." He nodded politely at Frankie.

"He brought company," Hattie said. "This is Frankie Daniels. She's the new deputy."

"Well, now, if they'd been hiring pretty deputies like you when I was younger I would have signed on as a police officer." He shook her hand. "Dennis Webber.

Glad to meet you, Frankie. Everybody calls me Denny 'cept my wife—she calls me 'Hey Stupid.'''

They all chuckled. Hattie shook her head. "The things you say, Denny. Please sit down, Frankie. Dinner is almost ready. Would you like a glass of iced tea?"

"I'm fine for now, thank you." Frankie took a seat on one end of the sofa, and Matt sat on the other. His parents took chairs opposite them.

"Frankie has been living on mostly junk food," Matt said. "I thought it would be nice if she had a decent meal."

"I hope I won't put you to any extra trouble," Frankie said, wishing Matt wouldn't speak for her.

Hattie shook her head emphatically. "Oh, heavens no. We're always glad to set an extra place at our table. How long have you been in Purdyville, honey?"

"Only a few days."

"She was supposed to rent the Gibbses' house on Elm Street," Matt said.

"I was so sad to hear about the fire," Hattie replied.

"A tragedy," Denny said. "I know Irma and Homer depended on the extra income. Do you have any leads?"

"Nothing I can prove in a court of law, but we're working on it." Matt slid closer to the edge of the sofa and clasped his hands together. "We're planning a little social event next Friday night. To raise money for the Gibbses'."

"I'm sure they'll appreciate it," Hattie said.

Denny frowned. "Not Irma. You know how she is, stubborn old mule. Anytime someone tries to help her, she acts insulted. She would starve on the street before she would ask a neighbor for a slice of bread."

"That's true," Matt replied, "but that doesn't stop folks from trying."

"Where do you come from, Frankie?" Denny asked.

"Atlanta. I worked for the police department there for ten years."

"Uncle Dell was her captain."

"Well, now, it *is* a small world," Denny said.

Hattie nodded. "I'm afraid my brother and I don't keep up with one another as we should. Is Dell still grouchy?"

Frankie wondered if Hattie avoided him because of his drinking. "As grouchy as they come. But he was good to me."

"What made you decide to move to Purdyville?" Hattie asked.

"I got tired of big-city life," she said. "I was looking for a change."

The other woman smiled. "Well, you're in the right place if you like small towns. I can't imagine living in a big city. All that traffic, my goodness! The only time we have traffic here is when there's a parade." She stood. "Excuse me while I check on dinner."

"Is there anything I can do to help?" Frankie offered.

"No, honey, but I appreciate your asking." She hurried out.

Frankie, Matt and Denny made small talk about the weather, crops and economy. Frankie got the impression Matt was close to his family, and she envied him. She suddenly wished her relationship with her mother was better. As she studied the room, she noticed a picture of an attractive young girl in a picture frame. A family member, perhaps? An old girlfriend of Matt's? She was intrigued.

"Dinner's ready," Hattie announced, standing in the doorway wearing a plaid apron. "Frankie, I hope you don't mind eating in the kitchen. We're not a formal bunch here."

"Actually, I prefer it," Frankie said. "I don't like formality."

Denny laughed. "We should get along just fine."

Frankie's eyes widened in disbelief when she saw how much food was on the table. "Oh, Hattie, you've gone to so much trouble."

"This is nothing," Matt said. "You should see how much she cooks on Sunday. Only reason people go to the same church she does is 'cause they hope they'll get invited to dinner afterward."

The woman blushed. "Hush, now, Matt, you're embarrassing me. Frankie, you can sit right here next to me."

They settled themselves at the table. Matt's father asked the blessing and then passed a platter of sliced ham to Frankie. She chose one slice, only to be encouraged by Hattie to take another. There was macaroni and cheese—the best Frankie had ever tasted—a sweet potato casserole with pineapple and nuts on top, a large bowl of collards, corn that Denny bragged came from their own field, and a pan of hot corn bread.

Frankie had never tasted such wonderful food. "I wish I could cook like this," she said.

Hattie looked surprised. "You don't cook?"

She shook her head. "Never really had time to learn. And when I joined the Atlanta Police Department we ate on the run."

"Oh, honey, I can teach you to cook."

Matt chuckled. "Frankie doesn't appear to me to be the type of woman who'd go for that sort of thing."

"Your son is right," Frankie said. "I'm not a kitchen person."

The woman looked amazed. "What do you do when you get hungry?"

"Grab a burger. Call out for pizza."

Hattie smiled and nodded as though it made complete sense.

An uncomfortable silence ensued. "How's work, son?" Denny asked.

Matt told them about Mrs. Blubaker and Smiley, the dachshund, and Frankie found herself laughing as loud as the others at the story. "It was hard to keep a straight face," she said, "and by the time we left, I think Mrs. Blubaker was ready to adopt Smiley and raise him as her own."

Finally, Denny regarded her, a quizzical expression on his face. "I heard you whipped Willie-Jack's behind."

Hattie gasped. "Dennis Webber, I can't believe you would bring that up. And at the dinner table, of all places." But she looked at Frankie curiously. "Did you?"

"I was defending myself," Frankie said.

Matt grinned. "She beat the hell out of him."

"Such language," Hattie said, shaking her head sadly. "Which reminds me, Matthew, you have not attended church with us for more than a month. The reverend has been asking about you."

Matt winced. "I've been busy chasing hardened criminals, Mom."

"On Sunday?"

"That's the worst day. They just seem to come out of the woodwork."

"Matthew Webber, you don't have me fooled for one minute."

"I'm sure Willie-Jack deserved what he got," Denny said, returning to the previous subject. "That man has been trouble since the day he was born. The whole bunch is nothing but white trash."

"You're passing judgment, dear," Hattie pointed out.

"Any judge in the world would agree."

"Tell us about your family, Frankie," Hattie said. "Were you born in Atlanta?"

"Yes, ma'am," she said politely, having heard Matt answer his mother in such a way, "born and raised. My father was a policeman. He was killed in the line of duty when I was eleven years old."

"Oh, I'm so sorry. And your mother?"

"She lives in a retirement community in Florida."

"Are the two of you close?"

Matt held his hand up. "Okay, Mom, enough already."

Hattie looked offended. "I wasn't trying to pry, son." She gave Frankie an apologetic look. "I'm sorry if I sound nosy, honey. I'm just curious. I hope you don't take offense."

Frankie shrugged. "That's okay. I don't mind questions." At least Hattie's seemed harmless. "My mom and I are—" She paused, trying to think of a way to describe her relationship with her mother, when she didn't understand it herself. "She's very protective. She worries about me a lot. Too much, I think."

Hattie and Dennis exchanged looks, and Frankie thought she saw sadness pass through their eyes.

"It's only natural to worry about your children," Hattie said gently. "You never stop." She gazed toward a photograph on the wall, the same young woman Frankie had noticed in the living room earlier.

"May I ask who the lovely girl in the picture is?" Frankie said.

Hattie didn't hesitate. "Why, that's Mandy, our daughter. Matt's twin sister. She's with the Lord now."

Frankie looked around the table. All faces, including Matt's, were turned to the photograph. "Oh, I'm so sorry. How long has she been…uh…gone?"

"Two years now. That's her high school picture. She

was the prettiest little thing. So tiny. So dainty. Like a bird.'' Hattie looked wistful. ''She weighed little more than a bird when she came into the world, just the opposite of Matt, who was such a strong, healthy baby. Nine pounds, he was. But Mandy was sickly.''

''We were lucky to have her as long as we did,'' Denny said, ''considering her health problems. She was born with a defective heart. The heart specialists managed to control the problem with medication for many years, but in the end, it would have taken a transplant to save her. Mandy wouldn't hear of it. She was a very spiritual girl who believed that whatever happened was God's will, and we honored her decision.''

His wife nodded. ''Yes, we were truly blessed.''

Frankie looked at Matt, who had suddenly taken an interest in lining up his silverware beside his plate, but the tense lines on either side of his mouth told her he was uncomfortable with the conversation. She wondered what was going on in his mind, wondered what it had been like losing his twin. She felt like reaching out and touching his hand, but it would only prove awkward for them both.

Finally, Matt pushed his chair from the table and patted his stomach. ''That was a great meal, Mom.''

''You're not finished! My goodness, you always ask for seconds.''

''I'm watching my waistline.''

''Oh, pshaw! You've always been in good shape. You're just trying to impress Frankie here.''

''I think I've eaten enough for both of us,'' Frankie said, wishing she could unbutton her jeans.

Frankie and Matt cleared the table while Hattie cut a pie and served coffee. ''Sit down, now,'' the woman ordered. ''I'll put those in the dishwasher later. I don't hold much stock in dishwashers, but Matt bought me one for

Mother's Day, so I feel guilty if I don't use it once in a while." She pointed to the refrigerator. "He bought that, too. See all those fancy gadgets in the door? I told him he was foolish to spend so much money on extras that his daddy and I don't even use."

Denny laughed. "I've got a riding lawn mower out there that'll do everything but plant my garden. I still haven't gotten used to all the fancy gadgets, but Matt insisted on buying it for me. Truth to tell, I preferred the old one."

"The old one kept breaking down, Dad," Matt reminded him.

"Yeah, but the more gizmos you have on something the more likely you're going to have trouble with them." He looked at Frankie. "I have to call the boy every time something goes wrong. You'd have to be a rocket scientist to understand the directions on how to use it."

Matt shifted in his seat uncomfortably, refusing to meet Frankie's gaze.

They ate their pie and sipped coffee as Hattie regaled Frankie with stories of Matt's youth. "He was a handful in high school," she said, "getting into one scrape after another. Denny and I spent as much time in the principal's office as the man himself. Mandy was the opposite. Never gave us a minute's trouble. Studied hard, brought home good grades. She received a full scholarship—"

"She really applied herself," Denny interrupted. "Became a college professor."

Frankie was beginning to grow weary of the subject of Mandy, although it had nothing to do with the girl herself. She doubted the Webbers had a mean bone in their bodies, but they had yet to say anything positive about Matt, and she was embarrassed for him and almost angry with his parents. She was suddenly ready to escape but had no idea how to do it without appearing rude. She only hoped, should she ever have kids, that she would be more sensitive to their feelings.

"I wasn't big on school, either," she said finally. "I just wanted to graduate and get out into the real world."

Finally, Matt gave a wide yawn and looked at her. "You ready to go, Deputy? It's been a long day."

The Webbers walked them to the door. Hattie hugged Frankie and made her promise to visit again soon. Frankie noted the smile on her face, while warm and inviting, did not hide the tinge of sorrow in her eyes. She realized the Webbers were still grieving, and she silently forgave them for some of the hurtful words that had come out of their mouths. She knew what it was like to grieve, to hurt so badly it felt as though everything inside had died. She had heard losing a child was the worst thing a person could go through. If that were the case, if the Webbers had known even more sadness than she had, she could almost forgive them anything.

"I'll be back," she promised.

Matt was unusually quiet as he drove Frankie back to the motel. "Your parents are very nice," Frankie said, "and the meal was wonderful. Thank you for inviting me."

"I'm sorry they asked so many questions. That's just the way they are."

"Do you think it was because you brought a female to the house?"

"Who knows? They're used to seeing Buster or Cooter." He chuckled. "They ask them a lot of questions, too. I suppose it comes from being retired and living out in the country, where nothing much ever happens."

"I was surprised to hear you were a twin," she said softly. "You must miss your sister very much." He nod-

ded but kept his eyes on the road, and Frankie wondered
if he was trying to keep his feelings to himself.

"It was hard losing her," was all he said.

"So now you feel guilty that you made it and she
didn't, and you try to compensate by buying your parents
new appliances and riding mowers." She saw his jaw
harden and wished she hadn't spoken.

"I bought the stuff because they needed it," he said
tersely. "My mother would sooner store food in an ice
chest than spend money on a new refrigerator. She refuses
to have a clothes dryer in the house. Says the wash smells
fresher if she hangs it on the clothesline. It doesn't matter
that her fingers grow numb with cold in the winter." He
paused, then took a deep breath. "But, yeah, I guess I
have tried to make up for their loss, even though I wonder
if they appreciate it. It's difficult to measure up to my
sister when they think of her as a saint."

Frankie was surprised he'd opened up. "I know what
it's like to feel as though you don't measure up. My mom
takes every opportunity to tell me how I've disappointed
her. But I don't think your parents mean any harm. They
just don't know any better."

"It's in the past. I loved my sister very much, but I had
to move on or let it eat me alive. My parents are still
struggling."

"Everyone has to grieve at their own pace." She knew
that from experience.

"I hope you didn't feel too uncomfortable. I just
wanted you to have a home-cooked meal and meet a couple of nice people, so you wouldn't think the whole town
was filled with rednecks like Willie-Jack."

They made the rest of the drive in a comfortable silence. Frankie could tell Matt was caught up in his own
thoughts, and she wondered at them. She felt relaxed for

the first time since arriving in Purdyville, and she was disappointed when he pulled into the parking lot of her motel. "I'll see you in the morning," she said, opening the door to climb out. "Thanks again for inviting me."

He dipped his head slightly. "Anytime, Deputy. I'll wait until you're inside."

Frankie hurried to her door, unlocked it and went in. At the sight before her she gasped and turned for the door. Matt was already pulling away. She curled her thumb and middle finger between her lips and gave an earsplitting whistle.

Matt brought the car to a screeching halt as soon as he heard the sound. He stopped and turned in his seat. Frankie was racing after him. He opened his window as she neared the truck. "What is it?"

"My room," she said. "Somebody's been in my room."

"Are you sure?" Dumb question, he thought. She was a cop; of course, she was sure. Matt backed his truck quickly and parked. He hurried in, Frankie right behind him.

The room was trashed. The screen on the TV had been shattered. Shards of glass were scattered across the carpet and flashed beneath the light, jagged and wicked-looking. The mattress on the full-size bed had been slashed and the stuffing pulled out, reminding Matt of an old rag doll that had belonged to his sister, after the family dog had chewed it. Someone had even gone through Frankie's suitcase, shredding her clothes.

"Holy hell," he muttered. "Stay put while I check the bathroom." He was back in a few seconds. "I'll be right back."

"Where are you going?"

"I'm going to radio for backup. I want this room dusted

from top to bottom. I also want to notify the motel owner.''

Frankie looked at her clothes. She felt as though she'd just been raped, violated, by the person who'd gone through her suitcase and touched her personal belongings. For the first time, she truly understood what it was like to be a victim, and she remembered all the other victims who'd suffered at the hands of someone evil—people who'd lost children, women who'd been raped and brutalized or worse. Men who'd been beaten and robbed or killed for less than twenty dollars. She'd remained uninvolved, merely interested in solving the crime. She'd seen it all from a distance because she had not wanted to feel their heartache.

Her sense of violation turned to anger. She literally seethed with it. The mess before her had Willie-Jack's name all over it. *Bastard.*

Matt arrived back a few minutes later. ''Jimbo and Hurley are on their way.''

Her look was hostile. ''Jimbo and Hurley?''

''They work the night shift. I checked out your car, everything's fine. Whoever did this must have felt it was too risky to commit a crime out in the open.'' He noted her look of open hostility. ''Look, I don't blame you for being upset.''

''Upset?'' She almost shrieked the word. ''Everything I own is ruined! And the son of a bitch responsible for this is laughing his ass off as we speak.''

''From his jail cell,'' Matt reminded her.

''It doesn't matter. He knows people. What is this, some kind of mountain mafia at work?''

The owner stepped through the door and came to a dead halt. ''What in tarnation happened here!'' he demanded.

''Someone came into my room while I was out,'' Frankie replied, wishing she could remember the man's name. "Don't you have any security people on your staff? And look at this flimsy-ass lock. A two-year-old could break in."

He swallowed hard, as if trying to keep his anger at bay. "This is a respectable place. I never had any trouble till you got here."

"Just hold on, now," Matt said, maintaining his usual calm composure. "Al, did you hear or see anything tonight? Have any of your guests complained of noises coming from this room?"

"Chief, you know I don't have a lot of business this time of year. Not till the leaves start turning. I got a couple of truckers, but they're in the back. As for myself, I've been watching TV and I didn't hear a thing. 'Course, I'm a little hard of hearing to begin with, Vietnam and all, but you already know that. I keep the volume up high on the television set. Like I said, I don't ever have any trouble." He cut his eyes at Frankie. "Trouble must follow you everywhere you go."

She tossed him a withering look but remained quiet.

"I'll have one of my men question the guests, just in case. I have a feeling I know who's responsible for this."

Al looked at Frankie. "I'm sorry, Miss Daniels, but I'm going to have to ask you to leave. I don't care if you *did* beat Willie-Jack's butt, I can't have this sort of thing going on. Makes business look bad."

"This isn't my fault," she said. "What am I supposed to do, sleep on the street?"

"I'm sorry, miss, I mean, Deputy. I just don't want no more trouble."

She lit a cigarette and curbed an impulse to blow smoke in his face. *Asshole.*

"I could order you to give her another room," Matt said.

Frankie took another drag of her cigarette. "I don't want to stay where I'm not wanted."

"We'll work out something," Matt said.

Two deputies stepped into the room. "Dang, what happened here?" one of them asked.

"Vandalism," Matt said. "Jimbo, Hurley, you haven't met our new deputy, Frankie Daniels."

They nodded briskly. The one named Jimbo brightened. "You're the one who—"

"Yes," she said, finishing his sentence for him. She wondered if people would always refer to her as the woman who beat up Willie-Jack Pitts.

"Looks like somebody's trying to settle a score with you," Hurley said. "Could be one of Willie-Jack's hangers-on."

"I want you and Jimbo to dust the room and see what you can find," Matt said. He turned to Al. "This room will be off-limits for a couple of days."

"Who's going to clean up this mess?"

"You've got housekeepers, don't you? Besides, I wouldn't worry about that right now. This is a crime scene, and we have to investigate. I don't want anyone else to step inside this room until we've finished. Understand?"

Al looked disgruntled.

Jimbo sighed. "I reckon we ought to get started. I'll grab a kit from the car."

Matt looked at Frankie. "You need a place to sleep tonight. Come with me."

"Where?"

"Just do it."

She was not pleased with his tone. Frankie didn't like

being told what to do, especially in front of another deputy, but this was no time to put up a fuss. She followed Matt outside. "Where am I going?"

"My place."

"You're kidding, right?"

"I'm too tired to argue with you, Daniels. For once, just do as I ask."

"I'm taking my car. I can't risk something happening to it."

They were on their way a few minutes later, Frankie following Matt's newer-model pickup truck. She suddenly felt weary. Seemed there was no end to her problems. No wonder her blood pressure was on the high side. Ten minutes later, Matt turned onto a dirt road, and she continued close behind, having no idea where she was or where they were going. Finally, he led her into a driveway, where a simple frame house with a wraparound porch sat behind a stand of tall loblolly pines.

"You live here?" Frankie asked, once she climbed from her car and joined him on the front walk.

"I must. This is where my bills are delivered."

A lanky hound was sprawled on the porch. Folds of reddish-brown skin hung about his face, and the wrinkles above his eyes gave him a sad look. He flicked his tail once at the sight of Matt.

"This is George," Matt said, stepping around the dog when the animal refused to move out of their way. "My watchdog."

"And a good one at that."

Matt unlocked the front door and flipped on a switch just inside. The living room lit up. "You want a cold beer?" he asked when Frankie followed him in.

"That sounds good," she said, hoping it would calm her strained nerves. She glanced about the sparsely furnished room. A beige couch and chair, and a battered coffee table were the only furniture.

"Have a seat. I'm afraid I haven't gotten around to decorating the place," he called back over his shoulder as he headed toward the kitchen. "No time. No talent."

She was half sprawled on the sofa when he returned with the beers and handed her one. "How long have you lived here?"

"Couple of years. An old friend of mine built it. I sort of helped. It gave me something to do in my spare time after Mandy died."

"You live here alone?"

"Yep. Just George and me."

The sofa was comfortable, despite the bland color. "This is nice."

"Thanks. It's quiet out here. A nice place to come home to after chasing dangerous criminals all day."

He and Frankie shared a smile. "I've always wanted my own place," she said, "but all my money was spent on high rent."

"I have a garden out back," he said. "Nothing big. I grow roses, too."

She took a sip of beer. "You're kidding."

"I like roses."

"You don't look the type."

"What type do I look?"

"I figured you spent all your spare time chasing women."

He shrugged. "Well, I'm not much of a fisherman, and I don't hunt, so—" He paused and shrugged again.

"How come you never married?"

"I came close once. You?"

She shook her head. "I'm not the marrying type."

"What type are you?"

"I'm like you. I just love 'em and leave 'em."

"Somebody has given me a bad rep."

"Hey, I've seen you in action."

"I've done nothing improper."

"Women don't smile at a man like they smile at you unless they know what the man looks liked naked."

He laughed out loud. "You've got me pegged all wrong, Daniels. I'm a good guy."

"You're probably very good. That's why they smile."

"You're embarrassing me."

"Give me a break, Chief. You love it."

"Okay, so I have a past. What about you?"

Frankie automatically stiffened. The last thing she wanted Matt Webber to know was that she'd been duped. "Let's just say I'm not as pure as my mother thinks I am."

"Interesting. Care to share?"

She set her beer on the coffee table. "I'm really tired."

Matt looked disappointed. "Just when it was getting good." He stood. "I'll show you your room." He gave her a come-hither look. "Unless you'd rather not sleep alone."

Frankie met his gaze. It was difficult to tell whether or not he was being serious. Nevertheless, he was as cocky as they came. "Actually, I prefer it."

He shook his head. "You're a tough one, Daniels."

"Because I don't simper?"

He led her upstairs. "The room isn't fancy, but you should be comfortable enough," he said, opening a door.

The bedroom held an old iron bed, an oak dresser and a matching night table, all of which were antiques and probably given to him by his parents. A homemade quilt covered the bed, and Frankie wondered if Hattie had made it. All in all, it was inviting.

"There's a bathroom through that door," he said. "It connects to another bedroom. My room is downstairs." He looked at her. "You'll need something to sleep in."

She shook her head. "I sleep in the nude, but thanks." She had the pleasure of watching that cocky smile falter.

Matt looked at her a full minute, trying not to imagine her crawling between the sheets wearing nothing. "The...uh...bath towels are in the linen closet in the bathroom. Let me know if you need anything else."

"Thanks, Chief."

He paused. "You know, that sounds rather formal under the circumstances. You can call me Matt."

"I prefer calling you Chief." Besides, it set limits between them, and she suspected a man like Matt Webber needed limits.

"Well, good night." He closed the door behind him.

Frankie looked about the room. Why had he built such a house for just himself? Well, he had mentioned almost getting married. Perhaps he and his fiancé had planned to live here. She shrugged. What did it matter? It was none of her business. A hot shower and a comfortable bed was all she cared about at the moment.

Frankie had been awake for some time when Matt knocked on her door early the next morning. Awake and wondering where she was going to live, now that she'd been kicked out of the motel.

"Are you naked?" he called out from the other side of the door.

She pulled the sheet to her chin. "You can come in."

He was already dressed in his uniform, and his eyes immediately went to the bedsheet. Matt tried not to let his thoughts run amok. "I'm going to run by the office and see what's going on, then I thought I'd go by the motel and get your suitcase. You can see if any of your clothes are salvageable.''

Frankie groaned inwardly. The thought of buying a new wardrobe was not a pleasant one. Not that she really had that much, since she mostly wore jeans and T-shirts. She had a couple of dresses for weddings or funerals, but that was about it. ''How long will you be? I have to start looking for another place to live.''

''Why don't you talk to my cousin, Sissy?''

''Sissy?''

''That's what we call her. The two of you would get along well.''

''Do you even know if she wants a housemate?''

''I'm sure she could use the extra money. Like I said, her place is pretty decent compared to what you're going to find, as far as rentals go. I can take you by there when I get back.''

Frankie realized she didn't have much choice. ''I'll take a look.''

''Help yourself to anything you need,'' he said. ''I made coffee.'' He closed the door.

A moment later, Frankie heard him pull out of the drive. Slipping into the clothes she'd worn the night before, she made her way to a spacious kitchen. The oak floors were bare of rugs, and the beige walls held no pictures. The kitchen was neat, the white cabinets standing out against a hunter-green wall, the only room that had been given a definite color. She found a coffee mug in one of the cabinets and filled her cup, then sat on the back deck, sipping and smoking her first cigarette of the day. She should have enjoyed the peaceful scenery—the woods behind the house, the sound of birds chirping in the trees—but her mind raced. So much had happened since she'd arrived in Purdyville, and she wondered if it was a sign that she should move on.

By the time Matt arrived with her suitcase, Frankie had drunk the entire pot of coffee, smoked more cigarettes than she should have and taken a quick shower. She was lighting another cigarette when he walked through the door. She knew she smoked too much and had been thinking of giving it up once her life settled down, but she had serious doubts that would ever happen.

"You okay?" Matt asked, setting the suitcase beside her.

"Yeah." She opened the suitcase and rummaged through it. Her dresses had been pulled from the closet and were folded neatly on top of her clothes. Everything else had been destroyed. Her anger flared. "I'd like to get my hands on the SOB who did this."

"We'll find him. In the meantime, why don't we drive over to my cousin's place so you can take a look? She's expecting you."

Grabbing her pocketbook, Frankie followed Matt in her car. She had tossed her suitcase in the back seat of her car, reluctant to part with it at the moment. Thank goodness she had moved her stereo and TV to the trunk.

Fifteen minutes later, Matt pulled into a ranch-style brick house. Frankie noted the mums growing in the flower bed as she pulled in beside him. The grass had been cut. At least this Sissy person kept the place up.

A redhead met them at the door. She wore leggings and a tie-dyed T-shirt. She was exceptionally pretty, tall and thin with only a smattering of freckles across her nose. Frankie suspected she and Sissy were close in age.

"Sissy, meet Frankie Daniels, Purdyville's new deputy," Matt said. "Daniels, this is my cousin, Sissy Burns."

"Nice to meet you," the woman said, shaking hands with Frankie. "Matt says you were looking for a place to stay. Come on in."

Frankie stepped inside and came to an immediate halt. From the outside the place had appeared normal. Inside, it was anything but. In fact, it looked like something straight out of the late sixties or early seventies. "Who…uh…decorated your place?" she asked Sissy, exchanging looks with Matt, who appeared slightly amused.

"I did it myself," Sissy said. "And at a reasonable price. The Salvation Army almost *gave* me the leopard sofa and lava lamps."

"No kidding?"

"I'm a die-hard Elvis Presley fan. Mama took me to one of his concerts when I was just a child, and we've toured Graceland three times. I was trying for that certain ambience."

Matt looked around and nodded. "I'd say you succeeded very well."

"Please sit down," Sissy said. "I just made a batch of my special herbal tea. I'll be just a minute." She hurried away.

Frankie looked at Matt as they sat on the sofa. The coffee table was an old tree trunk covered with thick coats of shellac. The walls were adorned with posters of Elvis; bookshelves were crammed with the King's memorabilia.

"You never mentioned your cousin had a knack for decorating," Frankie muttered under her breath.

"Okay, so she's a little different," he whispered.

"What does she do for a living?"

"I'm in human relations," Sissy said, sailing into the room with a tray of teacups. She set it carefully on the coffee table. "Didn't Matt tell you?"

"No, he didn't mention it." Frankie saw the cups were

of a leopard design as well. She picked up one and tasted the tea. Had she ever tasted seaweed, she would have imagined the tea contained it. "Mmm," she said.

"Great tea, Sissy," Matt said.

"Drink up, there's plenty more."

Frankie set her cup on the tray. "Human relations? What does it involve?"

Sissy glanced at Matt. "Well, you might say I'm a counselor of sorts. I listen to problems and try to help people out. I work at home, except on weekends, when I work at Virgil's. Speaking of which—"

"Yes, I beat the hell out of Willie-Jack Pitts," Frankie said.

"Good for you. I hate that man. Always causing trouble." Sissy folded her hands in her lap. "All those jobs are just sidelines. Actually, I'm a model."

Frankie was impressed. "Oh?"

"Well, I *was* a model when I worked at Wal-Mart. They use their employees in all the ads. Anyway, everyone kept saying what a natural I was, so I decided to start working on a portfolio. It's not cheap hiring professional photographers, which is why I work two jobs. Would you like to see my portfolio?"

Matt cleared his throat. "Why don't you do that later, Sissy? I think Deputy Daniels is feeling pretty frantic right now, what with not having a place to live."

Sissy suddenly looked abashed. "Oh, honey, I'm so sorry. Here I am talking about myself, and you're homeless."

"I'm not exactly homeless," Frankie began.

"Of course you're not," Sissy interrupted as though she'd just realized her blunder, "but let me show you around, anyway. This is a big place. My mother, bless her heart, left it to me when she died. It wasn't fixed up like it is now." She stood. "Let me show you the spare room."

Frankie stood, giving Matt a quick glance before she followed Sissy down the hall. "I'm afraid I never got around to decorating the guest bedroom," she said, throwing open a door. "I can only afford to do one room at a time."

After seeing the living room, Frankie was thankful of that. The simple bed and matching furniture in the guest room was a welcome sight.

"The bathroom is right across the hall," she said, opening a door so Frankie could peek into a lemon-yellow bathroom with a psychedelic shower curtain. Sissy had obviously found time to decorate that room as well as the living room.

"I have my workout room in the spare bedroom, which you're welcome to use. Most of the equipment came from the Salvation Army, but it works."

They toured the kitchen, which had been painted the same yellow as the bathroom. "I plan to do this room next," Sissy said.

"We should probably discuss the rent," Frankie replied.

"Can you afford seventy-five dollars a week, including utilities? You'd be responsible for your own groceries, of course. Oh, and you won't have to pay a deposit since you whipped Willie-Jack's butt. You did me a real favor. The only thing I ask is that you keep your gun out of sight. I'm terrified of weapons. On the other hand, I'd feel safer knowing you're here."

"That sounds fair," Frankie told her. "When can I move in?"

"How about today?"

"Sounds like a plan."

"It's all settled," Sissy announced to Matt when they reentered the living room. "Frankie has decided to become my new housemate."

Matt looked relieved. "Great. That's one less thing she'll have to worry about." He looked at Frankie. "Now all you have to do is buy a new wardrobe."

Frankie groaned, then pulled money from her wallet and handed Sissy seventy-five dollars. The other woman thanked her and laid the money on the coffee table. "Now, what's this about a new wardrobe?"

Frankie explained.

Sissy looked at Matt. "Do you have any suspects?"

"I'll know more when I talk to the crime lab. We're still trying to figure out who burned down the Gibbses' rental house."

Sissy pressed her lips into a grim line. "Doesn't take a rocket scientist to figure that one out."

"Maybe not. But it does take evidence."

Sissy nodded and turned to Frankie. "So you need clothes, huh? Well, you've come to the right place. I'll be glad to take you shopping."

Frankie looked at Matt, who quickly glanced away. "I'd better get going," he said. "Why don't you take the day off so you can take care of everything?"

"I need to stop by the station later on to see if my uniform has come in. Hopefully, it'll be my size this time."

He started for the door. "I'll see you ladies later."

"Oh, Chief?" Frankie stepped closer. She suddenly felt shy. "Thanks for putting me up last night."

He regarded her. He hoped he'd made the right decision by suggesting she move in with Sissy. "No problem. I only hope things turn around for you soon." He closed the door behind him.

"Well, now," Sissy said. "Have you and Matt got something going?"

Frankie arched both brows. "You're kidding, right?"

"No, I just saw the way he looked at you and assumed—"

"He let me stay at his place last night because the owner of the motel kicked me out." She explained further. "I think he feels sorry for me."

"Oh." Sissy seemed disappointed. "Well, I couldn't help feeling hopeful. It's about time Matt got on with his life. He's too good-looking to spend his Friday nights watching cable TV."

"I'm sure he has his share of dates."

"Yes, well, he does have a way with women. Thank God he didn't end up marrying the one he was engaged to."

"Why do you say that?"

"She was all wrong for him. When Mandy died, he called off the wedding out of respect for her. Never set a new date. After six months, his fiancée moved."

"I guess that explains why he lives alone in that big house."

"He's better off." She cleared her throat. "Now, I only have one rule here," she said, changing the subject abruptly. "I work mostly at night as far as my human relations job goes. I would appreciate it if you'd limit your calls during that time. Or, if you think you're going to stay for a while, I'll add another line."

"No problem. I don't know anyone around here to call."

"If you happen to answer the phone during the evening, and I'm out for some reason, don't get into any conversations with them, okay? Just take a number and tell them I'll call right back."

"Okay."

Sissy gave her a quizzical look. "Tell me the truth. Did Matt say anything to you about what I do for a living?"

"No, why?"

"Maybe I should tell you. You may want to rethink moving in here."

"I'm listening."

"Honey, I work for one of those one-nine-hundred numbers. I talk to lonely men. Horny men. Men who can't...um...get off any other way."

Six

Frankie just looked at her. For once, she had no words.

"I have my favorites, you see. I'd get fired if the company knew, but some of the men have my number and know they can call on certain nights."

"They have your home number?" Frankie asked in disbelief. "Isn't that dangerous?"

"It's okay. I've been talking to these guys for a couple of years. They don't want anyone to know about this any more than I do. One is a senator, another is a CEO of a Fortune 500 company. I deal with a lot of professionals, pillars of their community. Only, they have a few hangups."

"Matt knows about this?" Frankie asked, wondering why he hadn't said something.

"We've never actually discussed it, but Matt and I have always been close. I feel certain he knows. Of course, he would never breathe a word of it to anyone."

Frankie sank onto the sofa. Was it *her*, she wondered. How come she always found herself in the middle of something weird? How had she managed to end up sharing a house with a woman who talked dirty to men for money?

"You don't have to stay," Sissy said.

Frankie pondered it. Where would she go? "How in the world did you get mixed up in something like this?"

Sissy sat in a chair across from her. "I don't have a lot of skills. I enjoyed working in the jewelry department at Wal-Mart, but I got laid off when business dropped. I began working for a telemarketing firm, since that allowed me to work at home, and I got friendly with some of the girls. One of them told me about the job and how much she made.

"It's just something I'm doing while I add to my portfolio. I plan to send it to every modeling agency in New York. I want to get the hell out of Purdyville. This is nothing but a two-bit town with a bunch of gossips. My goal is to live in one of those high-rise apartments in a big-city like Atlanta."

Frankie was tempted to ask Sissy if she planned to take the leopard sofa. "Those are mighty big dreams," she said, wondering if Sissy had considered the age factor. Frankie knew nothing about modeling, but she was pretty sure agencies preferred much younger women.

"So, do you want your money back?" Sissy asked. "Now that you know what I do?"

Frankie shook her head. "No. I figure that's your business. But I have to give this phone number to the office, as well as my mother. If I should get a call from one of your...uh...clients, I'll take a message like you asked."

"Well then, it's settled." Sissy stood and picked up the tray. "I'm free for a couple of hours. Why don't we go shopping?"

Frankie waved her off. "Oh, I can go alone. I just have to pick up a couple of pairs of jeans, T-shirts, and underwear."

"You're going to the benefit next Friday night for Irma and Homer Gibbs, aren't you?"

"I suppose."

"Then you'll need a party dress. Give me a second to change clothes."

* * *

They were on their way in a matter of minutes. At Wal-Mart, they each took a cart and made for the women's area. Frankie grabbed several pairs of jeans, and a half dozen T-shirts that had been reduced, a pair of sneakers and strappy heels.

"Don't you want a couple of nice blouses?" Sissy asked. "And maybe a pair of slacks? You can't wear jeans all the time."

Frankie shrugged. "I guess." In the end, she found a pair of dressy khaki slacks, a navy oxford shirt and a camel blazer she could wear with anything. Sissy insisted on picking out a dress for the upcoming benefit, as well.

"Aren't you going to try everything on?"

"No, they'll fit. If not, I'll bring them back."

Sissy shook her head sadly in the lingerie department. "Don't tell me you're buying cotton underwear." She led her to the next aisle, where matching bras and panties of satin hung from the racks. "Look, they're thirty percent off. Is this your lucky day or what?"

Frankie argued with her for several minutes before she gave in and made her selections, tossing them into her basket. Sissy smiled prettily. "Okay, let's check out the makeup department."

"I don't wear much makeup."

"We'll see." She paused. "I should have asked if you could afford all this?"

"I'm okay. Besides, what choice do I have?"

"Well, you've got the essentials. You can add to your wardrobe as time goes on."

By the time they left the store, Frankie's shopping cart was full. The two women stopped by the station on the way home, and Sissy waited in the car while Frankie hurried in to check on the status of her uniforms. They had arrived, both in size ten. Matt spied her and came out front.

"Willie-Jack's old man just bailed him out of jail."

"Oh, great," Frankie said, sarcasm filling her tone.

"We're still investigating the arson, but Willie-Jack has a good alibi. Seems he met up with a lovely woman at the Fillin' Hole Lounge, and they spent the night together."

"He probably threatened to sleep with her again in order to get her to lie."

Matt grinned.

"Why didn't you tell me what Sissy does for a living?" Frankie said.

"I figure it's her business. She's not breaking any laws."

"Don't you think it's a little strange?"

"I've seen stranger." He smiled. "So did you buy something pretty for Friday night?"

"A dress."

"Play your cards right and I might ask you to dance."

"I don't know how to dance."

"Lucky for you, I do. See you tomorrow morning, bright and early." He turned for the door leading to his office.

Back at the house, Frankie began putting away her clothes. Sissy brought an iron and ironing board to her room. "What's that for?"

"You'll need to iron your uniforms. You *can* iron, can't you?"

"If I have to."

"I thought we might grab a barbecue sandwich at Virgil's place for dinner. I have to run out for groceries afterward.''

''Me, too. Don't you have to work?''

''Later. I don't usually get calls until after eight or nine o'clock.''

Frankie was surprised to find Matt sitting at the bar when she and Sissy walked into Virgil's place at six o'clock. He was out of uniform, dressed in jeans and a blue short-sleeve shirt that brought out his blue eyes. Sissy hugged him. ''Hey, are you following us?''

An easy smile tugged the corners of his mouth before he shifted his gaze to Frankie. He stood, and she was impressed by his manners. ''Somebody has to keep an eye out for you wild women.'' His gazed remained fixed on Frankie, and the light in his eyes told her he was glad to see her. It was almost sensual, emphasizing his handsome features. Frankie wondered if it came naturally or if he'd practiced it in front of a mirror, because her stomach did a small flip-flop in response. No wonder women were drawn to him. When he dressed in civilian clothes, it was easy to forget he was her boss.

''Actually, I'm keeping an eye out for Willie Jack. I don't want him coming in making trouble. First night out of jail and all.''

''Mind if we join you for a cold one?'' Sissy asked.

''Be my guest.'' He pulled out two stools.

Frankie sat down, and he grabbed the stool beside her.

Abby appeared instantly. ''Sissy, don't you see enough of this place on weekends?''

''Yeah, but I love the barbecue.''

Abby glanced at Frankie, and her eyes widened. ''Well, now. I believe I'm going to have to personally buy you a drink.''

"How about me?" Sissy asked, giving a pout.

"Forget it. You didn't take on Willie-Jack." But she was smiling. "You should have seen this woman at work. Kicked the crap out of him." She turned to Frankie. "You've obviously taken a few self-defense classes. I've never seen someone make those kinds of moves. And so fast."

"I know a little bit about defending myself," Frankie said. "It comes with the job."

Matt gave a grunt. "She knows more than a little bit. She's an expert."

"You don't have to tell me. I watched the whole thing from the window. Willie-Jack will think twice before messing with her again."

"I doubt it," Frankie said. "One has to have a brain to think. Willie-Jack is missing something vital in that department."

Abby laughed as she went for their beers, which Matt insisted on buying.

Sissy leaned forward and regarded Matt. "Don't ever go shopping with this woman," she said, motioning to Frankie. "Can you believe women still buy cotton underwear?"

"Sissy!" Frankie felt her face burn.

"He's my cousin."

"Well, he's not mine."

"I finally talked her into satin."

Frankie caught Matt's amused look and turned her head in the opposite direction. She could feel his eyes on her, and she suspected he was giving some thought to what she would look like in her underwear. She suddenly felt like wringing Sissy's neck.

"Satin, huh?" he said, thinking how cute Frankie looked when she blushed. He wouldn't have expected it from someone like her. "I hope you helped her pick out her dress."

"Yes, I did. A slinky black number and sexy high heels to match."

"She'll be the belle of the ball."

"Excuse me," Frankie said. "Could we discuss something else?"

"I taught her to iron."

Frankie groaned and reached for a menu. "Why don't we go ahead and order?" she suggested to Sissy. "We're supposed to go grocery shopping, remember?"

"Uh-oh, here comes trouble," Abby said.

Frankie didn't have to turn around to know Willie-Jack Pitts had just walked through the door. She took a sip of her beer and studied the menu, but she knew exactly when the man sat down. She heard the bar stool scrape against the wood floor.

"I'll have the usual, Abby," he said. "Oh, look who's here. Hello, Chief," he said in a way that sounded like mockery. "I would never have figured you for a drinking man."

"Is that you, Willie-Jack?" Matt said. "I didn't recognize you. Guess I'm used to seeing you on the other side of iron bars."

Frankie raised her menu higher so nobody would see the smile on her face.

Willie-Jack chuckled. "Hello, Sissy. You still talking dirty to horny old men?"

Frankie looked at Sissy, whose face was scarlet. How did Willie-Jack know about Sissy's night job?

Sissy regained her composure. "Eat dirt and die, Willie-Jack."

"Why don't you just keep your mouth shut?" Matt told

the man. "I don't want to have to sic Deputy Daniels on you."

This time Willie-Jack looked embarrassed. "Look, I just came in for a cold one. Don't start any shit with me, Webber."

"Let's move to a table," Sissy suggested. "Matt, why don't you join us for dinner?"

"Be glad to." Once again, he met Frankie's gaze. She didn't look happy at the prospect, which made him all the more determined.

"Just grab a seat anywhere," Abby said.

Sissy chose a booth. "Oh, my sneaker came untied." She leaned over to tie it. While Frankie waited for her to finish and scoot over, Matt looked up from his side. "You can sit next to me. I won't bite."

"Damn shoelace," Sissy said. "There's a knot in it. Oh, now look what I've done."

Frankie felt dumb just standing there. Finally, she took a seat next to Matt, making sure she was as close to the booth's edge as she could get. Nevertheless, she could feel the heat emanating off his body.

Sissy sat up, holding part of the shoelace. "It broke," she told Frankie. "Help me remember to buy a pair at the store, okay?"

Virgil, who'd been in the kitchen up till now, carried their menus over. "Hi, folks," he said, then directed his attention to Matt. "How did you get lucky enough to sit with the best-looking women in town?" He winked at Sissy and Frankie.

"Guess it's my lucky day. If you're our waitress, I'm going to have to complain. I was expecting someone with pretty legs, in a short skirt."

Virgil laughed. "Business is slow. I let the waitress go home so she could spend time with her family." He glanced toward the bar. "Abby said Willie-Jack was running his mouth."

"We're ignoring him," Matt said. "Everything is fine."

"I'll throw him out of here if he acts up." He smiled at Frankie. "Or maybe you'll throw him out. By the way, dinner is on me tonight, young lady."

Matt shifted slightly in his seat, and Frankie felt his thigh brush hers. She tried to make herself smaller. "You don't have to do that."

Virgil smiled. "I insist. As I recall, the last one ended up in my parking lot."

They ordered the country rib plate and switched from beer to iced tea. Once Virgil took the order, he hurried away, stopping by the bar briefly. Abby delivered their beverages, while Matt told Frankie what was going on with the investigation at the motel.

"There are a million fingerprints in that room," he said, "but none of them match up with Willie-Jack's buddies. I would never have believed they'd be smart enough to wear gloves, but it looks that way."

"What I'd like to know is how Willie-Jack found out about my phone work," Sissy said. "I'm sure it's all over town by now."

Matt shrugged. "Since when have you cared what people thought, Sissy? It's nobody's business. Besides, who would believe Willie-Jack in the first place?"

"He had to find out illegally," she insisted. "How do I know he hasn't been listening through an open window?"

"I can investigate, but it'll draw more attention. You two need a dog. A big one with a loud bark. And security lights front and back. I can pick them up and install them this weekend."

Sissy shook her head. "I'm not mature enough to take care of a dog. I have trouble keeping houseplants alive."

"I could always lend you George," Matt said, grinning.

Frankie rolled her eyes heavenward. "Forget it. We can take care of ourselves. I've got a G-U-N."

Sissy shuddered. "What? Do you think I can't spell? You know I'm terrified of guns."

"Yes, but wouldn't it be worth watching me shoot Willie-Jack between the eyes?"

"I could probably get over my fear long enough to watch that."

Matt chuckled. "Yeah, but where would you dispose of the body?"

Virgil arrived with their plates and set them on the table. Frankie suddenly remembered she hadn't eaten all day. The ribs were the best she'd ever tasted. They chatted about the upcoming fund-raiser for Irma and Homer Gibbs.

"I'm making pasta salad," Sissy announced. "It always goes over well."

Matt shrugged. "I'll do my usual baked beans."

"You're taking the easy way out as usual, cousin."

"Should I plan to bring something?" Frankie asked.

"It's up to you, honey. The pasta salad can be from both of us."

"I'll bring a cake," Frankie said.

Matt and Sissy looked at her doubtfully.

"I don't plan on baking it myself," Frankie informed them. "I'll pick one up at the bakery and just pretend I baked it."

"Frankie's going to turn a lot of heads come Friday night," Sissy said. "I don't think there's going to be a man in town who cares whether or not she can bake."

For some reason that didn't sit well with Matt. "She's

already promised to save me a dance. Guess I'll have to wait in line.''

"Who's playing?" Sissy asked. "Please don't tell me it's the Slattery Brothers.''

Matt looked apologetic. "They're the only ones we could get on such short notice.''

"All they play is country-western.''

"Did I mention they're doing it for free?''

"They should be paying people to listen to them," Sissy complained. "I wouldn't give them ten cents to play at my funeral.''

Frankie listened to the banter between the two. "How are the Gibbses doing?''

Matt sighed. "Irma is still upset, but she has her hands full with Homer, so she doesn't have much time to think about it. She wasn't real happy to hear about the fund-raiser. Said she didn't want folks thinking she and Homer were charity cases. Stubborn woman. Always has been. You're going to be as bad as her when you get old.''

She shot him a dark look. "Any leads yet on who started the fire?''

Matt shook his head. "No prints, no witnesses. And like I said, Willie-Jack has an airtight alibi. We're trying to find out if the Gibbses had any enemies, but Irma insists she has no idea who would intentionally set fire to the place.''

"Maybe it was teenagers," Sissy said. "If they knew the house was empty, it would be a good place to party. It could have been accidental.''

Matt shook his head. "The gas cans tell a different story. Somebody had a score to settle with the Gibbses. Buster checked the hardware stores. The cans weren't bought locally.''

Abby stopped by and refilled their tea glasses, just as

Willie-Jack left the restaurant. "Oh, good, he's gone. I can relax tonight."

"Why doesn't Virgil get a restraining order against him?" Frankie asked. "Keep him out of here."

Sissy grunted. "That would probably make him even more dangerous."

"Virgil does ask him to leave when he starts trouble," Abby said, "which seems to be on a regular basis these days." She sauntered away.

"We'll keep an eye on Willie-Jack and his pals," Matt said. "All it'll take is a belly full of beer before they start bragging. Abby is going to let me know if she hears anything. Actually, I'm trying to give the SOB enough rope to hang himself. I'd enjoy nothing better than to let him rot in prison. In the meantime, I'm going to have the guys make regular passes by Sissy's place day *and* night, just to be on the safe side."

"Do you think my being there will cause danger for her?" Frankie asked.

"Don't worry about me, honey," Sissy said. "I've got a baseball bat with Willie-Jack's name on it, right beside my bed."

Matt shifted once again in his seat, his arm pressing against Frankie's. "This is just an added precaution. I think Willie-Jack will lie low for a while. He probably misses sleeping in his own bed."

"I look stupid," Frankie said the next morning as she modeled her uniform for Sissy.

"You *don't* look stupid," the woman said. "You look very professional."

Frankie shot her a look. She already felt like she'd known Sissy for years. "This coming from a woman who tells men exactly what they want to hear over the telephone.''

The other woman chuckled. ''Damn right. And I make a lot of money doing it.''

''Maybe I should go into that line of work,'' Frankie said glumly. ''My mother always said I had a dirty mouth.''

''I could probably get you on,'' Sissy said. ''In the meantime, there's nothing wrong with the uniform. Of course, a little makeup wouldn't hurt.''

''I'm wearing makeup.''

''Oh. Then, why don't you let me give you a touch-up? Just enough to give you a little color. It'll boost your confidence.''

''Do I look like I have a problem with self-confidence? Besides, I can't go in looking like a floozy. I'm a professional.''

''Trust me.''

When Frankie viewed herself in the mirror a few minutes later, she had to admit that Sissy had done a good job. ''Not bad.''

''It was easy. You have deep-set eyes and high cheekbones. Most women would die for them. All I did was enhance those features. I could show you how to do it. One more thing. Speaking of professionalism, you really should pin up your hair. I'll show you an easy way to do it.''

Frankie tried not to grumble. She had always worn her hair down. But Sissy was right, she would look more professional. In two minutes flat, Sissy had Frankie's hair pulled into what Eve called a French twist. Frankie plopped her cap on her head. ''Do I look like a cop now?''

''You *are* a cop, honey. A pretty one at that. The men in town will probably break the law on purpose, just to have you give them a ticket.''

* * *

Matt did a double take when he caught sight of Frankie. "Lookin' good, Deputy," he said. "Let's take a ride. We've got a tough job ahead of us."

"Did something happen last night?"

"It's a fresh crime. We have to move fast on it."

Frankie felt a rush of adrenaline as she climbed into the patrol car next to Matt. "You mind filling me in?"

"You'll see. I need your advice on how to handle it."

Frankie remained quiet on the ride. It was obvious Matt didn't want to talk about it. She wondered what the crime involved. Must be bad, she thought. And Matt was counting on her to help him solve it. He left the city limits. Ten minutes later, they reached a dirt road that ran through a heavily wooded area. "Would you at least give me a rundown on the victim?"

He looked at her. "Name is Molly. She's six years old."

Frankie felt a sense of dread. She hated crimes involving children. Perhaps the little girl was missing, kidnapped—or worse. The wooded area opened up, and she saw a farm up ahead. Matt pulled into a long driveway that led to the house. Two men, one slender in overalls, a heavier man in jeans and T-shirt, hurried toward the squad car.

"Glad you're here, Chief," the one in overalls said as Matt and Frankie stepped out of the car. "Poor Molly is scared to death."

Frankie sighed her relief. Molly was alive. "You found her?"

Both men gawked, as if noticing Frankie for the first time.

"Weldon, Sam, I want you to meet my new deputy. This is Frankie Daniels. Frankie, meet Weldon Evans and Sam Bone."

Frankie nodded. "You haven't touched the crime scene, have you?"

The men continued to look at her strangely. All except Matt, who glanced in another direction.

"What crime scene?" Weldon asked. "Caesar jumped the fence again, and we ain't seen hide nor hair of him. We've got poor Molly locked in the barn until we find him."

"Your daughter is in the barn?" Frankie said in disbelief.

This time the men looked at Matt. "What in God's green acre is she talking about?" Sam asked.

"Why is your daughter in the barn?" Frankie insisted loudly. "Why is she not in the hospital?"

"Molly isn't my daughter," Weldon said. "She's my heifer."

"Your heifer!"

"Caesar jumped the fence to get to her. Broke the fence and almost broke Molly's back trying to hump her. She's not even in heat, though I suspect she's close."

Frankie was growing more confused by the minute. "Who is Caesar?"

"My bull."

"Your bull!" Frankie turned to Matt. "What's the meaning of this?"

Matt looked at her. "We've got to find Sam's bull before he goes after Molly again. He's huge. Way too large to mate."

Frankie glared at him. "You led me out here to look for a bull?" she shrieked. "I thought we were looking for a missing child, for God's sake!" She noted the men's stares and took a deep breath. "May I have a word with you, Chief?" she said, trying to calm down.

He followed her to the patrol car. They climbed inside. "What?"

"Do you get some kind of sick pleasure out of making me look like a fool?"

"I don't know what you're talking about."

"Oh, hell yes, you do. I'm sick and tired of being dragged to these asinine crime scenes. I know what this is all about. You're jealous of me."

He arched one brow. "Jealous?"

"That's right. I've got a helluva lot more training than you, and your male ego can't handle it."

"That's ridiculous."

"It pisses you off that you've spent ten years dealing with all this silliness while I've worked the hard stuff. How many *real* criminals have you collared, Webber? You don't know shit-from-Shinola about what it's like on the mean streets, because you're too busy swaggering along the sidewalks like the town stud in this one-horse town. I'm sick of your 'Andy of Mayberry' routine."

His dark look seemed to drill right through her. "If you're such a hotshot, why the hell are you here? Why did my uncle practically beg me to take you? What's the real story, Daniels?"

Frankie felt as though she'd just been slapped in the face. Had Dell Wayford been so desperate to get rid of her that he'd pleaded with Matt to take her off his hands? She had never been more humiliated.

"You want to know why I'm here?" she almost shouted. "I'm here because I was doing the police commissioner's son-in-law, that's why. It was either move to Purdyville or work in a doughnut shop. Welcome to my world, Webber."

He looked stunned. "You had an affair with a married man?"

"With three kids, to boot. You got a problem with that?"

Weldon Evans and Sam Bone had walked to the front of the patrol car, and were staring through the windshield as if watching Matt and Frankie's exchange on a TV screen. The two men exchanged looks. Finally, Weldon pulled a cigar from his pocket, bit off the tip and lit it. Sam reached into his pocket for a tin of chewing tobacco.

A shadow of disappointment and annoyance fell over Matt's face. "Look, I don't have time to listen to the sordid details of your love life. We're here to do a job."

The censure in his eyes sent anger surging through her. "You want to find Caesar-the-bull, then you go after him. I'll wait for you in the car."

"You take your orders from me, Deputy."

"Not anymore. I quit."

Seven

Frankie waited in the car for more than an hour before Matt returned. She would gladly have walked to town had she known the way. He climbed into the driver's seat, his uniform stained from sweat and dirt. Without a word, he started the car and pulled from the drive.

He didn't speak until he'd pulled onto the main road. "I'm sorry you find your job so boring," he said. "Perhaps I should have someone killed to make it more interesting."

"That's a moot point now," Frankie replied. "I've already quit."

"I'll need a two-week notice."

"Forget the notice. Fire me."

Matt pulled into the parking lot of an abandoned gas station. He turned off the engine and faced her. Exasperation twisted the corners of his mouth. "Look, I'm sorry if I made you feel silly back there. I was trying to have a little fun with you. You take things so damn seriously."

"I don't like being the brunt of your jokes. I'm a professional, and I demand to be treated like one."

A long silence ensued.

"I made a mistake, and I'm sorry. It's just—well, you're a regular ball-buster, Daniels, you know that? You come into town like you own the place, and, yeah, you can be a little intimidating at times. And that mouth of yours ought to come with a warning label.''

The last thing on earth Frankie had expected from him was an apology. It left her feeling disconcerted. She crossed her arms and pointedly gazed out the side window.

''I don't want you to quit, Frankie.''

He had used her real name, and that was more mind-boggling than anything. ''I don't belong in Purdyville, and I don't think I can continue working with you.''

''Because you find me attractive?'' he asked.

She snapped her head around and found a slight smile on his face. He was teasing, but it still irked the hell out of her. ''I saw the look you gave me back there when I told you the truth about why I was here. You, of all people, have no business passing judgment.''

''I was angry. Not because you'd had an affair, though, but because you were the one who took the rap. That *was* the case, am I right?''

''Yes.''

''Did you know he was married?''

''He told me he was separated and in the process of a divorce. And I was dumb enough to believe it.'' She paused. ''In the end, he got what was coming to him. I'm not the only one who suffered.''

''Were you in love with him?''

She continued to stare out the window. ''I thought so at the time. The truth is, I don't know a damn thing about love.''

''That's too bad, because I'm attracted to you.''

She felt a momentary wave of panic as his words set in. At the same time a strange surge of excitement coursed through her body, causing her pulse to race. Matt Webber was attracted to her? She had no answer so she remained quiet, despite the topsy-turvy emotions going on inside her.

"I like the feistiness in you," he continued, "although I suspect you're not as tough as you act."

Frankie was silent for a long moment. "This isn't going to work, Matt. I'm not going to make the same mistake I made before."

"You think getting involved with me would be a mistake?"

"A big one. And I'd take the fall, just like before."

"Are you going to spend the rest of your life comparing every man to the jerk in Atlanta? That's in the past."

She eyed him. "I don't want to forget. I lost everything as a result of poor judgment. Besides, your reputation isn't exactly sterling at that."

"If I'd done half the things folks said I have, I wouldn't have time to keep law and order in this town." His voice softened. "Think about it, Frankie. Have you really lost all that much?"

She looked at him. "What do you think? All those years of training, and for what? So I can chase bulls?"

"Our job is to serve and protect. This is about helping people, not making yourself look good."

"Great speech, Matt, but it's also about me working my ass off all those years so I could make detective. And I was good at it." She could feel the sting of tears behind her eyes.

Matt didn't miss the emotion in her voice. "You are a good detective."

The compliment surprised her. "How would you know?"

"I've read your file, remember?"

She sniffed. "I *was* good."

"The problem is, you don't feel you'd be doing important work here. I grew up here, Frankie. I know these people personally. I've witnessed their good times and their hardships. I've sat with some of them all night after delivering the worst news they could ever get. A teenage son killed in an auto accident. A daughter who ran away and was never found. This isn't about big-city life where crime occurs on a daily basis. It's not about case numbers. It's about real people. People who will dig deep in their pockets to help someone like Irma and Homer Gibbs. I may not have worked the *mean streets,* as you refer to them, but I've seen a lot, and I sometimes have trouble falling asleep at night.''

Frankie remained quiet, even as her eyes filled with tears.

"I recently told you I knew where I belonged. I think you belong here, too.''

Her throat was full. "I care about people, too, Matt. But I'd rather find the guy responsible for selling crack to teenagers. Not just some flunky passing off a joint to his buddy. I want to take down the man at the top. I want the name of the pimp who lures young girls into prostitution, girls who sometimes end up dead if they don't do as they're told. When I visit a crime scene and see what people are capable of doing to others, I don't sleep until they're behind bars. I don't care about socializing; I care about solving crimes and taking dangerous people off the street.''

He looked sad as he started the engine. "Maybe I was wrong about you. Maybe you don't belong here, where you have to look at the people who were hurt or brutalized. Maybe you're better off working with case numbers, but I prefer dealing directly with the human beings involved.'' He sighed. "It's up to you if you want to quit, but I would appreciate a couple of weeks' notice. If you've already sent out your résumé, you can have people call me, and I'll give you a good reference.''

"Thank you."

They made the drive back to the station without speaking. Frankie realized she may have acted rashly by quitting a job without having one lined up, but she had to look after her own interests. She and Matt would never be able to work together. She was as attracted to him as he was to her.

Matt tried not to show his disappointment as he walked into the station, Frankie beside him. Velma was waiting.

"I was about to radio you. I just this minute got a call from Piney Grove Nursing Home. Darnell Peters passed away less than an hour ago, and there's been a bad accident on Highway 26. Bad morning, Chief. Really bad.''

"Where's Doc Linton?"

"He's on his way to the accident scene. Supposed to be fatalities. Cooter, Buster and Abe just walked out the back door.''

"Who's Linton?" Frankie asked.

"Our coroner and medical examiner."

"He does both jobs?"

"Small town," Matt said.

Velma cleared her throat. "On top of everything, Earlene Peters called while I was on the phone with Piney Grove. She plans to file a complaint on willful neglect. She wants the staff questioned immediately. I'll tell you, it's been the worst five minutes of my life.''

"Is the body still there?"

"Yes. The staff doctor pronounced him dead due to heart failure. Darnell was on nitroglycerin before he was admitted to Piney Grove. Earlene made such a fuss that the director of the home told them not to move Darnell until he was seen by you or Doc Linton.''

"We'll ride over and take a look. I'm sure Earlene is overreacting, as usual. If the folks at Piney Grove claim Darnell was bruised falling out of bed, that's good enough for me.''

"Why are you so easily convinced?'' Frankie asked.

"My grandparents spent several years in Piney Grove, and I sort of grew close to the staff. If you're interested, I'd like you to help with the investigation. I don't know that I could be impartial.''

She nodded. "Let's go.''

They started for the door. "Velma, keep me informed about the accident,'' Matt called over his shoulder.

Piney Grove Nursing Home sat on the outskirts of town, a sprawling, ranch style, brick structure that looked more like a private residence than a home for the elderly. A massive lawn with flower beds and towering pine trees gave it a picture-perfect look. Frankie wondered if it was too perfect, but then, she was trained to see things in as many ways as possible.

A veranda stretched the length of the front of the facility, where patients sat in weathered rocking chairs, obviously enjoying the late-morning air. Several wheelchairs claimed space, a couple of the occupants dozing while others talked among themselves. They became quiet when they spied Matt and Frankie.

"Is something wrong?'' a man asked Matt.

Matt smiled. They obviously didn't know about Darnell's passing. "No, sir, everything's fine. We're just visiting. My deputy is thinking of putting her mother here.''

Frankie smiled as well, trying to put everyone at ease. "I understand Piney Grove has a wonderful reputation.''

An overweight woman with silver hair shrugged. "The food ain't that great, and they seldom serve desserts."

"That's because they've put you on a diet, Doris," another woman said. She was bone thin with angular lines. "The rest of us eat just fine. The staff serves a lot of fruits and vegetables, but at night we get milk and cookies."

"You can't get a decent cup of coffee," Doris added. "Everything is decaffeinated."

"We'll keep that in mind," Matt told her as he and Frankie went through the front door. She noticed that the carpet was worn, the furniture lumpy, as they made their way to the receptionist's desk. Frankie wondered if Piney Grove Nursing Home was having financial difficulties.

A pretty receptionist looked up from the counter and smiled broadly at the sight of Matt. "Why, Matthew Webber, you devil. It's about time you came around."

"Hi there, Melinda. Haven't seen you in a coon's age."

"Not since your poor sister was called home, bless her heart. Looks like you would have taken the time to visit us once in a while." She leaned closer and whispered, "I suppose you're here because of Mr. Peters. The patients haven't been told. They think he has the flu, so they won't go near his room." She looked sad. "They get so depressed when we lose someone."

"My grandparents used to be the same way." He nodded toward Frankie. "This is Deputy Daniels."

"Nice to meet you, Deputy," the woman said without taking her eyes off Matt. "Are you planning on going to the gathering Friday night, Matt?"

"I thought I'd stop by."

"I'll be sure to save you a dance."

"My feelings would be hurt if you didn't. But your husband is bigger than me. What if he gets jealous?"

Melinda batted her eyelashes. "Johnny-Lee and I are separated."

"I see."

"I'm free as a bird."

"Just don't fly too far away," Matt replied, giving her a hearty wink, which brought a blush to her cheeks. "Let me ask you something, Melinda. Was Mr. Peters well liked by the staff or was he a complainer, like that woman sitting out front?"

"You must mean Doris. Big woman?" Matt nodded. "Doris is never happy. It's like my mama used to say about one of the deacons in our church. She said, 'Melinda, that man wouldn't be happy if he was hanged by a new rope.'"

"I've met a few people like that myself."

Frankie wondered if he was referring to her, wondered if Matt was trying to put on a show for her, so she'd think he was irresistible. Never mind that a man lay dead and was suspected of abusive treatment by the staff. She tapped the toe of her shoe impatiently.

"Mr. Peters was different," Melinda said. "He liked everybody and everybody liked him."

"What about his wife?"

"We…uh…tolerated her, if you know what I mean. You know she accused us of hurting him."

"Who found him?"

"Shirley."

Matt looked sad. "Where is she now?"

"She's in the chapel. Been in there ever since Earlene left."

"Thanks."

Matt and Frankie walked to a set of wooden doors. "Do you want me to go in with you?" she asked.

"You're part of the investigation team."

"Matt?"

He paused with his hand on the doorknob. "Yeah?"

"I'm sorry about what I said earlier. I had no right to say those things. When I get angry, I don't think."

"My skin is tougher than you think, Frankie. Don't worry about it."

But she would. There were times people said things in the heat of anger that could never be taken back, and insulting him as an officer of the law was unforgivable. Regardless of whether or not she stayed, she planned to make it right between them.

They found Shirley sitting in the front pew, staring straight ahead. Matt took a seat beside her; Frankie took the pew directly behind. Shirley was a big woman with gray hair and old-fashioned glasses. Frankie could smell the starch in her white uniform.

"How're you doing, Shirley?" Matt asked softly, taking her plump hand in his.

"Hello, Matt. I was hoping you'd come." She squeezed his hand. "I'm better than I was. Earlene really tore into me. Accused me of not taking proper care of her husband. She's threatening to sue the nursing home for patient neglect. Like she cares. She only visited her husband twice a week. His son either called or came by every day."

"Earlene's nothing but a bag of hot air," he said. "But I need you to tell me what happened before I take a look at the body. Has anyone touched it?"

"I checked Mr. Peters's pulse the minute I found him. He was already dead. There was blood coming out of his nose. He obviously took a hard fall, but not a soul heard him. There was quite a ruckus going on in the hall shortly before I found him. One of the patients accused another one of stealing her teeth. Anyway, I covered him with a sheet and gave strict orders that no one was to enter that room."

"Good thinking."

Frankie pulled out her notebook and Matt nodded at her. "By the way, Shirley, meet Deputy Daniels."

The woman wrenched her head around and offered Frankie a sad smile. "I heard there was a pretty new deputy in Purdyville. I'm Shirley Waters. Welcome, Deputy Daniels."

Frankie returned the smile. "I'm sorry we had to meet under these circumstances, Mrs. Waters."

"When did you discover Mr. Peters, Shirley?"

"Hour and a half ago. I wrote down the time on his chart. Dr. Russ signed the death certificate, but he was called to the hospital. I understand there's been a bad wreck on the highway."

Matt nodded. "Why don't you give me a little background on Mr. Peters."

Shirley's eyes glistened, and her voice broke. "He hadn't been feeling well for weeks. Said his lower stomach was cramping, as if he was having gas pains. Dr. Russ gave him something for it, but it didn't seem to help. There was a stomach virus going around at the time, so we attributed it to that. He had no appetite. The only thing we could get him to eat was the banana pudding his wife brought in. You never saw a man who loved banana pudding as much as Mr. Peters. But after a while, he couldn't even tolerate that. Everything he ate came right back up." She paused and frowned. "Not to change the subject, but do you believe that Earlene told us to throw out the pudding she brought in yesterday, as well as his belongings? I guess she's afraid someone will eat her precious pudding or wear Darnell's clothes.

"I'm sorry, I shouldn't be talking like that. Where was

I? Oh, yes, then Mr. Peters's hands and feet started to swell, and Dr. Russ gave him something for that. But swelling is common when patients spend so much time in bed. I tried to encourage him to get up and join the others, but he said it made him dizzy. He just became so weak. Dr. Russ figured his weakened condition was making it difficult for Mr. Peters to recover from the stomach virus, but it hung on for weeks, even after Dr. Russ sent him to the hospital for tests.''

"What did the hospital find?"

"Two of his arteries were blocked, which could have caused the weakness and dizzy spells. He'd had a heart condition for years, you know. But the doctors were hesitant to operate while he was still recovering from the stomach virus. And, of course, his age was the main consideration. Mr. Peters was almost ninety and very frail.''

"Anything else?"

Shirley nodded. "His color wasn't good. He became jaundiced, and I noticed a rash. Sometimes medication causes rashes, but Dr. Russ didn't like the looks of it and scheduled him for more tests at the hospital. Mr. Peters was to go in by ambulance this afternoon." Once again, tears filled her eyes. "Only he didn't live long enough."

"What do you think happened?"

Shirley took a deep sigh. "I think he was having stomach cramps again, and he tried to get up and go to the bathroom and fell trying to climb over the guardrail. Or he could have had a dizzy spell. He had strict orders not to get out of that bed without help."

"He didn't buzz anyone?"

"No. Mr. Peters was afraid of being a burden to us. He would run out of water, but do you think he'd call someone and ask for more? No, he waited until one of us came in and noticed. We're short-staffed—have been for years—so he seldom asked for anything. That's one reason we didn't know he was sick in the beginning. He never complained. Not once. But he was scared of hospitals. Terrified. I think he had some kind of phobia. Or maybe he was scared to leave us because he knew we loved him. He'd plead with Dr. Russ not to send him, and the doctor would hold off, hoping he'd get better. I was supposed to ride in the ambulance with him today so he wouldn't fret so much. He said, 'Shirley, if you'll promise to go with me, I'll go. I know you won't let nothing bad happen to me.'"

"He obviously trusted you very much," Matt said. "Who else visited besides his wife?"

"His son, Jody. That boy was devoted to his daddy. I personally called him with the news, because he and I have grown close over the years. Naturally, he's beside himself right now. He wanted to rush right over, but I convinced him to stay away for the time being, since we were calling you and Doc Linton. He promised to go home and try to calm down."

"Anyone else?"

"A man by the name of Blaine, who was his best friend. Blaine Freeman. Mr. Peters once told me they'd been friends since grade school. I still can't believe it happened." Shirley began to weep.

Finally, Frankie spoke up. "Mrs. Waters, why don't you let someone take you home? You're in no condition to work."

"I'll see. I just want to sit here awhile longer. Like I said, we're understaffed. There've been budget cuts."

Matt squeezed her hand and let it go. "We're going to go have a look at Mr. Peters now."

"He's in room eight," Shirley said softly.

Frankie followed Matt out of the chapel and down a

polished hallway. The nursing home needed a face-lift, but it was clean. "I feel so sorry for her," she whispered.

Matt nodded. "She has a tendency to get personally involved with her patients. I know my grandparents loved her dearly. That's why I could wring Earlene Peters's neck for making accusations. Shirley would chase a fly out of her house before she'd swat it."

Matt paused before a closed door bearing the number eight. He stepped through first, and Frankie followed. True enough, the body was covered with a sheet. He lifted it, taking great care not to disturb anything else. "Aw, hell," he said, as they knelt beside the late Darnell Peters.

Frankie felt her gut tighten. She had seen her share of bodies, but the poor old man looked so pathetic lying there, facedown. The blood from his nose had begun to coagulate. She allowed herself to feel crummy for a minute before her instincts kicked in.

Matt sensed the change in her. "Tell me what you see." When she didn't say anything, he prodded her on. "What are you thinking?"

"I've seen this sort of thing before. Twice, actually. But I'm not qualified to say."

"This is off the record, Frankie."

"Off the record, I'd say he's been poisoned." She glanced at Matt, and they made eye contact. "Arsenic. It's as old as time."

Eight

Matt didn't look surprised. "Explain your reasoning."

"Like I said, I'm not qualified, and I could be all wrong, but there are too many similarities. Gastritis, vomiting, weakness and dizzy spells. Check out his coloring—he's almost yellow." She looked at Matt. "What do you think?"

"I think you're right on target."

Her brows puckered. "You already knew, didn't you?"

"I had my suspicions. I'm no expert, either, but I think he was slowly being poisoned."

"And the hospital tests didn't show it because they weren't looking for it."

Matt covered the body, and they stood. "I also knew something else you didn't know."

"Yeah?"

"Peters owns a fertilizer plant. That's where he met Earlene."

"You held out on me."

"His son, Jody, runs it now. Peters handed it over to him once he retired."

"Shirley said the two were close. Could he be a possible suspect?"

"It isn't likely. I met Jody a couple of years back when there was a theft at the plant. He seemed nice enough.

There were pictures of him and his dad all over the place, the two of them fishing and hunting together.''

"Any other children who might be jealous that Jody got the plant?''

"No. Peters had money, but you'd never know it from the way he dressed. Jody is much the same. He and his wife live in a simple log cabin. He showed me a picture. They could afford better, but they just don't worry about material things. At least, that's the way Jody struck me.''

"So who else stands to gain anything from Peters's death?''

"Earlene.''

Frankie was suddenly jolted by a thought. "Oh, shit.''

"What?''

"The banana pudding! What if—''

"Don't jump to conclusions, Daniels.''

"It all fits. Why would Earlene tell them to toss it?''

"Because she's a selfish bitch, maybe?''

"We need to get our hands on that pudding.''

"Let's go.''

They closed the door behind them and hurried toward the cafeteria. "Be careful,'' Matt warned. "We don't want to alarm anybody.''

A minute later they found the chef kneading dough. He was a balding man who carried too much weight, obviously a result of eating his own cooking. "Tom Gilmore,'' he said, by way of introduction. He glanced about. "You're here over the Peters guy, right? Sorry I can't shake hands at the moment. We're having chicken stew tonight, and the patients will pout if I don't serve home-made biscuits with it.''

Matt sniffed the air. "Smells good.''

Frankie didn't waste any time. "Mr. Gilmore, we're

looking for the banana pudding Mrs. Peters brought in for her husband.''

''It's gone.''

''You've already thrown it away?''

He chuckled. ''Are you kidding? I never made it as far as the trash can before one of the staff grabbed it.''

''Who?''

''The dishwasher. Name's Patrick Bower. We call him the human garbage disposal.''

Frankie felt a sinking sensation in her stomach. ''Where is he now?''

''Probably taking a smoke break out back.''

Frankie stared at him. ''How long ago did he eat the pudding?''

Tom shrugged. ''I don't know. A half hour ago, maybe. Why? Is something wrong?''

''I'll find him,'' Frankie said, heading for the back.

''Do you have any milk?'' Matt asked quickly. Tom looked at him oddly, but he pulled a gallon-size plastic container from the refrigerator and handed it to Matt.

Frankie found the teenager standing outside, puffing on a cigarette and talking to a deliveryman. ''Are you Patrick Bower?''

He looked alarmed as he glanced her way. ''Who wants to know?''

''Just answer the question.''

''Yeah, I'm Patrick, but I haven't done anything wrong.''

''That's not why I'm here. Come inside, please.''

Patrick flicked his cigarette onto the driveway and followed. Matt was waiting for him with a gallon container of milk. ''Did you eat the banana pudding that Mrs. Peters left here for her husband?''

The boy looked from one to the other. "Yeah. Am I under arrest?"

"Did you eat it all?" Frankie asked.

"No, just half. The other half is in the walk-in refrigerator." He pointed to a large, stainless-steel door. "I didn't steal it. Tom told me to throw it away, but I figured there was no sense wasting it."

Frankie made her way to the cooler and opened it. She grabbed the pudding from the shelf.

"Radio for two ambulances," Matt said. "No, better make it one. They might need the other for the traffic accident. It's for Peters, so you can tell them there's no rush." He handed the milk to Patrick. "Come with us. And don't stop drinking this milk until it's empty."

"The whole gallon? I don't like milk."

"You do now."

Patrick drank as he followed them to the patrol car. Matt put him in the back seat, and they screeched from the parking lot, siren blaring.

"Could somebody tell me what's going on?" Patrick asked.

"You may have ingested poison when you ate that banana pudding," Matt told him.

"Poison?" The kid paled.

"We don't know that for sure, but we have to take every precaution, so stop talking and keep drinking."

Matt radioed Cooter as they sped toward the hospital. Cars pulled off the road to let them by. "How bad was the accident?"

"Three fatalities, Chief. We've already sent the injured to the hospital in an ambulance."

"Is Doc Linton there?"

"He just left. We've got a couple of ambulances here loading the bodies now."

"I'll see you at the hospital." Matt radioed Velma. "Get a deputy to the hospital fast. Call the crime lab. Tell them I'm sending a banana pudding over. I want it tested immediately. We suspect poison—tell them to test for arsenic. Hold on. What's your phone number, Patrick?" The kid blurted it out and Matt repeated the number to Velma. "The name is Bower. Find his parents and tell them to come to the hospital."

"Holy crap," the kid said from the back. Frankie glanced over her shoulder and saw that Patrick had already finished more than half the milk.

They arrived at the hospital in record time. "Bring the pudding," Matt told Frankie. Inside, he spoke briefly to the receptionist, and she buzzed someone in back. A doctor pushed through a pair of doors marked No Admittance and asked Matt and Patrick a few questions before leading the teenager back. Matt returned to the receptionist. "Can you give me any information on the people who were brought in from the car accident on Highway 26?"

"I haven't heard anything yet, Chief. I'll let you know as soon as I do. This sure has been a busy day."

A deputy arrived, listened to Matt's instructions, grabbed the pudding and left.

Matt and Frankie sat down to wait. He looked at her. "And here you thought all we did was chase bulls."

"My mistake."

Cooter arrived, nodding at Matt before heading to the receptionist's desk. He spoke with her briefly before joining Matt. "The ambulances are unloading the bodies in the back so they can be taken straight to the morgue. Nothing on the injured yet. They were from out of state. Tourists just driving through." He looked tired. "What a day. And it's not even lunchtime yet."

Patrick's parents arrived, wearing panicked expressions,

and Matt filled them in. Mrs. Bower looked as if she might faint. "We don't know that your son was poisoned, but we're not taking any risks. Mr. Bower, you need to talk to the receptionist."

Frankie helped Mrs. Bower to a chair. The fear in the woman's eyes was palpable. "May I get you something, Mrs. Bower?" she asked softly. The woman didn't answer. Frankie wondered if she was in shock. She took her hand. It was cold and clammy. "Mrs. Bower?"

Finally, the woman looked at her.

"Mrs. Bower, we don't know that your son was poisoned," she repeated, "but if he was, the dose was so minute that it was probably lower than the toxicity level."

Mrs. Bower could hardly form the words. "How...do you...know?"

"We're working on a case where a gentleman may have been slowly poisoned. But I'm talking over a matter of months."

"Did he die?"

"He was ninety years old and had heart problems. He showed signs of poisoning, but we won't know for sure until the medical examiner performs an autopsy. We have every reason to believe the gentleman suffered cardiac arrest," she added, trying to sound optimistic. Mrs. Bower nodded, but Frankie wondered if she was taking it in. She could not imagine what the woman was going through, but the devastation on her face tugged at Frankie's heart. "Your son is very healthy and was treated within minutes of eating the food in question. The doctor has pumped his stomach. We have every reason to believe he's going to be okay."

Mrs. Bower sucked in a long, shaky breath. "I appreciate your telling me, Deputy Daniels. You don't know how that eases my mind. Would you mind sitting here with me?''

''Of course not.'' Frankie squeezed her hand. ''I'll stay with you as long as you need me.'' Although she had avoided getting emotionally involved with cases since she'd become a cop, she couldn't leave the woman in her state. Matt was right. It was difficult not to get emotionally involved with people in Purdyville. At the same time, she had to manage a degree of detachment. If Patrick Bower died, she would have to deal with the loss, as well. And that would raise questions in her head. What could she have done differently?

Patrick's father rejoined them. ''Are you okay, Madeline?'' he asked his wife.

She nodded wordlessly.

Dr. Russ appeared shortly afterward. They stood, each of them anxious to hear what he had to say. ''Good news. The blood work came back negative.''

''Oh, thank God.'' Mrs. Bower began to cry.

''He's going to have a sore throat for a few days because of the tube we inserted in his esophagus to get to his stomach, but other than that, he's fine. I'm going to release him.''

Moments later, Patrick stormed through the door, tossing Matt and Frankie a dark look. ''Do you know what the hell I just went through back there, only to find out the whole thing was a hoax? They stuck a giant tube down my throat and into my stomach and sucked out everything but my a-hole.''

''Patrick!'' Madeline Bower had obviously regained her composure. ''I think the words you're looking for are *thank you*.'' The boy turned and walked out of the emergency room without another sound.

"I'm sorry," the boy's father said, obviously as embarrassed as his wife.

Matt chuckled. "Don't worry about it. I'd probably be mad as a hornet if I'd just come out of something like that. I hate that he had to go through it."

"We would much prefer having him go through that ordeal than losing him," Madeline said. She hugged Frankie. "How can we ever thank you?"

"You just did," Matt said.

The men shook hands and Madeline hugged Frankie again. Once they'd left, Matt turned to Frankie. "I want to hang around a bit longer, find out how the accident victims are doing."

"I'm going outside for a smoke," Frankie said as he started for the receptionist's desk.

The sun was warm on her face as Frankie stepped outside and found a designated smoking area. She pulled a crumpled pack from her back pocket and lit up, having waited hours for a cigarette. She couldn't smoke in her office or the patrol car; it seemed every place was off-limits. She was going to have to start wearing a nicotine patch before long.

She sat on a bench, smoking and thinking. There had been little time for pondering her situation since she'd given her notice, and now she was beginning to wonder if she had done the right thing.

She did not belong in Purdyville—of that she was certain. No matter what Matt had said about the people there, she had been telling the truth when she'd confessed solving crimes was her top priority. She was glad she hadn't grown up in a small town, as Matt had. She would not want to have to tell an old friend, or someone she'd grown up with, that they'd lost a child to a violent accident or sit with parents whose daughter was missing. She didn't want to get to know the people and see the pain in their eyes because their daughter had never come home and was, in all likelihood, dead.

How long she sat there, she didn't know. Matt came out and joined her on the bench. "Anybody ever tell you that you smell like a burning barn?" he asked.

"Anybody ever tell you that you wear too much aftershave?"

"It's Obsession."

"Way too strong. Especially first thing in the morning."

He frowned. "How come you never said anything?"

"Because I knew you'd start harping on how I smelled like a burning barn."

They just looked at each other. Frankie tried to ignore the way the sunlight hit his hair, the light stubble that had already begun to grow back on his jaw, the way his eyes seemed to look right through her, as if he'd already figured out all her secrets.

"You're wearing makeup. And clear nail polish. Any specific reason?"

"I was hoping to turn you on."

"It's working."

Frankie put her cigarette out. "Actually, this was Sissy's doing."

He laughed. "She'll have you wearing fake eyelashes before long."

"No. I will stick my revolver in my mouth before I allow that."

"Well, you look cute in that cap."

"I'm not supposed to look cute. I'm supposed to look like a cop." She lit another cigarette, uncomfortable with the compliment. "No news yet?"

"They're still in ER. A couple of them have serious

fractures, the other one is pretty much fighting for his life.'' He paused. ''I spoke with the crime lab. They put a rush on the tests and found nothing.''

She shrugged. ''There went that theory.''

''You should be glad. I know I am.''

''I *am* glad, but this is going to make me look like an idiot.''

''I was in this, too, Daniels.''

''Yeah, but everybody likes you. You'll come out looking like a hero.''

''I'm sorry.''

She looked at him. ''For what?''

''That Patrick Bower didn't die of arsenic poisoning so you'd look good.''

She saw the amusement in his eyes. ''That's not what I meant, and you know it.''

''You still going to quit on me?''

''I'm thinking about it.''

''Anything I can do to talk you out of it?''

Frankie didn't answer.

''I don't want you to leave.''

Once again they looked at each other. Frankie could not read the expression in his eyes. ''Matt, there's no place for me here, and a relationship between us is out of the question.''

''You might change your mind in time. I have a way of getting under a woman's skin.''

''Oh, you get under my skin, all right. Like a chigger bite.''

He laughed. ''You're not going to find a nicer boss than me. Besides, where would you go?''

She sighed. ''I know this is insane, but I may go to Florida so I can be closer to my mother. She drives me up the wall, but she's not getting any younger, and we should probably work on our relationship. I'm sure I could get on with one of the larger precincts there.''

Matt opened his mouth to answer but was interrupted when a brand-new Mercedes squealed into the parking lot and came to a halt on the curb. Earlene Peters slammed out of the car and marched up to Matt and Frankie, hands on her hips.

''Just who do you think you are, sending my husband's body to the morgue for an autopsy. His funeral is day after tomorrow.''

Matt shrugged. ''Guess you'll have to put it off.''

The woman looked as though she might have a stroke. ''And what is this business about the banana pudding? I was just informed you suspect there was poison in it. Are you accusing me of trying to kill my own husband?''

Matt stood. ''We have reason to believe that your husband has been ingesting arsenic over a period of months. We can't be certain until the medical examiner takes a look, and he has more pressing matters at the moment. I don't know when he'll get to Mr. Peters.''

''If you suspect me of a crime, I suggest you either arrest me right now or release my husband's body immediately.''

''Can't do that.''

''I'm going to call my lawyer. Better yet, I'll call Judge Davies.''

''You certainly have that option.''

''How dare you treat me like this? Can't you see I'm grieving over my husband's death? Why are you putting me through this ordeal? The man was ninety years old, for heaven's sake.''

''I am responsible for upholding the law in this town, Mrs. Peters,'' Matt said calmly, ''and I'm doing the job I'm paid for. I don't care if you have friends on the Supreme Court. If I think a death warrants an autopsy, I have the authority to order it."

She shot him a menacing look. "You're going to regret this, Chief Webber. I can promise you that." With her head high, she turned for her car.

"By the way," Matt said. "The speed limit is five miles per hour. I suggest you adhere to it so I don't have to ticket you."

"Well, I have never!" She climbed into her car and pulled away.

"Nice lady," Frankie said.

"Trust me, we haven't heard the last of her."

Nine

Frankie sat in her office for a long time after she and Matt had returned, wanting to kick her own butt. Velma had given her a self-satisfied smirk when they had walked through the door, and Frankie had overheard a couple of deputies snickering as she passed one of the offices. She assumed they were discussing what had happened at Piney Grove Nursing Home and the crime lab findings.

Frankie called Alice Chalmers, only to discover she was in a session. But Alice called back within fifteen minutes, and Frankie told the woman about her day. "Everybody is laughing at me."

"Matt was in on it, too," Alice pointed out.

"Yes, but this town loves him. Except Earlene Peters, who will probably end up suing the department."

"Answer this," Alice said. "If you had it to do all over again, would you?"

Frankie considered it. "Yes. I wouldn't risk the life of another human being, no matter how ridiculous I might look in the end."

"There's your answer." She paused. "Listen, Frankie, I know Earlene Peters. She can be vile at times. Everybody in town knows she married poor Darnell for his money. She was a nothing and a nobody until she became Mrs. Darnell Peters. She wears that name like a crown, and she's a regular pain in the butt.

"Now. Let's plan on meeting for lunch. When's a good day for you?"

They settled on the following Wednesday, at the same place they'd met before. When Frankie hung up the phone, she found Matt standing in the doorway. He held two cups of coffee. "Mind if I come in?"

Frankie shrugged. "Sure. You're the only one in the building who isn't laughing behind my back right now."

He closed the door with one elbow, handed Frankie her coffee and sat in the chair next to her desk. "I just got off the phone with Judge Davies. He's on our side. He said he would be afraid to eat Earlene's banana pudding, too."

"So why is Velma looking at me as though I'm some dolt, while the others are snickering behind doors?"

"Velma and Earlene attend the same church."

"Now, there's a pair."

"And the others are probably jealous of you, because I'm the one who's been working with you instead of assigning you to one of the other deputies." He took a sip of his coffee. "I spoke with Darnell's son, Jody. He's calmed down some, but he's asking questions about the investigation. Doesn't know anybody who'd want to hurt his father, not even Earlene."

"That's interesting."

"So, have you been working on your resignation?"

"No, I've been talking to my therapist."

"Alice Chalmers is a good woman."

"How did you know I was talking to her?"

"Someone saw the two of you at lunch, deep in conversation. We don't have many therapists in Purdyville."

"Can't a person do anything in this town without it getting around?"

"You can get away with anything if you're discreet enough." He smiled. "You have anything in mind?"

Frankie cocked her head to the side. "Are you flirting with me, Webber?"

"I'm interrogating you. If you're thinking of doing something kinky and wild, I may have to cuff you and take you to my place for your own protection."

"Matt?" Her look was serious.

"Yeah?"

"You're full of shit."

"Yeah, I know. But at least I'm honest enough to admit it. Does that mean you'll rethink your resignation?"

"I don't want to talk about it."

He sat there for a moment, studying her. "I never would have figured you for a quitter."

"That's not going to work."

"You're not even trying, Frankie. Are you going to the dance tomorrow night?"

"No." She had no desire to show her face in town if she didn't have to. She would wear her party dress another time.

"See what I mean? It would be the perfect way to get to know people."

"So Earlene Peters can publicly ridicule me?"

"You're above all that. We both saw something suspicious at the nursing home, and we acted on it. What if the pudding had been poisoned and Patrick Bower had died? He's just a kid. How would you have felt then?"

"That would have been hard to live with," she admitted.

"Besides, the *Gazette* has already called. I told them I couldn't discuss the incident because it was still under investigation, but I also told them we had a new deputy, who we were lucky to have in the department. I bragged about your credentials and expertise in investigations. They were impressed and suggested they do a story on you.''

''They'll want to know why I left Atlanta.''

''I already covered that. Told them you were burned-out with big-city life and wanted to work in a small town where you could feel like part of the community.''

She frowned. ''I wish you hadn't said that part, because we both know it isn't true.''

''You should get out more, Frankie. Meet nice people. It's a shame you had to run into Willie-Jack and Earlene so soon.''

''Alice is very nice.''

''She isn't the only nice person in Purdyville, and contrary to your opinion, there are a lot of educated professionals in this town, if you took the time to meet them.'' He stood. ''But you don't seem interested, so I'm not going to push.''

Frankie watched him exit her office, a look of disappointment on his handsome face. He was right. She wasn't even trying.

That evening, Frankie told Sissy about the conversation she and Matt had shared earlier.

''He's right, you know,'' Sissy said. ''You need to get out and meet people. I think you'd change your mind about Purdyville if you did. Think about Virgil, who'd give you the shirt off his back if you needed it. And your friend Alice. The two of you hit it off right away. She's one of the nicest, most respected people in town.'' Sissy paused and smiled brightly. ''And then there's me. What's not to like?''

Frankie chuckled. The two had grown close in a short time. ''That's true.''

"Not only that, I don't have a date for tomorrow night, and if you don't go, I won't go. I'm not about to stand around by myself hoping someone will ask me to dance. Besides, you might meet a good-looking man."

"I'm not really interested in men at the moment." Frankie had already told Sissy why she'd been forced to leave Atlanta.

"Not all men are assholes, Frankie. Sure, they come in and use the guest towels instead of the ones put out for drying their hands. They leave the toilet seat up, and they have a tendency to clean their fingernails with their pocketknives, but they can't help it. It's up to us to train them."

"I don't have the patience or the desire. I've been on my own all my life. I sort of prefer it that way."

"You ever been in love?"

"I was once, for a while, back when I was attending the academy. But he decided to go into the FBI. Sometimes I regret not going, too."

"What about this guy you had the affair with in Atlanta?"

"I thought I was in love, but it was too easy to get over him, so it must've been lust. What hurt most was having the entire department find out about it. I should have been smarter."

"If I had a dime for every man who's dumped me, I'd be rich."

Frankie was surprised. "How can that be? You're gorgeous."

Sissy gazed down at the floor. "I'm too needy, and a man senses that right away in a woman. Someone has always taken care of me. My parents weren't wealthy, but they always bailed me out financially. Paid my rent most of the time. When my daddy died, my mama insisted I move in here to take care of her.'' She smiled. ''She's not the one who needed taking care of.

''They left me everything, but I blew it on clothes and trips and skin-care products. I've got enough shoes to start my own store. Not that I need them. I don't go out much anymore. I've pretty much gone through all the men in this town, and after one date, they don't ask me out again. Like I said, I'm too needy. If a guy asks me out, I start thinking about marriage and babies, and that's the last thing on their minds. I'm not like you. If a man thinks a woman doesn't need him, he'll fight all the harder.'' She sighed. ''I wish I could meet a decent man like Matt.''

Frankie grunted. ''Matt is a womanizer. I've seen him in action.''

''He's a flirt, Frankie, I'll give you that. But Matt Webber is a good man once you get to know him.''

Frankie wondered. Perhaps Sissy didn't know her cousin as well as she thought she did. ''Why do you suppose Matt and his fiancée never rescheduled the wedding?'' she asked.

''Who knows? Maybe he wasn't ready. Maybe Mandy's death affected him more deeply than we'll ever know. Part of it could have been for professional reasons. Jenna—that was her name—was a defense attorney. Matt's job is bringing criminals to justice, and Jenna's job is getting them off. I think Matt secretly resented that. Perhaps he was having second thoughts. Or maybe he didn't like the idea of Jenna making more money than he did. Some men are like that. Then Mandy died, and the wedding was postponed. Even though Matt was devastated, I think he used it as an excuse to get out of marrying Jenna. That's my opinion, for what it's worth.''

''What about the house?''

''Matt had already bought the land, and he and Jenna

had hired an architect, but everything came to a screeching halt with Mandy's death. Matt designed the house later and helped build part of it. He did a damn good job, as far as I'm concerned.''

''And Jenna?''

''She went to a big law firm in Virginia. Have you ever thought of painting your toenails?''

The sudden change of subject caught Frankie off guard. ''Not recently.''

''Ever had a pedicure?''

''No.''

''You've *never* had a pedicure?''

''It wasn't a top priority in my life.''

''I suppose you've never had your nails done, either.''

''Let's face it. I'm a slouch.''

''You most certainly are not! You're a beautiful woman, Frankie, but it wouldn't kill you to...well, you know.''

''Do something with myself? You remind me of my mother.''

''Who has left half a dozen messages, none of which you've returned.''

''I'll get around to it sooner or later.''

''The two of you don't get along well, do you?''

''Not especially.''

''It's none of my business, of course. Say, how'd you like to order a pizza, and I'll give you a pedicure?''

''The pizza sounds good.''

''You're getting a pedicure whether you like it or not.'' Sissy picked up the telephone. ''I usually order the works. What about you?''

''That's fine. No anchovies.''

Sissy placed the order and hurried from the room. A few minutes later, she carried in everything she would need for the pedicure, including a foot massager that she filled with hot water as soon as their pizza arrived.

Frankie noted various clippers and sharp objects. "Looks like you're going to perform surgery."

"It won't hurt."

They watched a game show while they ate their pizza. The phone rang twice, and Sissy carried the portable to her bedroom. Frankie suspected she was working. Once they'd finished their pizza, Frankie found herself soaking both feet in the foot massage while Sissy continued her phone conversation.

"I'm hot for you, too, baby," Sissy whispered. She looked at Frankie, stuck her finger in her mouth and pretended to gag.

Frankie rolled her eyes and tried to concentrate on a TV sitcom. Sissy's voice had changed from the perky one Frankie was accustomed to. She spoke softly, but there was a huskiness that was almost lulling. Frankie grimaced and grabbed the remote control. She switched to a channel that carried detective stories.

"You naughty boy," Sissy said, and chuckled into the phone. "What am I wearing? Well, since I knew you were calling this evening, I decided to slip into something more comfortable. Like nothing."

Frankie shook her head, and Sissy shrugged. She had changed into capri pants and a baggy shirt that had somehow met with a bleach bottle. Obviously, it was important to her callers what she wore. Probably helped in their fantasies.

"I spent the evening soaking in a hot tub." She chuckled. "Of course I washed *there*. I always do." She sighed. "I thought about you. Yes, that would feel nice. Better than nice. Oh, you *are* a bad boy!" She giggled. "I like it when you're bad."

Sissy knelt before Frankie, pulled one wet foot out of the massager and dried it on a towel. She reached for the toenail clippers. Frankie continued to watch TV.

"I like the sound of that, sweetie. Keep doing it. Slow at first, like always."

Frankie tried not to think what was happening on the other end of the line, but her thoughts ran amok. Sissy went on as if it were no big deal, filing Frankie's toenails neatly.

"Okay, faster, baby," Sissy said. "I love it when you breathe heavy. It turns me on."

Perspiration beaded Frankie's upper lip.

"That's it, baby, go for it."

Frankie wiped her brow and wished she were anywhere but there. She would have gotten up and left the room had Sissy not already begun painting her toenails.

"How did that feel, sweetie? Mmm. I think my little boy needs a shower." Sissy covered the phone with her hand and looked at Frankie. "Do you like this color okay?" she asked.

Frankie simply nodded.

"I can go a shade darker."

"This is fine," she whispered in a choked voice.

Sissy went back to her conversation. "Oh, sweetie, I'm so glad I was able to help you. Now, you be a good boy. Yes, I got your check for ten sessions. Thank you for paying in advance. Sweet dreams." She hung up the phone. "Okay, look at your pretty feet," she told Frankie.

"My feet look great," Frankie said, "but I think I need a cold shower."

Sissy waved off her statement. "You'll get used to it. It's business. Now, let's give you a nice manicure."

The phone rang. Sissy looked up from her supplies.

"You don't mind if I keep working while we do this?"

Frankie shook her head wordlessly. The words just wouldn't come.

Frankie noted the work that was being done when she passed the courthouse square the following morning on her way to the police station. A stage built of thick plywood sat near the bandstand, folding tables had been set up across the lawn, and metal chairs were being unloaded from trucks. She felt a stab of guilt. The community was really coming together to help the Gibbs family, and she, as a citizen—albeit temporary—wasn't showing her support. Perhaps Matt was right. She wasn't trying hard enough to fit in. She drove on, passing the small shops that surrounded the courthouse. They had names like O'Henry's Barbershop, Cards Galore, Fannie's Flowers, Macon's Meat Market, and she wondered about the people who owned them.

She pulled behind the station and parked. For a moment, she just sat there. Had things been different, perhaps she wouldn't have resented being in Purdyville. It certainly wasn't the fault of anyone who lived there that she had been ordered to leave Atlanta. She had secretly resented the town and its occupants because of a mistake *she'd* made.

She wasn't being fair, Frankie thought as she climbed from her car and made for the back door, but for some reason her heart wasn't in it. Matt called out as she passed his office. "You'll be working with Cooter today," he said. "There was a domestic disturbance last night. The night shift took care of the call, but we need to follow up." He winked. "This will give you and Cooter a chance to bond."

Frankie saw that he was scraping mud off his shoes over his wastebasket as he spoke. "What happened?"

"I had to go out and help find Caesar again at six o'clock this morning. We found him in the creek."

"How's Molly?"

"Still hiding out in the barn. Seems Caesar has been struck by Cupid's arrow, as far as Molly is concerned." He smiled disarmingly. "I don't know if she's playing hard to get or she just isn't interested, but Caesar is one determined bull. Problem is, he's way too large for mating. He'd end up breaking her back."

"Why doesn't his owner castrate him?"

"Because Caesar is a prize bull. Weldon has done everything to collect sperm from him, but Caesar won't have anything to do with the usual methods. We've come up with another idea."

"I'm almost afraid to ask."

"Going to get one of those fake heifers and attach it to Sam's pickup truck. May paint the contraption to look like Molly. Caesar will get his thrill, and Molly will be artificially inseminated."

"Is this sort of like one of those blowup dolls you find in adult magazines?"

"Yep. Only this one is more expensive." Matt grinned. "The end result is the same." He studied her. "Have you made up your mind about our big social event tonight?"

"Nothing personal, but I think I'll sit this one out."

He shrugged. "That's your choice." He picked up the phone and began dialing. Frankie decided she'd been dismissed. She was somewhat disappointed that he hadn't pushed.

Some minutes later, Frankie climbed into a squad car next to Cooter. He filled her in on the happenings of the night before. "Domestic dispute. Husband was drunk and abusive. We locked him up, but someone will bail him out by noon. We need to follow up on the wife. She was pretty shaken, from what the report reads." He pulled into a subdivision where small houses had been built too close together. Frankie followed him up the front walk and stood there silently as he knocked on the door.

Frankie had seen battered women before, so the young, attractive woman who opened the door gave her little pause. Her bruises were clear evidence of the trauma she'd suffered the night before.

Cooter introduced them. "Ma'am, I'm Deputy Calvin Rines from the Purdyville Police Department, and this here is Deputy Daniels. We're following up on last night's disturbance."

The woman did her best to smile. "I know who you are, Cooter. You and I struggled through biology at Purdyville High, remember? I'm Vicki Godley. It's Vicki Morris now."

Cooter broke into a grin. "Vicki Godley, I can't believe it! I don't know why I didn't recognize you. You haven't changed a bit."

She blushed and touched a bruise on her cheek. "I've changed some, I reckon."

Now it was Cooter's turn to look embarrassed. "Well, now, you can't help that. But that's why we're here. Your…uh…husband, Chuck, will be arraigned this morning, so there's a good chance he'll be out of jail by lunchtime. Do you have any place you can go?"

She shook her head, and her eyes glistened. "I would have gone a long time ago if I'd had a place. But I don't. No money, no place to go. I was fired from my last job because Chuck called all the time and showed up drunk once. He never liked it when I worked. Last night he came in smelling like a bottle of Wild Turkey and just lost it. It was my fault, really, because I'd fallen asleep on the sofa and didn't have dinner on the table. I've been under the weather for a few days.''

"You know it wasn't your fault, Vicki," Cooter said gently.

Frankie had investigated domestic violence many times before she had been promoted to detective in homicide. "Mrs. Morris," she said, as gently as she could. "I'm sure there's a shelter you can go to where it will be safe." She looked at Cooter for confirmation.

He nodded. "We can take you, Vicki. You'll be safe."

She shook her head. "Chuck will find me. There's no place safe." She swallowed hard. "Besides, a night in jail is probably just what he needed to change his ways."

"Sounds like you've already given up," Frankie replied.

"I'm just so scared." She started to cry. "I can't seem to do anything right. Who's going to give a job to someone like me?"

Frankie planted her hands on her hips. "Boy, he's really done a number on you, hasn't he? Made you think you're worthless. And you've bought right into it."

Cooter glanced Frankie's way. "Deputy Daniels, I don't think—"

Frankie ignored him. "If Mrs. Morris chooses to remain a victim, there's nothing we can do here. Except come back when it's time to put her in a body bag."

Both Cooter and Vicki looked stunned. "I'm going to talk to Matt about this," Cooter said under his breath.

Frankie shrugged. "I don't care if you go to the pope. You know the stats on this sort of thing. Mrs. Morris thinks her husband's going to change and that's crap." She looked at Vicki. "How long has this been going on?"

The other woman hung her head. "Since I married him."

Frankie looked at Cooter. "There's your answer. You ready to roll?"

It was obvious Cooter was angry with Frankie, but he was enough of a professional to keep it at bay, at least for the time being. He pulled out his wallet and withdrew a card. His hands trembled. "Vicki, I want you to call me if you need something," he said, handing it to her. "They can't keep Chuck in jail forever." He and Frankie turned toward the squad car.

"Wait!" Vicki cried out.

They turned in question.

Tears spilled down the woman's cheeks. "I don't want to be a victim anymore."

"Great," Frankie said. "Let's start packing some clothes."

Ten

Two hours later, Cooter and Frankie stood in Matt's office. They'd managed to get Vicki into the women's shelter, but Cooter was still annoyed at Frankie for mouthing off. Once he'd told his side of the story, Matt looked at her.

"Don't you think you were a little harsh, Deputy?"

"The situation called for harsh measures. What was I supposed to do? Pat her hand and tell her everything was going to be okay? Sympathize with an abused woman so that she can feel even more helpless?"

Cooter broke in. "Daniels acted like she didn't care. Like we were wasting our time."

Frankie regarded him. "People have to be willing to rescue themselves, Cooter. They can't just sit around feeling like a victim and do nothing about it."

"The woman was already beaten down, both physically and emotionally," he replied. "Don't you know anything about battered women's syndrome?"

"I could tell you stories that would make you pee in your pants, Deputy."

Matt cleared his throat. "Don't be a smart-ass, Daniels." He looked at Cooter. "I'll take this up with Deputy Daniels. You can go."

Cooter shot Frankie a dark look as he closed the door behind him.

"Take a seat," Matt said.

Frankie did as she was told. "Go ahead and chew my head off and get it over with."

Matt chuckled as he leaned back in his chair and regarded her. "You're something else, Daniels, you know that? Things were running fairly peacefully until you joined the department."

"Are you insinuating that I'm a troublemaker?"

"You have done nothing but make trouble since you got here."

"So fire me and save me the trouble of writing out my resignation and working a notice."

"I can't fire you. I need someone like you here to keep the others on their toes. I like your style."

Frankie's jaw dropped. The last thing she had expected from Matt Webber was a compliment. "I don't belong here. Cooter resents me, the others are laughing at me behind my back. Velma wishes I would crawl in a hole and die."

"What was it that you just said about people feeling like a victim?"

Frankie made eye contact with him. "I'm doing the job I was hired to do. I can't satisfy everybody so I don't even try."

"You could try to get along with people instead of carrying that chip on your shoulder."

"I don't have a chip on my shoulder."

"Sure you do." He checked his wristwatch. "I believe you have a lunch date with Alice. If you don't hustle you're going to be late."

"How do you know about that?"

"I know everything that goes on in this place. Besides, Alice called to confirm it. I told her I'd remind you."

"You really piss me off, you know that?"

He smiled. "Then I can rest easily, knowing I've done my job today. I'll see you at the party tonight, Daniels."

"I'm not going to that stupid party."

"Don't forget to save me a dance. Once you're in my arms you'll never want to let go."

Frankie almost slammed out of his office. She found Cooter close by, grinning.

"From the look on your face, I reckon the chief just read you the riot act," the man said.

"Yeah, my ass is in a sling. Satisfied?"

The grin faded from Cooter's face as she turned and walked away.

"What do you mean, you're not going to the party?" Alice asked. "It'll be a lot of fun."

"I'm having a bad day," Frankie said. "I don't feel like socializing."

"You want to talk about it?"

Frankie gave a short version of what had happened with Vicki Morris. "The other deputy wasn't happy with the way I handled it. He went straight to Matt."

"You accomplished what you set out to do. I think you should give yourself a pat on the back. You know, I hold a group therapy session at the women's shelter once a week. I'll keep an eye out for Vicki."

"Thanks, Alice."

"Now, about that party. You need to go, Frankie, and hold your head high. If you don't, folks will think you have something to be ashamed about."

"I won't fit in."

"People need time to get used to you, Frankie. The other deputies probably feel threatened. They'll come around in time." The waitress appeared, and they placed their order.

Frankie scanned the room, thinking how different it was to be eating in a nice place, when she had literally crammed cold hot dogs down her throat in Atlanta so she wouldn't have to stop working. Her life had certainly changed.

"Have you seen or heard anything from Willie-Jack?" Alice asked.

"Surprisingly, no. I think he's probably lying low at the moment. Maybe he did us a big favor and left town."

"I doubt it. He finds pleasure tormenting people here. You'll never believe this, but there was a time when Willie-Jack Pitts was one of the best-looking men in town."

"You're kidding."

Alice shook her head. "He turned a lot of heads. Just like Matt."

"What happened to him?"

"Too much booze, too many barroom brawls. He pretty much let himself go, but you'll never convince him of that. He still thinks he's God's gift."

"So does Matt."

Alice chuckled. "Well, he is about the best-looking thing we've got going in this town."

"And don't think he doesn't know it. Let's change the subject."

Alice gave her a funny look. "Okay. Let's see. Did you know Hep Whitfield is building an arcade next door to his pool hall? I ran into him at the grocery store, and he told me all about it. I know you had something to do with that. Why didn't you tell me?"

"Cooter was mostly responsible."

"That's not what Hep said. We need a safe place for our children to go after school. Hep is a good man. He figured it was better allowing the kids into his poolroom after school for a couple of hours instead of letting them wander the streets unsupervised. He may not have chosen the best place to entertain them, but he meant well. Now he's on this campaign to provide good clean fun for our youths.

"You've been saying you don't belong here since you arrived, but if you'd just look at what you've accomplished in such a short time, you'd see how desperately we need you." She chuckled. "If for no other reason than to kick Willie-Jack's butt every now and then."

Frankie thought about it. "You always manage to make me look at my life more closely," she said. "I'm lucky to have you as my friend."

Alice patted her hand. "I knew there was something special about you the minute I laid eyes on you. I consider you my friend, as well."

"I appreciate what you've said, Alice, but I'm seriously thinking of resigning."

"Have you told Matt?"

She nodded. "He asked for a two-week notice."

Alice looked hurt and stunned. "Oh, Frankie, I wish you wouldn't."

Frankie waited until the waitress served their lunch before answering. "I have my reasons. I probably shouldn't tell you this, but I'm...well...I'm—"

"Attracted to Matt?"

Frankie shook her head. "Sometimes I think you're psychic."

"Is the feeling mutual?"

"He says it is, but who knows with him? He's such a flirt."

"Flirting is one thing, but Matt is very careful when it comes to matters of the heart. If he told you he's attracted to you, you can believe him."

"But where would it lead? I can't afford to get involved

with the man I work for. I've been there, done that, remember?"

"I think I just lost my appetite," Alice said, pushing her plate aside. "Do you have a cigarette?"

Frankie arched one brow. "I didn't know you smoked."

"I used to years ago, but Rand complained until I quit. I think I could use one right now."

Frankie handed Alice her pack. "I'm sorry. I've upset you."

"What does Matt say about your leaving?"

"He's disappointed. He doesn't think I've given this place a fair chance."

Alice lit the cigarette and inhaled deeply, as though she'd never quit. She coughed once. "Neither do I, but you don't look the type who can be talked out of anything once you've made up your mind. Where are you going?"

"I don't know. I was considering Raleigh or Ashville. Then I start guilt-tripping and think I should go to Florida so I can be closer to my mother."

"You don't have a job offer yet?"

"No, but I have a lot of experience, and Matt promised to give me a glowing recommendation."

"You're awfully brave, Frankie. Quitting a job before you have another one lined up."

"Maybe *desperate* is a better word."

"Or scared."

"Yeah, that's probably the best word. I wish you wouldn't smoke, Alice. It's a nasty habit, and I don't want to be the cause of you starting back. I've cut down dramatically since I came to Purdyville. And please eat something."

"Do you need money?" Alice asked, changing the subject. "I've tucked away a little here and there. Started doing it when my husband and I were having problems, and I've gotten into the habit.''

Frankie was surprised, not only by the offer of money but the fact Alice had just admitted things hadn't always been perfect in her marriage. ''I have some savings,'' she said. ''I'll manage. How are things now? With your marriage?''

''We've managed to work out most of our problems. We both made mistakes, but that's in the past.''

Suddenly, Frankie wasn't very hungry, either. They asked for a to-go box and she insisted on paying the check. They parted ways, and Frankie promised to call Alice soon. It amazed her that she'd been in Purdyville less than a week and had already grown close to the woman. And then there was Sissy. She really liked Sissy. She would miss them.

Matt was pacing the lobby when Frankie returned. ''How long does it take two women to eat a salad?'' he demanded. ''I was going to give you about three more minutes before I radioed you.''

Frankie was caught off guard. ''Is there a problem?''

''Yes. Let's go.''

Frankie hesituated. ''This doesn't have anything to do with Caesar the bull, does it?''

''No.'' He pushed the door open and Frankie followed. ''Are you going to tell me where we're going?''

''To the morgue. Doc Linton wants to meet with us.''

Frankie perked up. ''Does this have something to do with Darnell Peters?''

''Yes.''

They found Dr. Donald Linton in his office, located in the hospital basement, studying slides beneath a microscope. Matt introduced Frankie, and they shook hands.

"What's going on, Doc?" Matt asked.

"This place is a madhouse, what with that accident yesterday. I haven't had time to autopsy Peters, but I had my assistant take fingernail and hair clippings yesterday. They tested positive for arsenic."

Matt and Frankie exchanged looks.

"So Peters *was* being poisoned," Matt said. "Wonder why the teenager from Piney Grove Nursing Home didn't get sick?" He told Linton about their suspicions over the banana pudding and rushing Patrick Bower to the hospital. "Tests proved negative."

"So the kid is okay?"

Matt nodded. "Maybe you were looking in the wrong place," Linton said.

Matt looked at Frankie. "Guess we'd better head back over to Piney Grove."

Shirley seemed much better when they arrived. "We've cleaned Mr. Peters's room and put his personal belongings in a plastic bag."

"Mind if we take a look?" Matt asked.

"Not much to see. His wife picked up most of his dirty clothes last time she was here."

"Doesn't Piney Grove take care of the patients' laundry?"

"I guess that wasn't good enough for Earlene. Whenever she came in, she brought fresh pajamas and those furry footies. Mr. Peters's feet stayed cold due to poor circulation." She led them to a closet. "There's a change of clothes hanging on the rack there for hospital visits. That bag contains a pair of pajamas, his footies and underwear."

"Has anyone touched them?"

"I wore plastic gloves, what with it being a police matter and all."

"Thanks, Shirley."

Matt and Frankie returned to the car with Peters's belongings. "What else do you know about arsenic?" he asked once they opened the trunk and reached for plastic gloves. They slipped them on. "I understand it can be ingested through the skin."

"It can also be inhaled when it's in the form of a dust."

"Perhaps Mrs. Peters put some in those footies or whatever they are."

They were both quiet as they searched through the bag. Frankie pulled out two used handkerchiefs and met Matt's gaze. "Maybe this would be a good place to start looking."

"I'll drop everything by the crime lab," Matt said once they climbed back into the car and were on their way. "You need to go home and take a hot bubble bath."

She looked at him. "Why?"

"So you'll look nice for the party tonight."

"I'm not attending. How many times do I have to say it?"

"You're still working for the department. I expect all my deputies to be there to support the Gibbses' cause."

"You can't force me to go."

"I'm the boss, remember? And the one who will be writing your recommendation."

Frankie's jaw dropped. "That's blackmail."

"You planning on pressing charges?"

Frankie remained silent for the rest of the drive. She walked inside. Velma stopped her. "You have messages, Deputy Daniels."

Deputy Daniels? Frankie looked at the woman. What had happened to *hey you?*

"One is from your mother, who says call or else. The other is from Vicki Morris, who wanted to thank you for all your help. Said she could never have found the courage to leave her husband if it hadn't been for you. She left a number, in case you want to call her back."

"Thank you, Velma."

"You're welcome, Deputy."

Matt followed Frankie through the door leading to the back. He headed for the crime lab as Frankie made for her office. She almost bumped into Cooter when she turned the corner. She thought she saw him blush.

"Did you get your messages?" he asked. "Vicki...I mean, Mrs. Morris was real impressed with you. Said you more or less embarrassed her into leaving, but she's glad she did."

"I'm glad I could be of service, Cooter, but you're her friend, and I think you showed a lot of compassion. Not all cops would take the time."

He gave her a slight smile. "Guess it doesn't matter who did what. We got her out of there. Her husband has called me a couple of times, accusing me of sticking my nose into their business. I keep threatening to lock him up on some trumped-up charge and throw away the key. He's not real smart, I think he believes me."

"If he was smart, he wouldn't have been beating his wife."

"What's happening with the Peters's case?"

"Dr. Linton hasn't had time to perform an autopsy, but nail clippings proved positive for arsenic poisoning. Matt just took Mr. Peters's belongings to the crime lab, so now we wait."

"Earlene Peters is the biggest bitch in town." He blushed. "Pardon my language."

"Hey, I've said worse."

He grinned. "I have no doubt of that. You going to the Gibbses' thing tonight?"

Frankie sighed. "I'm thinking about it."

"I'm bringing chips and dip," he said. "How about you?"

Frankie had forgotten they were supposed to bring something. "I haven't decided. Maybe I'll bring a cake."

Cooter laughed. "For some reason, I can't imagine you in an apron mixing cake batter."

"Who said I was going to bake it?"

As Frankie headed toward her office, she felt a sense of lightheartedness for the first time since coming to work for the Purdyville Police Department. Perhaps Matt was right. She hadn't really tried to make friends with the locals. She wrestled with indecision. Not that it mattered. She had already given her notice, and Matt had accepted it.

And Matt Webber was one of her reasons for leaving.

She was drawn to him in such a way that she knew it could only spell heartbreak. Matt liked women; it was as simple as that. He enjoyed their attention, and they gave it freely. They doted on him. But what woman wouldn't? He was the best thing Frankie Daniels had ever seen. But it wasn't just his looks. She liked the way he handled himself. He was strong and confident. Fear didn't seem to have a place in his life.

She seriously doubted he had ever sat in a corner in his shower and cried.

Of course, that didn't mean he hadn't grieved in his life. Losing his twin hadn't been easy, he'd admitted that much, but he had allowed himself to feel the pain, whereas she had always tried to block it out. And sometimes failed miserably.

Frankie entered her office and closed the door. She

needed time to sort through things in her mind. From the moment she'd been ordered to leave Atlanta, her life had been in constant turmoil, and she had not been able to take stock of herself, her life, something she would rather have ignored, if possible.

She was a fake. It wasn't easy to admit, but that's what she was. She pretended to be strong, even when her guts shook and her palms grew clammy. She led people to think she really didn't need anybody in her life, even though her soul cried out for it at times. She pretended nothing bothered her, and if it did, she played games with her head. She had walked into crime scenes that had sent even the most seasoned detective searching for a place to get sick. But she'd swallowed it back because she had learned to look at the scene with a different eye. Victims had become stick people in her mind, nothing more. She'd pretended they weren't significant, refused to consider how they'd looked when they were alive, or what their lives had been like. Sometimes she had even pretended she was back at the academy, where they used fake bodies and set up situations to teach would-be cops how to respond to an emergency.

It may not have been a healthy way to deal with all she saw on a day-to-day basis, but it was *her* way, and the only way she could live with it. If she had allowed even one ounce of emotion to get in, she wouldn't have been able to do her job, and doing her job well meant everything to her. She had overcompensated, not only because she was a woman, but because she felt she had to be as good as her father. It hadn't been easy trying to follow in his footsteps. He was a veritable legend, as far as the APD was concerned. It hadn't been easy seeing his picture the past ten years on a wall devoted to heroes, cops who'd given their lives in the line of duty.

That hadn't stopped her from trying. For some reason, she had to prove to everyone on the force she was as good as her father. She had succeeded. She had been labeled a tough cop by the best of them.

Tough. She was able to handle any call, no matter how grisly. After all, she was Frank Daniels's daughter.

She'd never expected it would carry over into her personal life. That's why she was such a loner. Her friends had been mere acquaintances, and the men in her life… She paused and reflected. Had she compared every man to her father, at least subconsciously? Was that why they had never measured up? Was that why she had sabotaged every relationship that came along?

She knew the answer.

But Matt Webber made her vulnerable. She couldn't explain it any more than she could count the stars in the sky, but she sensed the strength in him. It was real. Matt was real. He measured up.

If she weren't careful, he would get too close, and he would see right through her. He would know that her entire life had been a sham, that deep inside, in a place where she seldom went, there hid that eleven-year-old girl who had lost the most important thing in her life. That same little girl who had decided never again to love and suffer the pain of loss.

Eleven

"**Y**ou look fantastic," Sissy said as they prepared to leave for the Gibbses' benefit. "In fact, you look like something right out of *Cosmo*."

"You're spreading it on mighty thick, Sissy. But I have to admit, you did a good job with my hair and makeup."

"Honey, it was easy with your looks."

"Thank you." Frankie was not accustomed to compliments. She supposed it had to do with the fact she'd tried to dress like one of the guys for so long. Now she felt feminine, and although it was not as bad as she'd thought it would be, she still had to get used to it.

The phone rang as they started out the door, Sissy with her pasta salad and Frankie with her cake. She had stopped by the bakery on her way home and purchased a German chocolate cake. Sissy had put it in a plastic container so it would look homemade. Sissy sighed when the phone rang a second time.

"I'd better get it. I can always come up with an excuse for them to call back." She answered, then held the phone out to Frankie. "Your mother," she said.

Frankie rolled her eyes and took it.

"Where have you been, and why have you not returned my calls?" Eve Hutton demanded as soon as Frankie answered. "I called the motel and learned you'd checked out because someone vandalized it. I had no idea if you were hurt or living on the street or what. Had to call that nice woman in dispatch to find out what was going on. Francis, why can't you just live like a normal person? And what is this vandalism thing? Who's mad at you now?''

Frankie wondered which question to answer first. ''The vandalism was a fluke. Had nothing to do with me.''

''I find that hard to believe. You're always getting into something. I go to bed at night wondering what's going to happen to you next. I should come up there so I can see firsthand what's going on.''

''Not a good time, Mom. I just started a new job, and I'm trying to get moved in to my new place. Besides, my housemate uses the phone a lot at night. She's a…telemarketer.''

Sissy shot Frankie a thumbs-up.

''That is no excuse for not returning my calls.''

''Mom, I don't have time to go into this. I'm on my way out.''

''You have a date?''

Frankie knew it was the only way to get her off the phone. ''Something like that, yes.''

''You're lying.''

''Whatever.''

''Who is he?''

''A wealthy doctor. You've always wanted me to marry a doctor.''

Silence. ''I don't believe you. I can always tell when you're lying. What's his name?''

''Mother!''

''I can find out on my own, you know. I always do.''

Frankie shot Sissy a desperate look. ''His name is Dr. William Williamston.''

Sissy rolled her eyes and shook her head.

"Who would name a child that? What kind of doctor is he?"

"If you must know, he's a proctologist."

Sissy burst into laughter and slapped her hand over her mouth to curtail it. Frankie tried to keep from laughing, as well.

Eve sighed from the other end. "Oh, Lord. How will I ever tell my friends? Couldn't you find a nice general practitioner?"

Sissy opened the door and rang the bell.

"Oh, there he is, right on time. I'll call you later, Mom."

"Dr. William Williamston?" Sissy asked, still laughing. "Couldn't you come up with something better than that?"

Frankie grabbed her cake. "I had to think fast, okay? My mother will be so glad I'm seeing a doctor that she'll leave me alone for a few days."

They looked at each other. "Yeah, right," they said simultaneously.

The courthouse square had been transformed. Tiny white lights adorned the trees and bushes, and the stage had been set up with band equipment. Crisp white tablecloths covered more than a dozen folding tables, now laden with food. At least one hundred people crowded the lawn; another fifty were lined up at the tables. The area was roped off, obviously so no one could sneak in. A number of men stood along the sidewalk collecting money and handing out tickets. Sissy and Frankie paid and carried their food to the designated table.

"Oh, Lord, there's Macon Comfy," Sissy said, hiding behind Frankie. "I don't want him to see me."

"Who is he?" Frankie asked, noting a beefy man with long sideburns who was looking in their direction.

"The town butcher. He's had a crush on me for years. Oh, shit, he's coming this way."

"Sissy, get a grip!" Frankie stepped aside as the man approached.

"Well, would you look at that? Miss Sissy, you are about the prettiest thing I've ever laid eyes on." He looked at Frankie. "No offense, ma'am. You look nice, too."

She simply nodded.

"Hello, Macon." Sissy's voice was dry. "I don't suppose you've met Frankie Daniels. She's our new deputy."

"I haven't had the pleasure, but I've certainly heard about her." He pumped Frankie's hand. "Welcome to Purdyville, ma'am."

"Thank you."

His gaze fell on Sissy once more. "Is that a new dress you're wearing?" he asked.

"No."

"Well, you'd look good in a burlap sack, honey. Now, why don't I get you ladies a cup of punch?"

"Oh, that would be so nice of you," Frankie replied, and saw Sissy cringe.

"I'll be right back. Don't run off."

"Thanks a lot," Sissy muttered as soon as Macon was out of earshot. "How are we going to meet new men if Macon tags along?"

"I didn't know there were any new men in Purdyville. Besides, it's obvious Macon adores you."

"He smells like raw meat and bad cologne. Not only that, he's overweight."

"Not by much. Twenty or thirty pounds, maybe? You could work that off of him within a week."

"Do you realize he's the deacon at the First Baptist Church? I'll bet he doesn't even talk dirty in bed."

"You could always keep your night job."

Sissy shot her a look.

"Here we go, ladies," Macon said, trying to balance three plastic cups of punch.

Frankie shot him a big smile. "Why, thank you, Macon." She took a sip. "Oh, this is wonderful. Isn't it wonderful, Sissy?"

"Yeah, wonderful."

"I understand you're a butcher, Macon."

"Yes, ma'am. You don't find fresher meat anywhere else unless you slaughter something yourself."

"I'll remember that."

"Thank you for the punch," Sissy said, "but Frankie and I must be running along now."

"You're not leaving?" he protested, looking disappointed. "Not without promising me a dance."

Frankie felt a presence and turned. Matt stood there smiling. "I don't believe my eyes. You came."

"Did I have a choice?"

"Of course you did. You wouldn't be here if you hadn't wanted to come, and you wouldn't be wearing that pretty dress if you hadn't wanted me to notice. You look like a million bucks."

"I'll sleep better tonight knowing you approve. Would you excuse me?"

"I was going to do the gentlemanly thing and get you a glass of punch."

She smiled pleasantly. "I've already had punch," she said, holding out her empty cup, "but thanks just the same." She turned.

Sissy shot her a frantic look. "Where are you going?"

"I thought I'd walk around. I'm supposed to mingle with the locals."

"I'll go with you."

"Don't bother," Matt said. "I'll escort Ms. Daniels wherever she wishes to go." He cupped her elbow and prodded her in the direction of the food. "I hope you're hungry, because I am. Let's see what we have. Oh, fried chicken. I'll bet it's not as good as yours, but I'll have to take my chances."

"Very funny," she said, looking at the fare. There seemed to be enough food for a small country. Frankie would have made excuses to get rid of Matt had she not been so hungry. He handed her a plastic plate, took one for himself, and they got into line.

"It's a beautiful night," she said, trying to make conversation. It wasn't easy. She was used to seeing him in uniform, and his civilian clothes made her feel shy and awkward.

"Beautiful," he said, his gaze roving the length of her body, lazily, enjoying every inch of her. She had never looked lovelier than she did at that moment, and he wanted to commit it to memory so that every time he closed his eyes he would see her standing beneath the tiny white lights looking like something out of a fairy tale. The simple black dress she wore defined every curve, giving her a softness and highlighting her translucent complexion. He wondered if she had any clue how beautiful she was.

Frankie felt Matt's eyes on her. His gaze was like a caress; it was as though she were cocooned within an invisible warmth. The night air seemed warmer, charged with a current that sent a ripple of pleasure through her. He looked very male in simple dress slacks and a white oxford-cloth shirt, and although she tried to shut out her awareness of him, it was impossible. She couldn't fault the women who looked his way as they passed—he was as good-looking as they came, but oddly enough, he seemed oblivious to it.

"Well, look who showed up, after all," a female voice said.

Frankie turned and found Alice and Dr. Rand Chalmers beside them. "Yes, I was badgered into coming," Frankie said, "but I'm glad I did."

"And you look wonderful. What did you do to your hair?"

"Sissy forced a curling iron to it."

"Very classy, I must say. Frankie, you remember my husband?"

"Hello, Dr. Chalmers."

He shook her hand. "Call me Rand. Have you been checking your blood pressure regularly?"

"Yes."

"Rand, this is no time to play doctor," Alice said. "We're here to have a good time."

"Yes, ma'am." He grabbed two plates and handed her one.

"The line is moving slowly," Matt told them. "I'm just hoping I get a piece of fried chicken before they run out."

"I've never known this town to run out of fried chicken," Alice said, "but I'm holding out for Virgil's barbecue. I smelled it a block away. I may just have to go off my diet tonight."

Sissy joined them, with Macon on her heels. She didn't look pleased as she grabbed a plate.

"Hello, folks," he said, shaking everybody's hand. "Nice evening, isn't it?"

"Perfect," Alice said.

"Speaking of perfect, that pork loin you ordered arrived this afternoon—prettiest piece of meat I've ever seen. And I found that apricot stuffing you were looking for."

"Thank you, Macon. I'll pick it up in the morning."

They'd arrived at the first table, which contained salads of every kind. Frankie bypassed it. Sissy stuck a fork into a sliced tomato and put it on her plate. She looked bored.

"Don't be so shy, honey," Macon told her. "This is an all-you-can-eat event."

Sissy offered him a condescending smile. "That doesn't mean I'm going to eat all I can. I'm watching my weight."

He scanned her closely. "And doing a very good job of it, I might add." He patted his belly. "Might not be a bad idea if I cut down."

"You know, that thought never once occurred to me."

Frankie nudged her. "Be nice," she whispered.

As they filled their plates, members of the band stepped onto the stage and began testing their equipment. Matt spied an empty table and hurried toward it, saving it for the others. Once everyone was seated—Macon taking a place next to Sissy—a woman carrying tall plastic glasses of iced tea on a tray came by and passed out their beverages.

"So, Frankie, what do you think of Purdyville?" Rand asked.

"I haven't met a lot of people," she said, "but those I have met seem nice enough."

"Are you enjoying your new job?"

Frankie didn't know how to reply. "There are interesting aspects of it."

"Not quite as exciting as Atlanta, I'll bet."

"The past couple of days have been fairly busy."

"So they have. I was called to the ER after that awful wreck on the highway."

"How are they doing?" Frankie asked.

"They're still critical, but they're alive."

"I drove out later and saw the vehicles," Matt said. "Worse accident we've had in years. I'm surprised any of them made it out alive."

"It was bad, all right," Rand agreed before turning his attention back to Frankie. "I suppose accidents like that are an everyday occurrence in a place like Atlanta. You won't find excitement like that here."

"I'd hardly call it exciting," she replied, "but it wasn't my job to respond to automobile accidents. I worked homicide."

Matt spoke up. "Frankie is fitting in very well here, despite the lack of excitement. We're lucky to have her."

She warmed at the compliment. "Thank you, Chief."

He grinned. "I'm just trying to butter you up so you'll dance with me later."

"I don't dance."

"Sure you do."

They chatted as they ate. Frankie looked at Sissy and saw the unhappy expression on her face. Macon had not stopped talking about the rising costs of beef since they'd sat down.

Finally, Sissy looked at him. "Excuse me, Macon, but do I look like someone who gives a damn about beef costs?"

He burst into hearty laughter as he gazed about the group. "Isn't she something else? Talk about personality."

Sissy shook her head sadly and gnawed on a rib.

Alice looked at Matt. "How are the Gibbses doing?"

"I've called Irma a couple of times. She sounds tired."

"I don't imagine it's easy taking care of an invalid."

"She could ask for help. Hospice would come in for free. She heard about the benefit, and she didn't like it one bit."

"Some people carry pride a bit too far," Rand said.

Matt nodded. "That's why I'm going to deposit the money right into their checking account."

"Do you have any idea who burned down their rental house?"

"It's still under investigation. I can't believe the neighbors didn't see anything."

"I know you can't talk about the case," Alice said, "but I heard Willie-Jack Pitts had a score to settle with her."

"Willie-Jack has a score to settle with everybody in this town. Unfortunately, I can't put him at the scene. He has an alibi."

"Which is probably a lie," Macon said. "I've had problems with him myself." He grinned. "I'm thinking of hiring Frankie to whup up on him."

Frankie shook her head. "I'll never live that one down."

"Probably too embarrassed to show his face," Rand said.

"I'd be embarrassed to show my face if I looked like him," Sissy replied.

The band started playing "Brown-Eyed Girl." Frankie didn't think they were half bad. The crowd had grown since she and Sissy had arrived. People were still lined up at the food tables.

Virgil stopped by the table to greet them. "How are the ribs tonight, folks?"

"Virgil, I believe these are the best you've ever cooked," Alice said.

''There's plenty more,'' he told them before he moved to the next table.

''I'm going up for seconds,'' Macon said. ''Sissy, can I get you anything?''

She shook her head wordlessly. As soon as Macon disappeared, she looked at Matt. ''Can you arrest Macon for stalking me?''

Matt chuckled. ''He's got a crush on you, Sissy. You could do worse than Macon Comfy.''

''Thanks for your support, cousin.''

''No problem.''

The band started a slow number. Matt stood and held his hand out to Frankie. ''I believe they're playing our song.''

''I told you, I don't dance.''

''I'll lead.''

''Oh, go dance with the man,'' Alice said.

''Yes, dance with him,'' Sissy insisted. ''No sense sitting here being miserable like me.''

They all had their eyes on Frankie. She looked at Matt. ''Well, okay, but if I step on your feet, you deserve it.''

She took his hand and he led her to a portable dance floor, one that could be folded and taken to the next event. It was already filled, so people were dancing on the grass.

Frankie felt her breath catch in the back of her throat the minute Matt took her in his arms, curling his fingers around her hand. His wide palm pressed the small of her back, pulling her close in a possessive gesture. His fingertips caressed her spine, and she shivered as all her nerve endings snapped to attention.

''Are you cold?'' he whispered, his mouth at her ear.

He said it in such a way that Frankie knew he was aware that her body was merely responding to his, and it irked her that he had such an affect on her. "No, I'm fine," she muttered.

"Relax," he said in a voice that sounded as though honey dripped from his vocal cords.

Easy for him to say, Frankie thought, trying to ease the tension and stiffness from her body. He knew damn well what he was doing. He wasn't dancing, he was trying to seduce her. He moved gracefully, but she could feel the muscles rippling beneath his shirt, his thighs brushing hers, and his chest pressing against her breasts as they danced to an old Patsy Cline song. She felt small and feminine and vulnerable. Their gazes met and locked for what seemed an indeterminable amount of time, although Frankie was sure it only lasted a matter of seconds. His look said it all. He wanted her.

He held her too close. "I don't think we should be doing this," she said.

"Why? Because it feels so good?"

It felt much too good, his lean body flush against her softer one. She had not realized—well, maybe she had— what a big man he was. Big and solid and warm.

"Matt?"

"Hush, pretty lady. I only asked for a dance, not a roll in the hay. Although I'm not opposed to a roll in the hay, if you were to insist."

She didn't respond. Instead, she glanced over her shoulder, trying to concentrate on what was going on around them instead of what was happening inside of her. Macon was obviously trying to get Sissy on the dance floor, because he was leaning over the table with a hopeful look on his face, and she was shaking her head emphatically.

Matt chuckled, his breath soft as a whisper as it fell on her ear. "You know, you could loosen up a bit and pretend to enjoy this. Or maybe that's the problem—you're enjoying it more than you care to admit.''

Once again, she remained quiet. What could she say? He was right, of course. She was feeling things she shouldn't, and that scared her.

She stepped on Matt's toe. ''Sorry.''

''That's okay, I'll be able to collect disability now.''

She tried to relax, sink into his embrace, enjoying the feel of him despite warning signals flashing in her head. ''I'm not real good at this,'' she confessed.

''You could have fooled me. Or maybe we're just good together.'' He paused. ''You look stunning tonight. Did I mention that?''

''I believe so.'' It was hard to keep up her end of the conversation when her emotions were playing havoc with her body.

''Then I'll keep telling you. I just want to know one thing.''

Once again she looked into his eyes. ''What?''

''Did you even once think of me while you were primping for this event?''

''You're embarrassing me.''

''I'm sorry. I was just being hopeful.''

She glanced away. ''Maybe I did. I just wanted to feel like a woman tonight instead of a deputy.''

''I never had a doubt you were a woman, Frankie. I know this is going to sound strange, but you exude sensuality, even in uniform.''

The dance ended and immediately started into another slow number. Matt didn't make a move to leave the dance floor; in fact, he held Frankie more tightly.

''What would you say to coming by my place afterward?'' he asked.

''Not a good idea.''

"What if I promised to behave myself? We could sit on the back porch and just talk. Unless you don't trust yourself," he added.

"People might get the wrong idea."

"Since when have you cared what people thought?"

"Since I was asked to leave my job in Atlanta."

He sighed. "You can't live in the future if you refuse to let go of the past. I've made mistakes, too, Frankie. I've had my share of regrets. It's called life."

She thought about it as they danced in silence, each of them content to be in each other's arms. She had made a mistake by getting involved with Jim Connors, and it had cost her. No, she shouldn't have to pay for it for the rest of her life, that much was true, but whatever was happening between her and Matt was happening too fast. She had never been more attracted to a man, and she knew, unlike her affair with Connors, this was more than physical. If she were smart, she would pack her bags and leave town first thing in the morning.

Suddenly, they both realized the music had stopped, and they were still dancing while other couples drifted back to their tables. "The dance is over," she said self-consciously, trying to pull away.

"Not for me," he said. "Please come by tonight." His look beckoned her.

She felt impaled by those blue eyes. The silence lengthened between them. Frankie fidgeted. "I'll think about it."

They returned to the table. "Ya'll were the best couple on the floor," Alice said, giving Frankie a knowing look.

It took Frankie a moment to regain her thoughts. She smiled, feeling shy in front of the group. "Thanks."

"Has anyone seen Sissy?" Macon asked. "She went

to the ladies' room and never came back. Must be a long waiting line.''

"I hope she returns," Frankie said. "We rode together."

"I can drop you off on my way," Matt said, "but I'm sure she'll show up."

"Excuse me," a woman's fruity-sounding voice said, causing everyone at the table to look in her direction. She was elderly, with a mass of white hair that reminded Frankie of cotton candy. The men stood out of respect. The woman eyed Frankie. "Did you bring that German chocolate cake?"

"Yes, I did. Why, is something wrong with it?"

"I would certainly think so. You're obviously trying to pass it off as a homemade cake."

"I beg your pardon?"

"Frankie, meet Edna Rose," Matt interjected. "Edna, this is Deputy Frankie Daniels." He looked at Frankie. "Edna bakes the best cakes in Purdyville."

The woman hitched her chin high. "That's right. My cakes have taken the blue ribbon at the county fair three years in a row. I brought my famous German chocolate cake tonight, but folks can't stop talking about yours. Don't think I don't know a store-bought cake when I see one."

Frankie looked at Matt. "Is this for real?"

"Quite serious," he replied, although he looked amused. "I may have to haul you in for trying to pass off a counterfeit cake."

"Edna, I'm sure Frankie meant no harm," Alice said. "She was probably too busy to bake a cake. Surely you've heard all that's been going on this week."

"I don't even know how to bake," Frankie confessed.

Edna didn't look at all placated. "You deliberately put

GET 2

HOW TO GET YOUR
2 FREE BOOKS AND FREE GIFT!

1. Peel off the MIRA sticker on the front cover. Place it in the space provided at right. This automatically entitles you to receive two free books and an exciting surprise gift.

2. Send back this card and you'll get 2 "The Best of the Best™" novels. These books have a combined cover price of $11.98 or more in the U.S. and $13.98 or more in Canada, but they are yours to keep absolutely FREE!

3. There's <u>no</u> catch. You're under <u>no</u> obligation to buy anything. We charge nothing – ZERO – for your first shipment. And you don't have to make any minimum number of purchases – not even one!

4. We call this line "The Best of the Best" because each month you'll receive the best books by some of today's hottest authors. These authors show up time and time again on all the major bestseller lists and their books sell out as soon as they hit the stores. You'll like the convenience of getting them delivered to your home at our special discount prices . . . and you'll love your *Heart to Heart* subscriber newsletter featuring author news, horoscopes, recipes, book reviews and much more!

5. We hope that after receiving your free books you'll want to remain a subscriber. But the choice is yours – to continue or cancel, anytime at all! So why not take us up on our invitation, with no risk of any kind. You'll be glad you did!

6. And remember...we'll send you a surprise gift ABSOLUTELY FREE just for giving "The Best of the Best" a try.

SPECIAL FREE GIFT!

We'll send you a fabulous surprise gift, absolutely FREE, simply for accepting our no-risk offer!

Visit us at
www.mirabooks.com

BOOKS FREE!

Hurry!

Return this card promptly to GET 2 FREE BOOKS & A FREE GIFT!

YES! Please send me the 2 FREE "The Best of the Best" novels and FREE gift for which I qualify. I understand that I am under no obligation to purchase anything further, as explained on the back and on the opposite page.

385 MDL DH5Y   185 MDL DH5Z

FIRST NAME	LAST NAME

ADDRESS

APT.#	CITY

STATE/PROV.	ZIP/POSTAL CODE

▼ DETACH AND MAIL CARD TODAY! ▼

(M-EB3-02) ©1998 MIRA BOOKS

The Best of the Best™ — Here's How it Works:

Accepting your 2 free books and gift places you under no obligation to buy anything. You may keep the books and gift and return the shipping statement marked "cancel." If you do not cancel, about a month later we will send you 4 additional novels and bill you just $4.74 each in the U.S., or $5.24 each in Canada, plus 25¢ shipping & handling per book and applicable taxes if any.* That's the complete price and — compared to cover prices of $5.99 or more each in the U.S. and $6.99 or more each in Canada — it's quite a bargain! You may cancel at any time, but if you choose to continue, every month we'll send you 4 more books, which you may either purchase at the discount price or return to us and cancel your subscription.

*Terms and prices subject to change without notice. Sales tax applicable in N.Y. Canadian residents will be charged applicable provincial taxes and GST.

If offer card is missing write to: The Best of the Best, 3010 Walden Ave., P.O. Box 1867, Buffalo, NY 14240-1867

THE BEST OF THE BEST
3010 WALDEN AVE
PO BOX 1867
BUFFALO NY 14240-9952

POSTAGE WILL BE PAID BY ADDRESSEE

BUSINESS REPLY MAIL
FIRST-CLASS MAIL   PERMIT NO. 717-003   BUFFALO, NY

NO POSTAGE
NECESSARY
IF MAILED
IN THE
UNITED STATES

it in a plastic container so that folks would think you'd made it from scratch.''

Matt patted the woman's shoulder. ''Aren't you overreacting a bit, hon?''

''I have a reputation to uphold in this town.''

Frankie had had enough. ''This is the most ridiculous thing I've ever heard in my life. Let me just get the damn cake off the table.''

''It has already been devoured,'' the older woman said, ''and not one soul has touched mine. I will never be able to show my face in this town again.'' A faint thread of hysteria ran through her voice. ''I can just imagine what folks are saying. They're saying, 'Why, Edna Rose has lost her touch. She's too old to bake any more cakes.' Next thing I know they'll be knocking on *your* front door for donations for the cakewalk at our annual charity bazaar. I demand a public apology.'' She had to pause to catch her breath.

Frankie blinked in total confusion. ''Lady, you need to get a life.''

Edna Rose's face reddened. ''Well, I have never!''

''Nor have I,'' Frankie replied, ''and I hope I never do again.''

The woman stalked away. She was joined by a group of ladies her age, who stared at Frankie as though she had just committed an unspeakable act. Frankie looked at the group at her table and found everyone wearing an amused smile. Matt looked ready to break out into hearty laughter any moment. ''I don't believe what just happened,'' she said. ''Those women look mad enough to take me behind the courthouse and kick butt.''

Alice waved the statement aside. ''Oh, don't mind Edna Rose. She's just an old woman with nothing to do but bake cakes.''

Matt nodded. "Alice is right. Edna lost her husband a few years back, and she's become a bit disagreeable."

Frankie crossed her arms and sat there wordlessly while the others joked about some of the town's characters. "You'll meet them all," Matt said.

Frankie gave him a deadpan look. "I can't wait."

Macon got up. "I don't know about the rest of you, but I'm worried about Sissy. I think I'll go look for her."

The evening wore on. Frankie agreed to dance several times with Matt. She was delighted when others stopped by the table to ask her for a dance, but she politely refused. Twice on the dance floor, the same man tapped Matt's shoulder, and he made a gallant show of backing off and allowing her to dance with him. But the look on his face, as he returned to the table, was anything but pleased.

"Frankie's very popular tonight," Alice said. "I'm glad she decided to come."

"Yes, well, I wanted her to get out and meet people," a stony-faced Matt replied. "I just had no idea so many people would want to meet her."

"She's a beautiful young woman," Alice replied. "Naturally men are going to want to meet her."

"Uh-oh," Rand said, trying to see over the crowd of people. "Macon just found Sissy sitting at a table with some guy. He must be new in town, because I don't recognize him."

"Maybe she'll have a good time, after all," Matt replied, trying to keep his eyes on Frankie. When the dance stopped, she allowed her dance partner to lead her to his table where a group of people seemed eager to shake her hand. She laughed and talked with them and allowed the same man to lead her onto the dance floor again.

Matt realized Rand was saying something about a new

doctor in town, and he pretended to listen, but he was more interested in what Frankie was up to. Not that it was any of his business, he reminded himself. She was free to dance with anyone she pleased—as long as she knew he was taking her home.

"Oh, my Lord!" Alice said, her face taking on a twisted expression. "The snake has finally crawled out from under his rock."

Matt turned and followed her gaze as Willie-Jack Pitts and his buddies strolled through the crowd, no doubt seeking trouble.

Twelve

Matt tried to gauge Willie-Jack's mood as he watched him. The man was drunk. Matt had seen him in that condition enough times to know. The group paused to gaze at the dance floor, and Matt knew the minute Willie-Jack spied Frankie. He simply stood there, watching every move she made. Matt picked up his radio.

"Cooter, are you there?"

A moment of static. "Yeah, Chief, what's up?"

"Willie-Jack just arrived with his pals. From the looks of it, they're intoxicated."

"Imagine that. Well, there are five of us here—seven, including you and Frankie—so I reckon we'll be able to head off any trouble. Where are they now?"

"Near the dance floor."

More static. "Don't worry, we'll keep an eye out."

Rand looked at Alice. "It's time we left."

"I won't let them start any trouble," Matt said, surprised at the cold expression on Rand's face.

"I may have to live in the same town with that piece of garbage, but I don't have to attend the same functions." Rand stood. "Are you ready, Alice?"

"Yes." She grabbed her purse and stood, as well. "I'm sorry to run out on you, Matt, but it's getting late, anyway. Rand and I are usually in bed by this time."

"Let's go." Rand took her hand and led her away, in the opposite direction of Willie-Jack.

Frankie finally returned to the table, slightly out of breath. "I don't think I've danced this much in years."

Matt eyed her. "I thought you didn't dance."

"That was a long time ago."

"Willie-Jack is here."

"Damn. Do the others know?"

"I radioed Cooter. They're watching him."

"Speaking of the lowlife scumbag, here he comes now."

Matt turned. Sure enough, Willie-Jack and his entourage were headed their way.

"Evening, Ms. Daniels," Willie-Jack said. "Chief," he added with a nod. His words were slurred.

"That's Deputy Daniels, Willie-Jack," Matt corrected him.

"I ain't never seen a deputy look that good." He eyed Frankie as though she belonged on the dessert table. "I thought maybe you'd let bygones be bygones and save me a dance."

"You can take a flying leap into hell, Pitts. I don't want you in my presence, and I sure don't want your hands on me."

The guys behind him snickered.

"Is that any way to talk to a man who has decided to change his ways?"

Matt saw Cooter and Hurley Ledford from the night crew draw closer. From the corner of his eye he noted Jimbo Taylor, also from the night shift, talking to Orvell Dean, but he was watching Willie-Jack, as well.

"I don't want any trouble out of you, Pitts," Matt said. "I'd rather lock you up than look at you."

Willie-Jack shot him a menacing look. "You think you

own this town, don't you, Chief? You like strutting your stuff down the sidewalks behind that badge, because it gives you a sense of power, and because it turns the women on. Gets you laid on a regular basis, don't it?''

Matt stood. Cooter, Hurley and Jimbo closed in. ''You know, Willie-Jack, that would really piss me off if it weren't coming from the town's biggest loser. But I'm going to let it slide because I don't want any trouble. I suggest you and your boys get back into that rusted heap of junk you call a pickup truck and go home before I lock all of you up for public drunkenness.''

''You can't lock me up. I ain't done nothing yet.''

''I'll just charge you for being ugly as cow dung, how's that?''

The man looked around as the deputies closed in. ''Oh, I see you've called the boys. You afraid to face me alone, Chief?''

Matt smiled. ''As I recall, I stomped your ass in the ground years ago. I'll do it again if it pleases you.''

''Let me do it,'' Frankie said.

Willie-Jack offered her a menacing look. ''What are you, some kind of bull dyke?''

Matt grabbed him by the collar and startled several people who were watching the exchange. ''Leave or I'll haul you in and make sure you have an accident while you're behind bars. And I suggest you put somebody sober behind the wheel, so I don't have to arrest you on a DUI charge.''

Willie-Jack shrugged free. He was clearly in a rage. ''Don't worry, this is not my kind of party. A bunch of old farts dancing to shitty music.'' He motioned to his friends. ''Let's get the hell out of here.''

Cooter looked concerned. ''He's mad *and* drunk, Chief. No telling what he'll do. You want one of us to tail him?''

"Yeah. And if you can come up with a reasonable excuse, shoot him."

All three deputies grinned. "I think the fact that he's breathing is good enough reason to put a hole in his head," Hurley said. "Me and Cooter can follow him."

The two deputies walked away together. Jimbo stood there. "You want me to go with them or hang around?"

"I think they can handle it."

Frankie noted the thinning crowd. Sissy returned, a handsome man on her arm. "This is Joe," she said, and then proceeded to introduce Matt and Frankie. Joe pulled out her chair, and she sat.

"Why don't I grab us some iced tea?" he offered. "I'm pretty warm after that last dance."

"Thank you, Joe," Sissy said sweetly. Once he left, she regarded Matt and Frankie. "Isn't he just about the best-looking thing you ever laid eyes on?"

Matt nodded. "I've got goose bumps all over me."

"I think he's handsome," Frankie said, "and very nice. Is he new in town?"

"Only been here a couple of days. He's heading up the construction crew that's adding a new wing to the hospital. Said he hasn't had this much fun since his high school prom. Invited me to the Huddle House for coffee later."

"Don't forget I rode with you," Frankie said.

"Joe can drive me home, and you can take my car."

"I'll take Frankie home," Matt offered. "You don't know this guy. I think it would be better if you had your own vehicle."

"You worry too much, cousin. I'm a big girl. I can look after myself." She winked at Frankie, who gave her the thumbs-up in return. Sissy looked at Matt, and it was obvious he didn't approve. "Okay, okay, I'll take my own car."

The band had stopped playing and was in the process of packing up while others broke down the folding tables and began carrying them to several large trucks. A number of men were hard at work, unstringing lights, others picking up trash. A few stragglers still remained, chatting with one another.

"Should we help clean up?" Frankie asked.

Matt shook his head. "Not when they're being paid to do it."

Cooter and Hurley arrived back. "I reckon Willie-Jack decided to call it a night," Cooter said. "His friends dropped him off at his trailer."

"So the rodent is back in his hole," Hurley said. "You want us to hang around till they're finished getting this place in order?"

"You and one of the other guys can hang around," Matt told Hurley. "Cooter, you go on home. You've already worked your shift, I don't expect you to work all night as well."

"Yeah, just don't forget you owe me overtime."

Sissy and Joe left, leaving Matt and Frankie at the table. "You have a choice," he said. "I'll take you home or we can go by my place and have coffee on the deck."

Frankie knew she was too wound up to go home and sleep, but she questioned whether or not it would be wise to go home with Matt. "I should probably go home," she said reluctantly.

"Playing it safe, huh?" His smiled mocked her.

"Webber, the day I'm afraid of you will be the day I hand in my badge for good."

"Let's not talk about badges or all that has gone on

this week. Let's go to my place and talk about something simple. Let's just relax, Frankie.''

"Relax?''

"Yeah, you've heard the word before, you just don't do it enough. But I saw a different side of you tonight. A beautiful lady who let her hair down and enjoyed herself.'' He wouldn't mention the fact she had danced with at least a half dozen other men.

Frankie pondered it. "Okay, maybe for just a little while.''

He smiled. "Okay.''

Frankie noted the warmth in his eyes. The man had charm; she had to admit that much. She followed him to a low-slung sports car that appeared to be a classic, surprisingly. "Where's your truck?''

"At home. I only take this out on special occasions.''

"It's beautiful, Matt.''

"My dad and I bought it for a song and worked on it. New engine, new everything. It has sentimental value.''

He opened the door and Frankie slid onto a leather seat. "I feel honored to be riding in it.''

He chuckled. "I'll have to show you pictures of what it looked like when we bought it.''

He drove to his house, and Frankie could not help but admire how big his hands looked on the steering wheel as he expertly guided the car down the dirt road, avoiding potholes and bumps along the way. He pulled into his driveway fifteen minutes later.

"Sit tight. I'll get your door.''

"That's not necessary.''

"It is to me.''

He led her inside the house and to the kitchen, where he began making coffee. "I should have asked if you'd like a beer instead?''

"No, I prefer coffee."

"It's my special blend. I only pull it out for special people."

"Once again, I'm honored."

"You should be. Just to be in my presence."

She laughed. "You need to be humbled, Webber."

"Yeah?" His look challenged her. "Think you're woman enough?"

"I'm not touching that one." She gazed at him while he prepared their coffee. He looked nice in civilian clothes. Hell, the man would look great wearing a fig leaf. Which was why she had chosen to dance with other men. She had not wanted him or anyone else to think she was his date for the evening and start more tongues to wagging. She had already made an enemy out of Edna Rose and her bunch.

"Would you like a snack to go with your coffee? I have carrot cake."

"You bake?"

"I don't have to. Every little old lady in town does it for me."

"That's because you're irresistible."

He turned and gazed at her. "Am I irresistible to you, Frankie?"

"Matt, we don't need to go there."

"Why not? We're not on duty. Right now I find myself looking at a beautiful woman in a slinky black dress with knockout legs. A woman who has intrigued me from the day I laid eyes on her."

"I thought we were here to relax."

"I just happen to be great at giving massages."

Her stomach dipped. "I don't doubt that for a minute, but I'm not interested. You invited me for coffee and simple conversation."

He made eye contact. "That's about as simple as it gets, Miss Daniels. Attraction between a man and a woman."

"What makes you think I'm attracted to you?"

"I know." He sighed. "Frankie, you drive me crazy. You're stubborn, pigheaded, and you have a mouth on you that would send most men running for shelter. You smoke like a chimney, you cuss like a truck driver, and you think you're smarter than everybody, including me, but I'm still crazy about you. I think it's those qualities that do it to me. But then I see this feminine part of you, and I realize there's a soft side of you that I'd like to get to know, as well."

"You're wrong about me, Matt. I've hardened over the years. I've seen enough violence that I'm immune to it. I can't get close to people."

"Which is why you held Mrs. Bower's hand at the hospital when we feared her son had ingested poison. You care, Frankie. You just don't want to, because it scares you to death."

Just as she had suspected, he was learning more and more about her. "I'd rather not discuss it."

"You'd rather spend the rest of your life alone?"

"I feel safer."

"Tell me about him."

She knew he was referring to her father. He was so adept at picking through her emotions. For some reason, she wanted him to know about the man who'd been her best friend.

"His name was Frank, and I was determined to be just like him. I even changed my name—well, not legally— but I decided it was a name I could be proud of."

"I already know that from looking at your file, Francis."

"I hate that name."

He poured two cups of coffee. They didn't speak until they had reached his deck and sat on a padded chair big enough for the both of them. "So you tried to take your father's place," he mused.

"And failed miserably."

He gave her an odd look. "Is that what you think? You underestimate yourself."

"He was a hero, Matt. Everybody looked up to him."

"You think people don't look up to you? Why do you think my deputies are so jealous? Hell, you've forgotten more about the law than they'll ever know."

"Your uncle Dell didn't make things easy for me. No matter how well I did, it was never enough."

"He called me a couple of days ago to see how you were. Your ex-lover has been demoted."

"Why didn't you tell me?"

"Maybe I was afraid you'd call Dell back and see if he could find another place for you. Or maybe I was afraid you still had feelings for that guy. I should have said something. Not very professional of me, but neither is jealousy, and that's exactly what I was feeling tonight when you danced with those other men. I've never been jealous. *Jealousy* is another word for *insecurity,* and I don't like feeling that way."

"I let the department down when I got involved with Connors," she confessed. "All that hard work, and I blew it." She sighed. "Worst of all, I let myself down."

"Maybe you've set such high standards for yourself that it's hard to reach them. There's only one Frank Daniels, and there's only one Frankie. You can't keep comparing yourself to him or it'll make you crazy. Believe me, I tried to make my parents as proud of me as they were of Mandy, but she was the apple of their eyes."

Frankie took a sip of her coffee. It was good. She smiled. "You think you've got me all figured out, don't you, Webber? If you're so smart, why are you living in this big house alone and chasing every skirt that walks by your office?"

"I like pretty women, and I don't mind looking now and then. That doesn't mean I act on it. As for choosing to live here alone, I thought it a good decision at the time."

"Because of Mandy?"

He didn't answer right away. "That certainly had a lot to do with it, but there were problems between Jenna and me. She's the woman I was engaged to," he added. "Professional problems that led to personal ones."

Frankie knew some of it, but she hadn't heard it from him. "You want to talk about it?"

He shrugged. "She was a defense attorney, and a damn good one at that. I'd bring in the criminal, and she'd get him or her off. Simple as that."

"She was doing her job."

He leaned back in the chair and crossed one leg. "Yeah, that's what she kept reminding me. Only I got tired of busting my hump trying to bring someone to justice and then having her show up in court, trying to make me, my deputies or the witnesses look like fools. She had great aspirations. I don't think she was long for this town, anyway. She preferred designer labels, exclusive restaurants, the best salons, and Purdyville just didn't meet her standards.

"I'm a simple guy, I guess. That doesn't mean I'm stupid. But I believe in right and wrong, and I believe people should be punished when they break the law. Nowadays, it doesn't much matter what you do, if you're rich.

You pay a highfalutin attorney enough money, and they'll get you off. But Jenna went too far.''

"What happened?"

"We had two little girls disappear almost three years back. The evidence pointed to Bud Combes. I don't know if you've heard of the family, but they live in the historical district. Got money coming out their butts. The boys and I worked for months on that case, put Bud under surveillance. Everything pointed to him. When we found the bodies, there were fibers on them from Bud's car. Only, Bud was smart enough to call dispatch that night to report his car had been stolen. We found it out in the woods, and the bodies less than a hundred yards away.''

Frankie shuddered. "I hate crimes involving children.''

"You just confessed a weakness." He smiled. "That makes two of us. Nothing like that had ever happened in Purdyville. Everyone was stunned. Bud's old man must've paid through the nose because Jenna got him off. She had experts flown in from all over the country. By the time she finished with me I looked like chopped meat. Bud Combes walked out of the courthouse a free man. I was still reeling from that when Mandy died.''

"That sucks.''

Matt nodded. "It gets worse. Two weeks later they found another little girl in Blossom City, not far from Purdyville. Same MO. Jenna knew she'd never get Bud a fair trial here so she moved for a change of venue. The case garnered a lot of press, which was exactly what she was hoping for. But this time Bud was convicted. He pled guilty to a lesser crime and got life. They should have fried his ass.''

"So the two of you broke up?"

"I kept putting off the wedding. I went into a shell, I guess. Jenna kept calling, but I wouldn't talk to her. I couldn't. The whole thing left a bad taste in my mouth. She was offered the job in Virginia, and I told her she should take it because I just couldn't see us spending our lives together. She asked me to give it a shot, but I couldn't. I'm old-fashioned or naive enough to think marriage should be for keeps. We would never have made it."

"I'm sorry, Matt."

"I'm not." He looked at her. "I know we need defense attorneys, but it was obvious who killed those girls. Jenna knew it, too, but it was more important that she win the case, and because of that, another life was lost. Now, Jenna's where she wants to be, and I'm exactly where I want to be."

Frankie pondered his words for a long moment, and she realized how much she respected the man beside her. Matt Webber cared about people, cared about protecting them, at any cost. "I'm proud of you," she said.

He looked surprised. "That's something I never thought I'd hear come out of your mouth."

"It's true. You held fast to your beliefs even though it caused you personal pain."

"You want to hear something that'll make you laugh?" She nodded.

"You think I'm some kind of wild man who flirts and chases women. I haven't been with a woman since... well...a long time. I haven't *wanted* a woman."

"I find that hard to believe."

"It's true." He smiled at her. "But don't tell anyone, it'll ruin my image."

"Hey, this is me you're talking to. I've seen how you operate when it comes to the opposite sex."

"It's all in fun. I'm not saying I don't get tempted... hell, I'm still a man. But I've learned where to draw the line. That way nobody gets hurt.'' He sighed. He only wished he'd learned that lesson earlier instead of using women to heal his wounded ego.

''She must've hurt you pretty badly.''

''It wasn't just Jenna. It was everything, I guess. I needed time to sort out things. Sometimes it's best to be alone. But I've reached a point in my life where I want a woman in my life again. Not just any woman. I want you, Frankie.''

Thirteen

She could only stare at him. His gaze fell across her, soft as the evening breeze that caressed her cheek and brought with it a late-blooming flower she couldn't put a name to. A faintly sensuous thread seemed to be tugging at them, unseen, but as real as the stars that twinkled in the night sky. Matt pulled her closer. Frankie saw the sincere look on his face, the need in his eyes as he ducked his head and touched her lips for the first time. She remained still, so caught up with the taste and scent of him that she could do little more. She tasted the coffee on his tongue when he slipped it inside and touched her own for the first time. It was a gentle kiss, as though he were merely taking a small sample, while at the same time waiting for her to respond. When he raised his head, he was smiling.

"Are you going to kiss me back or slug me?"

Frankie blinked. "I don't know what to do."

"I think I'll take my chances." With that, he captured her lips once more, only this time he pulled her into his arms. He was warm, comforting against her cool skin. She relaxed against him, her head falling back against one broad shoulder. He began to explore, this time boldly, her lips, the delicate inside of her mouth, and Frankie, her body tingling clear down to her toes, responded.

It was a perfect kiss, so perfect it almost brought tears to her eyes. His mouth never stilled, even when he rearranged her so that she was half lying in his lap. Matt slipped his arms around her waist and caressed the small of her back before sliding his fingers upward, touching each vertebra, causing her to shiver when he reached the nape of her neck, where the tiny hairs stood on end, seeming as eager as the rest of her for his touch.

The kiss deepened; they were so caught up in each other that they were oblivious to anything else. The world and all its worries slipped away, leaving behind a man and a woman who could not get enough of each other. Frankie wrapped her arms around his neck, and he tightened his hold on her. Her breasts flattened against his wide chest, and once again she marveled at the size of him. He had appeared so tall and lean before, but in his arms she felt dwarfed beside him. She had never felt more feminine, more desirable in her life.

After a moment, Matt pulled away and pressed his lips in Frankie's hair. His breathing was labored. "Lord, you taste good," he said, his voice a mere whisper that felt warm on her face.

"You, too," she confessed. She felt shy and vulnerable, unable to process what was going on between them. Her mind, usually sharp and alert, had abandoned her entirely, leaving her feeling defenseless.

Somehow, though, it felt right.

In one easy move, he pulled her onto his lap, cradling her in his arms as his lips sought the hollow of her throat and traced a path to her jaw. He kissed her closed eyelids, her temples, and nibbled her earlobes. His mouth was hot, leaving a delicious warmth behind as he moved, leisurely, almost unbearably so, to her breasts.

Matt paused, wondering what to do next. She had responded to him, and that knowledge warmed his belly. He'd had no idea what to expect when he'd brought her here, but she had kissed him back, and that had to mean something.

She felt surprisingly small in his arms. She was no longer the tough, hard-as-nails detective who'd worked the mean streets of Atlanta, who'd seen more than any human being should have to witness. He ached for that part of her, the mental pictures that would never go away. His only hope was that they would become less vivid in time.

But right now, she was a woman—sexy and delicious and responsive to his touch. She was everything and even more than his wildest dreams.

And he had never wanted a woman so badly in his life.

He searched her face and found uncertainty. "Frankie, I want to make love to you," he confessed, not knowing any other way to put it. "This is not why I brought you here, but I swear, it's all I can do to keep my hands off you." He released her, raking both hands through his hair. "But this is your call, baby, because I'm not thinking straight at the moment. If you don't want this to go any further, I'll take you home right now."

Frankie was touched. The man was not playing games; instead, he was laying it on the line. He was prepared to back off, despite the desire, the sheer need she saw in his eyes. If he felt anywhere close to what she was feeling, it could not be an easy decision.

Frankie stood. She pulled the pins from her hair, letting them drop, one by one, on the floor of the deck. She shook her hair, and it fell just past her shoulders, giving her a wild, come-hither look. Then, in one fluid motion, she reached around, unzipped her dress and slid it down her shoulders until it fell at her feet.

Matt's eyes almost popped out at the sight of her in black bikini panties and matching lace bra. She wore black thigh-highs. He had thought her on the skinny side, but as he raked his eyes boldly over her, he noted every curve. Her skin was flawless. "Oh, Lord. I'm a dead man."

Wordlessly, Frankie opened the door and made for his bedroom. A smile of satisfaction curved her lips as Matt followed. For some reason, it was important that she be in control. She swept the covers aside while he undressed. He slipped off his boxers, and she gazed at him longingly.

For a moment they simply stared at each other. Frankie rose up on one elbow. "I want to make something perfectly clear," she said. "This has nothing to do with work."

Matt could hear his own heart beating. "Actually, work is the last thing on my mind right now."

"I just want that understood."

"Duly noted, okay?" He slid into the bed beside her and pulled her into his arms and kissed her, hungrily this time, surprised by his own need. She returned his kiss with the same ardor, snuggling against him, soft as a kitten. He slid his hand across one shoulder and down her back, delighting in the feel of her. Suddenly, he could not get enough of her. He dispensed with her bra and panties, choosing to leave on the thigh-highs because, truly, they were the sexiest things he'd ever seen. He gazed at her, seemingly unabashed in her nakedness, and he knew he would die if he didn't touch her, taste her.

Frankie saw the fever in his eyes as he kissed the hollow of her shoulders, his lips feather-light and tantalizing. He smoothed his rough hands along the lengths of her arms, turning them slightly so he could nibble the underside. Her flesh prickled, and every nerve ending seemed to come alive, as if they had been buried in some dark place for a long time. His touch was so agonizingly slow, so soft, that her flesh literally ached for more. She slipped her fingers through his dark hair and sighed.

Matt was on fire for her, but he didn't want to rush her. For some reason it was very important that she be okay with what was happening between them. Even though his own need was so great, he did not want Frankie to have regrets later. He'd tasted enough of it in his life to know what it could do to a person.

He lifted his head, and the desire in her eyes made his gut tighten. He had never seen her like this; warm, loving, passionate. "Are you okay?"

"Make love to me, Matt." Her voice was husky.

"I want to make love *with* you, sweetheart."

Frankie pulled his head to her breasts, and he covered one nipple with his warm, wet mouth. He tongued it. She sucked in her breath sharply, as the sensation seemed to cause her lower belly to contract. She skimmed her hand lightly over his chest, feeling the curls tickle her fingers. She stroked his nipples, and they hardened much like her own. His belly was hard and flat as she explored, and when he pressed himself against her thigh, his desire was evident. He moved to the other breast, and Frankie rolled her head to one side, giving in to the sheer pleasure. He kissed her abdomen, her stomach, and finally parted her thighs, burying his head between them.

Nothing could have prepared her for the sensation, the touch of his tongue, wet and warm, soft as dandelion fluff against her. She whimpered as he reached beneath her hips and pulled her closer. She arched against him, and he applied more pressure, tasting her, circling her pleasure point with the very tip of his tongue. Frankie gave in to the magic he worked. She was lost in a world of sensation and a longing so great that it shook her. She wanted him, wanted to feel him deep inside. She reached for him, but he refused to budge. He tongued her thoroughly and expertly, until all control was lost, replaced by a white-hot sensation. She tried to hang on, balanced precariously on the precipice until there was no holding back. Her orgasm was powerful and shattered all common sense.

Matt knew the moment Frankie had given herself over to him, felt her shudder beneath his lips. He continued to kiss her until she, once again, cried out his name.

His own need was great as he entered her. She was tight and warm, and he groaned aloud as her muscles gripped him and moved him to new heights. He filled her, and she grabbed his hips and pulled him closer, opening herself like a flower. She moved against him, meeting each thrust until he thought he would go mad. He could no longer think; all he could do was marvel at the sensations. Soon he lost himself, pressing deeply, his movements frenzied and mind-boggling. He looked directly into her eyes as he emptied himself, all the pent-up desire draining into her.

Afterward, he held her for a long time, stroking her, whispering her name. Their coupling had left him deplete. All he could do was hold her close, trying to let her know how special, how precious the moment had been for him. He pulled her even closer, and she rolled onto one side, so that her hips were pressed against him. He wrapped his arms around her, thinking he had tasted heaven for the first time.

They didn't speak. Matt felt himself drifting off, half dozing but very much aware of her warm skin against his body. When he opened his eyes sometime later, he knew she had fallen asleep, as well, her steady breathing making him smile in the darkness. He closed his eyes.

Sometime during the night, Matt felt Frankie reach for him. He instantly perked as she nibbled his jaw and trailed her fingers down his chest, his abdomen, before closing her palms around him. He was instantly hard. He reached for her, but she climbed on top, straddling him. She guided him inside of her and slid down the length of him, sighing her contentment as he filled her. She was slick and tight.

She rode him. Matt searched for her breasts in the dark, cupping them in both hands, teasing the nipples with his thumb and forefinger until he heard her sigh of pleasure. They moved in unison. Finally, he heard her cry out, and he let go, filling her with his juices. She slumped against him, and he held her, stroking her hair, her back, cupping her hips in his palms.

"Frankie?"

"Shh. Don't say anything."

He remained quiet. Finally, she rose and lay beside him, falling asleep in his arms.

Matt stared into the darkness for a long time. He had seen a side of Frankie Daniels that surprised him. She was cool and controlled on the job, but she gave her all when it came to making love. He had never met a more uninhibited woman, and he'd enjoyed every minute of it.

He was falling for her, and it frightened him. She had fought him all along, letting him know from the beginning she would take no crap from him. There were times that he wondered who was really in charge at the office, but he had to admire her spirit and spunk.

Now, as he listened once more to her breathing, he wondered if Frankie had made love with him simply to fill her needs and nothing else. Would she be so accommodating with her emotions, with her heart?

When Matt awoke, he reached out and found Frankie's side of the bed empty. He glanced around the room. The bathroom door was slightly ajar, but the light was off, and there was no sound of the shower running. He climbed from the bed, found his boxers and slipped them on.

A note waited by the telephone.

You were sleeping like the dead, didn't want to wake you. Sissy picked me up. Hope you have a good day. F.

Matt frowned. *Hope you have a good day?* That was it?

He made coffee and drank it on the deck, pondering the situation. How could she have just left without saying goodbye, without letting him at least make her breakfast? He grumbled as he moved through the house, which suddenly felt empty without her. Damn. He was still grumbling to himself as he drained his cup, walked into the bathroom and turned on the shower.

"I'm not asking any questions," Sissy said as they turned into her driveway.

For that, Frankie was thankful. "Good. Because I don't have any answers."

"But for your information, I suspected you were with Matt. I've seen the way you look at each other."

Frankie paused with her hand on the door handle. "What are you talking about?"

"Aw, come on, girl, the guy is hot for you and you are for him."

Frankie said nothing.

Inside, the house smelled like disinfectant. "I've been cleaning since five-thirty this morning, which is the only reason I answered the phone when you called. Joe is stopping by for lunch."

"Is he nice?"

"Very. In every way. And don't look at me like that, I did *not* sleep with him on the first date. But I almost swooned when he kissed me good-night."

"I have to grab a shower and get out of here so I'm not late for work."

"What are you going to say to Matt when you see him?"

"What do you mean?"

"Well, you know. Things are a little different now."

"Not as far as I'm concerned. It'll be business as usual." Frankie headed for the bathroom for her shower.

Matt was waiting for Frankie when she arrived at the station. "Would you come in and close the door, please?"

"Certainly."

"Have a seat."

Frankie sat before him. It was hard to make eye contact after what had happened between them the night before, but she forced herself. "Yes?" she said when he didn't speak for a moment.

"You left this morning without saying goodbye."

"Did you see my note?"

"It's not really the same as a goodbye kiss."

"Chief, I'd rather not go into that at this time. I was hoping you'd have news on the Peters case."

"I was just wondering if you enjoyed yourself?"

"I would think the claw marks on your back and the bite mark on your inner thigh should be proof enough. Now, back to Mr. Peters."

He gazed at her for a moment. She had resumed her cool, no-nonsense attitude. "The autopsy results proved positive for arsenic poisoning. Earlene Peters's fingerprints were all over those handkerchiefs."

"Yes!"

"Cooter is obtaining a search warrant as we speak. I'd like for you to be there when we go in."

"No problem. I want to see the look on Earlene Peters's face when we serve her."

"Won't do much good to lock her up. Her attorney will have her out of there in five minutes flat."

"When are we going in?"

"Soon as Cooter gets back with the search warrant."

"I'm looking forward to it."

"Oh, by the way, Hep Whitfield called me from the pool hall. He knows who vandalized that house you and Cooter checked out."

"Oh, yeah?"

"He and the kid have already spoken with the owners. They agreed not to file charges and allow the boy to make restitution."

"Has Hep decided to become a social worker?" Frankie wished she could take back the words the minute they'd left her mouth. Matt frowned, and she didn't blame him. She was a smart-ass, simple as that.

"He's a good man, Frankie, and he's taken an interest in the teenagers in this town. I wish we had more people like him. Besides, the kid has never been in trouble before, and he's a straight-A student. He was trying to fit in with the wrong crowd. Did it on a dare. He returned the missing items."

"I'm sorry for mouthing off, Chief. I just blurt out things before I stop to think."

"Yeah, you do. You need someone like me in your life to teach you good old Southern manners."

"This is me you're talking to. I don't know the meaning of good manners."

There was a knock at the door. Cooter opened it and held up several papers. "Got it, Chief."

Matt stood. "Let's go."

Fourteen

Earlene Peters was in the middle of her bridge game when Matt knocked on her front door. Cooter and Frankie were right behind him. "Mrs. Peters, I have a search warrant signed by Judge Davies."

"A search warrant?" The woman looked as though she would drop into a dead faint. Several of the middle-aged ladies sitting at the card table in the living room joined her in the foyer.

"Is something wrong, Earlene?" one of them asked.

"They're going to search my house," she said, motioning toward Matt and the others.

"Whatever for?"

Earlene looked at them. "Whatever for?"

"Arsenic. We have reason to believe you were responsible for your husband's death."

"Murder," Frankie said.

Earlene's eyes rolled back in her head as she staggered. Matt caught her before she hit the floor, causing quite a stir among the ladies. He lifted Earlene and placed her on the sofa. "Earlene, open your eyes," he said, slapping her lightly on the cheek.

Her eyes popped open. She took a moment to gather herself together. Finally, she rose, and her shock turned to anger. "Chief Webber, you have just embarrassed me in front of all my friends. Search the place all you like, but you will not find what you're looking for. Now, if you'll excuse me, I'm going to call my attorney.''

Frankie looked at the group of women standing there, curiosity mixed with horror. ''You ladies may want to finish your bridge game another time,'' she said. ''I don't think Mrs. Peters is in the mood for company.''

Astonishment showed on their faces as they filed out the door, one by one, without a word.

John Zimmerman, Earlene's attorney, arrived in less than ten minutes. Matt and Frankie were searching the kitchen and laundry area, Cooter had gone out to the garage.

''Hello, John,'' Matt said, shaking the man's hand. ''I haven't seen you since the Jaycee barbecue.''

''Myra's pregnant, and she's been having a time of it. Doesn't much feel like going out these days.''

''Congratulations.''

Earlene cleared her throat. ''Excuse me, gentlemen, could we get on with this?''

The attorney nodded. ''Chief, I understand you've served Mrs. Peters with a search warrant.''

Matt handed him the papers. The other man looked through them and turned to Earlene. ''Mrs. Peters, everything seems to be in order here. You have no choice in the matter.''

She drew herself up sharply. ''Fine, let them search, but I want you here, because I plan to sue them for harassment as soon as this is over. Now, if you don't mind, I'd like to lie down.''

''Better lie on the sofa, Earlene,'' Matt said. ''We're going to have to search your bedroom, as well.''

''Then get on with it. The sooner you're out of here, the better.''

They searched for more than two hours. Frankie went through Earlene's bathroom, spooning talcum powder into plastic bags and marking them carefully. She checked beneath the cabinets, in all the drawers, and then went through the bedroom. She repeated her search in the guest baths and bedrooms. Damn, the woman had a big house. When she came downstairs, she found Cooter coming in through the back door, carrying more plastic bags. His uniform was filthy.

"I've looked through the garage and storage shed," he said. "Gathered everything I saw that could pass for arsenic in liquid or powder form."

Matt found Earlene's attorney in the dining room, briefcase open, talking on a cell phone and making notes on a yellow legal pad.

"We're finished here, John," Matt said. "Thanks for your cooperation."

"No problem, Matt. Would you notify me if you find something suspicious?"

"Sure thing." They shook hands. "Give Myra my best."

"Will do."

Earlene was sleeping on the sofa. Matt decided not to wake her. They filed through the front door and made for the patrol car, neither of them saying much. Back at the station, Matt shook his head at the sight of Cooter. "You look like you just crawled through gopher hole. Did you mark the evidence you collected?"

"Sure did, Chief."

"I'll take it to the crime lab. You need to go home and grab a shower."

Frankie followed Matt inside, and waited while he sifted through his messages.

Velma looked at the plastic bags they held. "Anything on the Peters case?"

"Still working on it."

"She wouldn't hurt Darnell, Chief. I know there's a big age difference, but Earlene loved that man dearly."

"Which explains why she seldom visited."

"She would have gone more, but he didn't want her to see him in that condition. Mr. Peters had his pride, you know."

"We'll see what happens," he replied. He started for the door leading to the back with Frankie behind him.

"Deputy Daniels?" Velma called out. "You have a message from your mother."

Frankie sighed and took the slip of paper Velma was holding out. She followed Matt to the crime lab. She had only been there a couple of times. It was minute compared to the one in Atlanta, and the cop inside was working on a crossword puzzle. "I've got something for you, Jennings," Matt said.

The other man looked up. "More tests for arsenic?"

"Yeah. How long will it take?"

"You got a lot of bags there, Chief."

"Call me when you're finished."

Matt and Frankie stepped into the hall. "Why don't we grab a quick lunch? I believe I heard your stomach growling on the way back."

"Lunch sounds good."

They notified Velma on their way out. "Radio me if something comes up," Matt said. "We won't be gone long."

Velma nodded.

Matt pulled into the Dairy Queen a few minutes later. "You know what I'm craving?" he said. "A foot-long hot dog with onions, chili and sauerkraut."

Frankie nodded. "I could go for that."

They went inside and ordered. Matt found a table and Frankie joined him. "So, what do you think?" he asked.

"About Earlene Peters? All the evidence points to her."

"It doesn't always work out that way, though. Notice she didn't seem the least bit concerned about us finding anything? She was more interested in suing our pants off."

"Maybe it was just her bitch act."

"Or maybe she didn't do it. Maybe we need to look elsewhere." Matt radioed Velma and asked for messages, then told her, "We're going to run over to the fertilizer plant and talk to a few people. We'll be back in an hour or so."

Jody Peters was eating a sandwich at his desk when Matt and Frankie arrived. He greeted them warmly, but there were dark circles beneath his eyes. "This is a coincidence," he said, once he had offered them a seat. "I just tried to reach your office, and Velma said you were headed out here."

"Was there anything specific you needed?" Matt asked.

"Well, I've tried to get information from Doc Linton at the morgue, but he's always tied up. I wanted to see if you had any news on the investigation."

"Jody, your dad tested positive for arsenic poisoning."

The man looked stunned. "Who would do something like that?"

"That's what we're trying to find out. We searched Mrs. Peters's house today."

"That must be why Earlene called. My secretary said I had an urgent message from her, but I haven't returned the call. Earlene thinks it's urgent if she finds a mouse in the house. Last time that happened, I was expected to run over there and catch it for her."

"What do you think of her?"

"I've never been crazy about her, but I would never have said anything to my dad and caused trouble between us. I guess my wife and I tolerated her. She has these highfalutin ways about her, you know?"

"Do you think she would poison your father?"

He looked shocked. "I don't know, Chief. Like I said, I can't imagine anyone wanting to hurt him. He was good to everybody. Earlene always treated him kindly, at least in front of me."

"Did you say Earlene once called you to catch a mouse?" Frankie asked.

Jody smiled. "Lord, that woman is terrified of them."

"Did she ask you to put poison out?"

"No, I set a couple of traps with peanut butter. Naturally, she called, all upset, when the trap got him. So I had to drive over there and dispose of the nasty thing."

"Tell me something, Jody," Matt said. "Who all stands to inherit money from your father's death?"

"Earlene, I suppose. And I know he's leaving a healthy portion to Piney Grove Nursing Home and to Shirley, as well, because she was so good to him. He told me that much. He settled with me when he gave me this plant so I wouldn't have to pay inheritance taxes. He was a generous man, always has been."

He grinned. "I don't think Earlene appreciated that side of him. From what I understand, she had it rough growing up, and I think she fears going hungry again. That's why she calls me to take care of her pest control, even though she can more than afford to pay a service. Of course, then she'll turn around and have the bakery make all these fancy finger sandwiches and pastries to serve her bridge club."

"You don't begrudge her for marrying your father?"

"My mother died when I was just a tyke. I don't remember her much. But I know my dad was lonely. Earlene was his secretary, and they just ended up together. There's a big age difference, but I think Earlene genuinely loved him, and she took good care of him before he went into the nursing home a few years ago.''

"Can you think of anyone else your father may or may not have settled with?" Frankie asked. "Or perhaps someone who thought your father owed them and didn't receive anything?"

"I don't know what all he gave away. I know the employees here got a generous bonus, depending on how long they'd worked here. I'm sure he took care of his friends."

"What about Blaine Freeman?"

Jody nodded. "Oh, Dad settled with Mr. Freeman long ago, about the same time he did with me. I remember Mr. Freeman showing up in my office with tears in his eyes, and the check in his hand."

"Do you remember what the amount was for?"

"One million dollars. The exact amount I received, except I was given the plant, as well."

"That's a lot of money," Matt said.

"Blaine Freeman was like a brother to my father, and he ran this company right alongside him. My dad was president, and Mr. Freeman was his VP." Jody reached for a photograph. "This is him with my dad and me on a hunting trip." He put the photo back. "I've been on the phone with Mr. Freeman on and off since it happened. He's taking it real hard. That's one of the reasons I haven't had a chance to return Earlene's call."

"You seem to be handling it okay," Frankie said.

His look sobered. "It broke my heart at first. I mean, he was my best friend, too. My dad took a lot of pride in himself, and he hated being incapacitated or having strangers wipe his behind like they did one time at the hospital. He said he'd rather be shot than have to go through something like that again.'' Jody glanced at the photograph of his father and touched it, as though reaching out for the man himself. ''He's in a better place now.''

''I know you miss him,'' Matt said. When the other man nodded, Matt went on. ''Wonder if you'd do me a favor and give me Blaine Freeman's address and phone number.''

''You don't suspect him of anything?'' Jody said, shocked.

''Oh, no, nothing like that. But he may have some ideas on the case that would help us.''

Jody flipped through an address book and began scribbling the number. ''Just go easy on him, Chief. He's not really stable right now, and the last time I spoke with him I think he may have been drinking.''

''Is he a heavy drinker?''

''At one time. But he joined AA some twenty years ago and stopped.'' He handed them a card. ''How long do you expect the investigation to last? Earlene's got her caterer on standby, says she plans to send my daddy off in style.''

Matt replied, ''We'll be in touch,'' then he and Frankie left the building and made for the patrol car. ''What do you think?'' Matt asked.

''I don't think he's taking it that hard.''

''Sometimes death brings relief.''

Frankie pondered it. ''I suppose if someone has suffered a long time.'' Her mind was working. ''Have there been any other suspicious deaths at Piney Grove Nursing Home?''

''None. I don't know anyone on that staff who would so much as snap at a patient.''

Blaine Freeman lived in a simple brick ranch-style house that was reminiscent of the late sixties. The grass was neatly trimmed, the sidewalk and driveway edged, and an older model Ford sat in the driveway. Frankie followed Matt up the front walk. "For an ex-VP and a millionaire, Mr. Freemam doesn't exactly live high on the hog."

"Darnell Peters didn't move into his grand house until after he married Earlene. You'd be surprised how many rich folks don't care about money. They just work hard and live simply, tucking the money away until one day they have more than they ever dreamed."

Matt knocked on the door several times, but there was no answer. "Let's look around back." The screen door leading to an enclosed porch was ajar. Matt stepped inside and banged on the back door, trying to peer through a curtained window. They waited. From inside, they heard a moan. "Someone's in there." Matt banged harder. They heard glass shattering, then someone cried out.

"I'm going in," Matt said, twisting the knob. Surprisingly enough, it was unlocked.

Frankie followed. The smell of whiskey assailed her as she entered the kitchen, the counters lined with empty whiskey bottles and plates of uneaten food. She followed Matt down a short hall and into a bedroom that smelled of urine and dirty clothing. A man was sprawled on the bed, dirty and disheveled, his white hair standing up in tufts. He held a whiskey bottle in one hand, a broken glass in the other. Blood dripped from his palm.

"Are you Mr. Freeman?" Matt inquired.

The man looked up, as if suddenly realizing he wasn't alone. "I'm bleeding." He slurred his words badly.

Frankie found the bathroom and gathered up peroxide, gauze and bandages. While Matt questioned the man, she cleaned the wound. "It's not deep," she said.

Mr. Freeman watched her as if in a daze. "Why are you here?" he asked. "Am I in trouble?"

Matt looked at him sharply. "Why would you be in trouble?"

The man shook his head and lay back on a pillow. "Trouble everywhere these days. Everywhere you look."

Matt and Frankie glanced at each other. The man wasn't making sense.

"Jody Peters was worried about you," Matt said. "He asked us to look in on you. Said you'd been upset ever since Darnell died."

"I don't want to talk about Darnell," Freeman said loudly, angrily.

Matt was undeterred. "I have a few questions to ask you. You can either answer them here or at the police station."

Freeman closed his eyes. Tears streamed from each corner. "Darnell was the best friend I've ever had."

"Jody told us," Frankie said softly, once she'd bandaged the wound. "That's why we're hoping you can help us. Your friend was poisoned, Mr. Freeman. You may be able to give us information."

"I can't help anybody," he all but wailed. "I can't even help myself."

Frankie noticed how thin he looked. His face hung in folds. "How long since you've eaten, Mr. Freeman?"

He looked at her. Red veins stood out in the whites of his eyes. "I don't remember." He sighed. "I can't hold food down."

Matt noted the empty bottles. On a desk sat a wide round vase filled with colorful chips that resembled poker chips. Matt recognized them as AA chips. There were dozens of blue chips, signifying years of sobriety. "Looks like you're doing okay in the booze department."

The man looked ashamed. "I only meant to take one. One turned into another."

"How long have you been on this binge?"

"Ever since Darnell died."

Frankie patted his hand. "What do you think Darnell would say if he were able to see you right now?"

Freeman buried his head in his hands and began to cry. "He's the one who helped me get sober in the first place. I reckon he would jerk me up by my collar and drag me to a meeting. I just don't feel strong enough right now."

"Everyone has to deal with loss at one time or another," Frankie said. "And it's hard, Mr. Freeman. It's one of the most difficult things we have to go through. But we have to go on." She wondered if she was trying to convince him or herself.

"You don't understand," he said, and started to cry.

"Understand what?"

"I can't live like this. I never wanted to go through with it, but I swore on an oath I'd do it, and now I have to live with it."

Frankie and Matt exchanged glances.

"What was it you never wanted to go through, Mr. Freeman?" Matt asked. "Why are you trying to drink yourself to death?"

The man looked up at them, misery lining his face, the pain in his eyes so intense it seemed to have sucked all the life out of him. "I killed him." He burst into tears.

Fifteen

Frankie put on coffee and made a sandwich. When she reentered the bedroom she found Matt had brought in a washcloth and towel and was in the process of cleaning up the man.

Freeman was trembling so badly he couldn't hold his coffee cup. Frankie held it to his lips so he could sip it slowly. Then she broke off part of his sandwich, but he turned his head. "I'm not hungry."

"You need to get something into your stomach, sir."

Matt scooted a chair close to the bed. "Mr. Freeman, we're going to get you to the hospital in a minute. I have a couple of questions, but I'll wait to follow up when you're in better shape. Would you like to call your attorney first?"

Freeman nodded.

"I understand you and Mr. Peters were best friends."

"For almost eighty years." He looked sad. "Neither of us expected to live this long. Nobody should be forced to live this long when all they do is hurt." He looked up. "I was his best man both times he married. I watched him marry his first wife and bury her while Jody was still in diapers. And I pretended to be happy when he told me he planned to marry Earlene years later. I didn't give a hill of beans for that woman, but Darnell never knew it. I just wanted him to be happy."

Frankie held the cup to his lips once more and he took another sip. He gagged and looked as though he might go into a spasm. "Pour some whiskey into his coffee," Matt said, afraid the man would go into convulsions before they could get him into detox.

Frankie did as she was told. Freeman managed to take a long sip of the coffee.

"If you loved him so much, why did you kill him?" Matt asked.

The old man looked right into Matt's eyes. "He asked me to."

"And you just agreed to do it?"

"Hell, no, I didn't agree. But he kept after me. He'd already spent two and a half years in Piney Grove, and he knew he wasn't getting any better. Told me about patients who'd been in there for five or six years or more. Parts of their bodies had become deformed because they'd laid in bed so long, even though the staff was careful to turn them.

"He'd had enough, Chief, and that's all there was to it. He felt bad all the time, hated being incapacitated. Got to where it was too much trouble to be wheeled outside. Darnell was a proud man. Said it was no kind of life. He didn't speak to me for months when I refused to help him. Finally, I agreed. He would have done the same for me."

"Where did you get the arsenic?"

Freeman didn't so much as flinch. "At the plant. I go in every so often just to bug people or take cookies. It's boring around here now that my wife and most of my friends are gone. People at the plant act like it's no big deal, and I can go anywhere I like. I packed some arsenic in a couple of pill boxes on the dresser there and carried them with me to the hospital."

"You dusted the handkerchiefs?"

He nodded. "I wanted to give him one big lethal dose and get it over with, but he was afraid folks would get suspicious, so I took my time."

He started to cry. "When I noticed he was getting sick, I told him I was pulling out, but he pleaded with me, Chief. He begged me to see it through and I did." Tears streamed down the man's face. "Because I loved him."

Matt and Frankie sat there quietly for a moment as he sobbed. Frankie reached for a box of tissues and handed it to him. She felt sorry for Freeman, despite the fact he'd taken his friend's life. She had investigated assisted suicides before. She wondered if people like Darnell realized what they put family members and friends through when they asked for that one last favor.

"Call for an ambulance," Matt told her.

Once Freeman had calmed down, Matt helped him into his shoes. "Mr. Freeman, I'm afraid I'm going to have to arrest you for the murder of Darnell Peters. I'm not going to cuff you, and you'll be put in the hospital instead of jail, but I'll have to put a deputy at your door until we get things straightened out. Are you sober enough so that you can understand everything I'm telling you, because I'm going to have to read you your rights?"

Freeman nodded sadly.

Frankie was quiet on the ride back to the station. She stared out the window, watching the passing scenery, thinking of Blaine Freeman. What would she have done under the circumstances?

"You okay?" Matt asked, noting her silence.

She sighed, feeling as though her insides were lined with lead. The whole episode had left her depressed. "I don't think he should have been arrested."

"He took a person's life."

"He was Peters's best friend. He was acting out of love."

"Would you have done the same thing?"

She looked at him. He had read her thoughts. "I've been wondering. If someone I loved was wasting away in a nursing home, without hopes of getting better, and they were in constant pain—" She paused. "I honestly don't know what I'd do."

Matt stared at the road before him. "I'm not saying I don't sympathize with Mr. Freeman, but he committed murder. A judge will have to decide his fate."

"What if it had been Mandy? Would you have allowed her to suffer because you couldn't live with the guilt of helping her end it?" Frankie cursed herself silently the moment the question left her lips.

"I will never know the answer to that question," he said sharply. "Mandy died before I had a chance to say goodbye."

Frankie pressed her fingers against her forehead. "I'm sorry, Matt. That was a shitty thing to ask."

"Yes, it was. Very shitty."

"I said I was sorry." She felt miserable.

Matt gripped the steering wheel tightly. "Do you think I *wanted* to arrest Freeman? What do you take me for, some kind of hard-ass who doesn't care about people's feelings? I care a lot, Frankie, but the man committed a crime, and like it or not, I have to follow the law."

"I've seen you bend the law."

"Not on murder charges. Besides, I think Freeman would have ended up killing himself with booze within a matter of days or weeks." He looked at her. "The judge will go easy on him, Frankie. Blaine Freeman will get the help he needs."

"Think, Matt. Darnell Peters gave him one million dollars. It's going to look like Peters paid him to do it."

"That money was handed over before Peters moved into the nursing home. He settled with Jody as well."

She didn't respond.

They arrived back at the station. Matt pulled into his slot and parked. "Look at me, Frankie."

She turned and met his gaze. "What?"

"Do you trust me?"

She shrugged. "Yes, I suppose."

He looked offended. "You *suppose?*"

"Okay, yes."

"Then let me say this much. Blaine Freeman will not spend one night in jail. You have my word."

"But—"

"Trust me."

She did. "I believe you."

"Are you planning on dropping by the house later?"

Frankie was surprised by the abrupt change of subject. "I don't know. I don't think that's a good idea. The first time it just happened. I don't think we should get into the habit of planning something. It seems like…I don't know. Like we're sneaking around."

"Is seven o'clock good for you?"

She reached for the door handle. "Yeah, that'll work."

Frankie arrived home and found Sissy lying in her bed wearing her bathrobe, eyes red and swollen. An empty wineglass sat on her bedside table. "What's wrong?"

"Nothing's wrong. Except, once again, I made a fool and a slut out of myself today."

"What are you talking about?"

"Joe's getting ready to leave town for the weekend, and he wanted to spend the day with me. Here. In bed."

"Okay, so?"

"He's going home this weekend for his wedding."

"Oh, damn."

"Yeah, ain't that special?"

"He told you this?"

"He kept getting beeped. Seemed his fiancée was worried he wouldn't make it back in time for the wedding rehearsal and dinner."

"He told you all this?" she repeated.

"He made the call in the kitchen. He was very sneaky about it, closed the bedroom door so I wouldn't overhear. I thought it odd so I picked up the phone in here and listened to every word."

"You eavesdropped?"

"Damn right. The guy couldn't seem to get enough of me. I mean, I'm going to have to take a sitz bath after today. He used me."

Frankie sat on the bed. "So why are you blaming yourself? The man's a jerk. You're lucky to be rid of him."

"Don't you get it, Frankie? I have a reputation in this town. I'm easy."

"That's bullshit. You've obviously had too much to drink."

"You're not that naive. I am what I am. Just look how I make my living. I talk dirty to old men on the telephone so they can get off. I'm no better than a paid whore."

"I'm not going to listen to you put yourself down. I hope you kicked him out on his royal ass."

"Damn right I did. *After* I slapped him from here to kingdom come. Left claw marks on his handsome face. He's going to have a tough time explaining *that* to his bride." More tears.

"Stop feeling sorry for yourself, Sissy. She's the one

we should take pity on.'' Frankie picked up the wineglass. ''I'm going to make you something to eat.''

''I'm not hungry. I just want to go to bed. I've already popped a sleeping pill. Hoping I'll wake up and discover it was all a bad dream.''

''You took a sleeping pill on top of wine?''

''I do it all the time. Works quicker that way.''

Frankie shook her head sadly. ''I'm still going to make you something to eat.'' As she made her way to the kitchen, she experienced that leaden feeling in the pit of her stomach again.

Frankie arrived at Matt's shortly before eight and explained why she was late. He looked concerned.

''I knew she tended to drink too much at times, but I had no idea she was mixing pills with it. What do you think brought it on?''

''A man, what else? Joe whatever-his-name used her like a blowup doll all day, but he forgot to mention he was getting married this weekend. Bastard. Just another man out to get laid.''

''Hold on, Frankie.''

''Why should I? It's the truth, isn't it? Tell me something, what was the first thing you noticed about me when we met?''

He smiled. ''You want the truth?'' She nodded. ''I liked your butt.''

''There you have it.''

''Does that make me weird?''

''No, it means you're like every other man on this planet. Do you know what a woman notices first? A man's eyes.''

Matt smiled as he took in her tight jeans and sweater. ''If you wanted me to notice your eyes you shouldn't have dressed like that.'' She opened her mouth to respond, but he held his hand up. ''But that's only part of it. There's a lot more to you than your physical side. You're witty and intelligent and spirited. And yes, I've noticed your eyes. They're beautiful. As well as your hair.''

She closed her mouth. It felt good to be complimented as a woman instead of a deputy. But she couldn't get Sissy off her mind. She knew what it was like being used.

''A man will say anything to get what he wants.''

''Is that what you think?''

''I know.''

''Look, I'm not going to be the kicking post for Connors or this Joe guy. Sissy has a habit of choosing the wrong kind of men.''

''Where are the good ones?''

''You're looking at one of them. Now, do you want to stand there and stew over something that has nothing to do with us or do you want to help me with dinner?''

''Who said anything about dinner?''

''I figured you'd be hungry. I'm marinating steaks, and I've already put potatoes in the oven to bake. All you have to do is make the salad.''

''I wasn't planning on staying for dinner.''

''I just assumed—''

''You assumed wrong. We're adults, I think you know the real reason I showed up.''

''You're not using me just for sex, are you?'' This time he looked amused.

''Don't act like you haven't done the same thing.''

''What if we discover there's more to it?''

Frankie felt something flutter in her stomach. ''That isn't going to happen.''

Their gazes locked, and Matt saw the determination in

her look. She tried so hard to be tough. Was she so scared that she couldn't let her guard down for one moment?

"Okay, Frankie," he said, deciding to play her game. He began unbuttoning his shirt. "You came here to get laid. Let's do it."

Frankie followed him into the bedroom, where the covers were still in disarray. "You forgot to make your bed."

Matt kicked off his shoes and dispensed with his socks. "I figured there was no sense making it seeing as how we were going to mess it up again, anyway." He shrugged out of his shirt and unzipped his pants. "Why aren't you undressing?"

Without hesitating, Frankie stripped down to nothing. She saw his look of appreciation as he removed his boxers. He sat on the bed and pulled her between his thighs. He was already hard. "I like your style," he said, cupping her hips and pulling her closer so he could tongue one nipple.

"My style?"

"You know what you want and you go after it. A man doesn't have to send you flowers or buy chocolates, silly little things that don't mean much to begin with."

Frankie blinked rapidly as he moved to her other breast, but it was difficult to concentrate as her body began to respond to his touch. He pulled her onto his lap and kissed her hard, hungrily. He laid her gently on the bed and wasted no time, tonguing her navel and the downy curls between her thighs, before taking her. His entry almost took her breath away. He thrust deeply, prodding her on.

"Come on, baby," he said, almost gritting his teeth as he looked down at her flushed face. "This is what you came for."

Frankie did as she was told, and he pushed harder,

faster. Her orgasm was powerful and mind-boggling. Matt shuddered violently before rolling off of her. They lay on their backs, staring at the ceiling, waiting for their breathing to become steady again.

"I could get used to this," Matt said, sitting and reaching for his boxers. "You sure know how to make a man burn."

Frankie glanced his way, wishing he would stay with her for a moment. Some of her anger had dissipated and she wanted to reach out, but he was already standing. "Are you planning to shower here or wait till you get home?"

Was he trying to get rid of her so quickly? She wanted to talk, but he didn't seem to be in the mood. "I'll wait. Would you hand me my clothes?"

He tossed them to her. "I don't want to appear rude, but I'm going to light the grill. I'm hungry."

"You're going to light the grill in your underwear?"

"I'm surrounded by woods. Who's going to see?"

Frankie watched him go, feeling both a sense of relief and loss as he went. Well, what did she expect? She had pretty much laid out the rules. He was simply following her lead. They had filled a need in each other, and now it was time for her to go.

So why did she suddenly feel so empty?

She found him in the kitchen drinking water. She didn't quite meet his gaze. "I'm going now."

He appeared indifferent. "Hey, thanks for stopping by. You know you're always welcome."

She nodded. "Matt, I may have overreacted."

He put his hands on her shoulders. "You don't owe me an explanation, okay? We both had a good time, and that's what counts."

Frankie squared her shoulders. "Later, then." She left

him in the kitchen and made for the front door without looking back. Hot tears stung the backs of her eyes as she got into her car and drove away. She felt dirty. Used. Matt had not made love to her as he had the night before. He had not cuddled her and held her against his chest. He had not kissed her hair.

Well, why should he? The man realized he was wasting his time, that's all there was to it. She had already told him she was incapable of love, of having a relationship, so he had obliged her with good sex and sent her on her way.

What man wouldn't agree to such a plan? Matt had confessed he found the thought of flowers and chocolates silly and unnecessary. Why waste time on the niceties when they weren't needed? Both of them knew what they wanted, simple as that.

Yet, it wasn't so simple. Frankie felt no different than she had after sleeping with Jim Connors, and that's what hurt worst of all. She respected Matt, not only as a cop, but as a man. And he'd respected her in the same vein.

The tears streamed down her cheeks. Frankie only managed to get halfway down the road before she gave in to them. What the hell was wrong with her? Why had she gone to Matt's in the first place? She had ruined everything. If Matt had seemed cool and distant, it was because he was protecting himself, just as she was.

She folded her arms on the steering wheel and sat there with the engine running. Would there ever come a time when she could accept love or kindness from another human being without distrusting their motives? Had she seen so much ugliness in the world that she had forgotten good people still existed? She had trouble loving her own mother, for heaven's sake.

There was something wrong with her, some deficiency,

perhaps some genetic disorder. Or maybe she was going crazy. She had no idea where she belonged anymore. Her half-written resignation was still lying in her desk drawer at the station, and she had not bothered to put together a résumé. She had no place to go and no idea where to look.

She was vaguely aware of the sound of an approaching vehicle. She turned her head in the opposite direction, hoping the passing motorist would not stop and ask if she was having car trouble. The last thing she needed was for someone to see Purdyville's newest deputy in the throes of a nervous breakdown. She heard a door slam. "Shit," she muttered under her breath, wiping her eyes.

"Frankie?" Matt's voice was soft.

She refused to look his way.

"Are you having car trouble?"

"Nothing I can't handle."

"Look at me."

"No."

"Look at me, dammit!"

She turned and glared. "What!"

"You've been crying."

"So?"

He leaned inside her window. "You're a real piece of work, hotshot, you know that?"

"Go away, Matt."

"No way, kiddo. I'm not letting you get away. I'm going to get inside that head of yours if it kills me."

"Why?"

"Because I—" He paused. "Because I have no choice. You mean more to me than anything else in this world or I wouldn't put up with half the crap you dish out. Maybe I'm crazy, but I think there's a chance for us."

She couldn't think of a response.

"We've had a bad day, Frankie. Let's go back to my

place and start over. I want to make dinner for you. I want
to cuddle on the sofa and talk. I want to make love to
you, but I refuse to reenact what just happened between
us. I want to hold you and talk to you because, oddly
enough, I'm interested in more than a piece of ass.''

"How do I know that?''

"Today you said you trusted me when I told you I'd
make sure Blaine Freeman wouldn't go to jail. You're
going to have to trust me again.''

She shook her head. "It's so hard.''

"I know, baby, and I wouldn't ask if I weren't serious.
Come back and spend the evening with me. Hell, spend
the night, that's even better.''

"I'm scared.'' There, she had admitted it.

His eyes softened. "You don't have to be afraid anymore.''

Sixteen

"Now, here are the ingredients for the salad," Matt said. "Everything has already been washed. Do you think you can handle it?"

She gave him her eat-dirt-and-die look.

"I'll take that as a yes."

Frankie began to tear the greens into bite-size pieces and drop them into a large wooden bowl. "I never really learned to cook," she confessed. "But I can tune my own car, if money is tight and I can't afford to take it in."

"I'll remember that."

"I can tell you're impressed."

He glanced at her. "I like an independent woman who can take care of herself but doesn't hesitate to ask for help if she needs it."

"Yes, well, that's a little difficult for me."

"It's only difficult if you allow it to be. There's nothing wrong with asking for help now and then. It doesn't make you a needy person. We all need a helping hand once in a while."

Frankie supposed he was right. "My mother was very needy, always expecting some man to take care of her."

"Is that why you don't like her?"

"It's not that I don't like her. It's just—she meddles in my business too much. I'm supposed to account for my every move. I have to back off from time to time because she can be suffocating. I know it has to do with losing my dad. She's afraid of loss."

"That's normal, don't you think?"

Frankie wondered if he was thinking about his sister. "To an extent. But there comes a time when you have to let go."

"Have you let go of losing your father?"

Frankie looked up, caught off guard by the question. She had just criticized her mother for fearing loss when she feared the same thing. Hadn't fear of loss kept her from forming lasting relationships? "I still miss him," she confessed.

"You need to slice that celery a little thinner, Deputy Daniels."

"Who's doing this, you or me?"

He turned and looked at her, an amused smile in his eyes. "I have a similar question. What are you doing to me?"

She glanced up. "Bringing confusion into your life?"

"Other than that."

"I'm not sure I understand the question."

"You understand. I want to know how things stand between us."

She paused. "Matt—"

"The truth."

"Okay." She put her knife down. "I care about you more than I should. I think about you more than I should. When I moved here, having a relationship with a man was the last thing on my mind. But I feel comfortable with you. It's just happening too fast."

"I think about you, too." He took her in his arms, and their gazes met. "Listen, I don't expect you to fall in love with me right away, but would you please at least let me in?"

"Let you in?" She was confused.

"In your head and in your heart. Can you trust me enough to allow me that much?"

She grinned. "You don't ask for much."

"We'll take it slow. Baby steps. Just don't shut me out, Frankie."

"What about our jobs?"

"I want you to keep working with me. You're too good at what you do to give it up, and I need someone with your experience. We'll just have to try to remain professional at the office, although I think a few people probably suspect something is going on between us. There won't be a problem unless we let personal feelings get in the way of our work."

"It won't be easy."

"But we can do it. It's worth it." She felt good against him. He would have loved nothing better than to sweep her up and carry her into the bedroom. "I'd better put on the steaks before things get out of hand."

"You're assuming we'll end up in the sack. Your ego is as big as your—" She stopped herself.

He arched both brows. "You were about to say?"

"Forget it, Webber."

"Why, Miss Daniels, I believe you're blushing. And what a pretty sight it is to behold." He picked up a dish towel, swung it around and snapped it in the air. "I have ways of making people talk."

"You wouldn't dare."

"You're right. I don't want to bruise that delicious fanny of yours."

"The steaks?"

"Oh, yeah." He disappeared out the back door and lit the grill. Damned if the woman didn't get to him in every way. And he couldn't seem to get enough of her. If only he could gain her trust. But he wouldn't push and risk losing her. It was obvious she needed more time. He wanted to do it right.

Frankie finished up the salad, but her mind wasn't on it. She became flushed all over each time Matt looked at her, each time he put his arms around her. She felt safe with him. For the first time in her life, she wanted to open up, share that part of her that she had done everything in her power to protect. Of course, it could leave her vulnerable. Thinking of Sissy, she wondered if she was doing the right thing by giving Matt so much power over her heart.

They dined, upon Matt's insistence, by candlelight, in the large dining room he claimed he never used. Frankie wished she'd dressed up a bit instead of wearing her jeans and sweater, but the way Matt looked at her, she decided it didn't matter.

"I have never tasted a better piece of meat," she confessed. "Everything is delicious."

"I'm pretty good on the grill, if I may say so myself."

"Did you and Jenna grill out much?" Now, what had gone and made her ask a question like that?

If Matt was surprised, he didn't show it. "Not as much as I'd have liked. Jenna had her heart on making senior partner, which meant she had to put in a lot of hours to prove herself."

"Did she make it?"

"Yeah."

"I'm sure it meant a lot to her."

"It did. She put herself through college and law school. Despite the scholarships she was awarded, she'll probably spend the rest of her life paying on her student loans."

Frankie took another bite of her steak. She suddenly

felt insignificant compared to the woman Matt had asked to marry. "She must've been smart."

He stopped eating and smiled. "You're asking a lot of questions about my ex-fiancée. I'll bet your next question will be if she was good in bed."

Frankie pretended to be insulted. "Of course not."

"You're dying to know, Daniels. Don't pretend otherwise."

"It has crossed my mind," she replied with a shrug. "I mean, if she was so smart and beautiful, not to mention all her other assets, I'm surprised you let her go."

He took her hand and gazed into her eyes. "Frankie, you are without a doubt the best lover I've ever had. It has to do with chemistry. Don't think for a minute I'm not curious about your past lovers, but in the end I'd rather not know." He let go of her hand. "I admired Jenna for her achievements, but I suspected no matter how well she did it would never be enough. And I didn't see myself becoming a top priority in her life."

"But her career meant a lot to her."

"That's true. We all have goals, Frankie, but your mate should come first. I'm sorry if that sounds selfish, but it's the way I feel."

"As long as the other person doesn't feel smothered."

"Love is supposed to enhance your life, not hinder it."

She pondered that as they finished their meal and carried the dishes into the kitchen. Frankie stepped outside for a cigarette while Matt loaded the dishwasher. She thought about her mother.

Perhaps the woman hadn't been as needy as Frankie had thought. Maybe she had loved the men in her life and had only sought to make them as happy as they made her. If she thought back, she clearly remembered how her mother would sit up all night for her father, waiting for him with a snack. If he got a call at dawn, Eve made sure he had a thermos of coffee and a slice of pound cake to take with him, although he fussed at her for getting up. Eve had taken care of everything: the yard work and housework, budgeting and paying bills, seeing that the family car was taken in for repairs, running errands, cooking her husband's favorite meals so that his time off was his own. She took an hour for herself near the end of the day, at which time she bathed, changed into a pretty dress and met him at the door with a kiss and dinner on the table.

Frankie's ideas were different from her mother's. She believed a man and woman should have a little space, to accomplish those things that were important to them, instead of the woman devoting every waking moment to her family.

The back door opened and Matt stepped outside. Frankie stubbed out her cigarette in a metal ashtray. He stepped behind her and slipped his arms around her waist and nuzzled the nape of her neck. "You know what I was thinking we might do?"

Frankie suspected she knew the answer. "Tell me."

"I thought we might curl up on the bed and watch a video. I rented a couple just in case."

Frankie tried to hide her surprise. Jim Connors had never watched videos with her, and he had never prepared dinner for her. She would never again compare the two men. "That sounds nice."

"You can wear one of my T-shirts to sleep in, and there's an extra toothbrush in the bathroom with your name on it."

"You've thought of everything."

"Not everything, Miss Daniels. I'm still trying to figure

out how to make you fall in love with me. Not right this minute, but I want it to happen in the very near future.''

Frankie leaned against him, loving the feel of him, the heat from his body. ''Oh, Matt,'' she said with a sigh. ''You make me feel so special.''

''Silly woman. You *are* special, and you know it. You're still reacting from what happened in Atlanta.''

''I'm trying to get past it, but it's not going to happen overnight. I felt I'd been cheated, not only by losing my job, but as a woman as well. I should have been more cautious.''

''What you should do is stop blaming yourself. Some men can be very persuasive.''

''What about you?''

''I haven't always been honest with women, Frankie. I've said things I didn't mean because I thought that's what they wanted to hear. But after seeing how deeply hurt you were over being treated dishonestly, I feel guilty as hell about it.'' He pulled her closer. ''I can't change the past. All I can do is try to be a better man in the future.''

''Don't ever do that to me—say things you think I want to hear.''

''Are you kidding? I have too much at stake here. Besides, you'd pistol whip me if you found out.''

They went inside. Matt cut the lights. In the bathroom, Frankie pulled on Matt's T-shirt and brushed her teeth. He waited until she was finished before doing the same. He shoved a video into the VCR and hit several buttons. Frankie tried not to notice how good he looked, the way the muscles in his back and shoulders flexed each time he moved. She was as fascinated with his body as she was with the man.

Curled in Matt's arms, Frankie fell asleep halfway

through the movie. Matt chuckled and turned it off. He much preferred snuggling against her soft body than watching a movie. He buried his face in her hair. She made a sound in her sleep, and he smiled. He could get used to this.

When Matt awoke the following morning, he found Frankie had turned on her side and kicked off the covers during the night. His T-shirt had crept above her waist, leaving her long legs and behind exposed. His body responded immediately.

He moved closer and nibbled an earlobe. She made a noise but didn't wake. He ran his finger lazily down the small of her back before palming the swell of one hip.

"Cut it out" came a sleepy voice.

He smiled and nuzzled her neck, where her hair had fallen away during the night. He inched his fingers between her thighs and sought the little bud that seemed to bring her so much pleasure when he tongued it. She squirmed. He feather-touched it and felt her arch against his hand. He stroked it until she became fully aroused, then dipped his finger inside and closed his eyes when he found her wet.

"I want to taste you," he said.

"I'm asleep."

"You're hot and wet, and you want me as badly as I want you. Face it."

Frankie turned over. She stroked his dark hair, letting it slide through her fingers. He stroked her thighs, and she sucked in her breath. He parted them.

"Show me where you want me to lick you."

Unabashed, Frankie reached down and opened herself to him. "Here," she said.

He touched her gently with the tip of his tongue and heard her gasp. He slid his hands beneath her hips and lifted her, covering her with his mouth so that he could taste as much of her as he liked. Her scent made him dizzy. He dipped his tongue between the pouting lips and Frankie moaned aloud and grasped his head. She rode his mouth, losing herself when the sensations became too much. Her orgasm was powerful, and she quaked from the intensity.

"Lie back," she said, pushing against his chest so that he had no choice. She kissed him once before running her tongue across each nipple, dipping inside his navel and finally lower. Matt groaned aloud as he felt her lips and tongue on him. She teased the ridge of his penis, paying special attention to the underside where he was most sensitive. Just when he thought he could handle no more pleasure, she put him in her mouth.

"Oh, Frankie." Her name was a half-choked gasp.

Frankie slid her lips as far down as she could go, wrapping her fingers tightly against the base of his penis. She moved slowly at first, loving the taste and texture of him.

"Baby, I want to be inside of you. Please." It was the plea of a dying man.

Frankie lay down and opened herself to him once more. His thrust was hard and deep, taking her breath away. She cupped his hips as they moved against each other, slowly at first, until each of them lost control. They climaxed together. Frankie wrapped her legs around his waist as he emptied himself inside of her, riding the wave of heat that pulsed through her body.

Afterward, he took her in his arms. Their breathing was ragged, their bodies sweat-soaked. The erotic smell of their coupling lingered. Matt raked his hand through his hair and found it wet.

"Woman, what are you doing to me?" he demanded.

"I could ask you the same question."

"We're good together, babe."

He spoke the truth. "Yeah, and we're also late for work."

Frankie arrived home to find Sissy lying on the sofa with an ice pack on her eyes. "How are you feeling?" she asked.

"Like shit. And you?"

"You're giving this Joe guy far too much power, you know. He isn't worth it."

"Easy for you to say. You've got the most eligible bachelor in town wrapped around your little finger."

"It's not about men, Sissy. I've spent a lot of time alone, believe me."

"Weren't you lonely?"

"I had my bad days. Why else would I have gotten involved with a married man? I must have been desperate at the time or I would have seen the warning signals. Or maybe I saw them and chose to ignore them, I don't know. I would hate to think I had intentionally become involved with a man with a wife and three kids. But the answer to your question is yes. I have been lonely. So lonely that even my skin ached."

Sissy struggled with her words. "I wish I would die, Frankie. I mean, I wouldn't do anything so stupid as to take my own life, but what have I really got to live for?"

Frankie realized the depths of her friend's despair. "You've got plenty to live for, Sissy, namely yourself. Why don't you talk to Alice?"

"Alice Chalmers?" Sissy gave a snort. "Why should I want to take my troubles to someone who has it made? She's got a handsome husband who loves her more than life itself. She's got a career and makes good money. Her life is perfect. I have nothing."

"Nobody has a perfect life." Frankie walked into the kitchen and dialed Matt's number. He was getting ready to walk out the door. "I'm going to be a little late this morning," she said.

"Is Sissy having a tough time?" he asked.

"Yes."

"She goes through this every once in a while. Stay with her as long as you need to."

Frankie hung up the phone and put on a pot of coffee. She returned to the living room and sat on the sofa beside her friend. "What do you enjoy doing most?"

"Do we have to have this discussion right now?"

"Surely you have some kind of hobby."

The woman sighed and motioned toward a brochure on the coffee table. "I used to like participating in the little local theater. They're holding auditions this week for *Steel Magnolias*. I usually get the lead role because nobody else can act their way out of a paper bag."

"Sounds like you need to go to the audition."

"I've lost interest, Frankie."

"I could go with you. I've never acted before, but hey, I could do something backstage, maybe."

"Does this mean you're going to stay in Purdyville?"

"I haven't really made up my mind, but I'm going to give it a chance."

"Matt is worth it, Frankie."

"It's not just Matt. I think I need to take time to see what I really want."

"You need to go to work instead of baby-sitting me."

Frankie was torn. The woman appeared to be so despondent. And Frankie suspected there were more tranquilizers in the house. "Promise me something, Sissy. Stay off the pills and booze today and don't do anything to hurt yourself."

"I'm not stupid. Well, maybe a little stupid where men are concerned. Now, get out of here so I can feel sorry for myself a little while longer."

Frankie felt better as she showered for work.

Seventeen

Matt called Frankie into his office as soon as she arrived. "Is everything okay with Sissy?"

"She'll be okay. I asked her to call me if she needed to talk." Frankie told him about the auditions the little theater was holding. "Perhaps it will take her mind off her problems."

"And keep you in Purdyville longer."

"I've decided to hold off on my resignation, if that's okay with you. Unless you've already found my replacement."

"You can't be replaced. Any particular reason for your decision?"

"I know you think it has everything to do with you."

"Aw, so my assumption was correct."

She was accustomed to his wit by now and ignored it. "Actually, I'm trying to find myself."

"Are you lost?"

"I think I have been for a long time. Perhaps this will give me time to sort through a few things."

"Your mother called. I told her everything was okay, but we'd had a lot going on the past week. I assured her you were in no danger, just busy trying to get settled. In other words, I saved your butt. Give the poor woman a call, Frankie."

"I'll call her tonight."

"Before or after you come to my place?"

"I think I need to spend time with Sissy."

"You're probably right. Oh, I almost forgot. You came in through the back, didn't you?" When Frankie nodded, he smiled. "There's someone in the lobby who wants to see you."

Curious, Frankie made her way toward the lobby. She found Vicki Morris sitting in one of the plastic chairs. The woman looked entirely different, dressed in a starched skirt and blouse. "Mrs. Morris, what a surprise. You look wonderful."

Vicki stood. "I wanted to thank you, Deputy Daniels, for helping me make up my mind to get out of an abusive marriage. The volunteers at the shelter have been so kind. I'm in therapy."

"That will help you a lot. Where's your husband?"

"He's staying with his parents in Georgia. He sent me a letter through one of our friends, asking me for another chance, but I've given him too many as it is. As soon as I save enough money, I'm filing for divorce on grounds of physical abuse."

"Do you think he'll try to hurt you?"

"An advocate for the shelter has already taken me to the courthouse where I took out a peace bond. If he comes anywhere near me, they'll lock him up. He's scared of going to jail, believe me."

"So you're okay?"

Vicki smiled. "I have a new job. I just started yesterday."

"Congratulations! What will you be doing?"

"I'm the new receptionist at Burke Photography Studio," she said proudly, "and soon I should have my own place. One of the women who works at the shelter is looking for a housemate."

"I couldn't be happier for you," Frankie said. "I know it wasn't easy for you, but you've come a long way in a short time."

"I'd been wanting to get out for a long time. Thank you for what you did."

"I didn't do anything. You did it all on your own."

"You don't understand, Deputy Daniels. I was so caught up in self-pity that I couldn't put one foot in front of the other. I'd been told so many times how worthless I was that I believed it. But you showed up and refused to feel sorry for me. You made me realize that I had made a choice to stay in a bad marriage because I was too scared to do anything about it. It's not up to me to change my husband. I can only change myself." She blushed. "I'm sorry to ramble on, but I'm so excited with my new life and all the possibilities." All at once, she hugged Frankie.

Frankie hadn't seen it coming and was taken by surprise. She found herself hugging the woman back. "I'm so proud of you, Vicki."

The door opened and Cooter walked through. He paused at the sight of Vicki. "Well, look who has gone and gotten herself all fancied up."

Vicki blushed a deeper shade of red. "I have a new job. I'm on my lunch hour, and I wanted to come by and say thank you for getting me out of that mess."

"How long do you have left on your lunch hour?"

"About forty-five minutes."

"Then allow me to escort you to the Half Moon Café. This calls for a celebration."

"Are you sure you have the time, Cooter? I was just going to grab a sandwich."

"I'll have time if you don't stand there arguing with

me. Let's go. If you behave yourself I might let you play with the flashing blue light in my patrol car.''

Vicki waved to Frankie as the two hurried out the glass doors. Frankie turned and found Velma smiling.

''Well, would you look at that?'' the woman said. ''I'd say Cooter is smitten.''

Velma had never singled Frankie out or shown much kindness, and she was taken aback by it. ''Yes, he does seem to be attracted to her.''

''It's not even spring and romance is in the air,'' the woman continued, ''most of it going on right in this building.'' She shot Frankie a knowing look.

So much for being discreet, Frankie thought.

Frankie arrived home at precisely five-thirty, picked up the telephone and called her mother. She heard the shower running as she dialed and was glad Sissy had decided to get out of bed.

''Who is this?'' Eve Hutton asked as soon as Frankie spoke. ''Do I know you? I once had a daughter who sounded like you, but I don't know what's become of her, because she never calls.''

''It's good to talk to you, too, Mom. Now that things have settled down a bit, I'll be able to call more often.''

The woman on the other end of the line went silent for a moment. ''Well, it's good to hear your voice. Is everything okay?''

''Couldn't be better. I'm meeting a lot of new friends, and I think I'm making headway with my job.''

''What about the doctor?''

Doctor? Frankie blinked. Lying was not easy for her because she could never remember what she had said. ''He and I sort of parted ways.''

"And I had just gotten used to the idea of having a proctologist for a son-in-law."

They talked for a good twenty minutes before Eve mentioned she had dinner plans. "Thank you for calling me, honey. I hate to be such a nuisance, but I just worry."

"I know you do, Mom. But, honestly, I'm okay."

Frankie hung up the phone as Sissy hurried out of the bathroom a moment later, wearing a towel. "One of the girls called in sick. I have to work. Virgil is having karaoke tonight so we'll probably pack them in."

"Are you feeling better?" Frankie asked.

"I'm okay. At least I'll be too busy to worry about it." She paused. "I turned off the ringer on the telephone so you wouldn't be disturbed tonight. Also, I've turned down the volume on the answering machine."

"No problem."

Sissy left shortly afterward. Frankie went into the kitchen, looked into the refrigerator, saw nothing appealing and closed the door. She made herself a peanut butter and jelly sandwich, and thought of Matt. She missed him already. She ran a tub of hot water, added bath salts and spent an hour soaking, the first time she could remember doing so. She read a magazine from cover to cover. She had never been big on clothes, but she examined some of the outfits with a critical eye. She noted hairstyles and makeup. One article gave tips on making a woman's eyes look larger. She'd have to ask Sissy about it. She spied a Victoria's Secret catalog and flipped through the pages as well, thinking about what Matt would do if he saw her in some of the lingerie and wishing she had pretty gowns instead of floppy nightshirts.

Perhaps it was time to make some changes in her life. She watched a crime show on TV. At ten, she could no longer keep her eyes open, and she switched off the lights. Matt Webber was her last coherent thought before drifting off.

Two days later, Frankie and Sissy arrived at the audition for *Steel Magnolias*. People of all ages and sizes filled the room. The two registered, sat down and waited.

"Oh, brother, this is going to be a tearjerker," Sissy said. "Just what I need at this point in my life."

"It'll take your mind off your troubles."

Some minutes later, a man in black leather pants and a purple cashmere sweater walked through the door.

"Okay, everybody take a seat, please," he called out loudly.

"That's Joey Smiles," Sissy whispered. "He's the director. Nice butt, don't you think?"

Frankie shrugged. The only butt she looked at these days belonged to Matt, and it was indeed a nice one. Her stomach fluttered as she thought about him beside her, warm and naked. Damn, she was turning into such a girl—eye makeup, nail polish, bubble baths, butterflies in her stomach.

Finally, the room quieted. Joey took center stage. "Okay, everybody, be quiet for just a minute. I think you're all familiar with the story we're doing." He paused when he saw Sissy. "Hello, Miss Burns. Nice to have you with us. I hope you'll consider reading Truvy's part for us."

"Actually, I was sort of hoping to read for Shelby, the part Julia Roberts played, since the two of us bear such a resemblance."

"But, sweetheart, Truvy has more lines in the script. The entire play takes place in her salon."

"I'll think about it. But I want my friend here to get a part, too. She's acted in a lot of off-Broadway plays."

Frankie shot Sissy a dark look.

"Well, now, I'm impressed. What plays have you been in, Miss—"

"Daniels," Frankie said. "I, uh—"

"She was an understudy for *Cats* and played in *Miss Saigon* and *Rent*."

"I *am* impressed. We have a real professional among us." A murmur ran through the crowd.

Frankie's face flamed. "They weren't big parts," she said. "Smaller than a bread box, actually."

"We must get together and discuss it sometime," Joey said, before a woman holding a clipboard walked up to him and captured his attention.

"What the hell do you think you're doing?" Frankie whispered to Sissy.

"Trying to get you a good part."

"I'm not an actress. I've never even been on a stage."

"He doesn't know that. And if you saw how these local-yokels acted, you wouldn't be so concerned. Just get up there and pretend you know what you're doing."

The director spent the next hour going over the play and explaining what he was looking for in each character. Frankie grew bored in no time. As was often the case these days, she found herself thinking about Matt. He *was* moving in quickly. Why? Was he afraid she would leave town without a forwarding address? She rather enjoyed being pursued by the best-looking man in town, but if he expected her to flounce around in skirts and dresses all the time, like the women who ogled him, he would be sorely disappointed.

She was not about to change her ways for any man.

Finally, Sissy was asked to read. Frankie watched as her friend took center stage and read from the script, while the others in the room stared in rapt silence. Frankie was amazed—the woman was truly awesome. When Sissy finished reading, the onlookers burst into applause.

"I think we have our Truvy," Joey announced proudly. "Miss Daniels, would you care to read for the part of Shelby?"

Frankie swallowed and it felt like a goose egg going down. "Well, I, uh, don't think—"

"Of course she will," Sissy said. "Frankie, go up there and show them what you've got."

A hush fell over the room as Frankie took the steps leading to the stage. She could feel her heart pounding as she glanced through the passages she was to read. It felt like the times she had been called on to read in history class, and she'd hated every minute of it. Dreaded it, actually. She dropped the script twice before she began. She took a deep breath and started reading from the section Joey had selected. After a few minutes of reading, she noted the strange look on his face and heard the shuffling of feet in the crowd, although she didn't dare look at the audience.

"I'm sorry, but I can't do this," she said, after stammering and stuttering her way through a number of lines.

"Is there a problem, Miss Daniels?" Joey asked. "You seem to have trouble putting emotion into the character."

"Well, of course she does," Sissy said, jumping from her seat. "The poor girl is exhausted. She just finished playing Lady Macbeth in New York. She's exhausted. Drained."

Joey looked skeptical. Frankie suspected he didn't believe a word Sissy was saying. Why Sissy was going to such extremes to get her a part in the play was beyond her.

"In that case, perhaps you'd like to bow out of this particular play," Joey said kindly.

"At least give her a small part," Sissy said. "Or I refuse to play Truvy."

Joey looked uncomfortable. "I have a part for Miss Daniels, but it's only a one-liner."

"Which line?" Sissy asked.

"Well—" Joey flipped through several pages. "Uh, here it is. All she'd need to do is sit in the chair, quietly reading a magazine while Truvy does her hair. Once finished, Miss Daniels will say, 'Truvy, I love what you've done to my hair.'"

Sissy looked at Frankie. "Is that okay with you?"

Frankie had her doubts. She felt queasy at the mere thought of being in front of an audience. But she had to do it for Sissy's sake. The woman needed to become involved in something that would lift her self-confidence. Surely she could remember one line.

"I'll do it," she said.

Joey looked relieved. "Very well, let's move on."

When Frankie arrived at work the next morning, Matt greeted her warmly. "I hear you've got a part in the upcoming play."

She blinked. "How did you know?"

"I just hung up from talking to Sissy. I made up a reason to call, just to make sure she was okay. She told me about the audition last night. Congratulations. I'm glad you're getting involved in the community."

"Well, it's not that big of a deal."

"Stop being modest, Daniels, it doesn't suit you. Sissy said you've got a main role in the play."

Cooter tapped on the door. "Oh, hey there, Frankie. I hear congratulations are in order. Matt said you got a big part in the upcoming play."

Frankie felt her cheeks grow hot as Buster joined

Cooter at the door, grinning from ear to ear. "I didn't know we had an actress in the department," he said. "I hope this doesn't mean you're going to end up leaving us and going to Hollywood. Next thing you know, they'll be asking you to put your hands and feet in that cement like they do other big-time celebrities."

Frankie felt the heat rise to the tips of her ears. "You guys are making a big deal over nothing."

"She's just being modest," Matt repeated.

Velma appeared in the doorway. "What's going on in here?"

Matt told her. Velma smiled. "That's good news," she said. "Deputy Daniels, you have a call. Alice Chalmers is on the line."

Frankie was glad for the distraction. She hurried into her office and picked up the phone. "Hi, Alice."

"I know you're busy," the woman said. "I just wanted to see if you're free for lunch."

"Sounds good."

"Okay. Same place, same time?"

"See you then."

Matt tapped on Frankie's door a few minutes later. "I've got to ride out to Weldon Evans's place. You want to come? Shouldn't take long."

"Does this have anything to do with Caesar the bull?"

He looked amused. "Yeah, they got some kind of new contraption they want me to have a look at."

"What kind of contraption?"

"Are you going with me or not?"

Frankie sighed. She knew she would use any excuse she could to be near him, even if she had to chase a raging bull through a pasture.

Matt didn't speak until they were in the patrol car. "I

missed you last night. That bed is too big without you in it.''

"I had to spend time with Sissy."

"I know. What about tonight?"

"I'll see how she's doing."

"You're not playing head games with me, are you?"

"Do you know how outdated that line is?"

"Yeah, well, look where you are. One day we'll all be as sophisticated as the folks in Atlanta."

She saw that he was teasing her. "I'll have my people call your people."

"Do you know how outdated *that* line is?"

They both laughed as they pulled into Weldon Evans's driveway a few minutes later.

"What in heaven's name is *that?*" Frankie said.

Matt shook his head. "Damned if I know."

She stared out the front window of the car as she tried to figure out what was going on in Sam Bone's pasture. Someone had put something that resembled a hide, of sorts, over the back section of a pickup truck. Sam walked around the truck, tugging here and there as if to test it, while Caesar remained chained to a large stake in the ground. Another man stood in the bed of the truck next to the front cab, talking to them.

The men looked up as Matt and Frankie approached. "Well, now," Matt said. "I don't believe I've ever seen anything like this before. What is it?"

"My cousin brought it up from Athens, Chief," Sam said. "Meet Bart Dixon. We call him Tailbird."

Frankie and Matt nodded toward the man. "What's this supposed to be, uh, Tailbird?" Matt asked.

"Well—" The man paused and spit. "I seen something like this in one of them there big-time magazines, and I remembered what a hard time Sam was having trying to breed Caesar, so I fashioned this here carcass. It's supposed to look like a heifer.''

"It doesn't have a head," Frankie said.

Tailbird grinned and spit again. "Don't need no head, ma'am. Ol' Caesar is going to be more interested in the rear section."

"We plan to collect sperm from Caesar using this thing," Sam said. "We tried putting him on a milking machine, but it makes him madder'n hell. S'cuse my language, Deputy Daniels. Then we tried sticking this electrically charged rod up his rectum, which is supposed to make him, well, you know—"

"That would work for me," Matt said wryly.

"I'll have to add that to my play toys," Frankie whispered. "So, how does this thing work?"

"Well, bulls ain't very bright," Tailbird said. "Caesar don't know this ain't a real heifer."

"And Molly's in heat, so Weldon is in his barn collecting her scent," Sam added. "We'll rub it right here in this here hole, and once Caesar gets a sniff he'll want to mount it. Hopefully."

Frankie's look was deadpan as she looked at Matt. "You brought me out here for this?"

"Hey, it's the latest technology."

"Here comes Weldon now," Sam said. "You got it?" he yelled as Weldon slipped through a barbed-wire fence, holding what look like an old T-shirt.

"Yep. You guys ready?"

Tailbird handed Sam four bricks. "Better put these in front of the tires to keep the truck steady. That's a big bull. Hope he don't put a dent in the back of my truck."

Sam took the bricks. "I put on the emergency brake." He positioned each brick in front of the tires.

"Everything ready?" Sam asked, once Weldon rubbed Molly's scent around the hole at the back of the carcass.

"I'm going underneath," Tailbird said, "so I can collect our...uh...specimen." He grinned and crawled beneath the hide. "Okay, let's get started," he called out, his voice muffled.

Sam carried the T-shirt to Caesar and let the animal get a whiff. The bull snorted loudly and yanked at the chain. The two men hooted.

Frankie and Matt looked at each other as Sam and Weldon pulled Caesar's chain from the stake. Weldon looked at Sam and winked. "Probably should have showed old Caesar some dirty pictures first," he said with a laugh. "You reckon he'll know what to do?"

"He'll know. Okay, Tailbird, here we come."

"I have to see this," Matt said.

Frankie glanced his way. "I don't know if I can take it."

Weldon and Sam led Caesar to the carcass, bringing his head down so the bull could get a good sniff. Caesar snorted again and, without warning, mounted the hide. He began humping wildly.

"I can't watch this," Frankie said, turning.

Matt chuckled. "You haven't been around many farm animals, have you?"

Caesar continued to snort and hump, his weight slamming hard against the carcass, the pickup truck bouncing on its tires.

"Glad I put those bricks in front of the tires," Sam said. "If this guy pushes any harder he's going to shove this here truck right into the next county."

Weldon laughed. "You okay in there, Tailbird?"

"Fine" came a muffled reply.

"Is it over yet?" Frankie asked Matt.

"I think he's getting close. Either that, or he's having a seizure."

Frankie could hear the ruckus going on and glanced over her shoulder. Caesar was breathing hard. Loud, urgent snorts filled the air. Suddenly, he went into a frenzy.

"You go, Caesar!" Sam said. "Show 'em what you're made of, boy!"

The bull made a loud sound and slumped from the carcass. "I got it!" Tailbird yelled from inside.

Weldon and Sam hooted, giving each other a high five. "We did it," Sam said. "I'm going to wring this bull dry before Tailbird heads back to Georgia. We'll have all your heifers pregnant before you know it, partner."

Caesar sat back on the ground as though exhausted. Tailbird climbed out from beneath the carcass, holding up a container. "Here it is, gentlemen."

Sam grinned at Caesar. "How was that, boy? Was it as good for you as it was for that fake cow?"

The men howled with laughter. "Ask him if he wants a cigarette," Tailbird said.

Frankie shook her head sadly as she and Matt made their way back to the patrol car. She looked at him as they strapped on their seat belts. "You know, it's times like this that I wonder what I'm doing here."

Matt patted her on the thigh. "You can wonder all you like, but I'm not letting you go anywhere, Deputy."

Frankie didn't argue.

Eighteen

Frankie thought Alice looked tired as the two were seated at what was becoming their favorite table. The woman had lost weight in the short time since Frankie had seen her. "Are you okay?" she asked her friend.

Alice nodded. "Just have a lot on my mind these days."

"Would you like to share? I've certainly poured out all my troubles to you."

Alice chuckled, but the look on her face remained weary. "Thanks for the offer, but I have my own therapist."

Frankie didn't know if the woman was joking or not. Alice seemed so savvy about life and its problems. She couldn't imagine her seeking help. "How's Rand?"

"Oh, he's staying busy. Spends a lot of time gardening when he's home, which isn't often these days. His practice keeps him tied up so much of the time."

A waitress appeared. They both ordered iced tea and chef salads.

Frankie sensed her friend didn't want to discuss her personal life at the moment. "Well, I've decided not to hand in my resignation," she said. "At least for now."

Alice looked pleased. "That's good news. Does this have anything to do with Matt?"

"Let's just say I'm becoming more acclimatized to the town."

"Are you in love with him?"

"I don't know that I would go as far as to say I was in love with him, but he has my full attention."

"I knew it. I could see it on both of your faces the night of the Gibbses' benefit. He's crazy about you. Does he know how you feel?"

"I've admitted having feelings for him."

"What are you waiting for?"

"I don't believe in love at first sight, Alice, and I don't want to rush into it. I haven't been here that long, and you know how my last affair ended."

"I thought you were past all that."

"Pretty much, but like I said, Matt and I haven't known each other all that long."

"When it's right, you know right away. At least that's how it was for Rand and me. I knew the first time I saw him I was going to marry him."

"The first time?"

"Uh-huh. I'm not saying it's been smooth sailing ever since. It's not easy being married to a doctor. But I can see the changes in you. You've softened."

"I'm probably more relaxed than I was."

"Has Matt said anything about how he feels?"

"Oh, yes. And that's what scares me. He's ready and willing for a relationship, and we get along surprisingly well on the job. If he needs my advice on something, he's not afraid to ask. I think he respects my opinions."

"And so he should. Matt's not one of those macho types who think they know it all. He's a nice man, Frankie." She paused. "That big house of his must get lonely at times."

"I suppose." Frankie noted the wistful look in her eyes

and wondered if Alice was lonely. "Has Rand been putting in a lot of hours at the hospital?"

Alice nodded. "This town is growing. They're adding on to the hospital, as you probably know, and we just had a new doctor join the staff, so that should take some pressure off Rand. So tell me, how do you like living with Sissy?"

Frankie wished she could tell Alice what was going on without breaking a confidence. "Oh, we get along well. We auditioned for the new play last night."

"*Steel Magnolias?*"

Frankie nodded. "Sissy landed the leading role. She's very good."

"I've seen her act. She's incredible. Are you playing a part?"

"Oh, yeah. Sissy got me a one-liner, but everybody at the department thinks I'm playing a major role, thanks to her." She rolled her eyes as Alice laughed. "I'm terrified of being on stage."

"What's the line?"

"I'm supposed to say, 'Truvy, I love what you've done to my hair,' or something like that." She pretended to gag. "I just wanted to help on the set."

"You'll probably end up doing both. We don't have many volunteers for our little theater."

Their order arrived. Frankie noticed how Alice picked at her salad. "Don't tell me you're on a diet."

"I just haven't had much of an appetite. I needed to take off five pounds, anyway."

"You look like you've lost ten."

"Even better."

"You can't afford to lose it. You're already too thin."

"What's that saying—a woman can't be too rich or too

thin? How are things going at the office?'' she asked, changing the subject. ''How's Velma?''

''Surprisingly enough, she's being civil to me.''

''And your mother?''

''She still calls in a panic if I don't check in every day. I'm trying to do better.''

Alice looked thoughtful. ''I wish my mother were alive. We were very close. We could talk about anything. There's something about mothers and daughters, you know? I've always wanted a daughter, but Rand and I were so busy with our careers. The time never seemed right.''

''Why not now?'' Frankie asked.

''I'm forty years old, Frankie. Rand is forty-five.''

''Women are waiting longer to have children these days.''

''It's risky.''

''So be a risk-taker. Besides, you can afford the best prenatal care. I'm sure there are excellent obstetricians in Raleigh.''

''I wouldn't mind adopting.'' She shrugged. ''At this point, I don't think Rand would go for either.''

Frankie wondered what Alice meant but didn't pry. The woman had once mentioned problems in her marriage. Had they returned?

Frankie finished her salad. Alice pushed her plate away. ''Rand and I were invited to a dinner party last night so I'm not very hungry.''

Although she said nothing, Frankie questioned if Alice was telling the truth. ''Alice, Sissy's telephone number is listed in the phone book. I hope you'll call me if you need to talk. You were the first friend I made when I came here.''

''Honey, I'll be okay. You know, it's probably premenopausal stuff. My mother went through it early, so I wouldn't be surprised if I did as well.''

"Have you seen your gynecologist?"

"No, but I plan to make an appointment soon."

Frankie wondered if that was what was bothering Alice as they left the restaurant and parted in the parking lot. Perhaps Alice was going through early menopause and having serious regrets that she and Rand hadn't started a family.

Something was going on, and Frankie suspected it wasn't good.

Matt called Frankie into his office later that day. "Blaine Freeman has been admitted to a psychiatric-care unit in Raleigh for observation. He has a daughter near there. I understand they're close."

"That's great news," Frankie said.

"Jody Peters convinced Earlene not to sue the department, but I doubt we can count on any more contributions from her."

"I suppose I won't be wearing a stylish uniform next year."

"What's wrong with your uniform?"

"Khaki does not look good on me."

"I know what looks good on you. Nothing."

Neither of them saw Cooter standing in the doorway until he cleared his throat. Frankie snapped her head around. From the look on his face it was obvious he'd heard what Matt had said. Frankie glanced away quickly. "If you have nothing else, Chief, I need to catch up on paperwork." She nodded at Cooter and slipped out the door.

Frankie avoided Matt the rest of the day, taking calls with Buster in order to avoid Cooter, as well. They broke up a fistfight in a local bar, assisted in a minor automobile accident and picked up a shoplifter at Wal-Mart. When they arrived back at the station, Frankie grabbed her purse from her office and slipped out the back to her car.

When she arrived at home, Sissy was pacing the floor. "Quick, grab a sandwich, we have rehearsals in twenty minutes."

"Again?"

"Yes, again. We'll have them several times a week from now until the play opens. Your mother called. I told her I'd give you the message."

Frankie barely had time to eat her sandwich and change clothes before they headed out the door. Those who had been chosen to participate in the play sat reading from the script. Joey headed toward Sissy with another woman. "You know Sheila Parks, I believe. She's going to be your understudy."

"Yes, we know each other," Sheila said, shooting Sissy a venomous look. "I've been Sissy's understudy several times."

Frankie arched one brow. It was obvious the woman was not pleased.

"Well, maybe I'll break a leg this time and you'll play the part," Sissy said. "In the meantime, we need to rehearse."

Frankie read her one line over and over, wondering if this was how Julia Roberts had gotten her start. Surely she wouldn't have to show up every night since her part was so small. She wished she had never agreed to act in the play. Perhaps she could back out now that Sissy was feeling better.

They arrived home after the rehearsals and discovered Frankie had two calls, one from her mother, the other from Matt. The phone rang before she could pick up and dial.

"Hello, baby, it's big daddy."

Frankie blinked, wondering if Matt was trying to disguise his voice. "Excuse me?"

"I've been sitting here with my glass of Scotch for more than an hour thinking about you. How 'bout you put on those black panties I like so much and—"

"It's for you," Frankie said, handing the telephone to Sissy and making her way to the bathroom for a shower.

Frankie was aware of the looks she received the next morning as she walked toward her office. Buster grinned outright, Cooter ducked his head and looked the other way. Frankie mumbled a hello, stepped inside her cubbyhole and closed the door.

She had gone and done it again. Just like before, all her co-workers knew she was sleeping with someone in the department, this time the chief. She leaned her head on her desk, wishing she could cry. But she was too damn mad to cry.

Someone tapped on her door, startling her. She sat up as Matt entered without waiting to be invited. He closed the door behind him. "I tried to call you a dozen times last night, but the line was busy."

Frankie pretended to be interested in the papers in front of her. "Sissy was working. She uses the telephone, remember?"

"You're upset."

"No shit."

"Okay, so the word is out. Big deal."

Frankie stood and planted her hands on her hips. "Maybe it's no big deal to you, Chief Webber, but it is to me. Everybody in this place is probably laughing behind my back. Just when I thought I was beginning to fit in. It's no different than it was in Atlanta. Seems my biggest problem is learning to say no to a man.''

"Look, Frankie, we can work this out.''

"For you, maybe, but not for me. You're the chief. People respect you, and they'll overlook something like this. But I'll be accused of sleeping with you to extract favors or whatever. The woman always comes out looking bad.''

"You're overreacting. I can take care of this.''

"Bullshit. The way news travels in this town, they're probably having a good laugh over it at the barber shop right now.''

"Look, we can't talk about this right now, obviously. Why don't you come by my place tonight?''

"I can't. I have to rehearse for the play.''

"Again?''

"I'm going to be busy, Matt, get it?''

"Is that what you really want, babe?''

"Yes. Because when the shit hits the fan, I'll be the one without a job.''

"That's not going to happen. I won't let it happen.''

She refused to look at him. If she did, all her resolve would weaken. "Like I said, I'm busy.'' She heard the door close softly as he left her office.

Frankie felt the tears forming behind her eyes, but she was determined not to cry. When another knock sounded, she almost barked her reply. Cooter stuck his head in the door. "Hep wants us to come by and take a look at the arcade. Seems he's been working on it like a madman. You want to take a ride?''

Frankie shrugged. "Sure. Nothing else going on around here.''

They made the drive in silence, Frankie staring out the

side window. When they pulled into Hep's place, she couldn't help but admire the work he'd done on the outside. The arcade had been painted a different color on the outside than the pool hall, and it had its own entrance so there could be no mistaking which door led where. Signs had been painted and placed over the doors, one reading Hep's Pool Hall, the other Hep's Arcade. A sign on the door of the pool hall was clearly marked: No One Under the Age of 18.

Frankie and Cooter found Hep polishing the glass on one of several pinball machines. He stopped when he saw them, grinned and held his arms out. "What do you think?"

Two pool tables sat in the center of the room, surrounded by computerized games of all sorts. The room was painted a dark blue with stars on the ceiling and walls. Soft drink and other vending machines offered snacks, and a coin machine had been added to make change.

"I put this coin machine in so the kids would have no reason to come inside the bar for change."

Cooter whistled. "You must have spent a fortune."

"Most of the computer games and pinball machines were put in free of charge. The vendors will collect on them, naturally."

"You've done a fabulous job, Hep," Frankie said. "And in such a short time."

"I had a lot of help. A bunch of kids talked to their parents and before I knew it there was a whole slew of people involved, cleaning and painting. I've received donations from several of the businesses and churches. Folks want a safe place for their kids, and I'm going to make sure there's no monkey business going on here. I've even cleaned up the pool hall and raised my prices to keep out the riffraff. I've talked to the owner of the Plaza Theater, and he agreed to put on more movies for kids.'' He grinned. ''And guess what? I've already been nominated for the good citizen award. Imagine that.''

''You've earned it,'' Cooter said.

Hep looked about proudly. ''It's the kind of place I'd feel good about my own kids coming to.'' He glanced at Frankie. ''I think you and Cooter should be the first ones to test out the equipment.'' He pulled a handful of quarters from his pocket. ''Enjoy yourselves. Just don't cause a ruckus 'cause I'll be checking in from time to time. I'd hate to have to call the chief and report the two of you for disorderly conduct.''

Cooter and Frankie spent twenty minutes in the arcade before they ran out of money. ''What do you think?'' Cooter asked, once they'd thanked Hep for his hospitality.

''I'm impressed. At least it should keep the teenagers off the street and give them something safe to do.''

''That's what's important,'' he said as they started out the door. ''Folks are real particular what goes on in this town. They value morality.''

As Frankie climbed into the car beside him, she wondered if he was referring to her and Matt's relationship.

Nineteen

Frankie spent the following week accompanying Sissy to the little theater. It was too soon to tell, of course, but with all the chaos going on, Frankie wondered how they would ever pull things together. There were bitter resentments between the actors, and most of them centered around Sissy because she always got the best part. They accused Joey of playing favorites behind his back, but when it was time to read, everyone seemed to put their pettiness aside and do the best they could. Which, in Frankie's opinion, was pretty good, considering she hadn't the first clue about acting.

They rehearsed from six until eight-thirty, three nights a week, after which Sissy flew home in order to receive her calls. Frankie usually spent time driving around, trying to get a better feel of the town, and trying not to think of Matt. She noted the questions in his eyes whenever they worked together, but he never voiced them. He seemed to sense she needed space.

One evening she found herself sitting in the dark on a bench in the courthouse square, feeling depressed. She missed Matt, but she knew she was doing the right thing by backing off. Alice Chalmers might believe in love at first sight, but Frankie was more practical. People needed time to get to know each other. She and Matt had simply become too close too fast. She couldn't allow herself to make the same mistakes as before.

Not that she didn't know Matt well, she reminded herself. They had spent a lot of time together working. She liked the way he dealt with people; his laid-back attitude inspired trust. He was a man who could be counted on, a man who would weigh things carefully before making a fair decision but would also move quickly in emergency situations. He suspected Willie-Jack of starting the fire at the Gibbses' place, but he was the type who would look under every rock, investigate every possibility before he made his move. The townspeople might become impatient, but they obviously knew that about him and respected him.

"Good evenin', Deputy."

Frankie froze, recognizing the voice immediately. It was as if her thoughts had conjured up the man. Willie-Jack Pitts sat down beside her.

"What's a good-looking woman like you doing out here all alone?" he asked. "Don't you know how dangerous it is, sitting out here in the dark?"

She could smell the booze on him. The square and the sidewalks were empty. Most people would be home, having dinner. The silence that she had enjoyed a moment before was now eerie. "Willie-Jack, I'm in no mood for chitchat tonight, okay? So move along."

"Hey, this is public property, Deputy," he said, making a mockery of her rank. "I have a right to sit here just as much as you do."

Her first impulse was to get up and walk away, but the last thing she wanted was for Willie-Jack to think she was afraid of him. She would lose leverage. Besides, she had kicked his butt before and she could do it again. Only she didn't want to mess up her nails, after Sissy had done such a good job painting them.

Oh, Lord, what was happening to her? "Then do me a big favor and keep your mouth shut."

"Bad day playing cops and robbers?"

She didn't respond.

"I know your type, lady. Think you're better than everyone else. You wouldn't believe how many highfa lutin bitches there are in this town. But when they get behind closed doors, they're no different from the rest of us. They like the hard stuff, and Willie-Jack knows how to give it to 'em. I may not be invited to their fancy soirees, but when their husbands are away, they call on old Willie-Jack."

Frankie's look was deadpan. "Excuse me, but do I look the least bit interested in anything you're saying?"

He laughed. "That's what I like about you, your spunk. I can't stomach a mealymouthed woman." He paused and looked her over. "You may not believe this, but we could actually be good together. I can take care of you, give you anything you want. You wouldn't have to sleep with Webber to keep your job."

Frankie was jolted by his words, although she refused to show it. Is that what people thought? It was already all over the department, but did everybody in town know they'd been intimate? She suddenly felt ill, but she would rip her own lungs out of her chest before letting Willie-Jack know he'd gotten to her.

She faced him. "You should have been born a worm, Willie-Jack. You know, they mate with themselves. The two of you would be perfect together. Now, get out of my face or I'll haul in your sorry ass for harassment."

He unfolded himself slowly from the bench. A smirk outlined his lips. "The truth hurts, doesn't it?" He spit on the ground. "The only difference between you and a whore is that a whore knows her place." He walked away without another word.

How long Frankie sat there she wasn't sure. She wanted to cry. Hell, no, she wanted to scream. She tried to remind herself the words had come from Willie-Jack Pitts, town scumbag. They stung, nevertheless. She longed to go to Matt, to ask him to hold her, but she feared she would never find the strength to go on if she leaned on him for even a moment. She was so damn tired of trying to be strong, and she wondered how she had ever lasted as long as she had in Atlanta. What had kept her going all those years, when at the moment she suddenly felt as weak as a new lamb?

She knew the answer, of course. In just a few weeks she had changed dramatically. She had made friends and opened herself up to the possibility of finding love. Without even knowing it, she had begun to let down her guard.

And in the blink of an eye, Willie-Jack had managed to get in and hurt her.

Matt sat on a rocker on his front porch, feet propped on the rail, listening to the night sounds, crickets chirping, an occasional bullfrog belching in search of a mate. Beside him, his coon dog snored. Any other time he would have enjoyed spending time on his porch in solitude, but he missed Frankie. When Mandy died, he had suffered a loneliness he thought would never end. Nothing had seemed to matter anymore, not even the woman he'd been engaged to at the time. As if a light bulb had gone off in his head, he'd suddenly realized how different they were, and he'd saved them both a lot of trouble by backing out of the relationship.

He'd found solace in women, and he'd done a lot of

smooth-talking in order to take the edge off his loneliness and get his physical needs met. He had hurt his share of women as a result. Women like Sissy, who'd been used by too many men and didn't need to be hurt any more than she had already been. Women like Frankie, who were trying so hard to be strong and rebuild their lives. Women like his own mother, who were good and down to earth and only looking to share their lives with a good man.

His shame had caught up with him, and though he enjoyed looking at a pretty set of legs, he'd stopped seeing anyone ages ago. He'd realized he couldn't count on someone else to make him feel better, because as soon as he climbed from a woman's bed, the empty feeling returned, and he hated having women call him, wondering what they'd done wrong. They hadn't done a damn thing wrong, he'd confessed. The fault lay with him.

He'd done a lot of soul searching and decided he needed to change his ways before he hurt anyone else.

The only good thing he had found in himself was that he truly cared about the people in Purdyville and wanted to protect them. At least he had that much going for him. He became more determined than ever to do his job as well as he could, and after a while, the gaping hole in his heart had begun to heal.

Then he'd met Frankie and he'd realized that, although he had come to terms with being alone, he wanted her in his life. She had shown him what he'd been missing all these years. He accused her of having a mouth on her, but he appreciated her forthright attitude and honesty. What you saw was what you got. She didn't care about the fancy trappings so many women were into these days. She didn't spend hours preening in front of the mirror. She was just Frankie. A proud woman—stubborn, too—but determined to make the world a better place.

Right now, she was angry. In her eyes, she saw little difference in what was going on between them and what had happened in Atlanta. He curled a fist in his lap, wishing he could punch the man in the face who'd hurt and embarrassed her and caused her to add more bricks to the wall she had already erected around herself.

Lord, he missed her. The way she smelled, the way her hair tumbled about her face when she awoke in the morning. He missed their lively banter, the way she felt in his arms, and the lovely expressions she wore when they made love.

Perhaps it had happened too fast, but he'd taken one look at Frankie Daniels and something inside of him had clicked. It was as though he'd waited all his life for her, that something within him, perhaps his soul, had recognized her as being *the one*. He couldn't explain it, even to himself, but he knew it as well as he knew the layout of the small town of Purdyville.

Obviously, she needed time. She was not like the other women he'd known, who were only happy to be with him. She had a mind of her own, and this time he was the one waiting for the telephone to ring. It was a humbling experience.

He wondered if Frankie was too bitter to ever give love a chance. Was she capable of loving him—or anyone else, for that matter? The fact that she might not be scared him.

He would have to be patient. He had no other choice but to back off and give her all the time she asked for.

And hope.

Frankie was awakened at 2:00 a.m. by the telephone. She ignored it, thinking it must be one of Sissy's clients. Finally, her sleepy housemate appeared at her bedroom door, holding the portable phone. "It's for you," she said. "It's Matt."

Frankie took the phone. "Yes?"

"The Gibbses' house is burning out of control. I need you there. Can you be ready in ten minutes?"

Her mind went blank. "The house they're living in?"

"Yeah. Just throw on a pair of jeans or whatever. I'm on my way."

"It's bad news, isn't it?" Sissy asked, once Frankie turned off the phone and handed it to her.

She nodded. "The Gibbses' house is burning."

"I'll put on coffee and have it in a thermos by the time you're ready."

Frankie hurried into the bathroom. She brushed her hair and pulled it back, splashed cold water on her face and brushed her teeth. Sissy carried in a cup of coffee as Frankie was climbing into her jeans. She grabbed a sweatshirt from a drawer, pulled it on and stepped into a pair of sneakers. She barely had time to smoke a cigarette and finish her coffee before Matt pulled into the drive.

"Here, take this," Sissy said, thrusting the thermos into her hand as Frankie started for the door. "And be careful."

"Go back to bed, Sissy. I probably won't be back anytime soon."

Matt had already thought about the coffee. He handed Frankie a tall plastic cup with a lid on it to prevent spilling. "Thanks," she muttered.

"Open the window if you want to smoke."

She did so. "What do you know about the fire?"

"The top floor is engulfed in flames. They've called firefighters from other districts. If this spreads to the woods, we're in deep trouble. We haven't had enough rain to fill a bucket."

''Are there any injuries?''

''From what I understand, Irma is okay, but they were trying to reach Homer in the upstairs bedroom the last time I spoke with Orvell Dean.''

''Who would have done this?''

''You know the first person who comes to mind, but I can't see him taking more chances—unless he just doesn't give a damn.''

Frankie told him about her run-in with Willie-Jack and saw Matt's fingers tighten on the steering wheel. ''Why didn't you tell me? I would love nothing better than to take that son of a bitch apart limb by limb.''

''That's exactly why I didn't tell you. I took care of the problem by myself.''

''Oh, that's right. You don't need help from anyone. You're tough.'' Matt wished he wasn't being such a jerk, but he couldn't help it. ''So, what you're saying is that Willie-Jack got pissed because you wouldn't have anything to do with him and set fire to the Gibbses' house?''

''Don't be a smart-ass.''

Matt knew he deserved it. He was scared of losing her. He vacillated between giving her the time she needed and giving up altogether. Why go through all this worrying? But he knew when he was wrong.

''I'm sorry,'' he managed. ''I have a lot on my mind.''

Like she didn't. ''Let's just drop it, okay?''

They were quiet for the rest of the drive, until they spotted a bright light in the distance. ''This is going to be bad,'' Matt said.

Bad didn't aptly describe it. When they turned onto the Gibbses' street, the entire house was ablaze. ''Oh, my God,'' Frankie whispered.

Matt parked a distance away so they wouldn't get in the way of the firefighters. A half-dozen fire trucks lined the road, as well as several emergency vehicles. They found Orvell Dean on the scene, sweaty and covered with soot as he drank from a gallon container of water. "Looks like you got your hands full," Matt shouted over the commotion.

"It's going to burn to the ground," Orvell said. "I was only able to get a few words from Irma before they rushed her to the hospital."

"How is she?"

"She was in shock."

"What about Homer?"

Orvell shook his head. "He didn't make it. They pulled him out ten minutes ago. The fire didn't get to him, but he's dead, obviously from smoke inhalation. He's already on his way to the morgue."

"Dammit!"

"Hey, Chief, we're doing all we can."

"I know. It's just…well…I'm sick about the whole thing."

"We all are. Seems like the past couple of years all they've had are problems. At least Homer doesn't have to lie in bed day after day anymore."

"What can I do to help?"

"We've got more than a dozen men on the job, trying to keep it from reaching the woods. Nothing we can do now except pray."

Frankie looked at Matt. She could not remember the last time she had prayed. Not since her father had died, she supposed. Why bother, she used to ask herself. She had hated the God who had allowed the person she'd loved more than anyone else lose his life at the hands of a career criminal who'd never done a damn thing for anyone.

"Looks like we're going to have to hold another benefit," Orvell said.

Matt looked at Frankie. "Let's take a ride."

"Anyplace in particular?"

"Willie-Jack's."

Twenty

Willie-Jack Pitts was nowhere to be found. His mobile home was badly mildewed; one would have had trouble figuring out what color it was. Matt pounded on the door a good five minutes before giving up. "He's probably watching the Gibbses' house burn from the woods," he said, "and no doubt getting some kind of sexual thrill over it, which is why a lot of arsonists set fires to begin with. I wish I had a piece of clothing. I'd call the K-9 Unit."

"We could break in."

Matt looked at her. "Yeah, we could." He tried the door. It was locked. "We need to look for a window."

They walked around the trailer, searching for a partially open window, but found none. Frankie tried the back door. It opened. "Well, I'll be damned."

Matt grinned. "You just made my job a whole lot easier. Keep an eye out for me, okay? I don't want Willie-Jack pulling up and finding me inside." He went in.

Frankie watched the road for any sign of headlights. It would not do for them to get caught ransacking Willie-Jack's home, especially not after the stink Earlene Peters had caused.

Matt was in and out in two minutes flat. "I went through his laundry basket. Found a couple of T-shirts. That ought to do it."

Matt got on the radio and called night dispatch. "Beemer, I need the K-9 Unit at the Gibbses' house pronto. Yes, I know what time it is. Just do it."

The top floor of the Gibbses' house had been reduced to cinders, and the firefighters were hosing down the first level as well as the wooded area surrounding the property. Several women had appeared with coffee and sandwiches. Matt recognized them as wives of some of the firemen.

The K-9 Unit arrived an hour later, two men bearing bloodhounds. Matt briefly explained the situation and handed them the T-shirts before they took off for the woods.

By dawn, the fire had been put out. All that was left was a charred structure, and the acrid smell of burned wood and ash. Matt felt sick at heart. "I don't know what Irma Gibbs is going to do now."

Orvell Dean appeared out of nowhere, wearing knee-length rubber boots and looking filthy and exhausted. "Whoever did this knew exactly what they were doing."

"So, you definitely suspect arson?"

"Hell's bells, Chief, I could smell the gasoline. I'm going to keep one of the trucks here, just in case we get another spark. I don't expect anything. What's left of the bottom floor is sitting knee-high in water."

"You should go home and get some shut-eye," Matt said, noting how weary Orvell looked. "You can always sift through the debris later. I'll send a couple of men from the day shift over to make sure nobody comes near the place."

"I need to go through the place first. Never know what I might find floating in all that water. Did you check out Pitts?"

"He wasn't home."

"Now, why don't I find that surprising? I still think he

set the last one. I don't know anyone in this town mean enough to burn down a house with two elderly people inside, especially one who was bedridden.''

''Problem is, I can't arrest him without proof, and I can't put him on the last scene. My men and I checked and rechecked his so-called airtight alibi for the last fire.''

Orvell sighed, and made for the house.

Matt radioed Beemer in dispatch. ''Call in the day shift. Tell them to meet me at the Gibbses' place.'' He looked at Frankie. ''I want to take a look around. Are you up to it?''

She nodded. ''I wouldn't be able to sleep after slugging down all that coffee, anyway.''

The two walked around the house, checking bushes and outbuildings that had been scorched by the fire but not burned. They found an empty gas can inside. ''I'm looking for more than one,'' Matt said.

Two patrol cars arrived within minutes of each other, and a pair of deputies climbed from each car and joined the search. A few hours later, a cop named Tevis Buford found three gas cans half buried in a ravine in the woods.

Matt nodded. ''That's what we're looking for,'' he said. ''Run them to the crime lab for prints.''

''Yes, Chief.'' Deputy Buford hurried to his car.

''I'm going to take you home,'' Matt told Frankie. ''We both need to clean up and rest a couple of hours. I'll call the hospital and see how Irma is doing.''

Frankie followed him to the car. They talked about the case, both careful to avoid anything personal. Matt dropped her off and drove home.

Sissy was asleep on the sofa when Frankie walked in. She awoke immediately. ''You need a shower.''

''No kidding.''

"And from the looks of it, a nap. You want me to fix you something to eat?"

"I'm too tired for food."

"What's the deal with the Gibbses' place?"

Frankie told her as she kicked off her boots at the door.

"Who'd do a thing like that?" Sissy asked. "No, don't tell me, I think I already know. If ya'll can't pin down Willie-Jack this time, it'd be smart to check out his old man. He's as mean as his son. Probably worse. If he thinks somebody cheated his boy out of money he wouldn't hesitate to go after them."

"Matt has already questioned Willie-Jack's family. No leads there."

Frankie showered, working to get the soot and grime from her hair. She pulled on a sleep shirt. Sissy was waiting in the kitchen with a plate of scrambled eggs and toast. "Sissy, you shouldn't have bothered."

"Hey, you have to eat."

"You're too good to me." Frankie hadn't realized how hungry she was until she tasted the eggs. She cleaned her plate. "I'm going to rest for a couple of hours," she said.

"I'll turn down the phones."

"Wake me if Matt calls." Frankie set her alarm clock and climbed between the sheets a few minutes later. She drifted asleep right away. When the alarm went off a couple of hours later, she felt somewhat rested. She dressed and left.

Matt was already in his office, talking on the telephone when Frankie arrived. He motioned for her to come in. "I spoke with one of the doctors at the hospital. Irma was in shock when they brought her in, but she's okay now. They gave her a sedative, and she's sleeping."

"Poor woman. Does she know about Homer?"

"The doctor said she was in no condition for more bad news."

"Where will she go?"

"She has no family. I'm going to call Shirley and see if they have a bed at Piney Grove. Irma won't like it, but she has no choice at the moment."

Frankie stood there a moment, shaking her head. Her gaze locked with Matt's, and she would have had to be blind to miss the longing in his eyes. She had missed him, too. "Do you have anything for me this morning?"

"Other than what happened at the Gibbses' house, it was a quiet night. Sam Bone called. Caesar has already artificially impregnated about half a herd of heifers."

Frankie laughed. "I guess he's making up for lost time. I'm amazed the carcass is holding up."

Matt chuckled. "I'm amazed the pickup truck is still in one piece. Oh, and Smiley, the dachshund, got out last night. Mrs. Brubaker is out posting signs this morning. Offering a fifty-dollar reward."

"She certainly changed her tune."

Matt stretched his hands behind his head. "That's about it. Looks like we're going to spend the day looking for Willie-Jack."

An hour later, Matt and Frankie pulled in front of a ramshackle cabin. It reminded Frankie of a scene straight out of *The Beverly Hillbillies* before Jed Clampett struck oil. A tall, lanky man appeared on the porch as soon as they climbed from the patrol car. He was dirty and unshaven. Matt introduced Frankie to Elder Pitts. The man didn't acknowledge her.

"We're looking for Willie-Jack," Matt said.

"Why?"

Matt shrugged. "Just want to ask him a few questions."

"You just missed him. He came for supper last night. Decided to sleep over."

"You mind if we take a look inside?"

"You'd be wasting your time."

"Maybe."

Frankie stepped forward. "Mr. Pitts, we can have a search warrant here in an hour. It's up to you." She noticed a shadow moving on the other side of the screen door. A woman stepped out, hands on hips, her appearance as unkempt as the man beside her. "Why are you always pickin' on Willie-Jack?" she demanded. "Poor boy can't so much as take a piss without the law comin' down on him."

"I'm waiting on an answer," Matt said.

Pitts gave him a menacing look. "Come on in, but make it quick. The wife is giving a tea party at ten."

"I hope you're serving scones," Frankie replied, stepping into a house that smelled of old grease and dirty laundry. "They're my favorite."

Matt looked amused. "Mind showing me where Willie-Jack slept last night?"

Pitts looked surprised. "His old room. Same place he always sleeps when he stays over. Upstairs in the loft. I done told you he ain't here." Matt and Frankie started up the stairs. "You're wasting your time," Pitts called out.

Matt and Frankie searched the room regardless. Pitts came up beside them, watching their every move.

"Your son is very thoughtful," Frankie said. "I see he made his bed before he left."

Pitts looked nervous. "His mama raised him right."

Matt was getting impatient. "Stop giving me the runaround, Pitts, and tell me where I can find him."

"I wouldn't tell you if I knew."

"I can't believe they let you out of prison."

"I can't believe you were hired on as Chief of Police."
He looked at Frankie, then back at Matt. "Is this your
latest screw?"

Frankie flinched.

Matt's face turned dark with rage. He grabbed Pitts by
the collar of his shirt. "Don't piss me off or I'll find a
reason to put you away for good. And don't ever mention
my deputy in a derogatory manner or I'll personally kick
your ass from here to Raleigh. You and your family are
nothing but trash. You know it, and everybody in town
knows it. You're like a scab that won't go away."

"Little touchy today, ain't we?" Pitts sneered.

Matt released him. He looked at Frankie. "Let's get
out of this rat hole before we get fleas."

They were on their way in minutes. Matt drove down
the long dirt drive leading out to the main road. It was
littered with beer cans, and rutted with potholes so deep
a large dog could have crawled into one and taken a nap.

"I'm sorry I lost it back there," he told Frankie. "I
was totally unprofessional. But I couldn't take him talking
about you like that."

She shrugged. "It's not your fault."

"I should have been more careful where you're concerned. I never meant for any of this to happen. I don't
blame you for being upset with me. Hell, I wouldn't
blame you if you turned in your resignation, after all."

"Is that what you want?"

He stopped the car and faced her. "Hell, no. I want
you in my life. I want to take you home with me and
never let go of you. I've fallen in love with you, Frankie,
it's as simple as that. I know it happened fast, but it happened regardless."

She fidgeted with her hands.

"But you don't feel that way."

"I didn't say that."

"Then tell me."

"I'm confused."

"Tell me, dammit!"

She snapped her head around so that she was looking directly into his eyes. "Okay, I love you!" she almost shouted. "Is that what you want to hear?"

He reached across her and unfastened her seat belt, then pulled her into his arms. "That's exactly what I want to hear." He kissed her hard, hungrily, his mouth literally devouring hers. When he pulled away, there was a question in his eyes. "So what's preventing us from being together? Surely not the town gossips."

Frankie leaned against him. "I haven't had much luck with men, Matt."

"Your luck is about to change."

"How do you know how you'll feel in five years? Or ten?"

He shook his head sadly. "You underestimate yourself. I don't ever want to lose you." He was silent for a moment as he toyed with an earlobe. "I wish you could just learn to trust. Trust me, Frankie."

Tears filled her eyes. "I'm trying."

Matt pulled her into his arms once again. "Oh, baby, try harder. Let go of everything else and give us a chance. We're worth it, Frankie."

"I have to work it out in my head. I want it to be right."

His look softened. "I'll give you a little more time because what we have is worth it. Just know in your heart that I'm the last person in the world who wants to hurt you." Finally, after kissing her once more, Matt released her.

* * *

Matt and Frankie spoke with a nurse before going into Irma Gibbs's room. "She's still sedated, but she can answer a few questions," the woman said. "Don't stay long."

They stepped into Irma's room a moment later. The woman seemed to be asleep, but she opened her eyes once they stood beside the bed. "Hello, Irma," Matt said. "How do you feel?"

Tears streamed from her eyes. "Like an old woman who just lost her house and her husband."

"So you know about Homer."

"Of course I know. I saw how bad the fire was. I couldn't reach him. I was in the bedroom across the hall." She paused. "When I woke up, the house was so full of smoke I could barely find my way to the stairs."

"You were smart to get out. You would never have been able to save him."

More tears. "I wish I'd died with him. I don't see much reason to go on without Homer. Sixty years, we were married."

Frankie took the woman's hand and squeezed it. "You'll always have your memories, Mrs. Gibbs. I know that doesn't sound like a lot right now, but nobody can take that from you."

Matt cleared his throat. "Mrs. Gibbs, I know you're not well, but I have to ask you a few questions."

"I didn't see nor hear anything if that's what you want to know. I'm a heavy sleeper. That's why I kept a monitor in my bedroom, in case Homer called out during the night. I just woke up coughing and gagging. I think the smoke was coming from Homer's bedroom."

"Did you lock the doors before you went to bed?"

"I've been asking myself that same question. I'm embarrassed to say I have caught myself forgetting to do things. Like turning off a burner on the stove or locking up. My memory isn't as good as it was.'' She closed her eyes. "I'm tired, Matt.''

He patted her shoulder. "I know you are, hon. Try to rest.''

Frankie and Matt ran into Rand Chalmers in the hall. He didn't look happy. "I take it you spoke with Mrs. Gibbs,'' he said. "She isn't doing well.''

Matt nodded. "She's had a big blow.''

"I hope to hell you're looking for Willie-Jack.''

"That's usually the first place I look when there's trouble,'' Matt said.

"I don't know why you let that maniac walk the streets,'' Rand snapped. "He and his family are a curse to this town.''

"I agree, Rand, but I can't lock him up without proof.'' He paused. "Was Homer a patient of yours?''

Chalmers nodded. "I've been treating Homer and Irma for years. But her life is nothing now. I want you to find Pitts, dammit, before he destroys this whole town.'' Rand stalked off.

Matt and Frankie exchanged looks. "I've never seen him so upset,'' Matt said.

"Do you think Dr. Linton has had a chance to perform Homer's autopsy?''

"Only one way to find out.'' They took the elevator to the morgue.

They found Donald Linton in his office making notes. "I know why you're here,'' he said, "and yes, I've performed the autopsy. Homer was a friend of mine. I came in as soon as I got the call. Hard to cut open an old friend.''

"What did you find?'' Matt asked.

"A big surprise.''

"Let us in on it."

"Homer Gibbs wasn't killed by smoke inhalation. His lungs were clean."

Frankie already knew what that meant. "You're saying he was dead before the fire."

"Best I can tell, he'd been dead at least twenty-four hours. Maybe longer."

Twenty-One

Frankie and Matt left the hospital and headed for lunch at the Half Moon Café. They requested a booth in the back, where they would be afforded more privacy.

"What do you think?" Matt asked as soon as they'd placed their order.

"Probably the same thing you're thinking."

"Okay, read my mind."

Frankie lit a cigarette. "When we talked to Irma Gibbs I thought it odd that she didn't hear a thing, that she claimed to be hard of hearing."

"Especially when she has a husband across the hall who may need her during the night. I'll have to check with Chalmers to see if Irma has complained of hearing loss."

"Secondly, most senior citizens don't usually forget to lock their doors before going to bed. Most I've known keep their doors locked all the time because they're so vulnerable, because of their age. Irma doesn't strike me as being senile. I think her mind is as alert as it always has been. Might want to run that by Chalmers, as well."

The waitress brought their beverages.

"Do you think she would have killed him? A mercy killing, like we just went through with Blaine Freeman?"

"Then burned down the house to cover it up?" Matt

arched a brow. "That sounds a little dramatic. Unless—"

"Unless she was desperate for money."

"And hoped to collect from her insurance company." Matt looked thoughtful.

Their lunch arrived, hamburger steak smothered in gravy and onions with vegetables on the side. Matt scribbled notes as they ate, and Frankie added a few more suggestions.

He put down his pen and looked at her. "You know, we make a good team."

"Of course we do, because I have to perform most of the work." She grinned to show him she was teasing.

He chuckled. "I think we make a good team, period. No matter what happens between us personally, I want to keep you on. I know the pay isn't the best, but I can get you more money."

"That would be nice. Then I could afford my own place. Not that I don't enjoy living with Sissy."

They finished their lunch. Frankie insisted on paying her share. "This is business."

"My other deputies and I take turns paying the check."

"Don't make me cause a scene, Webber, because I will."

They left a few minutes later. "I want to head back to the office so I can make some phone calls. I need to talk to Rand Chalmers."

By the end of the day, Frankie's butt was dragging. She and several other deputies had combed the area looking for Willie-Jack, but he was no place to be found. Back at the station, Frankie made her way to Matt's office.

"What'd you find out?" she asked.

"Chalmers was in surgery when I called and not expected to be out for several hours. His nurse, a personal friend of mine, checked Irma's chart. No mention of hearing problems or senility.''

''What's the plan?''

''I'm going to wait until tomorrow, then I'll question her again. Since Doc Linton has no problem holding the body until Irma is able to make burial arrangements, we've got time.''

Frankie shook her head. ''And I thought nothing ever happened in this town.''

Frankie was glad to see the day come to an end, even happier still that she didn't have to practice her part that evening. Only the main characters had to show for rehearsal. Frankie planned to take a bath and hit the sack early.

''Your mother called,'' Sissy said the minute Frankie stepped through the front door.

''I'm too tired to call her back.''

''You need to sleep, girl.''

''I'm planning on doing just that.''

''There's a casserole on the stove.''

''You're just too damn good to me, Sissy-Q. If you were a guy, I'd ask you to marry me.''

''I know a pretty nice guy who would do the same things for you.''

''Yes, well, we won't go there.''

Matt and Frankie stepped into Irma's room the following morning and found her sitting up in bed drinking hot tea. ''They're going to release me today,'' she said, looking directly at Matt. ''I understand you've made arrangements for me to go into Piney Grove. Am I to be some charity case?''

Matt sat on the edge of her bed, and Frankie took a

chair nearby. "You have no place else to go at the moment," he said, "but I need to speak with you about a more pressing matter."

She set her cup down on the roll-away table and folded her hands in front of her. "I'm listening."

"Doc Linton performed an autopsy on Homer." Irma winced. "He didn't die of smoke inhalation. In fact, he was already dead before the fire started."

Irma looked down at her hands. "You think I killed my own husband?"

"No. But I think you set the fire. I just don't understand why."

Irma looked at Frankie, who gave her a sad smile. "We just need to know the truth, Mrs. Gibbs. Perhaps we can help."

"I'm going to die an old woman in prison, aren't I?"

Matt took her hand. "What happened, Mrs. Gibbs?"

The woman took another sip of her tea. Her hands shook so badly Matt had to take the cup from her and set it in the saucer. Tears streamed down her cheeks. "You're right. Homer died the day before, and I didn't know what to do with his body. We could no longer afford our health insurance payments—they'd raised the premiums so high I dropped it. I couldn't even afford to pay our life insurance premiums. Our social security just wasn't enough. After the little house burned, there was no extra income, and the insurance company still hasn't sent us a check. All that red tape, you know? We'd gone through our savings and had nothing left. I set the fire because—"

"You thought you could collect on that house, as well?"

She hung her head. "Yes."

Frankie pulled tissues from a box and handed them to her. Irma dabbed her eyes. "Is there anything I can get you, Mrs. Gibbs?'' she asked. The woman shook her head.

''What about the first fire?'' Matt asked.

''Guilty.''

Matt and Frankie exchanged looks. ''How did you manage to get away in time? We had people on the scene in a matter of minutes.''

''The people across the street went on vacation. I know them well so I offered to water their plants. I had their garage door opener. I hid my car inside, hurried across the street and poured an entire can of gasoline on the floors. Tossed a match as I walked out the door.

''I saw everything that went on that day. Didn't leave the house until late that night when nobody was around. I gave Homer two sleeping pills so he wouldn't wake up for a while.'' She paused. ''I know what I did was wrong, Matthew, but I was desperate. At this point I don't care if I go to jail or not.''

Matt stood and crossed the room, gazing out the window as if he were searching for an answer in the clouds. After a few minutes he turned around, the expression on his face grave. ''I called the bank. The money from the benefit hasn't been touched. You're too proud to accept charity, but you're not above committing insurance fraud.'' The old woman refused to meet his gaze.

''I'm not going to arrest you, but I'll see that you never collect one dime of the money. You're going to spend the rest of your life in Piney Grove, but no, you're not going to be a charity case. You're going to sell the land and hand over the profits to Piney Grove. I'm going to give you a week to have your attorney do a new will. You'll pay for it from the funds we collected at the benefit, and it should be enough to hold you for a while because you won't need any money.''

She squared her shoulders. "So I'm going to die destitute and all alone in a nursing home."

"Only because you're too frail for prison."

Once again, she hung her head. Matt looked at Frankie. "Let's go."

Outside, Frankie looked at him. "Don't you think you were a little rough on her? She just lost her husband."

"The woman burned down two houses to collect insurance money that wasn't rightfully hers. If it weren't for her age, she would spend time behind bars over something like that. She and Homer own at least fifty acres of land, plus the lot on the rental house. They could have sold off some of that land to support themselves, but Irma was too proud, not wanting folks to think they were having financial problems. She preferred committing insurance fraud."

Frankie didn't respond.

Matt looked at her once they'd reached the patrol car. "You're not going soft on me, are you, Deputy?"

She shook her head. "No, I'm still the bitch from hell."

Matt chuckled as he started the engine and pulled from his parking space.

The next few weeks passed without incident. A liquor store was robbed, but the owner wasn't harmed and they found the culprit right away. Several car accidents occurred, but there were no fatalities. There were some minor skirmishes—domestic problems, a couple of bar brawls—but nothing earth-shattering.

The entire town of Purdyville was stunned when they read an interview that Irma Gibbs had given to a reporter from the *Gazette,* confessing her crime and her plans to make it right. She told of the hardships she and Homer had suffered, how she'd sat up with him the night of his passing, planning how she would burn the house as she had their rental home and collect the money from the insurance company.

"I have been a selfish old woman. People in town were more than willing to help me, but my silly pride stood in the way." She'd gone on to explain how she planned to sell the land and donate it to Piney Grove. "It won't be long before I meet my Maker," she'd added. "I have to get everything off my chest and make things right."

Frankie and Matt were impressed that she'd owned up to everything, even though they knew it had cost her. They were not surprised when Willie-Jack came out of hiding. Each time he passed Matt on the street he seemed to gloat.

Velma's bursitis began acting up, and Frankie found herself helping out in the front office as much as she could. Although Velma grumbled—Frankie couldn't seem to do anything right—it was obvious the woman appreciated the help. There was a time Frankie would have told Velma where she could shove her filing, but the more she came to know Velma, the more she realized the woman was just cantankerous. Except where Matt was concerned. She thought he hung the moon.

Actually, Frankie was glad for the respite, and she wondered how she'd managed the day-to-day stresses that occurred on a regular basis in Atlanta. At least she was getting enough sleep at night, and she'd put on a few pounds. Her face had filled out, so that she no longer looked gaunt. She practiced applying makeup, shopped with Sissy and tried to set up a couple of lunch dates with Alice. Each time she spoke with the woman, Alice seemed preoccupied and complained her schedule was too full for her to get away.

Rehearsals were going well, and the set now resembled

a real beauty parlor, thanks to donations from the salons in town, including two hair dryers that had been sitting in a storeroom for three years and were no longer working.

As opening night grew closer, Frankie became more anxious. "I know I'm going to screw up my line," she told Sissy as they were getting ready to rehearse one evening. Frankie spent much of her free time mumbling her line under her breath, although Sissy claimed it was driving her crazy. "Once I look out and find all those people watching, I'll forget every word."

"You'll do fine," Sissy said, not sounding at all enthusiastic. When Frankie asked if something was wrong, the woman frowned. "Macon Comfy called me today and assured me he was buying a front-row ticket. The whole place will smell like raw hamburger meat."

"I don't know why you say that," Frankie replied. "I've run into him in town several times, and he's neatly dressed and smells like after-shave. He always asks about you."

Sissy rolled her eyes as they headed out the door.

Matt called Saturday afternoon and invited Frankie to dinner. She hesitated. They lunched together often, even with some of the other deputies, but that was business.

"Are you still there?" Matt asked when she didn't answer right away.

"I'm thinking."

"Don't put a lot of thought into it. I'm just inviting you to dinner, not a porno flick and hot sex afterward."

"Okay."

"I'll pick you up at six. Wear something nice. I'm taking you to a decent restaurant, and I don't want to be embarrassed." He hung up.

Frankie heard the click in her ear and stared blankly at

the phone. Now, why had she gone and accepted a date with Matt Webber? They had backed off, and they were doing just fine. They worked well together, and as far as she knew, the rumors had died down. And what was this business about wearing something nice so she wouldn't embarrass him? Like she couldn't dress up if she had to. Oh, she could dress up. She could knock his socks off if she wanted, but she wasn't about to go to all that trouble over some man.

She headed for her bedroom, yanked her purse from the bed and turned for the hall, slamming into Sissy. "Where in the world are you going in such a hurry?"

"Shopping."

Sissy's eyes brightened. "Hold on. I'll go with you."

Frankie had already climbed into her car by the time Sissy locked the front door and raced out. "What's the rush, girlfriend? Are you out of clean underwear?"

"Matt thinks I don't know how to dress up."

Sissy eyed Frankie's worn jeans, sweatshirt and ratty sneakers. "Imagine that."

"I'm going to show him. I'm going to find something that'll have him drooling all night."

"What brought this on?" She listened as Frankie told her. "Honey, this calls for leather and a push-up bra. Turn right at the corner."

Fifteen minutes later they pulled up in front of a consignment shop. "Here?" Frankie asked.

"She carries leather. You can't afford this stuff straight off the rack, you know."

Frankie followed Sissy inside. Bettie, the owner of the store, greeted Sissy, who explained what they were looking for. She led them straight to a rack of leather slacks and skirts and animal-skin blouses.

"This stuff is so hot you have to wear oven mitts to

touch it," the woman said. "Get a load of this skirt. Still has the tag on it." She held it against Frankie. "Might be a little tight."

"Tight is good," Sissy said.

"I'll let you have it for twenty-five dollars."

"Try it on," Sissy said, "while I look for a blouse."

Frankie eyed the skirt doubtfully as she headed toward the back of the store. She stepped out of her sneakers and jeans and pulled the skirt on. It was snug, all right, and short at both ends, riding high on her thighs and low on her hips, showing her navel.

"I found something nice to go with the skirt," Sissy said, thrusting a lightweight sweater into the dressing room.

The sweater was too tight. Frankie could only fasten two buttons. It exposed not only the valley between her breasts but her belly button as well.

"It doesn't fit," she called out to Sissy.

Sissy pulled the curtain aside. "Ohmigod!"

"I need a size or two larger."

"No, darlin', you don't get it. That's the way it's supposed to look."

"But—"

"I have a Victoria's Secret catalog at home. I'll show you. And we can forget the push-up bra."

"My nipples are sticking out like pencil erasers."

"Precisely. And those spiked heels you've got will do the trick." She chuckled low in her throat. "I can't wait to see the look on my dear cousin's face when he gets a look at you in this."

"All finished?" Bettie asked as Frankie carried the out fit to the register. "What about the push-up bra and thong bikini panties? They're brand-new."

"Oh, she won't need panties," Sissy said.

Frankie's jaw dropped. Sissy reached up and pushed it closed. "Let's go. I have to do your makeup."

The telephone rang as soon as they walked through the front door. Sissy picked it up, and then offered it to Frankie. "Your mother," she mouthed.

"You haven't returned my calls," Eve Hutton said the minute Frankie answered.

"I was going to call tomorrow when the rates are cheaper."

"Are you hurting for money?"

"No, I'm just careful."

"You could always call collect if you really wanted to talk to me."

"Actually, I haven't had a lot of free time on my hands. We're rehearsing every night for the play. Then we all go out for coffee, and I don't get in until after ten o'clock."

"I don't go to bed until after the eleven o'clock news, but you already know that. I should have had more children, at least one of them would call me on a regular basis."

"I'm sorry, Mom."

There was silence from the other end. "I just like to know you're doing okay, Francis," the woman said after a moment, as though apologizing. "I know you're busy."

Frankie recognized the old guilt-trip routine. She *had* promised herself to call her mother more often but seldom found the time because she knew she would be on the phone at least an hour. "I'll try to do better."

"I wish I had a nickel for every time you've said that to me. Now, tell me all about the play. Sissy said you have a very important part. If I weren't going to that spa with the girls that week I'd be there, but we got a group discount."

"You've seen *Steel Magnolias*," Frankie said, "so you already know what the play is about."

"Do you know all your lines?"

"Yes."

"With your looks you could be an actress. I don't know why you waste your time in law enforcement when you have so many possibilities."

Frankie sighed. "I like to think I'm providing a good service. Mom, I have to go now."

"Of course you do."

"No, I'm serious. I promise to call you tomorrow. It's only five cents a minute on weekends."

"Of course you will."

"Bye, Mom." Frankie hung up.

Matt walked up the front walk leading to Sissy's house. In his arms were a dozen roses. He had tried to resist calling Frankie over the weekend but had failed miserably. He missed her, dammit. She could raise hell with him all she liked about needing more time, but he would go crazy if he didn't see her on a personal level.

He rang the bell and Sissy opened it, wearing her work uniform. "Roses! Are those for me?"

"You'll have to wait until your birthday."

She pretended to pout. "Well, I'd better get to Virgil's before I'm late. He's having karaoke again tonight so the place will be packed." She turned and called for Frankie. "Your date is here." She waited.

Heart pounding in her chest, Frankie stepped out of her bedroom in her new outfit. Her face was made up, and her hair fell about her shoulders in massive curls.

Matt stared, stunned. The leather skirt clung to her like skin on a snake. Her tight sweater exposed the sexiest belly button he'd ever laid eyes on. He felt motion behind his zipper. "You look...you look—" He paused and shook his head. "Like a million bucks." He handed her the roses. "Thought you might like these."

"Thank you," she said. "Let me put them in water real quick."

Sissy smiled as Frankie made for the kitchen. "Have a nice evening, cousin," she said as she started out the door. She paused and leaned over to whisper in his ear. "Thought you'd like to know. She's not wearing a damn thing under those clothes."

The color drained from Matt's face.

Matt led Frankie to the sports car he'd used the night of the Gibbses' benefit. He opened her door and waited for her to climb in. His gut tightened as he thought of what lay beneath that skirt.

It was going to be a long night.

Matt tried to concentrate as he headed for the highway, but he couldn't seem to keep his eyes off the woman beside him. Her scent was intoxicating, something light but powerfully sexy. It took all the willpower in his body not to turn the car around, head to his place and peel those clothes from her body.

But he wouldn't. All he could hope was that she wanted him as badly as he did her. He had to stop thinking about her in that way. She was a lovely woman, and he was simply out to show her a good time. Being in her company was enough. Well, it would have been enough, had they not already made love. Now all he could think about was kissing those luscious lips, burying his head between her breasts, tasting her and losing himself inside of her.

He grew hard just thinking about it.

"How was your day?" he asked politely, wishing that he didn't feel so awkward. This was Frankie. He worked closely with her, respected her skills, and was always happy to get her opinion. But this was different, and he felt as though he were back in high school.

Frankie glanced at him. She'd been staring out the window, trying not to notice how good Matt looked in dark slacks, a dress shirt and sports jacket. She filled him in on her day, told him how the play was progressing, and was surprised that he seemed so interested.

"I know you got involved with the little theater out of concern for Sissy," he said. "I appreciate all you've done for her."

"Thank you for inviting me to dinner, Matt." Frankie smiled.

His gazed locked with hers for a few seconds before he turned his eyes back to the road. "You're welcome. I'm glad you came. You'll certainly turn a lot of heads in that outfit."

She chuckled. "Do you think it's too much?"

"Frankie, I'd say it's just right. But you'd better stay close to me, because the first man who sees you like that is going to want to grab you and take you home with him."

"I wanted you to like it," she said softly.

Matt didn't know how to respond so he just smiled. He turned on the radio and pushed the buttons until he found something soothing. "Just relax, pretty lady. I'm going to make sure you have a wonderful time tonight."

They arrived at a large steak house some twenty minutes later. "Sit tight," Matt said, climbing out of his car and going around to help her out. "They have a piano bar here. I hope you like it."

"My dinner tonight was going to be chicken pot pie. I doubt I'll be disappointed."

Matt held the door open and Frankie stepped inside a

fashionably decorated restaurant where a hostess smiled pleasantly. "Reservations?"

"Webber," Matt said.

"Oh, yes, Chief Webber. We seated you close to the piano bar, as you requested."

Matt placed his hand on the small of Frankie's back, urging her to follow the hostess. He kept his hand on her protectively, noting the stares she was receiving from some of the men at the long mahogany bar. He didn't have to be psychic to know what they were thinking, and he almost wished he'd brought his raincoat to drape over Frankie's outfit. He only hoped she'd remember to keep her legs close together, and that thought was almost his undoing.

They were seated at a table draped in a crisp white cloth with a crystal candleholder in the center, giving off soft light. Matt looked at Frankie and thought she was the most beautiful creature he'd ever laid eyes on.

Finally, he chuckled.

"What's so funny?" she asked.

"I was just reminded how you looked the first time I saw you. Mad as a hornet and covered with mud."

"That was not a good day."

"I thought, now, there's a little spitfire if ever I saw one."

"You and Orvell seemed to enjoy the scene."

"You were adorable, despite the mud."

She smiled, and their gazes lingered on each other. The waiter appeared with water and a breadbasket. "Would you like to see our wine list?"

Matt nodded, checked through the selections and ordered a bottle. He and Frankie made small talk as they waited. The waiter reappeared with the wine and two menus.

"Our special tonight is prime rib," the man said. "Would you care for an appetizer before you order?"

"How about the Brie?" Matt looked at Frankie and she nodded.

Once again, they were left alone.

"Matt—" Frankie paused when he looked at her, his eyes gazing into hers deeply. "This is very nice of you. I'm sorry things have been strained between us lately."

"I understand," he said. "I don't want people talking about you any more than you do. That's why I was prepared to back off for a while." He reached over and touched her hand. "That doesn't mean I haven't missed you."

"People still have a very sexist attitude when it comes to what a man does in his personal life, as opposed to a woman."

"I know that, babe. It's worse in a small town. I never once meant to jeopardize your reputation. Never. I threatened to fire every deputy in the department if they uttered one unpleasant word about you."

Her face paled. "You did *what?*" Frankie did not realize she'd spoken so loudly until the couple at the next table glanced in their direction. She leaned closer to Matt. "You had no right to go behind my back and try to protect my reputation. I can take care of myself."

Matt leaned even closer. "Well, I did it, and you can be mad as hell, but I'd do it again. Do you remember how angry you were when that Joe fellow hurt Sissy like he did? I think you would have shot him at close range with a sawed-off shotgun if you could have caught up with him."

"We're talking about my professional life here. This is different. I don't need you defending me. My work has been more than adequate, and if the others have a problem with my personal life, they need to bring it to me. Hell, Cooter is seeing a married woman. He takes Vicki Morris to church every Sunday, and they always have lunch afterward. Do I say anything to him about it? No, because I think it's his own damn business. And Buster—''

Frankie closed her mouth as the waiter brought their appetizer.

''Let's get something straight,'' Matt said, his voice low. ''I told you in the beginning I was in charge. If I find my men are acting disrespectfully toward anyone else in the department, I'm going to call them on the carpet. And I'll do whatever is necessary to protect the woman I love, because you are a human being first and a deputy second.''

Frankie stared back at him, unable to reply. ''You really love me?''

''Yes.'' He didn't sound too happy about it at the moment. ''And if loving you means I've got to kick everyone's ass in Purdyville, I'm willing to do it.''

''Oh, Matt.'' Frankie felt tears fill the corners of her eyes.

''Does that surprise you?''

''I've never really had anyone who cared enough to go to battle for me. That's so…chivalrous.''

''You are the best thing that's ever happened to me, Frankie Daniels. I'm not going to allow you to leave Purdyville, and I'm not going to let anyone speak ill of you. That's just the way it is, whether you like it or not.''

The piano player sat down and began playing a slow number. Several couples stood and made their way to the dance floor. Frankie was still staring at Matt in awe.

''Now, do you want to dance with me or would you rather sit here and argue some more?''

''I would love to dance with you.''

Matt stood and offered his hand and she took it. On the dance floor, he pulled her easily into his arms. Their bodies fit together perfectly, as he knew they would. He could feel each curve as they moved together as one, could smell her sweet breath and fragrant hair. He ached for her, the touch of her fingers on his skin, the taste of her lips. But for now, all he could do was wait.

Frankie knew she was lost the minute she felt Matt's arms enclose her. It was like coming home, standing in front of a blazing fire after being in the cold. She leaned into his embrace, loving the feel of his strong body against hers. She had never felt more like a woman than when she was in his arms. He pressed his lips against her forehead, and she wished the dance would never end.

They dined on prime rib, tiny new potatoes and fresh asparagus. Afterward, they had fun sharing a dessert called mud pie and sipping coffee. And they talked. Not about work, but about growing up, things that interested them, their life goals.

"I haven't enjoyed myself like this since I don't know when," Frankie said, once Matt helped her into the car. "Thank you."

"You're welcome," he said. "I enjoyed it as well, and I really like your outfit. It shows just enough to drive me wild."

Frankie chuckled. "Actually, Sissy picked it out. But if you like it that much, I'll wear it to work Monday."

Matt shook his head. "I'll have to shoot the other deputies." He grinned. "So, what do you want to do now? It's still early."

"I wouldn't mind sitting in the courthouse square for a little while."

"That can be arranged." He drove toward town. His cell phone rang, and he frowned. "That's why I didn't take this inside with us.'' He answered it and listened for a moment. ''Hold on, Cooter, I'm getting a lot of static. Say it again.'' He continued to listen. ''How long ago?''

Frankie watched the expression on Matt's face. Something was wrong. It had to be bad.

''I'm losing you, Cooter. I'll be right there.''

He punched a button and pushed his foot on the accelerator. ''There's been a shooting. Just happened.''

She instantly perked up. ''Where?''

''Behind Virgil's place. Willie-Jack Pitts is dead.''

Twenty-Two

They arrived at the accident scene in almost half the time it had taken them to get to the restaurant. Matt parked in the back, where patrol cars formed a semicircle and lit up the area with their flashing lights. He and Frankie climbed out of the car and hurried over to the man sprawled on the ground. Willie-Jack's eyes were open, staring vacantly. The sneer was gone.

Onlookers milled about, filling the back doorway of Virgil's restaurant, some leaning against patrol cars, all trying to see what was going on. Virgil stood off to the side, wiping his eyes. Frankie thought it odd, but perhaps he was upset that the shooting had taken place in his parking lot.

The entire force was there. Frankie caught up with one of the night deputies whose name she didn't know. "Why hasn't the scene been secured?" she demanded.

He looked from her to Matt. "It just happened. Willie-Jack tried to take out his frustrations on some woman, and we were more interested in getting an ambulance in here."

"Did anybody see anything?" Matt asked.

"We've got men inside questioning people now. Virgil's real upset over it."

Once again, Frankie thought that was odd, but she didn't have time to worry about it.

"Get everybody out of here," Matt said, "and secure the scene."

Frankie made for the body. "I need a flashlight. Somebody give me a damn flashlight."

Cooter slapped one in her hand, and she and Matt knelt beside the body. Willie-Jack Pitts lay in a pool of blood, a gunshot wound to his chest. "Did anyone find a weapon?" Matt asked.

"No, Chief. We looked."

"Has anyone called Doc Linton?" Frankie asked.

"Haven't exactly had a chance," Cooter replied. "We've been questioning people and waiting for an ambulance."

"Please call him."

Frankie noticed a soft drink can and a cigarette butt not far from the body, the ashes still intact.

"I need a crime scene kit."

"Oh, those are from one of the customers in the restaurant," Buster said. "He was leaning over the body when we arrived."

Frankie couldn't hide her annoyance. "How many others have been near the body?"

He shrugged. "Half the people from the restaurant, I reckon. We chased 'em off as soon as we got here."

Frankie tossed an angry look at Matt. "Well, now that we know the evidence has been jeopardized, that should make our job a helluva lot easier." Her voice was thick with sarcasm.

"Hold on, Frankie," Matt said. "My men didn't just fall off a turnip truck. They know what they're doing. The crime just occurred, for Pete's sake."

"We were more interested in getting the victim to the hospital," Cooter said, eying Frankie's outfit.

Frankie looked up, caught Cooter's look, and remembered she wasn't wearing panties. She didn't have time to worry about it. "Was Willie-Jack fighting with someone?"

Cooter stepped closer. "Sissy Burns. I thought you knew."

Frankie felt her blood turn cold. "What about Sissy?" she demanded.

He looked from Frankie to Matt. "I thought you knew. Willie-Jack beat the hell out of her. She had serious injuries. We were more interested in getting an ambulance in here than worrying about this piece of shit who's already dead, anyway."

Frankie leapt to her feet. "Did you know about this?" she asked Matt.

He shook his head. "I couldn't hear half of what Cooter was saying when he called. How bad was she, Cooter?"

The man shook his head. "We didn't even recognize her. Virgil is beside himself with worry. Blames himself for the whole thing."

Frankie had no time for the details. Her knees felt weak. Shit. She couldn't faint. Not without wearing underwear. "I have to get to the hospital."

"I need you here right now," Matt said, not wanting her to run off in her condition. Besides, he wanted to see Sissy, too. "I can take you to the hospital as soon as we're finished."

"You don't need me. You know enough about this to do it in your sleep. I have to check on my friend." She didn't realize how loudly she was speaking. Why was he trying to prevent her from leaving? "I need the key to your car."

His gaze locked with hers. He was shaken, but he tried not to show it. He had no idea how badly Sissy was injured or whether or not she would even live after the attack. He didn't like the idea of Frankie going alone.

"Are you okay? You want somebody to drive you?"

"I'm fine. I can drive myself. You need your men here."

Matt didn't have time to argue with her. He fumbled in his pocket for his car keys. "Sissy is probably still in the ER. You won't be able to see her right away."

"Then I'll wait, but I want to be the first person she sees when she comes around."

Matt watched her make her way to the car. Frankie had once confessed she was more interested in solving a case than getting emotionally involved with the victim. True, Sissy was a friend, but he suspected there'd been a time when Frankie would have combed the crime scene looking for evidence instead of rushing off to check on someone who was injured, no matter who it happened to be.

It could only mean one thing. Frankie Daniels had changed.

Sissy did not come out of the emergency room for several hours after Frankie arrived. She sipped black coffee and waited, imagining all sorts of horrible things. She checked with the receptionist constantly. The woman looked sympathetic.

"Honey, your friend is going to be okay. You just have to have faith."

Faith. Frankie found that a hard one to swallow. She had counted on her own wits for so long that it was foreign to believe that she could allow a higher power to handle the situation.

Nevertheless, she prayed.

The receptionist finally called Frankie over. "Ms. Burns is stable, but they're moving her to ICU."

"Her condition is bad, isn't it."

"They want to observe her closely."

"When can I see her?"

"Only members of the family can visit."

"I'm her sister."

"I thought you said you were her friend."

"Well, of course we're friends." It never occurred to Frankie to tell the woman she was a cop.

The woman smiled. "I'll make a note on Ms. Burns's chart."

It was another hour before Frankie could look in on Sissy. A nurse led her in briefly. Frankie was appalled at the sight. Part of Sissy's head had been shaved and bore stitches. Her face was battered and bruised. Had Frankie not known it was her friend lying there, she wouldn't have recognized her.

"I understand she suffered a concussion," Frankie said. "Was there any brain damage?"

"You'll have to speak to Dr. Chalmers. He'll be by shortly to fill you in."

As if acting on cue, Rand Chalmers walked into the room. "I have one question," he said. "Is it true Willie-Jack is dead?"

"Yes."

"Well, thank God for small favors."

Frankie didn't answer. As much as she'd hated Willie-Jack, the loss of life was always tragic. "How is she?" she asked, looking at Sissy.

"Her tests revealed no swelling in the brain, which is exactly what we were hoping for. The sonogram showed a few internal injuries, but nothing life-threatening. Her wrist is broken, and you can see there are plenty of lacerations and contusions, but she's young and she'll pull through."

Frankie went weak with relief. "How long will you keep her in ICU?"

"She should be stable enough to move into a regular room tomorrow. We just want to keep a close eye on her tonight. I suggest you go home, Frankie. I'll have someone call if her condition changes."

Matt was waiting for Frankie when she came out. "I tried to get here as fast as I could, but we had a lot of people to question. How is Sissy?"

She repeated what Dr. Chalmers told her.

"I want to have a look."

Frankie waited outside. She felt responsible for Sissy's injuries. It was no secret the two shared a place. Had Willie-Jack taken some of his resentment toward Frankie out on Sissy? It was hard to believe the man was dead. She was certain a lot of people in town would be relieved, just as Rand Chalmers had been.

Matt looked sorrowful as he came out of the room. He sat down beside Frankie and sighed heavily. "He would have killed her if someone hadn't shot him."

"Nobody saw the shooter?"

"No. Or maybe folks just aren't saying anything. Virgil heard the shot from the kitchen. He was the one who found them."

"Does he have any idea what started the fight between Willie-Jack and Sissy?"

"Willie-Jack got drunk and started causing trouble, and Virgil put his foot down, told him he was permanently barred from entering the place again. Willie-Jack stormed out."

"What did Sissy have to do with the whole thing?"

"She refused to serve Willie-Jack. That's what started it all. Seems he called her every name in the book, and she slapped his face. Virgil told her to go out back and cool off. Willie-Jack obviously saw her on his way to his car.''

They were both quiet for a moment. Finally, Matt turned to her. ''Cooter said Virgil threatened to shoot Willie-Jack, said you were there and heard it.''

''I heard a man who was very frustrated. Cooter and I didn't take it seriously.''

''We searched the premises. We didn't find the weapon. I have a couple of deputies still searching the restaurant for the gun. Everyone in the restaurant was searched. Nothing. The place is surrounded by crime-scene tape. Nobody goes in. We'll keep looking.'' He paused. ''I hate to tell you this, but right now Virgil is our main suspect.''

''How can that be when we don't even have a weapon?''

''Virgil made threats against him, Frankie.''

''So have I.''

''But you have an alibi. Considering how loud the place was and how busy the staff, Virgil could have seen what was going on and put a bullet through Willie-Jack. You know how close Virgil and Sissy are.''

''Back to the missing weapon.''

''Who else knows the lay of the land better than Virgil? We may never find the gun. There's a lot of work to do. And I can tell you this much for sure. If we don't find out who killed Willie-Jack, his family is going to start trouble like you've never seen before.''

Frankie arrived at the hospital the next morning and waited for permission to go into the ICU. Sissy was conscious, but her outside appearance looked worse than the previous day. Her bruises were even more noticeable.

''Am I gorgeous or what?'' Sissy said, her tone humorous.

"You're not going to win any beauty contests in the next couple of weeks, but you're alive, and that's what counts."

"I have a gash on my cheek. They changed my bandages this morning, and I saw it. You know what that means. So much for my modeling career, but then, we both know I'm too old for that. People were too kind to point it out to me, but I knew."

Frankie's heart ached for her. "Sissy—"

"Don't look at me like that. I don't want anyone's pity. I know what I am. My house looks like a sixties reject, I spend every dime I have on facial creams and cosmetics because I want to have that something special that model agencies look for."

Frankie sat on the edge of Sissy's bed. "Stop talking like that, dammit. You're one of the most special people I've ever met. Look at me, Sissy." Her friend refused. "You're *alive*. Willie-Jack could have killed you. He was drunk and angry enough to do you in, right there in Virgil's parking lot, if someone hadn't killed him first."

Sissy's eyes widened. "Willie-Jack is dead?"

"Someone shot him. Don't you remember?"

Sissy looked thoughtful. "I heard a noise, but I don't know where it came from. The last thing I remember was Willie-Jack choking me. I felt myself blacking out. Then I woke up in this bed. I'd forgotten how I got here."

"Are you sure you didn't see anything?"

"I'd just had the shit beaten out of me, Frankie. All I saw was Willie-Jack's face. He looked dazed, as if he had finally lost it. I tried to fight back."

"You did fight back. You left teeth marks."

"Good. Too bad I didn't have a knife or I would have left a hole in his gut. Who do they think shot Willie-Jack?"

Frankie didn't want to upset her, but she knew Sissy would press. "Virgil is the prime suspect."

"Virgil wouldn't hurt a fly, and you know it," she said emphatically.

"I believe Virgil would kill to protect you."

"Will they arrest him?"

"They'll have to formally charge him, but I doubt he'll spend time behind bars, because he was defending you."

Sissy closed her eyes. "I can't believe this happened."

"The only reason I'm telling you is because I want you to try to remember what you saw, if anything."

A nurse appeared, signaling to Frankie that her time was up. She kissed Sissy on the forehead. "I'll be back as soon as they'll let me visit."

Matt was in a foul mood when Frankie arrived back at the station. "How's Sissy?"

"She's conscious, but she looks like hell. What's wrong?"

"The prosecutor is going after Virgil. I told you Willie-Jack's family would create a stink."

"There's no weapon, no proof."

Matt leaned back in his chair and sighed. "He likes the attention. He's running for district attorney next year."

"What are we going to do?"

"Find the killer, what else?" He didn't realize he'd snapped at her until he'd said it. "I'm sorry, Frankie, but I'll resign before I arrest Virgil Kellett. He's a good man, one of the best."

"Anything from the crime lab?"

"The bullets came from a .38 Smith & Wesson. They're trying to trace it now."

A knock sounded at the door. Cooter peeked in. "There's trouble out front, Chief. The Pitts family has arrived. And they look madder'n hell."

Twenty-Three

"**I** knew this was going to happen," Matt said. "How many are there?"

"'Bout twenty. You can tell they're kin. They're all ugly as the backside of a mule."

"Get Cooter and Buster out front." Matt picked up the phone. "Velma, get on the radio and find the deputies on patrol. Tell them we've got trouble at the department." He hung up.

Matt stepped outside a few minutes later, with Frankie, Cooter and Buster beside him. Pitts was standing at the front of the crowd holding a baseball bat.

"You got a problem, Mr. Pitts?" Matt asked.

"I want to know who murdered my boy in cold blood."

"Just so happens we're working that case now."

"You're wasting time, Webber. My boy is layin' on a slab in the morgue and not a damn one of you has given us any answers."

"I've made this case my top priority, I don't see how I can do any better."

"We all know who did it."

"Well, that's a relief, now I won't have to go looking."

"Virgil Kellett is as guilty as they come. It's all over town."

"We don't have any proof of that. Besides, the person who shot Willie-Jack was trying to protect Sissy Burns.

If Willie-Jack were alive, I would have sent him to the pen, anyway."

"I'll bet my last dollar she had it coming," Pitts said. "But she's alive, and my son is dead. My only boy. His mama can't stop crying. If you don't go after Virgil, somebody else will."

Matt's face darkened. "Are you threatening a citizen of this community?"

"I ain't *threatening* nothin'."

"Don't do anything stupid, Pitts. You'll regret it the rest of your life, I can promise you."

"I ain't got no life to speak of, now that my boy is gone. I ain't got nothing to lose. Not a damn thing." He looked at Frankie, his expression menacing. "I know how you talked to my boy. He told me every word. I don't know who you think you are, but you're going to wish you'd never laid eyes on him before this is over."

"You're too late, Mr. Pitts. I already wish I never laid eyes on your so-called boy."

Pitts's face turned so red Frankie thought he would suffer a stroke right on the spot. "Somebody needs to take you off that high horse you're on." He spit. "I'd watch my back if I were you."

"That's enough, Pitts!" Matt said loudly. "Say one more word, and I'm locking you up."

Two patrol cars pulled up at the scene and parked. Four deputies stood at the back of the crowd, waiting.

"If you and your army are here to start trouble, we're ready for you," Matt continued. "You need to go home and see to your wife."

Pitts tried to stare him down. "I'll give you twenty-four hours."

Matt crossed his arms. "I don't take orders from you.

Take your ugly kinfolk and get the hell out of here, before I arrest every one of you.''

Finally, Pitts mumbled something to the men behind him, and they drifted off. ''Twenty-four hours,'' he told Matt. He gave Frankie a hard look before walking away.

Matt was clearly shaken as he looked at her. ''You're not staying alone tonight.''

''I'm not afraid of that bastard.''

''Don't argue with me.''

The look on his face stopped her from making further comments.

Back in his office, Matt thumbed through his address book, picked up the phone and dialed. ''I need to speak to Clive Bibb,'' he said.

''What are you going to do, Chief?'' Cooter asked, having followed half the department into Matt's office.

''I'm going to arrest Virgil Kellett.''

Matt and Frankie arrived at Virgil's house an hour later. The man looked worried as he met them at the door. His wife stood beside him. ''Am I in trouble, Matt?''

''I have to arrest you, Virgil.''

The man paled. ''You don't think I killed Willie-Jack, do you?''

''Hell, no. I'm doing this for your own protection.''

''Willie-Jack's family is threatening me, aren't they?''

''You don't need to worry about that. You'll have twenty-four-hour protection. Now, shut up while Frankie reads you your rights. Ginni, you need to pack a bag for the two of you, say for three or four days.''

''Why are you arresting my wife?'' Virgil demanded. ''She wasn't even at the restaurant when it happened.''

''I'm trying to get the two of you out of town. Oh, Ginni, better pack bathing suits.''

Virgil looked worried and confused. "What's going on, Matt?"

"When was the last time you and Ginni had a vacation? Not only a vacation, but a free one?"

Virgil looked at his wife, then back at Matt. "I don't exactly remember."

"Well, I told the prosecutor I was going to arrest you, but on one condition. I'm sending you out of town. To a hotel. Frankie found a nice one."

"That's right," she said. "It has a swimming pool, a workout room and a hot tub."

"I'll have one of my deputies drive you. It's for your own protection. I don't want you calling anyone. Now, hurry up, Virgil. Ya'll have a long ride ahead of you."

"What about my restaurant?"

"You don't have to worry about that. I got it covered."

"Will we be able to order room service?" Ginni asked, looking excited for the first time.

Matt hugged her. "Honey, you can have anything you want. Now, get packed. One of my deputies will be here any minute to pick you up."

Back at the station, Matt paused at Velma's window. "Get somebody from the *Gazette* on the line, would you?"

"I am not staying at your house tonight," Frankie told Matt firmly at the end of the day. "I've got a weapon, and I'll use it if Pitts or one of his sidekicks shows up at my door."

"Then I'll stay at your place."

"That won't be necessary."

"I'm pulling rank on you, Deputy. I do not want you alone. You'll ride out to my house long enough for me to grab my things and feed my dog."

She folded her arms over her breasts. "You happen to forget that I'm a professional and a seasoned detective."

"I don't give a damn about any of that. You heard what Pitts said, and I'm not taking any chances." She opened her mouth to argue, but he interrupted. "I've been playing it your way long enough." Their gazes met. "I'm not backing down on this one, Frankie, so deal with it."

"I have to go by the hospital."

"I'll drive you."

Sissy had been moved from ICU into a private room. They found her watching a game show. Flowers adorned the room. Frankie recognized the big bouquet she and Matt had sent, but her eyes widened at the sight of a tall crystal vase containing a dozen red roses.

"Macon Comfy sent them," Sissy said.

"That was awfully kind of him. Did the two of you visit?"

"He was here for an hour, despite me telling him how tired I was. I finally pretended to fall asleep in the middle of some story he was telling me."

Frankie chuckled. "You're awful."

Sissy looked at Matt. "Abby and a couple of waitresses from Virgil's came by with chocolates and magazines. None of us can believe you arrested Virgil."

"I had my reasons, but I don't want to discuss them right now. You'll just have to trust me on this one, Sissy."

"Well, I don't mind telling you how upset everybody is. I hope you know what you're doing, because this town is going to be in an uproar when people find out. Besides, if Virgil did shoot Willie-Jack—which I'm willing to swear he didn't—he was merely trying to save my life."

"I know folks won't be happy, but I can't expect to win every popularity contest. Have you been able to remember anything?"

"Frankly, I'm trying not to think about it. Every time I close my eyes I see Willie-Jack's face." She shivered.

Frankie sat on the edge of the bed. "Do me a favor, Sissy, and close your eyes."

Matt tossed Frankie a curious look.

For once, Sissy didn't argue. She closed her eyes.

"You're in a safe place, and Matt and I are with you. Just keep your eyes closed and try to relax. If you feel uncomfortable, you can open them anytime."

Sissy seemed to relax, her facial muscles slackened.

"Okay, try to remember what happened after Virgil sent you out back to cool off after having words with Willie-Jack. Try to see it in your mind. You're standing in the alley. Do you smell anything?"

"Garbage. Virgil keeps the cans out back."

"Anything in particular?"

"Onions and old grease."

"And the weather?"

"It's cool on my arms, but I'm too pissed off to think about it. I'm mad as hell at Virgil for sending me out."

"What do you hear?"

Sissy shrugged. "Loud music from the karaoke going on inside. And people laughing and shouting because the person singing really sucks."

"Then what?"

"Next thing I know, Willie-Jack is standing there. I didn't even hear his footsteps because of the noise. I figure he heard Virgil send me out back right after he told Willie-Jack to hit the road."

"What does he say when he spots you?"

Sissy took a deep breath. "The usual. He calls me every name in the book. I mouth off. Next thing I know, he begins punching me."

Frankie noted a tear slip from one of Sissy's eyes. She

wouldn't press. "Okay, that's good, Sissy. You can open your eyes."

"What the hell was that all about?" Matt demanded.

"I want Sissy to keep going back. I know it's painful, but if she keeps pushing it out of her mind—"

"I know what she's doing," Sissy said ruefully. "She thinks I saw something." She looked at Frankie. "I've already told you, the only thing I saw was Willie-Jack before he bashed me in the face. I wish I could help you, and I wish I could help Virgil, but this hasn't been easy for me, you know?"

Frankie touched her shoulder. "I know. I'm sorry I put you through it."

Another tear slipped down Sissy's cheek. "I want to be alone right now, okay?"

Frankie kissed her on the head, and she and Matt left. "That was a little insensitive, don't you think?" Matt asked once they'd reached the lobby. "Are you a hypnotist now?"

"I don't know the first thing about hypnotism, but Sissy needs to try and remember what happened. Sometimes victims are so terrified they don't want to remember. Sissy may have very well seen something, but she's blocking it."

"What's worse than seeing Willie-Jack's face?" Matt asked.

"Nothing I can think of. But there's a chance she was still conscious when he was shot."

"You took a risk."

She stiffened. "I'm afraid for her."

He nodded. "So am I. The person who shot Willie-Jack may not want Sissy to remember."

"Precisely. And if that's the case, Sissy could be in

danger. But you're right. I'm not qualified to do what I just did back there. It won't happen again.''

Frankie was cool to Matt when they pulled into Sissy's driveway. She climbed from the car and made for the house, wishing she could just take a quick shower and hit the sack. She had decided to skip rehearsal again. She had called Joey to give him the news about Sissy, and the man had been distraught. Now that Sissy wouldn't be playing the main role, Frankie had no interest.

''How about I order a pizza?'' Matt said.

Frankie shrugged. ''Whatever.''

He placed his hands on his hips. ''Okay, hotshot, you can pout if you like, but you're just making it harder on yourself.''

Frankie crossed her arms. ''I don't appreciate your treating me as though I can't take care of myself. That's a direct insult when you consider my years of training.''

Matt threw his arms out as if surrendering. ''You know, I keep hoping we're going to get past this silliness.''

''It's not silly.''

''This has nothing to do with your skills as a professional. How many times do I have to say it, Frankie? I'm not acting as an officer of the law here. I'm acting out of love and concern. Deal with it.''

''You're shouting.''

''Has it occurred to you that Pitts might end up putting a gun to *my* head, and you'll be the one to have to shoot the SOB?''

She hadn't thought of that.

Finally, he shook his head, picked up his overnight bag and grabbed his car keys.

''Where are you going?''

''Home. You obviously don't want me here. If Pitts

shows up, put a bullet between his eyes and call me.'' He started for the door.

''Matt?''

He turned. ''What now?''

''Please don't leave.''

He sighed and his shoulders sagged. ''I can't go on like this, Frankie. I don't know where I stand from one day to the next. We have wild, incredible sex, we get along well, even at work. You know I have your best interests at heart, but it's not enough for you. I'm not going to fight a losing battle.''

''I love you, too, Matt.''

He looked at her, a challenge in his eyes. ''Prove it.''

Frankie knew it was up to her to make the next move. Matt had already laid his feelings on the line. Now it was her turn. They were standing at a precipice, and if she didn't act, she would end up alienating him or losing him forever. She could not risk it. For once she had to go out on a limb, whether or not it frightened her or made her feel more vulnerable than she ever had. She loved him. Every relationship she'd ever had paled compared to what she felt for Matt.

It was time to give love a chance.

Frankie closed the distance between them, took Matt's bag and keys and set them down. She turned to him, gazing into his eyes. She found the need and longing there, and it almost took her breath away. Finally, she reached up, slipped her arms around his neck and pulled his face to hers. She kissed him.

Matt moaned the minute her mouth found his, and he gathered her in his arms. He could not get close enough. The weeks without her had left him with a hunger that couldn't be filled in a simple kiss. He slid his fingers through her hair, cupping her scalp, anchoring her head between his wide palms so that he could continue kissing her. And kiss her, he did. He kissed her chin, her throat, her ears, her eyes, her forehead. When he recaptured her lips, he dipped his tongue deep inside, and the need for her only increased. With Frankie in his arms, he could forget everything else around them.

Frankie couldn't help but respond to Matt's lips. How could a man taste and feel so good? How could his kisses leave her yearning for more? All the muscles in her body went lax, and she leaned into his embrace. His big arms wrapped around her and steadied her. His breath was moist on her ear as he whispered endearments, each one filling her heart in places that had been hollow far too long.

"I want to make love with you, Frankie Daniels," he said.

She shivered at the huskiness in his voice. "I'd like to shower first."

"How about we conserve water and shower together?"

"Sounds like a plan." She was already unbuttoning his shirt and pressing her face against his chest. She knew the scent of him, the way his mouth tasted, the feel of his taut muscles beneath her fingers, but there was so much more she wanted to experience.

They played like children as they stood beneath the warm water, letting go of every single thought and concentrating only on the moment at hand. As they gazed at each other's naked bodies, their looks turned serious.

"You're beautiful," Matt said.

"My breasts are on the small size."

"Really?" Matt cupped them with his palms. "That's funny, they seemed to fit perfectly." He ducked his head and tongued one nipple.

Frankie's body responded, every nerve ending coming

to life. She grasped his shoulders for support. His brown skin felt good beneath her fingers.

Matt raised his head, and their gazes locked. "Do you have a washcloth?"

Frankie blinked and reached for a sponge and soap. Matt sniffed the soap and arched one brow. "It's girl soap," he said. "Do you have any guy soap?"

"No."

"If I bathe with this, will I want to wear your panties, too?"

She chuckled. "They wouldn't fit you."

"Turn around," he said. He lathered the sponge and began washing her gently sloping shoulders, kissing the back of her neck as he did so. Finally, he lifted her hair and washed the back of her neck before sliding down her back. He washed her hips, the back of her thighs and calves before returning to her hips. With the sponge in one hand, he slid his hand between the back of her thighs. Frankie gasped at the delightful sensation. He parted the lips of her vagina and touched the tiny nub lightly, making circular motions with his soapy finger. Her body went limp, and she whimpered. She leaned against him, and he encircled her with one arm, holding her steady.

He chuckled, the sound coming from deep within his chest. "I think you like this."

"I think you're right," she managed.

He waited until her breathing became sporadic before slipping a finger inside of her, still holding her securely within the circle of his other arm. He felt her muscles tighten as he pressed even deeper, brought her to full orgasm. She cried out and shivered against him, and her sounds excited him. He pressed his hardness against her soft hips so she would have no doubt what she did to him.

Once Frankie regained control, she took the sponge and

washed his back as he stood beneath the spray of the shower and washed his hair. His hips were lean and tight, his thighs and calves powerful. His feet, much larger than hers, were sturdy. He rinsed his hair and turned around. Frankie applied the sponge to his chest, watching the way his nipples reacted as she touched them lightly with her fingers. His belly was rock hard. She washed the black nest of hair that grew around his penis. He was hard. She took him in her hand.

"Oh, Frankie," he muttered sharply.

She palmed him with soapy fingers, moving up and down the swollen organ, admiring the beauty of him. She moved beyond and soaped his scrotum with a delicate touch. He closed his eyes. She allowed him to rinse before she knelt before him and put him in her mouth.

"Frankie, Frankie, you certainly know how to drive a man wild."

She tongued the tip of his penis, running her lips along the ridge and loving the feel of his hands on her shoulders, as if needing to anchor himself. She took him deeply into her mouth, and he moaned.

"I need to be inside of you," he said, his voice husky and urgent. He put his arms around her and lifted her. Frankie guided him into her, and he filled her. Still holding her, he climbed from the tub, ignoring the spray of water. They were wet and slick. He set her on the sink. She gripped the sides and parted her thighs wider so he could watch himself mate with her, sliding in and out, in and out. Her muscles gripped him tightly. He had never seen anything more erotic in his life and he thrust himself between her folds. Some primitive instinct took over as he entered and withdrew, taking her as he wished.

"Touch yourself," he demanded between clenched teeth.

Frankie steadied herself on the sink and with a free hand pressed her forefinger against the bud, circling it, rubbing it until she was as excited as he was. The desire in his eyes heightened as she brought herself to orgasm. Matt gave one deep thrust and drained himself inside her. His climax was powerful.

Once they'd dried themselves, they lay beside each other on Frankie's bed, spent. Matt kissed her. "Loving you is so...good."

"Mmm." It was all she could do to keep her eyes open. Her head on his chest, she drifted off.

A sound in the night woke them. Frankie felt a rush of adrenaline as Matt reached for his gun. She felt a tremor of fear as she imagined Pitts and his cohorts surrounding the house. She was thankful Matt was beside her. "Do you think it's him?" she whispered in a voice that was too low for anyone but Matt to hear.

"It's three o'clock in the morning. Who else would be snooping around out there at this hour?" He pulled on his jeans quickly as Frankie donned a nightshirt and grabbed her gun from the night table.

The doorbell rang. They looked at each other blankly. "I'll get it," Matt said, wondering what the hell was going on. He tucked his gun into the waistband of his jeans and walked through the living room, Frankie following close behind.

Matt unlocked the door and flipped the dead bolt as Frankie stood to one side, revolver pointed upright, ready in case anything happened. Matt kept the chain in place and cracked the door. An older woman with red hair stood on the other side. Her car must've broken down, Matt thought.

"May I help you?" he asked politely.

The woman's jaw dropped. For a minute she simply stared as if trying to recover from shock. "I certainly hope so," she said. "I'm looking for my daughter, Francis Daniels."

Frankie closed her eyes and swore under her breath. She almost would have preferred facing Pitts than the woman on the other side.

Twenty-Four

Matt undid the chain and Eve stepped in. She came to an abrupt halt at the sight of Frankie. Her eyes took in Matt's half-clad body and Frankie in her T-shirt.

"Uh, hello, Francis."

Frankie saw the hurt and disappointment in her mother's eyes, and she felt a sharp pang of sadness. "Mom, what on earth are you doing here?"

Eve's hand flew to her throat and she fidgeted with the collar of her dress, an olive silk that looked as wilted as the woman herself. "I wanted to surprise you, honey. I landed in Raleigh, rented a car and came right here."

"It's three o'clock in the morning!"

"My plane was late, and my rental car broke down halfway here." She kept glancing at Matt. "I suppose I should have called, but you know how impulsive I can be. I just had to see you. I obviously came at a bad time." She gave an embarrassed laugh. "Silly me. Honey, why are you holding that gun?"

Frankie felt something in her heart soften at the sight of her rumpled mother, who looked like she might start crying, either from embarrassment or exhaustion. Frankie hated herself for all the years she'd tried to protect the woman, who was still old-fashioned enough to believe a couple should wait for marriage before they became intimate.

Frankie gave her a hug. "Mom, you're welcome anytime. You just caught me by surprise, that's all." She glanced at Matt. "Matt, this is my mother, Eve Hutton. Mom, I...uh...want you to meet Chief Webber."

Eve perked. "We spoke on the phone once, when I was trying to find Francis after her little house burned. You're her boss."

Matt chuckled as he reached outside for a suitcase and pulled it in. "Well, I'm not sure anyone is capable of bossing your daughter around."

"Francis, where is your housemate, Sissy?"

Frankie wished her mother would stop calling her Francis. "It's a long story, Mom. We had a shooting the other night—"

"A shooting! I thought you said this was a safe town."

"It usually is," Matt cut in.

"Anyway, Sissy was badly beaten, and she's in the hospital. Matt was afraid I was in danger so he's spending the night."

Eve visibly relaxed as she regarded the two. "Oh, so you're offering my daughter protection?"

"That's right, Mrs. Hutton," Matt said, never missing a beat. "Frankie and I were expecting trouble when you knocked on the door. That's why we are both armed."

"Are we in danger?"

Frankie was thankful Matt had picked up his cue. "You have two armed police officers with loaded weapons on the premises. I don't think you have anything to worry about."

"Oh, I'm so embarrassed," Eve said. "I hate to say it, but I thought...well, I'm too embarrassed to even say it." She threw her arms around her daughter. "I'm just so happy to see my little girl." She hugged Matt as well. "And to know there's someone here to look after her."

Frankie and Matt exchanged looks. "Matt, why don't you make us a cup of coffee while I throw on some clothes. I feel silly standing here in my nightshirt."

"I'll be glad to," he told Frankie. "Eve, why don't you follow me into the kitchen. You look like you could use a cup of coffee about now."

Frankie hurried down the hall to her room, where she gathered Matt's belongings and tossed them on Sissy's bed. She dragged down the covers and mussed the pillows so it would look as though Matt had been sleeping there. In her room she sprinkled powder on the sheets and pillows, remade the side Matt had slept on, grabbed a couple of books from a battered bookcase and tossed them on the bed so it would appear as if she'd been reading before she'd fallen asleep. She sighed, wondering why she was going to the trouble. She was thirty-two years old, for Pete's sake. She couldn't keep pretending to her mother she was a virgin.

Frankie checked the bathroom, grabbing the two towels from the floor and stuffing them in the hamper. She could hear Matt and her mother chatting in the kitchen. She slipped on her jeans, checked the rooms once more, and then joined them. "I see the two of you are getting acquainted."

"Matt was just telling me all that's been going on the past few weeks. Frankie, why didn't you tell me?"

"Because I knew you'd worry."

"Is Sissy going to be okay?"

"She looks pretty bad, but she'll heal."

"Poor girl. I don't mind telling you I'm relieved this man was shot and killed. He sounds sick."

The coffee finished dripping through. Frankie reached into the cupboard for cups. "Matt, you don't have to stay up with us. Why don't you go back to bed?" Their gazes met briefly. "I don't expect we'll have any trouble at this hour," she added.

"I am kind of tired," he said, suspecting Frankie had moved his things to Sissy's room. "Be sure to keep your bedroom door open just in case. If you hear the slightest noise, come get me."

Frankie nodded. "Good night."

"It was nice meeting you, Mrs. Hutton," Matt said, backing out of the room. "I'm sorry we gave you such a fright."

"Please call me Eve. I'll see you in the morning."

Frankie spent the next hour listening to her mother's nonstop chatter. It was after five o'clock when she yawned. "We need to call it a night, Mom. I'm beat."

"Oh, that's right, you have to work tomorrow."

"I can probably go in late."

"Your boss seems very kind."

"He's okay."

"And handsome, too."

Frankie's look was deadpan as she went for her mother's luggage. "You think so?"

"Oh, Frankie, don't tell me you haven't noticed. How could you not? And that chest. If I were thirty years younger—"

"We work together, Mom. Simple as that."

Eve merely looked at her. She followed Frankie down the hall to her bedroom. "Oh, this is nice," she said. "I was afraid what it would look like after seeing that living room, but I didn't want to say anything."

"Sissy decorated the living room."

Her mother looked at her but was polite enough not to say anything. "Are you sure I won't be in the way?"

"There's plenty of room," Frankie said, placing the

suitcase on the bed so her mother could get what she needed. "As long as you don't mind sharing a bed."

Eve picked up the books on the bed. "Honey, what on earth are you reading?"

"Huh?" Frankie glanced up. "What do you mean?"

"*The Biography of Adolf Hitler* and *The Great Depression*?" Eve looked at her.

The books had obviously belonged to Sissy's parents. "I was nervous and couldn't sleep so I grabbed the first thing I could find."

Eve looked confused as she made her way to the bathroom, gown slung across one arm, a case of toiletry items in her hand.

Morning came too soon for Frankie. She smelled bacon cooking in the kitchen and knew her mother would have already showered and dressed and started breakfast. Eve believed in three meals a day, no snacks. Frankie slipped into a pair of jeans, lit a cigarette and headed in the direction of the smells. She found Matt sitting at the table with a cup in hand, listening to Eve go on about the activities offered at the retirement community.

"Good morning, darling," she said as soon as Frankie entered the room. "I thought you gave up smoking."

"I've cut back. Chief Webber maintains a smoke-free environment." Frankie reached into the cabinet for a coffee cup.

"Speaking of smokers, Dell Wayford asks about you all the time. Says he keeps meaning to call."

"How is he doing?"

"Fine. We talk on the phone a lot. He keeps promising to visit."

"That's nice." Frankie poured her coffee.

"He told me to give you a message. Somebody named

Connors or Connelly was fired. He thought you'd like to know.''

Frankie and Matt exchanged looks. He winked at her as she put the coffeepot back in place.

"Did Captain Wayford tell you he's Matt's uncle?"

Eve nodded. "Yes. He's just waiting for retirement, and then he's planning to come this way so he can see the mountains. He invited me to join him, but I'm so busy with all that's going on at home. And one of my neighbors, a retired airline pilot, has been giving me the eye. He's been all over the world and wants to go again. I certainly wouldn't mind accompanying him. I'm sure he gets a huge discount on his tickets, if he pays at all. Of course, I'd insist on paying for my hotel room."

Frankie sat across from Matt and wondered what he must be thinking. She caught his eye and smiled. He returned it.

The toast popped up. "Okay, Matt, your breakfast is ready," Eve announced, once she'd buttered the toast. She carried his plate to the table and set it down.

"Thanks, Eve," he said. "You can visit me anytime you like."

She smiled and looked at Frankie. "How do you want your egg?"

"You know I don't eat breakfast."

"That's why you've lost so much weight. If you'd stop smoking you'd put on a few pounds. I'm not saying this to hurt your feelings, Frankie, but you're too thin. If you lose any more weight people will think you have an eating disorder."

Frankie stubbed out her cigarette and lit another. "I'm not hungry, Mom," she repeated. "You go ahead."

Eve took her coffee cup. "I'll wait for you."

"Mom?" Frankie looked at her. "I don't eat breakfast."

The woman looked slightly hurt. "Well, okay, dear. I'll just boil myself an egg later. I'm watching my weight so I have to be careful."

She joined them at the table. An uncomfortable silence ensued. "I'd really like to meet your friend Sissy."

Matt looked at Frankie. "Are you going by the hospital this morning?"

She nodded. She tried to visit Sissy before work, at lunch and after work. "I try to go as soon as they'll let me in."

"That would be a perfect time for me to meet her," Eve said.

"She's a little depressed, Mom."

"Then we'll just have to cheer her up." She looked at Matt. "Is your family in Purdyville?"

He nodded. "My folks live out in the country."

"And your wife and children?"

"I'm not married."

Eve shot her daughter a look. Liar, it said.

He shook his head and tossed a piece of toast in his mouth. He nodded without going into details. "Eve, that's the best breakfast I've had in a long time. I hope you're planning on staying awhile, because I'll be over here every morning as long as you're cooking."

Frankie saw the amused look in his eyes and kicked him beneath the table.

"Actually, I'm in no hurry to go home. My lady friends and I were supposed to spend a week at a spa in Jacksonville, but one of them backed out at the last minute so we lost our group discount. I'm not about to pay full price."

Matt carried his plate to the sink. "I'd better head home

and shower for work," he said. "Seems I lost one of my socks."

Eve smiled prettily. "It's not lost, dear. You'll find it on the floor on the other side of Frankie's bed."

Sissy was lying in the bed staring at the ceiling when Frankie arrived with her mother in tow. She made introductions, and she could tell Sissy was trying to put on a brave face.

"Oh, sweetie, I am so sorry about what happened to you," Eve said, taking Sissy's hand. "Matt and Frankie told me all about it. I'm glad someone shot the man. But you are a beautiful woman, and you'll be back to your old self in a matter of weeks."

Sissy seemed to brighten. "You think so?"

"Honey, I know how to make this salve that will heal those wounds a lot faster than anything they've got at this hospital. When are they going to release you?"

"Tomorrow."

"So soon?" Frankie was surprised.

"They've done all they can. I'm supposed to go home and rest."

"Of course you are," Eve said, "and I'll be there to take care of you. Don't worry about a thing."

"Thank you, Eve." She looked at Frankie. "Have I gotten any calls?"

"They're on the answering machine."

"Do me a favor."

"Anything."

"Erase them."

"Okay."

"And call the telephone company. I want an unlisted number."

Frankie met her gaze. "I'll be happy to."

A knock sounded at the door. Macon Comfy peeked in. He looked embarrassed. "Oh, I'm sorry, Sissy, I didn't know you had company."

"Don't leave," Frankie said, rising from her place on the edge of the bed. "We were just about to leave. I have to get to work." Both she and her mother kissed Sissy on the cheek. "I'll see you at lunch," she said.

"I'll be here," Sissy replied.

Eve dropped Frankie off at work and promised to pick her up for lunch so they could visit Sissy together.

"I think I'll take a tour of the town and do a little shopping. Pick up a gift for that poor girl."

"That's nice of you, Mom." Frankie gave her the name of the shop Alice Chalmers had taken her to. That reminded her, she needed to call Alice and check on her. "It's just down the block, you can't miss it. Would you pick up a little gift for me to give her, as well?"

"Of course, dear. See you in a few hours."

Frankie nodded at Velma as she made her way through the lobby. She started past Matt's office, but he waved her in. "Okay, Hep," he said into the phone. "Why don't you come on in and we'll talk about it." He hung up.

"That was Hep Whitfield. He just called to confess to the shooting of Willie-Jack Pitts."

Cooter hurried inside. "Chief, you're never going to believe this. Alma Grimes from the Half Moon Café just called. She was crying like nobody's business. Told me she couldn't live with her secret anymore." He paused for breath. "She said she's responsible for the shooting of Willie-Jack."

The phone rang. Matt grabbed it. "What is it, Velma?" He listened. "Say what?" He was quiet for a moment. "Okay, tell him to come on in." Matt hung up the phone.

"Orvell Dean is on his way in to sign a confession for the shooting of Willie-Jack Pitts."

Frankie shook her head. "This is going to be a long day."

The next morning, the headline on the *Purdyville Gazette* read, Would the Person Who Did Not Shoot Willie-Jack Pitts Please Step Forward.

Elder Pitts was in Matt's office when Frankie arrived. Matt motioned for her to come in.

"...and I want to know what the hell you think you're doing," the man went on, as though Frankie hadn't entered the room. "Is this some trick?" he asked, shoving the newspaper in his face. "You trying to pull the wool over my eyes?"

Frankie sat down and listened quietly as the man ranted. Matt sipped his coffee in silence, obviously allowing Pitts to get his anger out of his system before he tried to talk to him. Finally, he set his coffee cup down and regarded the man quizzically.

"Pitts, what the hell do you want me to do? I have to investigate each confession."

"You're stallin' for time while my boy's killer walks the streets a free man."

"You keep forgetting something," Matt said. "Your son was trying to beat a woman to death when someone intervened and shot him. The fact the shooter left the scene of the crime isn't going to bode well for him or her, but no court is going to indict a person for trying to save another's life."

"You're just doing this 'cuz you're related to that slut. I know all about Sissy Burns."

"Get the hell out of my office, Pitts," Matt said, his

teeth clenched, "or I'm going to lock you up in Willie-Jack's old cell."

The man stuck a crooked finger in Matt's face. His nails were dirty and chipped. "I'm not finished with you, Webber." He glanced at Frankie. "You *or* your girlfriend." He stalked from the room.

Matt looked at Frankie. "Too bad he wasn't standing next to his son when the shooting went on."

"You think he's going to make trouble?"

"Are you kidding? Trouble is his middle name." He clasped his hands on his desk. "What time is Sissy being released?"

"Dr. Chalmers wants to check her out first. She's going to call me when she's ready for me to pick her up."

"I think all of you need to stay at my place until this thing gets settled." Frankie opened her mouth to say something. "Before you start arguing, let me say this. If it were just you and me, I wouldn't worry so much. But we've got Sissy and your mother to think about. Besides, I've got more room. I can't envision three females in a house with only one bathroom."

He had a point. "Let me think about it," Frankie said. "Sissy may want to sleep in her own bed."

He smiled that smile that made her heart flutter. "So your mother knows about us."

"I would think the sock was a dead giveaway."

"Does it bother you?"

"Not really. We haven't discussed it. I can't keep pretending I'm living a nun's life just to make her happy."

Sissy was amenable to spending a few days at Matt's. Eve packed her things while Frankie tossed her own things in a box, since she hadn't yet replaced the suitcase that Willie-Jack's friends had destroyed. The phone rang. Sissy glanced at Frankie before she picked it up.

"The phone company hasn't had a chance to change the number to an unlisted one yet. Should be today or tomorrow. I've been erasing all of your messages."

Sissy answered the phone. "Oh, hello, Macon. Yes, they let me out this morning, thank goodness." She told him their plans. "Is he mean?" she asked, drawing Frankie's attention. "Okay, bring him along. It can't hurt. And thank you for all you've done."

"I'm almost afraid to ask," Frankie said. "Is Macon sending a hit man?"

Sissy shook her head. "He has a Doberman he keeps in the store at night. He's going to bring him over."

Eve looked concerned. "Oh, my, does he bite?"

"Macon says he's a big baby unless he feels threatened, then he turns vicious. He wants to let him run loose on Matt's property."

"Sounds like Macon has become a big help to you," Frankie said.

Sissy actually blushed. "He has been kind, visiting me several times a day and bringing me flowers and chocolates. I'm not saying I'm attracted to that sort of man, but I consider him a friend, and he's going along with it for now. He must be wearing some new cologne, because he doesn't smell like a rump roast when he visits."

By lunchtime they had moved into Matt's house. Sissy was to sleep in the room Frankie had used during her brief stay, and Frankie and her mother were to share a room containing twin beds.

"This is a nice house," Eve said, giving Frankie a look that told her she was prepared to start planning her daughter's wedding at a moment's notice.

"Don't start, Mom."

Frankie checked on Sissy as soon as she was settled in. "Are you okay?"

Sissy almost smiled. "Fine. I thought I'd go crazy in the hospital."

Frankie was glad to see her depression had lifted. "I'm glad you're out, as well. Mom and I will take good care of you, and you're safe here."

"I'm not the least bit worried. Now, tell me what's going on with the play? I hate that bitch who is taking my place, but I can't very well participate looking like this."

"I haven't been back since you were hurt. I figured if you weren't going to be in it, neither was I."

"What!"

"It's no big deal, okay? Besides, it was only one line."

"It's a big deal to me. I want you in that play, Frankie. If I can't be in it, I want to watch my best friend perform."

Frankie just looked at her. "Sissy, please. You know I'm terrified."

"How do you think I feel having quit my night job? Do you have any idea the kind of money I was making? You're the one who told me I was somebody, and I could do anything. That's what kept me going while I was in the hospital. Now, I want you to suck it in and perform. Eleanor Roosevelt said we have to look fear in the eye and do the things that scare us most. Well, something along those lines. I read it in a book Macon brought me."

"I haven't been rehearsing."

"Lord, girl, you only have one line."

Frankie sighed heavily. She would have promised Sissy the moon right now, after what she'd been through. "Okay, I'll do it."

"And I'm going to be in the front row watching."

"I hate you."

"I know." Sissy smiled.

Eve knocked on the door. "Macon Comfy is here with a dog that could be saddled and ridden by most adults. Why didn't you tell me his name was Satan?"

Sissy perked. "Tell Macon to leave the dog outside, but he can come in." She glanced at Frankie. "How do I look? Not that it matters, really, but, well, you know."

"The makeup covers a lot."

Eve ushered Macon inside, and he brightened the moment he caught sight of Sissy. "You can stay for fifteen minutes," Eve said, giving the man a stern look. "Sissy needs her rest. She's been through enough today."

"Yes, ma'am," he said respectfully. He waited till she was gone. "Who was that?"

"The Gestapo," Frankie said before she left the room and closed the door. She found her mother searching through a cabinet of canned goods. She pulled out a can of chicken noodle soup.

Eve clucked her tongue. "Looks like I need to go to the grocery store. These bachelors. They never keep real food in the house. Matt Webber needs a good woman to take care of him."

"You might tell him to hire a cook and housekeeper."

"Don't get mouthy, Francis." She searched a drawer and pulled out a can opener. "Now, I'm going to prepare Sissy a nice cup of soup and insist she take a nap. After that, I'll run her a nice bubble bath. I'm sure she'll feel better."

"Mom, I appreciate all you're doing for her, but I don't expect you to play nursemaid. I can help Sissy. I'm sure you'd rather get back to your friends."

Eve looked determined as she regarded her daughter. "I'm not about to leave my only child if there's a chance she's in danger. Besides, Sissy needs me, even if you don't."

* * *

Frankie returned to work and found Matt and his deputies in the small conference room. She stuck her head through the door. "What's going on?"

"Come in and have a seat," Matt said.

The other deputies looked serious. "Something's happened," she said.

Cooter spoke. "Some son of a bitch shot Virgil's dog with a shotgun, not to mention all the windows out of his house and car."

Twenty-Five

Frankie sank into a chair. "Is the dog dead?"

"He was shot in the hip," Matt said. "The neighbor who was looking after him heard the shots and hid in her closet. She's older and lives alone. The poor woman was terrified. When she finally came out of the closet, she looked out her window and saw the dog lying in the front yard. She immediately rushed him to the animal hospital. Depends on how much blood he lost."

"So she didn't see anything."

Matt shook his head. "Nothing."

Frankie sighed. "Well, Pitts is making good his promises."

Matt rubbed his eyes with his thumbs. "I've got a couple of men covering all the windows in plastic."

"What do you plan to do about it?"

"I'm trying to figure that out right now. He must've caught wind that Virgil isn't behind bars, and that set him off. I could get a search warrant, but it won't do a damn bit of good. That shotgun is probably buried so deep in the woods we'll never find it. Pitts is an ex-con, and he's going to cover his tracks. He's meaner than Willie-Jack ever was."

"And there won't be no stopping him until he's as dead as his son," Buster said.

Frankie couldn't hide her disgust. "I thought with Willie-Jack out of the way everybody would be safer. I had no idea we'd have to face a whole slew of rednecks. What now?''

"I'm calling in extra manpower," Matt said. "If we were just dealing with Pitts I wouldn't be so concerned, but we could have a group of vigilantes on our hands."

They sat in silence for a moment. Matt looked at Frankie. "You got any ideas, hotshot?"

"I wish I did."

"How's Sissy, by the way?"

"Resting comfortably. My mother has appointed herself head nurse."

"I can't leave them alone."

"Macon dropped off his dog. George must've sensed something was going on, because they're both sitting near the front door."

"Hell, Pitts is likely to shoot both of them," Buster said.

"Hold on a minute," Frankie said. "How many men are jailed in back?"

"Only two," Matt replied. "A DUI and a purse snatcher."

"They have phone privileges, don't they?"

He nodded.

"Could one of them have tipped off Pitts? Told him Virgil wasn't behind bars?"

"Anything is possible."

"We need to get word out where Sissy and I are staying. Pitts will come after us next."

"I don't want to risk it," Matt said. "The man is crazy."

"It's our only hope. We'll have extra manpower inside ready to act."

Cooter straightened in his chair. "You're saying we

give him the bait and hope he takes it?'' He looked at Matt. "That might just work."

By the end of the day, Matt's house was crawling with cops. Sleeping bags and other gear, rolled tightly, filled one corner of the living room. Matt called out for pizza, and they took turns eating in the dining room, while others remained on lookout.

Nothing. Matt took Frankie to rehearsals, although she made him wait outside.

On Friday, Frankie awoke with a sense of dread. It was opening night at the little theater. She almost feared it as much as she did Pitts. She walked about the house all day, dodging cops and trying to rehearse her line in her head.

She practiced on Sissy and her mother until their eyes glazed over in boredom. She was getting ready to go when, all at once, she became ill. Sissy found her in the bathroom retching.

"Now look what you've done," her friend said. "You've gone and made such a big deal out of this that you're sick."

"I can't do it, Sissy. Please don't make me."

"There's no one else."

"It's only one line, for heaven's sake. Surely somebody can stand in for me."

Matt came down the hall. "Is everything okay?"

"Just a mild case of stage jitters is all," Sissy said. "She'll be fine."

"It's time to go," he said, checking his watch.

Frankie wiped her face. "You're going?"

"Sure. So are Buster and Cooter."

"And your mom," Sissy added.

"I thought you were watching the house," Frankie told

Matt, feeling more panicked at the thought of all of them attending.

"I think we have enough men to cover it."

"Can we go now?" Sissy said.

Frankie was silent on the drive to the theater. All she could hear was her heart pounding in her chest. The others made polite conversation, but she was only vaguely aware of what they were saying. Matt parked in back, and Sissy led Frankie through the stage door.

Joey hugged Sissy. "You look wonderful. So much better than when I visited you in the hospital." He leaned closer. "We're doing *Of Mice and Men* next time. You'll be playing the lead female role."

"Thank you, Joey."

Frankie headed for the room where two makeup artists were at work. One woman fastened plastic curlers in Frankie's hair, which were part of her costume. The main characters hadn't yet arrived. They would be given top priority. Frankie watched the woman add extra eye makeup and rouge to her face. She tried to pretend she wasn't there, that it wasn't really happening.

"I hear the place is sold out," the woman said.

Frankie was suddenly overcome with terror. "Would you excuse me?" She rushed to the bathroom. Sissy found her there several minutes later with a bad case of the dry heaves.

"What in heaven's name is wrong with you?" the woman demanded.

"I can't do it, Sissy," she cried. "Please don't make me."

"It's only one line."

"Exactly. It wouldn't take but a couple of minutes for someone else to memorize it."

"Stay right where you are," Sissy ordered, and disappeared.

Frankie pushed the seat down on the toilet, sat down and propped her chin on the porcelain sink in case she had to throw up again. She was still agonizing over her situation when someone tapped on the door.

"It's occupied, dammit!" she called out. "Use the men's room."

Matt opened the door and paused when he saw her condition. "Are you okay, babe?"

"No, I'm dying in here, can't you see? And I will never forgive Sissy for making me do this."

Matt closed the door and locked it. He wet a paper towel and knelt beside her, pressing it to her cheeks and forehead. "Nobody is forcing you, Frankie."

Tears filled her eyes. "You don't understand. The only reason I went along with this crazy harebrained scheme to begin with was to get Sissy involved in something after that Joe fellow dumped her. I have no business being here, Matt." She took the paper towel and mopped her face. "I'm too scared to throw up."

"I'm sure they can find a replacement for you, babe, and if that's what you want, I'll have Sissy talk to the director immediately. But I think you would only end up disappointed. You've always met challenges head-on. This is important to you or you wouldn't be so scared."

She was quiet for a moment. "The real reason I'm doing it is for my father." She met his gaze. "I know this is going to sound stupid, but when I was a little girl he referred to me as his star. He used to sing, 'There she is, Miss America,' every time I walked into a room." She realized she'd sung it off key, but she didn't care.

"Then do it for him."

She leaned her head against Matt's shoulder. "You

were right about me, Matt. I'm so tired of trying to be brave all the time. I've always thought I could tackle the world.''

''You can. You can do anything you set your mind to, and you know it.''

''That's just a facade. I'm really just like everyone else, and right now I'm scared to death.''

''So am I. I'm so scared right now that it feels like my heart is going to stop beating.''

She gave him an odd look. ''I've never known you to be afraid of anything.''

''Perhaps I have a reason to be.'' He reached into the pocket of his jacket and pulled out a black velvet box.

''Oh, shit,'' Frankie said, knowing what it meant.

He smiled. ''Why am I not surprised with your response?'' He opened the box, revealing a diamond ring. ''I'm scared you'll turn me down,'' he said.

Frankie raised her eyes to his, and the love she found there made her forget how nervous she was at the moment. ''Oh, Matt,'' she said softly, touching his face. ''I don't know what to say.''

''Say yes, Frankie. I love you more than life itself. I would do anything for you. I don't expect you to be brave all the time, and when you're frightened or anxious, I want to be able to hold you in my arms and kiss away your fears. I've seen through that tough exterior for a long time. I've seen you comfort those who were suffering, and I've watched you with Sissy. Besides, we make a good team, babe. Together we can accomplish anything.''

''I'm so…touched.''

''That's not the word I'm looking for. I want you to love me.''

''I do.''

''Then say yes.''

She hesitated, and wondered if this was how it felt before a person jumped from an airplane, before their parachute opened and they landed safely on the ground. Even with her heart pounding in her chest, she was ready to take the leap. She put her arms around him and drew him close. "Yes."

He slipped the ring on her finger and kissed her deeply. "Now you belong to me. I promise to be a good husband and father to our children. And right now I'm going to hold your hand until you step onto that stage. I believe in you, Frankie Daniels."

They exited the bathroom a few minutes later, holding hands. Frankie felt stronger knowing Matt was behind her all the way. Sissy was waiting. She winked. "Love your ring."

"You knew?"

"Honey, I helped him pick it out."

"Everybody take your places on stage," the director ordered. "The curtain goes up in five minutes."

"Go!" Sissy whispered. "I'll be throwing you kisses from the wings."

Frankie let go of Matt's hand and made her way in the semidarkness to the beautician's chair she was to occupy. She was weak-kneed and trembling, adrenaline gushing through her body like water through a fire hose. She sat down. The woman playing Truvy's character leaned over and whispered in her ear.

"Take a deep breath."

The curtain parted and the lights came on. Thankfully, the lights kept Frankie from seeing much of the audience. They appeared as shadows. The scene began. Frankie was only vaguely aware of what was being said as she listened for her cue. It would be some time yet, as the actresses were discussing an upcoming wedding. Shelby, the bride, and her mother would be arriving shortly, at which time there would be much fussing about the nuptials. In the background, shots were fired. The father of the bride was shooting at birds in a tree, to keep "bird droppings" from making a mess in the backyard, where the bride's family planned to hold the reception. Frankie jumped each time a shot was fired.

As the conversation went on around her, she began to relax. Truvy was saying her lines as she removed curlers from Frankie's hair. Frankie was amazed by how well the others played their parts. She had once imagined herself becoming an actress. She remembered dressing up in her mother's old clothes and high heels, strutting about the house like a famous movie star. Perhaps now that she had gotten over her initial stage fright she could enjoy herself.

The play went on as Truvy's character continued to fuss with Frankie's hair and converse with the others. Frankie smiled into the fake mirror as though she was enjoying every minute of it. She refused to look at the first row, where her mother watched, along with Matt and the deputies.

Finally, it was her turn to speak her line, but she had become so caught up in the play that she wanted to do more.

"Truvy, I declare," she said, "you have done wonders with my hair."

"Thank you, honey," Truvy replied.

"I just wouldn't think of going anywhere else to have my hair done. You have a magic touch, yessiree."

"Well, I try," Truvy went on, as though unshaken that Frankie had decided to change her lines.

"I don't know if I will be safe on the street looking as good as I do." She saw the other characters watching her and waiting their turns. "I may just have to hire me a bodyguard."

The audience chuckled. Frankie decided she was playing her part well. Ad-libbing was part of being a good actress. Joey had obviously not realized how good she was when he'd given her a one-liner. Well, she'd show him. By the time she finished, she and Sissy would be doing battle over who got the leading lady role in the next play.

"I must come in and have my color tinted," Frankie went on. "What would you think about adding red highlights?"

Truvy unsnapped her cotton drape and pulled it free. "I think it would look fabulous. Just make an appointment with the receptionist on your way out."

On your way out. They were already trying to get her off stage, when it was obvious the audience loved her. "You know, I just might be having a wedding of my own in the very near future." She noted the irritation in Truvy's eyes, and saw past her to the wings, where Joey was standing beside Sissy, motioning for her to cut. "Yes, I have been in love with Melvin T. Benefield since I was knee-high to a grasshopper, and I could do worse than Melvin, buh-lieve-you-me. Of course, I'd have to look under every rock in town."

More laughter from the audience. She obviously had stage presence.

"The problem with men these days is that most of them pay so much child support their idea of a fun evening is a chili dog at the Dairy Queen."

Truvy seemed a little stiff. "Well, we only do one wedding at a time, sugar, so you just call me in advance when it's your turn."

Frankie stood and made a production of brushing hair off her dress. At least that much was in the script. She sashayed to the receptionist's desk and pretended to pay her bill, as another character came through the door. Sissy was waiting for Frankie when she stepped backstage.

"What on earth was *that* all about?"

Frankie arched one brow. "I thought I did well. The audience seemed to think so."

"Those weren't your lines," Sissy hissed.

"I couldn't help it. I really got into character and decided my line sounded flat, so I improvised. Was I good?"

Joey came up to her, a strange look on his face. "Frankie, don't ever do that again," he admonished. "You could have thrown all the others off."

"Was I good?"

"Just great," he muttered as he walked away.

Frankie looked at Sissy. "I couldn't help it. Once I got out there and relaxed, the words just started flowing. I never thought I'd like acting, but then I remembered how often I'd dreamed of becoming an actress as a little girl. It just felt so natural being out there."

Eve Hutton noticed Frankie's ring right away. "My God, that's two carats!" She hugged her daughter. "This is what I've always wanted for you. And so romantic. Where did he propose?"

"In the ladies' room."

"What were the two of you doing in there, for heaven's sake?"

"I was sitting on the toilet trying not to throw up in the sink."

Eve shook her head. "I can't possibly tell that to my friends. I'll have to come up with something else."

"Let's celebrate," Matt said. "Not only is Frankie a star, she's agreed to become my wife."

They arrived at a fashionable restaurant half an hour

later. Frankie knew she was beaming. She couldn't stop looking at her ring. And she had accomplished one of the toughest fears in her life.

"What did everyone think of my performance?" she asked, once they were all seated, including Cooter and Buster, who had already offered their congratulations.

"I thought you were great," Matt said.

Sissy nodded. "*Great* doesn't come close to describing it."

"You certainly have stage presence," Eve said.

Buster and Cooter agreed as Frankie excused herself for the ladies' room.

Sissy regarded the group. "She was awful."

Everyone nodded, even Matt. "We can't tell her or it'll hurt her feelings."

Sissy nodded. "No, we can't tell her, but we can see that she never gets close to a stage again. Perhaps I can convince her to take square dancing lessons."

Twenty-Six

Frankie was still beaming when she arrived at work the following day. She showed Velma her ring.

"I never thought you'd last," the woman confessed.

"Well, I'm here to stay."

Velma actually hugged her. "I'm very happy," she said, "but you'd better be a good wife to Matt or I'll personally wring your neck."

"That's what I like about you, Velma. I always know where I stand."

The day seemed to fly for Frankie. When she arrived home she found her mother and Sissy talking on the sofa. "Is something wrong?" she asked, noting the serious look on their faces.

Sissy had tears in her eyes. "Your mother just offered to put me through beauty school."

"Oh, Sissy, that's wonderful! And just where you belong." She looked at her mother. "And it's very kind of you."

"That's not all," Sissy said. "Macon has asked me to go steady with him, and I said yes. He's the only man I've ever met who is more interested in me as a person than getting me into the sack with him."

The phone rang. Frankie answered. Alice Chalmers spoke from the other end. "Rand and I heard about the engagement," she said. "Congratulations. We want you and Matt to drop by the house tonight."

Frankie suspected they wanted to give a little celebration. "I'll talk to Matt and get back to you."

Matt and Frankie arrived at the Chalmers's home, an impressive colonial style, at precisely seven o'clock. A serious-looking Rand Chalmers let them in. "Thank you for coming," he said.

"Is something wrong, Rand?" Matt asked.

"Why don't we talk in the library," he suggested, ignoring the question.

Frankie and Matt glanced at each another, wondering what was going on. They followed him into a comfortable room filled with shelves that held an assortment of books. Overstuffed tweed furniture sat around a fireplace, where a coffee service, sandwiches and various pastries waited. Alice sat on a love seat and held a dainty handkerchief in one hand. It was obvious she'd been crying.

"Alice, what's wrong?" Frankie said, going to sit beside her friend.

"Rand and I have something very important to discuss with the two of you. Please, Matt—" She motioned toward a chair. Rand sat beside his wife and took her hand.

"Congratulations on your engagement," he said.

Matt nodded. "Thank you. But I have a feeling that's not why you called us out here."

Alice dabbed her eyes. "You're right." She sighed. "I've been living with a secret for a long time, and I can't go on and maintain my sanity." She paused, struggling. "I just don't know where to begin."

"Let me start, darling," Rand said. Alice nodded. He looked from Frankie to Matt. "Some years back, I became involved with a nurse at the hospital. We had a lengthy affair. I tried to break it off, but it wasn't easy. Alice and I weren't getting along at the time because my hours were so crazy I began sleeping at the hospital. Before long, I was spending nights with the other woman.

"Alice begged me to go to counseling, but I refused. Here I was, a wealthy, respected surgeon, and I thought I was above all that." He paused and looked sad. "Alice became pregnant a couple of times and miscarried. She grew despondent and I couldn't bear to see her that way, so I spent more and more time away from home. This went on for a couple of years. I never stopped to realize what I was doing to my wife. I've been trying to forgive myself ever since." He looked at Alice.

"I knew about the affair," she said. "I discovered Rand was not at the hospital the night I drove myself to the emergency room during my first miscarriage. I never told him. In a matter of months, I was pregnant again, but I lost that baby, also. I went into a deep depression."

Frankie listened closely, wondering where they were going with their story. "I'm sorry," she said at last.

"I wanted to hurt Rand as badly as he hurt me," Alice confessed after a moment. "I even planned to leave him. During this time, Rand had hired Willie-Jack Pitts to make repairs to our barn, which had been damaged in a storm. The man flirted with me shamelessly, and...well...I was so lonely and desperate for attention, I fell for it. Willie-Jack and I had a brief affair."

Frankie snapped her head up and found Alice looking off into the distance, as if seeing the whole thing in her mind. Rand stared at the floor. Frankie vaguely remembered Willie-Jack telling her about the affairs he'd had with some of Purdyville's most respected women. She hadn't believed him.

"I was so ashamed," Alice said. "I broke it off. Willie-

Jack went into a rage. He slapped me several times so hard he left bruises. I told Rand I'd fallen down the front steps. If only that had been the worst of it.'' She paused and swiped fresh tears.

"What happened then?" Matt asked gently.

"He decided to blackmail me."

They were all quiet for a moment.

"How long did this go on?"

"Ten long years." She looked at Frankie. "And I'm not the only woman in town who was paying." She took a deep, shaky breath. "It wasn't so bad in the beginning, but as time went on he kept raising it. I was a wreck trying to keep it from Rand. Then, two weeks ago, Willie-Jack asked for a payoff of fifty thousand dollars."

"My God!" Frankie said.

"He said he'd give me a couple of weeks to come up with the money, but if I didn't, he was going to make sure everyone in town knew about us. Finally, I had no choice but to tell Rand. I simply could not go on living with the lie any longer."

"Did you kill Willie-Jack?" Matt asked.

Alice nodded. "Yes."

Rand cleared his throat. "Before we go on, I think Alice needs to explain what actually happened that night." He slipped his arm around her. "Finish the story, darling."

"I did not go out looking for Willie-Jack with the intention of killing him. I didn't even know there was a gun in the car. But I'd had enough of his threats. I had suffered so long that I no longer cared who knew about our affair. I figured half the people in town wouldn't believe him, anyway. I drove to Virgil's, parked near Willie-Jack's car and waited. It didn't take long. Shortly after I arrived, Virgil escorted him out the door. I could tell Willie-Jack was drunk. I locked the doors, cut the lights and slowly followed him to the back of the restaurant. I intended to tell him I was no longer going to pay him, and he was free to say or do anything he liked.

"He was so drunk he never saw me following him, but by the time I pulled around he was already beating up Sissy. The poor girl fell to the ground and he began kicking her. I knew I had to do something. But I had nothing with which to defend Sissy or myself. I remembered the tire jack in the trunk, and I opened the glove compartment to pop the trunk. I saw the gun." She was quiet for a moment.

"I called out to him, told him to leave Sissy alone. I thought the girl was dead or near death. He laughed at me, then started for my car. He looked crazed. I warned him I was armed, but he kept on coming. I just shot him. I watched him fall to the ground, but I had no idea that I'd killed him until I heard it from a friend the next morning."

"Where did the gun come from?" Frankie asked.

"It was mine," Rand said. "I bought it off the street when Alice told me what was going on. I'd planned to kill Willie-Jack after what he'd put her through." He looked sad. "Unfortunately, Alice was driving my car that night because hers was in the shop. I wish I had been the one to kill the bastard."

"You had no idea she was paying him hush money?" Matt asked.

Alice answered for him. "I was cashing Certificates of Deposits I'd purchased with my inheritance. Rand never looks at the statements."

"Tell him the rest," Rand said.

Alice drew a deep breath. "Willie-Jack's father knew about the blackmail scheme. He called this morning and made it plain he expects payments to continue, despite his son's death.''

Matt remained quiet for a moment. ''Well, Alice, you were obviously acting in self-defense, so I don't think you're going to go to jail. I think you should call your attorney right away, though.''

''Is there any way to prevent the truth from getting out?'' Rand asked. ''Not that I give a damn what people in this town think, but my wife has been through enough, and I feel responsible for this. Not only for screwing up earlier in our marriage when Alice needed me—'' He paused and raised her hand to his lips. His eyes were unusually bright as though he were near tears. ''I should have killed Willie-Jack as soon as I bought the gun, but I could never get him alone.''

''You'll need a good reason for being at the scene of the crime in the first place,'' Matt told Alice, ''or it'll look bad.''

''I know a reason,'' Frankie said. ''She could have received a call from Sissy. Sissy could have called and told her she was depressed and needed to talk to someone right away. I have no doubt Sissy will back her up, since Alice saved her life.'' Frankie realized it would be altering the facts of the case, but it was important to protect her friend. Sometimes you had to bend the rules, she'd learned.

''That might work,'' Matt said, ''but I'd still call your lawyer and have him advise you. As for Pitts, I'll take care of him.''

It was not yet dawn when Matt, Frankie and several other deputies closed in on Elder Pitts's house, catching him by surprise. ''What the hell you mean coming around here this time o' morning,'' Pitts asked, still in his dirty underwear.

"I'm hauling you in," Matt said, slapping cuffs on the man.

"And charging me with what?"

"Does the word *blackmail* mean anything to you?"

"I don't know what the hell you're talking about."

"Alice Chalmers and I have had a real good talk. She recorded your voice on the phone threatening to blackmail her. You're going to be in prison for a long time, Pitts."

"That Chalmers bitch ain't gonna press charges against me. She don't want nobody in this town knowin' about her and Willie-Jack."

"That's where you're wrong, old man. She's already contacted her attorney."

The color seemed to drain from Pitts's face. He was quiet for a moment. "I'm too old to go back to prison. It'd kill me. And my wife—" He paused and wiped his eyes. "She ain't well. Cain't eat or sleep. She needs me here."

It was the first time Matt had seen any emotion on Pitts's face other than hatred. He wondered if Willie-Jack's death had finally broken him down. "I'm giving you a choice, Pitts," he said. "You've got twenty-four hours to get your ass out of town—out of this state—or I'll make sure you die in prison."

Pitts studied him a long time. "I want to know who killed my boy. Was it Alice Chalmers?"

"You killed him, Pitts, by raising him to be as mean as you. Besides, the person responsible for shooting him was trying to keep him from beating a woman to death, so if you're looking for revenge you're not going to get it. Hang around and I promise you're going to rot in prison."

"How do I know you won't send someone after me?"

Matt gave him an easy smile. "Depends on how well

you hide out. There are a lot of mountains in Tennessee. I reckon a man like you could crawl under a rock and never be found. In fact, I'm counting on it.''

Pitts looked him in the eye. "I raised my boy like my pa raised me. I did the best I could.''

Matt took off the cuffs. "Twenty-four hours, Pitts. My men will be watching the place. I expect you to be gone this time tomorrow." Matt turned to go.

"Hold it. Why are you doing this for me? You ain't never done a decent thing for this family.''

"Why am I doing it? You just lost your boy, and I'm showing a little mercy because of your wife." It was a lie. He knew it, and Pitts knew it. "But I don't have a whole lot of patience, and you don't have a whole lot of time.''

Pitts swallowed. "The sooner I'm out of this town, the better.''

"At least we agree on one thing." Matt and Frankie were on their way a few minutes later. One patrol car stayed behind. "You handled that well," Frankie said.

"Thank you. Coming from you, I consider that a great compliment.''

"And so you should. I don't know how you managed without my expertise.''

He chuckled. "I don't know what I'm going to do with you, Daniels.''

"As I recall, you *did* promise to make an honest woman out of me.''

He looked at her. "You fell for that? Hey, I was just trying to divert your attention so you'd get past your stage fright.''

"You diverted me all right. This is a pretty large diamond. I recognize good jewelry when I see it. I am my mother's daughter, after all.''

"I'm beginning to have doubts after seeing you on stage. I would have thought after your big debut you would be on the first bus to Hollywood."

"Sometimes we have to make sacrifices." She sighed. "But don't think I'm going to forget right away. I may have to hold it over your head for the next fifty years."

"Fifty years!" He looked at her. "You think I'm planning on hanging around until you get old and ugly?"

"You have no choice. I've got a gun, and I've probably had more target training than you."

"And that's another thing. I can't have my wife running around town telling everyone she's a better shot than me, even if it's true."

"Face it, Webber, you've met your match."

This time he laughed out loud. "Yes, I think I have." He reached for her hand. "We're going to do just fine, Frankie. Just fine."